Collected Christmas Horror Shorts 2

Presented by

Kevin J. Kennedy

Kevin J. Kennedy Presents

Collected Christmas Horror Shorts 2 © 2018 Kevin J. Kennedy

Story selection & formatting by Kevin J. Kennedy
Edited by Brandy Yassa
Cover design by Lisa Vasquez

First Printing, 2018

Kevin J. Kennedy Presents

Acknowledgements

I'd like to thank Brandy Yassa, Lisa Vasquez, all of the authors involved in the book, my wife, my mum, my dad and everyone else who keeps me involved in the writing world.

Table of Contents

Kevin J. Kennedy Presents

CHRISTMAS CURSE
BY
WESTON KINCADE

WEIHNACHTSTAG
BY
MARK FLEMING

SECRET SANTA
BY
VERONICA SMITH

THE JOYS OF CHRISTMAS

BY

LISA MORTON

Christmas Lunch
By
Amy Cross

I suppose it's that time again.

Reaching up to the top of the door, I slide the bolt across and then I pull the door open. The damn thing sticks slightly, probably swollen somewhat from the bad weather, but I get it open soon enough.

Immediately, I'm struck by the cold air of this snowy Christmas afternoon. I've never been a fan of snow, but I can't help leaning out for a moment and looking along the square. Fresh snow is falling, landing on the roofs of all those fancy-looking new cars, but otherwise the square is deserted and the only sound is the soft rustling sound of snow hitting the ground. Looks like a harsh winter's on the way, which means it was probably a cool summer too.

The house opposite has been painted.

Last year, number fifteen was a kind of dirty mottled gray color. Some time over the past year, it's been painted a nice bright new white. Too bright, if you ask me. I'm all for cleaning places up, but a little care and attention would be nice.

Apart from that, though, everything looks to be much the same as usual. This old town keeps ticking along with just a few changes every season. Somebody's apparently seen fit to string fairy lights up in one of the trees, which is a little tacky and modern for my tastes, but I can't complain if that's the worst of what's new.

I turn to go back inside, but then I hear distant footsteps crunching through snow.

Looking across the square again, I don't see anyone, not at first. The footsteps continue, though, and finally I spot a couple at the square's far end, wrapped up in thick coats and scarves and bobble-hats as they hurry toward the other pub. They make their way up the steps at the front of the Old Nag, and then they go inside. There are lights on in the Old Nag's window, and I'm sure their expensive Christmas lunch is well underway. I bet they're paying five or six bob now for three courses.

Good for them, but we do things a little differently here at the King's Head.

Letting the door swing shut, I start making my way back behind the bar. My hips aren't what they once were, but at least the pain doesn't get worse these days. It's just constant ache that hums along in the background, but on Christmas Day the discomfort always feels much worse. I have a few theories about that, but I don't bother thinking about any of it very much. Not these days. After all, what use would I have for perfect hips? It's not like I'd be out there running around. Still, I have to stop for a moment and lean against the bar, just to get myself together. Damn this old body of mine.

Suddenly I hear the door swing open, and I turn to see Bernard shuffling into the pub. Frankly, he doesn't look much better than I feel.

"Always first, you are," I mutter. "Always. I could set my clock by you."

"Being punctual is half the battle," he replies, grimacing slightly. He's an old man, like me, and he's in pain too, but he won't complain. Never does. Like me. "I'll have a pint of Nun's Delight to start

11

myself off, and then we'll see where we go from there."

He makes his way stiffly to the bar. I remember when Bernard Muir was a young lad, a few years younger than me even, and he'd be out on Christmas Day every year playing rugby. Now look at him. He's wincing and spluttering as he reaches the bar, and I can't help noticing that he's having to lean heavily on one of the stools as if he's having trouble keeping himself up. Sometimes, I think it'd be better for all of us if we'd just died young.

Heading to the taps, I start pouring him a pint.

"I hear John Laird's going to be joining us this year," Bernard says after a moment. "Now there's a name from the past, eh? I'm sure he'll spice proceedings up nicely."

"John Laird?" I pause, and it takes a moment before I can quite put a face to the name. After a moment, I get back to pouring. "I'm sure he won't come here," I mutter. "Why would he? I mean, this was never his local, was it? I could see him in the Old Nag more than I could see him in here."

"Mark my words," Bernard says with a faint smile as I set his pint in front of him. "Laird'll be here. And that's when the fun'll really get going." He keeps his eyes set on me for a few seconds, as if he's amused by my expression. "What's wrong, Charlie?" he asks finally. "For some reason, you don't look too thrilled by the prospect. Worried he might give you indigestion over your Christmas lunch, are you?"

"All the same to me, Bernard," I reply, trying not to let him see that I hate the idea of Laird showing up, even if I've long known his arrival one Christmas was inevitable. "All the same to me."

***

"I was down there the other day," Bobby Carpenter says, raising his pint to his lips and almost taking a sip, before lowering the glass again. "I'm telling you, they've knocked down the whole block and now they're building a supermarket."

"They're never," Colin Rice replies, clearly shocked. "What'd they have to go and do that for?"

"Progress," Bobby says, rolling his eyes and sounding deeply unimpressed. He raises his glass again, almost drinks, and then lowers it. "I've been spending a lot of time on the seafront and I'm telling you, nothing's how it was. You should all go down there some time and take a look for yourselves. Even the old scout hut's been got rid of."

"What for?" Colin asks, even more shocked.

"Buggered if I know," Bobby continues. "Maybe it's just 'cause it was old. People don't like old things anymore, do they?" He raises his pint, very nearly takes a sip, and then lowers it again. "They change things just 'cause they can. Not 'cause it'll be an improvement, but 'cause they can. I'm all for progress when it's real progress, but change for change's sake is not a good thing."

"Missed this?" a familiar voice asks, and I turn to see that Bernard has sidled over to join me. "You've been listening to them natter all afternoon.

14

Is this really how you want to spend your Christmas?"

"There's worse," I mutter, although I suppose he has a point. "I'm really -"

Before I can finish, the door creaks open and I spot a face I haven't seen in a long, long time. Looking somewhat dazed and confused – just like all those who come in here for the first time after the change – John Laird seems utterly lost. He glances around for a moment, looking at the tables where everyone's sitting with their plates of Christmas lunch, and then he finally turns and looks straight at me. I see a flicker of recognition in his eyes, and he lets the door slowly creak shut before coming this way along the saloon area.

"I'll leave you two to it," Bernard says. "You must have a lot to catch up on."

"You're all right," I tell him, but it's too late. He's already heading over to talk to the Catchworth sisters, and I can't avoid Laird now without making it obvious that's what I'm doing.

"Charlie," Laird says, stopping on the other side of the bar.

"John," I reply.

"What..."

He pauses, before looking along the bar and watching Bobby and Colin for a moment. He quite obviously doesn't understand what's going on, which means it must have happened fairly recently for him. His mouth's hanging open, and then at last he turns back to me. Still, though, he doesn't seem able to find the words.

"Let me guess," I say, pouring a pint of his favorite. "You were wandering past, and you heard us all chattering away in here."

"I did," he replies. He sounds so confused.

"And you thought you'd poke your head round the door."

He nods.

"And you didn't really expect to see us in here. You thought maybe you'd imagined it."

He nods again.

I finish pouring the pint, and then I set it in front of him.

"First one's always on the house at Christmas," I tell him.

"Even for me."

"Even for you." I pause for a moment. "How's Annie, anyway?"

"She's..." He seems frozen for a moment. "She's good. I think so. She was very good at the end. Always at the hospital, all day and every day. Took a lot out of her, though. She's in an assisted living place up at the other end of town now."

"You go and see her much?"

"I haven't quite..."

His voice trails off.

"I know the feeling," I tell him. "It's not easy, is it? You don't want to disturb them."

"Do you ever go and see your lot?" he asks.

17

I shake my head.

"Never tempted?"

"I'm tempted," I explain, "but then I think, what's the point? They wouldn't want me hanging around like a bad smell."

"Christmas is the time for families, though," he points out.

"Sure, but not when..." I try to think of the right way to phrase this. "Well, you know what I mean. There's family, and then there's family. I'll be happy enough if they go up to the cemetery some time over the next few days. Put some flowers down, that sort of thing."

"I don't check for flowers," he replies, and now a faint, wry smile is crossing his lips. "Too depressing."

"I'll drink to that," I say, and I raise my pint of soda water.

He raises his beer and almost drinks, but then he stops and stares down at the glass.

"Best to not try," I tell him. "Just one of those unwritten rules now. Most of 'em just sorta hold it in their hands like a prop, if you know what I mean."

"Looks like you've got all the old regulars in," he says, turning again and looking across the saloon towards the seating area. "I remember Christmas lunches here in the old days. The food was always good, Charlie, I'll give you that. I missed it after I stopped coming. Never found anywhere that did quite such a succulent bird." He pauses, before glancing back at me. "I found better company, though. That wasn't hard at all."

"You're welcome to go back there," I tell him.

"Nah, you're all right." He smiles again. "It's different when... I mean, the New Inn and the Nag and the Rose are all still open, aren't they? They're busy every day, and so modern now. Have you seen the New Inn lately?"

"I don't get out much."

"Don't blame you. They're ruining pubs these days." He pauses. "Charlie, I just want to say that

I'm sorry for the bad blood we got between us. It was silly, arguing over a woman like that. I'm not claiming I was a saint, but you've got to understand that nothing happened between me and Annie until well after you and her were divorced. *Well* after. I'd never have made a move on a man's wife. You must know that."

I open my mouth to tell him I heard different, but then at the last moment I realize there's no point. We went over and over this whole shebang back when it happened, and now it seems less important.

"I suppose we can let bygones be bygones," I tell him cautiously, surprising myself a little. "I wouldn't want to create any awkwardness, not on Christmas Day. You might even squeeze onto a table for lunch, if you're lucky. The Catchworth sisters are here, but I should warn you, they're as randy as ever. They might even -"

Suddenly I hear raised voices at the far end of the bar. I turn, worried that a fight might be about to break out, but instead I realize that a couple of the locals have started singing. Well, they're *trying* to sing, anyway, although it sounds more like a group of cats having an argument. It's enough to get some others to join in, however, and soon the entire pub is having a proper sing-along. Just like the old days, people are yawping and yelling in the middle of it all, and I have to fight the urge to stick my fingers in my ears. And then, to my utter shock, I hear a voice singing next to me, and I turn to see that Laird's having a go.

"Well!" he yells at me with a grin. "If I can't join in now, when can I? You should too!"

"I haven't got the voice for it!" I reply. "Even now!"

"You're not still embarrassed, are you?" he asks. "Of all the times to worry about stuff like that, surely now's a good time to just let it all hang out?"

"I'd rather just watch!"

I turn and look toward the seating area, and I listen to the dreadful, out-of-tune singing that's filling the entire pub. Honestly, after a year of being alone in here, I can't quite believe that the place is suddenly so noisy. I know I'm something of a stick-in-the-mud, and I know I shouldn't be so curmudgeonly, so I force myself to smile and listen as all my old regulars continue their carousing. After all, the place is only like this once a year, and I've got three-hundred-and-sixty-four other days to enjoy the silence. Today's different. Today's special.

Today's Christmas.

"You're smiling," Laird says.

I turn to him. "I am not!"

"Liar," he says with a chuckle. "I never thought I'd live to see the day when..."

His voice trails off for a moment, and then he raises his glass.

"Well," he continues, "maybe that was a poor choice of words. But you know what I mean. I never thought I'd see the day when Charlie Russell goes -"

Suddenly I hear the door creak open, and I turn just as the singing comes to a sudden halt. I didn't think anyone else would be coming today, and sure enough – to my horror – I see that a young man and woman, barely in their twenties, are standing in the open doorway, silhouetted against the snowy square outside. Wrapped up in warm jackets and scarves, they're staring in at the pub.

All the regulars, meanwhile, have become completely still and quiet, and they're sitting staring at the new arrivals. You could hear a pin drop.

"I told you," the young chap in the doorway says, "this isn't the one. It's the other one, at the other end of the square, the Old Nag. *That's* where we're meeting your parents for Christmas lunch."

"I know," the girl replies, before taking a step forward toward the bar, still looking around, "I just... This pub closed down about ten years ago."

Reaching the bar, she runs a finger along the top, wiping a line straight through the dust.

"It looks like it was one of those old-fashioned places for silly old duffers in flat caps," the guy says. "Come on, Lauren. Let's get going, I'm starving."

"But didn't you hear it?" she replies.

"Hear what?"

"The voices." She turns to him, as the locals continue to stare at her in complete silence. "The singing, Joe! People were singing in here, just a fraction of a second before I opened the door!"

"I might have heard something," he says, "but it could've been coming from someone's TV next door."

"No, it was coming from in here." She steps around the side of the bar, coming this way, and then she stops right next to Laird.

As Laird stares straight at her face, the girl looks at the beer taps.

"I didn't imagine it," she says, with a hint of fear in her voice. "I heard proper singing, Joe, and it was coming from in here." She looks this way, toward the old optics. She almost makes eye contact with me, but only almost. "It was like people were singing right here in the bar."

"Well, there's no-one here now," the guy replies, "is there? And it's not like they could have all run out the back in the time it took you to open the door. You must have just heard something else that *seemed* to be coming from in here."

She looks over at the old mirror above the fireplace, lost in thought, but then slowly she turns back this way. She looks at the optics, then at the sign above the old sink, and now she's once again almost staring straight at me. Her gaze moves past me and onto the pumps again, but then she hesitates. I watch her closely, and slowly – so slowly that I can barely telling it's happening – she turns back and looks at me. Straight at me this time. Straight into my eyes.

"Lauren!"

She gasps and turns, and now the guy has a hand on her shoulder.

"Can we *please* get going?" he asks, with a hint of a whine in his voice. "I'm so hungry, I think my stomach's started to digest itself."

"Sure," she replies, sounding shaken. "Sure."

She follows him past some of the silent customers and over to the door, but then she turns and looks back this way. Almost at me, but not quite.

"I just thought I saw something for a second," she adds. "It was only for a second, but it was like there was a..."

She pauses, and then she turns and follows the guy outside.

"Weird they left the door unlocked," the guy says, as he pulls the door shut. Then I hear him still talking as they trudge through the snow, until finally they're too far away.

Turning, I look at the customers. They're all sitting in complete silence, with their pale faces turned toward the door. It's as if the intrusion by those two living people made the entire pub come to a grinding halt.

"Come on, you lot!" I shout, finally breaking the silence. "I want all of you out by the time the church bells strike four! I'm sure you've all got other places to haunt!"

They start talking again, and I breathe a sigh of relief as I realize that the interruption is over and we're now back to normal. Well, as normal as things ever get around here these days. But as voices laugh and yell and argue all around me, and as Laird tries to talk to me about some old scrape we got into years ago, I excuse myself and head around the bar, making my way to the door. After all, it's so rare for all of us to get together again like this. Really only happens once a year. And as I peer out through the dirty glass and watch snow falling in the square, I realize that I actually *do* enjoy these little visits.

I slide the bolt across.

No more unexpected visitors, thank you very much. Not today. Not in our quiet little pub, when a few old friends are just trying to enjoy their Christmas lunch in peace.

The End

Kevin J. Kennedy Presents

Frau Perchta
By
Suzanne Fox

Snow creaked under each step of her sturdy, laced-up shoes as she crossed the road. It had been falling steadily for hours. Each flake merging with another until a thick, white layer carpeted the street, burying the piles of dog shit, and discarded beer cans and syringes. She was always pleased to see the arrival of the first snow, and she loved how its simple beauty purified the ravaged landscape of the Belfield estate.

She was following a star. It blinked in gaudy flashes of red and yellow from its location above the door of the mid-terraced house across the street. Each iridescent flicker illuminated the dilapidation and neglect of the council-owned building. Not that anyone from the council's housing department ever deigned to visit the estate anymore. It was a forgotten wilderness, bequeathed by fear to the rule of drug gangs and pimps. What had once been a haven for young families and the elderly was now a desolate battlefield where decent folks locked their doors before nightfall and never ventured out alone.

Her foot scooted on a patch of ice and a little yelp of surprise rose from her lips in a white cloud closely followed by a quiet giggle. "You silly old woman," she scolded. "How will you ever get your work done if you fall and break a hip?" She continued across the road making sure to set each foot down firmly before taking her next step. The wind that blew from the east was keeping most of the low-lifes indoors, giving the estate an air of abandonment.

The garden gate dangled from a solitary twisted hinge. Only a low drift of snow prevented it from swinging as an icy blast funnelled between the row of houses. She squeezed past it and made her way along the path. The thump of heavy bass rebounded through her chest as 50 Cent rapped, "Papi - what the fuck is the matter with your man?" It grew louder the closer she got to the house. Pulling her hand-knitted cardigan tighter across her chest, she raised an arthritically-gnarled hand and hammered on the door unsure whether the occupants would hear her over the rapper's rhyme.

She sensed rather than saw the eye peering through the spyhole - a sentry checking whether the Christmas Eve visitor was a 'narc' or a customer. Bolts clattered and scraped, and the door opened to reveal a face that hadn't seen daylight for a long time. Wary eyes glared at the uninvited visitor. "What you want, bitch?" The door opened wider revealing a beast of a man. Tree-trunk arms provided a living canvas of ink daggers and revolvers. A glint of gold shimmered from behind thin lips.

The old woman peered past the human wall into a haze-filled room. Blue smoke hung in clouds and a spicy scent drifted across to her. Drawing in a deep breath of the cold, but clean, outside air she stepped around the monster and entered the den.

"What the fuck?" The doorman looked on in disbelief as the stooped, slight figure walked past him. "Hey, bitch. You can't come in here." He reached out to grab her arm, but she waved him off, continuing on her way.

The room was a parody of Christmas. A purple, tinsel tree listed toward a mildew-stained wall and silver-foil wraps dangled by cotton threads from each of its bent branches. A plastic, festive cloth covered the table which was strewn with syringes, battered spoons and a nine-bar. A couple of dope-heads sucked greedily on glass bongs, belching smoke into the rancid air. In the furthest corner of the room sat the king-pin dealer who ruled the Belfield estate through fear and coercion. At his feet knelt a tattooed blonde, her bleached hair interwoven with sparkling, Christmassy ribbons. Her bare breasts wobbled with each bob of her head toward his groin. At the old woman's entrance, the blonde recoiled, but the dealer grabbed her hair and pulled her back to finish what she had started.

Unfazed, the dealer eyed his uninvited guest while the blonde resumed her duties. "Well, if it isn't the sour, old Kraut who's moved in across the street. Have you come to give us our Christmas presents?"

"I'd prefer you to show me some respect and call me by my proper name, Frau Perchta." The old woman slipped away from the sentry's grip as he made a lunge for her. "Get away." She glared at the big man and waited for him to react. He looked toward his boss for instruction.

"Get back to the door, asshole." He flicked his hand dismissing his minder.

"Mr. Carpenter. We need to talk," said Frau Perchta.

The dealer held up a hand to stop her from saying any more. His eyelids closed and fluttered as he tipped his head back, and a low groan rolled from his lips. The blonde lifted her head and wiped her mouth. Carpenter reached out, twisted her nipple until she yelped and pointed to the door. As she shrugged on a sweater and jacket, he adjusted himself and zipped up his jeans. "Better." He sighed and stretched. "Now, why are you here, sour Kraut?" He chuckled at his joke, pushed himself out of the seat, and stepped forward, invading her space. She took a hasty step back.

"My name is Frau Perchta-" She raised a hand to halt his advance and he paused, his brow wrinkled in a blend of amusement and irritation that she chose to ignore. "- and I have an *ultimatum* for you Mr. Carpenter."

Carpenter tensed. All amusement drained from his features, leaving behind a steeliness that rivalled any blade that was carried by the other occupants of the room. His stare would have reduced anyone else to a trembling wreck of humanity, but the dealer's unspoken threat was either ignored or not recognised by Frau Perchta. As if realising this diminutive, geriatric woman was no threat, some of the tension dissipated from his frame and his lips twitched in a semblance of a smile. "Do you think you're in any position to issue me a fucking ultimatum? I run this estate. Shit. I run this town." He stepped closer. The single, bare bulb that illuminated the room cast his shadow before him. It fell across his frail adversary.

Unfazed, Frau Perchta folded her arms and met his gaze. A similar steeliness was discernible beneath the faded grey of her irises and, despite the towering difference in sizes, she stood firm. Not a tremor betrayed any sign of weakness or distress. If she was anxious she concealed it well. "Mr. Carpenter." Frau Perchta shook her head. "This used to be a decent estate. A place where mothers and fathers raised their children. A place where they could grow old and feel safe in their homes. A place where friends were just as important and caring as family." She prodded a thin, bony finger against the centre of the dealer's chest and he stumbled backward as though he had been shoved by a brawny youth. "But, you, Mr Carpenter? You have infected this place like a virus. Everything you touch rots and decays. The lives you taint, moulder until the people resemble living corpses. Look at the scum that you surround yourself with. Viruses too."

Carpenter's eyes widened and darkened. Anger rode his face and body, stiffening his torso, and malice rolled off him in waves. His knuckles whitened as he flexed his fingers... fingers that itched to wrap themselves around the handle of a knife or the trigger of a shooter. Pulling himself up, he seemed to grow in stature, filling the room with his malevolent spirit. The other people in the room recoiled in anticipation of an explosion of rage. The dealer snorted like a bull and grasped the old woman by the throat. "Bitch! You come in here dissing me in my castle and in front of my people? Tell me why shouldn't I squeeze tighter until I snap your brittle neck to dust? I own this estate. I own all the people who live here, and a dried- up, miserable witch like you does not get to walk into my domain and call me out." He raised his arm, lifting Frau Perchta off the floor, and hurled her towards the door. She fell to the floor in a crunch of bone and ageing joints. "Get her out of here before I lose my good temper and finish the bitch off."

Frau Perchta shrugged away the hand that reached out to pull her up. Grasping the seat of a nearby chair, she pulled herself to her feet and staggered towards the door. "As it's the season of goodwill, I'm giving you a final chance to leave this place, Mr. Carpenter. A last chance to do the right thing and let the good people of Belfield reclaim their lives and futures." She stepped through the door. "I'll give you until midnight. Christmas day will be the start of something new and beautiful for this place."

"Get that bitch out of my sight!" Carpenter screeched across the room. The hulk who had opened the door and let her in, pushed her back through it and slammed it shut.

Frau Perchta hobbled along the path, through the gate, and followed her steps back the way she had come. The street was deserted and there was no one to witness the bowed, old woman as she picked her way through the deepening snow. No one noticed how, with each footfall, she grew taller as her spine straightened, or how each step was firmer and longer. When she reached the door of the house on the other side of the road, Frau Perchta was several inches taller and walked with purpose and determination.

Pushing against the unlocked door, she entered a dingy room. Paint peeled from the walls and dirty curtains veiled equally grubby windows. Her breath misted in puffy clouds that drifted into nothingness as they rose higher. Tears squeezed from the corners of her eyes as she surveyed the squalor and she shook her head, focussing herself in readiness for the long night that lay ahead of her. She sank down onto the dirty carpet and sat cross-legged. Closing her eyes, she drifted into a trance, like a frozen statue in the unheated room.

Hour after hour slipped by. Inch by inch the snow continued to fall, burying the estate in its wintry embrace. The only sounds disturbing the stillness of the night were the distant throbbing bass of the dealer's rap music, and the chiming of the nearby church bells heralding the change from Christmas eve to Christmas day.

Frau Perchta opened her eyes and rose with the effortless grace of a ballerina. She rolled her neck and stretched her arms wide as if welcoming the dawn of Christmas. Gone were her saggy grey clothes, replaced by a gown that flowed to the floor and sparkled like a glacier in the moonlight. Grey, wispy hair now shimmered in lengths of ebony, and porcelain-smooth skin supplanted the grooves and wrinkles of old age.

Frau Perchta walked upstairs to the bedroom. Yellow light from one of the few unbroken streetlights illuminated the room in a sickly haze. A large, dirty mirror listed against one of the walls and she stood before it, regarding her transformation. Even though it happened every Christmas, she never failed to be awed by the beautiful woman who looked back at her. As she stared, her large eyes clouded. Also reflected in the mirror was the former tenant of the house. He lay across the soiled bed, one side of his young face glued to the bedcovers by a dried pool of vomit. His left arm was blackened below a makeshift tourniquet, the needle and syringe that had delivered his lethal fix still dangling from a vein. Another victim of Carpenter's greed.

She turned and stroked a pale hand through the boy's matted hair. He was one of the many reasons she did what she did during the season of goodwill. There was no one to mourn him. No one to avenge his pointless death. No one cared.

Except her.

And she would wreak havoc on those who did wrong.

She hammered on the drug dealer's door for the second time. The muscleman drew it open and a leer twisted the edges of his mouth into a lecherous grin as he spied her. "You here to buy, or can I interest you in something extra?" He grabbed his crotch and thrust his hips toward her.

"I'm here for the organ-grinder, not his monkey." Frau Perchta pushed past the man who watched her with his mouth open and disbelief in his eyes as she entered the room.

Carpenter was sprawled across the sofa where the blonde girl had blown him earlier. This time he was alone, drawing deep breaths on a fat spliff. Curls of blue smoke drifted into the foggy haze that accumulated near the ceiling. Nodding, he waved her over to him. "Well, princess, what can I do for you?" He patted the cushion next to him and waited for her to join him.

Frau Perchta stood before Carpenter and stared down at him. "I gave you an ultimatum, Carpenter, and, it seems clear that you don't have the intelligence to heed a fair warning."

He started forward, a medley of emotions crossed his face – confusion, surprise, anger. When he was halfway to his feet Frau Perchta raised her hand to his chest and pushed him back down. "Sit!" Carpenter fell back against the stained cushions and the glowing joint tumbled from his fingers into the worn upholstery. His facial expressions melded into one... fury.

"Damn, bitch! No one marches into my place and pushes me around. You're gonna pay for that. That pretty face of yours is going scare kids at Halloween when I'm done carving it up." Carpenter looked toward a couple of his men. "Grab the whore and hold her down for me."

Two men, including the guy who had opened the door, rushed to do as they were told. Frau Perchta kept her eyes trained on Carpenter and raised a hand in the universal sign for halt. Both men stopped dead, as though they had slammed into an invisible wall, and they crumpled to the ground. She flicked her wrist and they slid across the floor, only stopping when they crashed into the closed door. The blood left Carpenter's face, and his mouth gaped in awe at the instant demolition of his best men. He pushed himself up from the sofa. "Stay!" Frau Perchta's voice was low but, held the terrible threat of a distant storm. He slumped back, paralysed and helpless, and she turned her attention to the two men who were attempting to clamber to their feet.

"I came here earlier and gave you fair warning." Her eyes darkened. The irises resembling pools of black oil. "I told you to leave this estate and the decent people who live here. You *chose* to ignore my request and now you will pay in full for all of the pain and misery you have dealt these people." The doorman had managed to pull himself upright and he drew a knife, its silvered blade twinkling in the garish flashing of the Christmas lights. Frau Perchta reached out her hand. The knife tore itself free from the man's grasp and flew toward her. She caught it by its handle and ran a finger along its razor-sharp blade. The man paled as he stared at the peculiar woman.

"Every Christmas I visit someone who has made bad decisions in life. Someone who has caused misery and suffering to others, and I give them a choice." She flicked her hand and the man fell to the floor again. "I give them the choice to leave, or to stay and face the consequences of their actions. Occasionally, they heed my advice. Unfortunately, more often than not, they don't." Frau Perchta turned a full circle looking at the three stricken men. "Sadly, you didn't and it's time to pay your dues."

"I don't know what shit you slipped us lady, but when I get up you're gonna feel pain like you never felt before. You're gonna squeal and beg me to finish you off, but I'll make it last a long, long time." Carpenter's eyes clouded with hatred and malice.

"Quiet!" Frau Perchta glared at the dealer and a small smile curled the edges of her lips when Carpenter's threats turned to muffled, throaty grumblings. As she watched, his lips melted and reformed into one thickened, pink scar as they fused together trapping his malicious promises inside his mouth.

Clenched in the icy grip of fear, he trembled at the sorcery that bound him to his seat and had robbed him of his mouth. Eye's bulging, he watched the woman approach his men.

They clutched at each other trying, but failing, to get to their feet. "Be still," she commanded, and both men froze. Frau Perchta bent over the first man who had opened the door to her, and she raised his shirt exposing his pasty belly. A thin line of hair trailed from the low waistband of his jeans to his navel. "Please, don't hurt me," he begged, but his cries went unheeded. Frau Perchta had abandoned mercy. Using the confiscated knife, she sliced into his abdomen, sawing through the layered muscles to reveal the glistening coils of his guts. Her hand plunged deep inside to grab the slippery entrails, and she tugged. Warm, red snakes spilled to the floor to a herald of screams. The second man screamed, too, afraid that the same fate was about to be delivered to him. However, he was forced to wait while his friend lay dying beside him.

Frau Perchta gathered rubbish and debris from around the room. She picked up discarded beer cans, fast food wrappers, an overflowing ashtray. *Some people are worse than animals,* she thought. She knelt beside the screaming, disembowelled man. "You are the detritus of the world. You waste your lives and destroy those of others. The only gift you will receive this Christmas is this." She pushed the gathered debris into the yawning abdominal cavity and the man's tortured wails reached a new pitch.

She turned her attention to the dying man's companion. "It didn't have to be this way. I gave you a choice." Ignoring his pleading and begging, Frau Perchta plunged the blade into his belly and repeated her task. She wasn't afraid of being disturbed as she completed her work. Fear kept the neighbours minding their own business. No one would call the police or dare to investigate the racket.

When the screams of the two men faded and they lay bleeding and dying, their entrails replaced by garbage, Frau Perchta turned her full attention to the dealer who was now a pitiful figure of abject terror. His sealed mouth attempted to form words which lay silent in his throat. Only his eyes were capable of pleading for mercy that was never going to be granted. She approached in silence holding the stained knife before her. Blood drenched her once white dress and splattered her fine, striking features, endowing her with a terrible beauty. She leaned forward, her nose almost touching his, and the acrid scent of his terror filled her nostrils. She ran a finger across the twitching, stretched skin that had been his mouth and whispered in his ear. "After tonight you will never harm anyone again. You will cease to exist, and the world will be a better place without you."

Tears poured from Carpenter's eyes as he begged in silence for his life. The knife carved through his skin and Frau Perchta sawed across his abdomen before casting the blade aside, its job done. The dealer's eyes rolled back, and tiny ruptured blood vessels patterned their surface when she thrust both of her arms, elbow deep, inside him. Her fingers hooked into the slippery, warm coils and she pulled them out in festive streamers before stuffing the remaining refuse she had gathered into the gaping hole. "Rubbish to replace rubbish." Her voice was soft and melodic, in contrast to the rawness of her task.

Her work completed, Frau Perchta left the house leaving Carpenter, barely alive, on the sofa. Grey tendrils of smoke began to rise from between the cushions where the dropped roll-up had fallen. Within minutes flames began to lick at his paralysed body. They would eventually cleanse the tainted building.

Frau Perchta strode through the deep snow, each footprint disappearing almost immediately as the blizzard danced and swirled all around her. If any of the estate's residents had dared to venture out, they would have seen a beautiful, blood-drenched angel of death walking on earth. She reached the end of the road and the flakes thickened, enveloping her slight body. Frau Perchta disappeared for another year.

The End

Kevin J. Kennedy Presents

Duende
By
Christina Bergling

The small box appeared on the porch, immaculately wrapped, three days before Christmas. The paper was black and embossed with striking silver snowflakes. The corners were folded crisply around the edges of the box. A thick, silver ribbon bound the present tightly.

When I opened the front door, the December air spat a flurry of snowflakes against my cheeks. I squinted against the glittery particles dancing in the sunlight. The waterproof material on my legs swished as my snow boots squeaked on the hardwood floor. With the wind tickling through my eyelashes, I cast my gaze down.

The beautiful little dark box greeted me. The perfect cube perched directly in the center of our welcome mat, miniature drifts of snow accumulating around its corners.

My snow boot hovered above the box, frozen in the intended step. Instead, I placed it on the icy stoop and crouched down to the strange present. My bulky blue mittens fumbled at it, unable to grasp the actual shape. I finally dug my teeth into the tip of my right mitten and tugged it from my hand.

The sharp edge of the cold air bit at my exposed skin, a stark contrast to the sauna created inside my winter wear. I traced the edge of the smooth paper with my fingertips until I located the gift tag, folded under the bow. I flipped the square of paper toward my face.

Merry Christmas, Maria.
Do not open until Christmas Eve.

The script was as impeccable as the wrapping itself. A smile stretched my face as I gathered the gift addressed to me into my bundled arms.

Forgetting my plans of building a snowman taller than myself, I turned on my rubber heels and stomped back into the house. My heart fluttered against my chest. I felt the thrill of the unexpected and mysterious gift chattering on my nerves.

Who could have deposited such a strange and pretty package on my porch? It was not the mailman. There was no box, envelope, or address. All of the gifts from my tias and tios and grandparents were already accounted for under the tree. I knew because I had counted, examined, and shaken them every day this festive month. My parents kept their gifts diligently hidden in the garage attic where my sister and I would not hazard a peek. And Santa would not be here for two more nights.

Who left this present for me on my porch?

The question in itself was a gift in the way it made my mind writhe with possibilities and my skin tingle in sympathy.

"What are you doing back inside so soon?"

The sound of Isabella's voice ground my excitement to a seizing halt. My bubbling emotions shrivelled back down into my chest. My shoulders tightened, and I felt myself clutching the box tightly.

"I don't see a snowman bigger than you out there. I don't even see any footprints out there," Isa snarled.

I pushed the present harder into my chest, until I could feel the corners of the box through my parka. I tried to obscure it with my arms, hide it from her. Her footsteps slammed on the hardwood around me.

"I knew you weren't going to do it. I told you that you wouldn't do it." She laughed, the way she always did, the way that made the fine hairs along my neck bristle.

Finally, she circled around to face me. I kept my chin tucked hard, still clutching my present. I knew where this was going.

"What is that?" she cried, as she caught sight of the shining snowflakes on the gift wrap.

She reached out to snatch it before the inflection finished passing her lips. I instinctively, and with practice, jumped back out of her reach.

"What is that? Give it to me!" She groped at me again, and I fell into the steps of our usual dance.

"It's mine," I cried, turning my shoulder to shield the gift.

I could feel my heartbeat climbing in my ears. My body heat bloomed below all my insulated layers. I began to sweat.

I turned around to flee, but my snow pants and boots were cumbersome. She grasped the edge of my sleeve and yanked me back until she could seize my arm. I could feel her impossibly tight grip through all my down layers. My younger muscles could not contend with her strength. Despite all my struggling, she simply moved me as she wanted.

I cried out as she wrenched my arm open, sounding out the familiar alarm, beckoning for reinforcements. Before I could hear footsteps from the back of the house, she stripped the present from my arms. She held it high above me, out of my reach, reading the tag.

"Merry Christmas, Maria," she mocked. "Do not open until Christmas Eve. Who gets to say when you open a present? Who would give a loser like you a gift like this? I'm taking this."

"No!" I shrieked, jumping futilely beneath her, grabbing for the box.

"What is going on in here?" our mother shouted, as her footsteps finally reached us in the hallway.

Isa immediately tucked the gift behind her back. I felt myself continuing to bounce up and down in full tantrum, but I could not resist the rolling swell of rage and frustration, the impotence I felt every time she took from me so easily.

"Maria, Maria, calm down, Mija," my mother soothed, placing her hands heavily on my shoulders to stifle my jumps. "Isa, what did you do?"

She turned to my sister with her fierce eyes of interrogation. Isa dropped her jaw and opened her eyes wide in feigned innocence. She nearly put her hand to her chest to express her offense, but she was too busy clutching my present.

"She took it!" I cried, through the tears I could not contain. "She stole my present!"

My sobs were embarrassing, but they had a mind of their own. Isa held the fake expression of shock and bewilderment. My mother tilted her head and looked at her from the side of her eyes as she began to strip off my winter layers.

"Isa," she said, allowing her tone to drop menacingly.

"Well, it's not hers," Isa replied.

"Yes, it is," I cried. "The tag says my name!"

"What tag?" A cold and clever smile slithered across Isa's lips as she brought the present from behind her back.

The tag was gone. Only the black paper and silver bow remained. I could hear the small scrap of evidence crumpling up in the hand still obscured behind her back. The rage flared in me once more, blazing over my senses.

"You took it!" I shrieked. "There was a tag. Mama, there was a tag, and it was to me! That's MY present! Give it back! Give it back, Isa!"

My mother stood and took the box from Isa. She rolled it over in her hands, examining it. She let the impeccable shape move along her fingertips as she searched for the name tag currently being squelched in Isa's ruthless palm.

"Dios, dame fuerzas," my mother mumbled to herself. "There's no tag here, Maria," my mother said to me softly.

I wanted to calmly and rationally explain to my mother how I had discovered the box on the porch and how the tag with my name clearly scripted was smashed in Isa's hand. I knew my explanation would be far more convincing than the lies Isa would sloppily spin. I knew my mother would hear the truth. Yet the emotions surged through my small body. The fury swelled my tongue with only incoherent sobs. The frustration at my emotional incapacitation only made the fit burn brighter.

"Maria. Maria, calm down, Mija," my mother soothed. She dropped my coat and snow pants in a heap beside us. "Sit down on the steps there. Count to ten, like the doctor said."

Another blast of outrage rattled up my skeleton, but I could only stumble over to the stairs. I dropped myself carelessly into a puddle of my own tears. I felt trapped by my own immature temper and my sister's narcissistic torment. I glanced up to meet Isa's eyes, a mix of condescension and enjoyment on her face. Her twisted smirk curled my stomach into tighter knots.

She was going to take this present from me. Isa took everything from me.

I gasped against the sobs and forced out the numbers.

"One, two, three..."

"Can I have my present back now?" Isa said.

My mother nearly rolled her eyes as she turned back to Isa. Isa stood sassily with her hand on her cocked hip and her head tilted. I could see the irritation tense along my mother's shoulders.

"No, Isa," my mother said.

"But it's mine," Isa whined. "I found it on the porch for me."

"No, it's not," I forced through my sobs.

"I'm not doing this, girls," my mother said. "No one is opening this present tonight. We are putting it under the tree, and we will deal with it on Christmas Eve, Noche Buena. And if I find that this present has been opened or is missing before then, I will donate all your gifts to charity."

I gasped, hard.

"Mom, no!" Isa shrieked.

"Dios ayúdame, I will make you deliver them yourself."

We fell silent. The edge on her voice made it clear she was serious. My mother never made hollow threats. When she said we would be forced to wear our father's shirt together until we stopped fighting, she watched our two heads poke out from the neck of his shirt for three hours. My tantrum froze at the threat and receded back under the edge of my control.

"OK, Mama," I said, mopping my cheeks.

"Fine," Isa huffed.

I clutched the spindles of the handrail and pressed my face against the wood as I watched my mother move to the tree. The twinkling lights reflected on the glass spheres suspended from each branch and the white wall beside our fireplace. She perched the perfect black and silver box on top of the rumpled gifts in red and white paper that arrived from our tia in Texas.

Isa moved up the stairs and stopped to lean over me. She brought her thick lips close to my ear until I could feel her wretchedly warm breath on my cheek.

"Nice job, psycho," she hissed.

Isa stomped up the steps until she disappeared into her room. Her ominous presence was replaced by the annoying mumbling of pop music through her closed door.

My mother returned from the tree and stepped up to me, placing her chin on the handrail above my head.

"Maria, Mija," she said gently.

"Yeah, Mama?" I put my head on my knees, refusing to look up at her.

"Are you OK?"

"It is my present, Mama."

"Mija, we are not going to deal with that now. It is under the tree until Christmas Eve. But that was an awful fit to have over a little present."

I took a deep breath and tried to keep the tide from swelling back into my brain. I squinted back the tears before looking up at my mother.

"She's just so mean, Mama," I replied. "She takes everything from me."

"I know it is hard to have a sister." My mother stepped around the banister and gathered me into her chest. Her touch was so warm and soft. I instantly felt the wave dissipate in my chest. "Your tias and I fought constantly growing up. We hated each other."

"That's why you live in different states."

My mother laughed wholeheartedly. The sound quivered down into her belly, making it full and rich. She hugged me tightly into her and planted a kiss on my forehead.

"Do not worry, baby. It will be a great Christmas."

She kissed me again, firmly, and gathered up the pile of my winter gear. As she moved down the hallway, I crept to the tree and crouched beside my gift. For some reason, this present captivated me above the others. Not knowing who sent it and the fact that Isa was determined to steal it elevated its importance. I would not let her take it from me.

I ran my fingers along the crisply folded edges of the box, explored the scratchy texture of the sparkling ribbon. The urge to disobey my mother and shred the wrapping in this isolated moment twitched in my hand. The impulse surged through me as rampantly as the tantrum had just gripped me.

"One. Two. Three. Four..." I counted as I replaced the present under the dangling edges of the pine needles.

I glanced over the mound of other gifts huddled beneath the branches. I knew, like every year before this, Isa would claim the items she wanted, regardless of gift tags or our parents' threats. The crying baby doll she had relieved me of Christmas morning only to return to me broken two days later. The Leapster game system she was four years too old for but requisitioned anyway and still kept idle in a drawer by her bed. Even the candy from my stocking if I didn't eat it fast enough or hide it well enough.

Isa took everything.

"Maria!" My mother hollered from the other room. "Time for bed, Mija."

I looked at the glinting lights on the tree once more before running up the stairs.

The next day, one more morning closer to Christmas, I bounded down the stairs in my pajamas. My sticky bare footprints hurried directly to the tree. The lights and the sweet scent of evergreen remained equally mesmerizing each morning, even if it was not yet Christmas, even if nothing had changed under the boughs. As the holiday excitement built, I needed to start my days close to the epicentre.

I scanned the same presents, the same contrasting patterns of festive papers, the same bows until my eyes met the dark present. I hesitated, squinted, looked again. I had to move closer and bring the box into my hands.

The gift tag appeared nestled below the silver bow, clearly printed, pristine, and unwrinkled. Just as it had looked when I first met the present on the porch, before Isa had gotten her thieving hands around it.

I didn't care how the tag had been recovered or replaced. It made about as much sense as Santa Claus coming down every chimney in the world in one night. The happiness and the faith were just as vivid as Christmas morning, and Santa Claus was still real to me. I smiled to myself and darted into the kitchen for breakfast.

The day whiled away uneventfully. Hours passed before I heard Isa's heavy steps stomp down the stairs. Once again, I did not go outside to construct a snowman larger than myself, though the flakes outside continued to accumulate in optimum conditions. Isa entertained herself all day by gluing her eyes and fingertips to her phone. I welcomed her distraction and the freedom to enjoy a day without harassment.

As twilight edged into the sky, I curled up on the couch in front of the traditional Claymation holiday classic Rudolph. I had the Grinch and Frosty queued up in my preparatory line-up. I cuddled down into my blanket and the couch cushions and watched both the characters on the screen and the fat snowflakes tumbling past the window.

"Maria!" Isa's shrill voice rang out down the hall.

I rolled my eyes, knowing she could not see me, and tossed the blanket aside. I chased the sound of her calls to the Christmas tree. She was clutching the mystery present. My mother had started a fire in the hearth beside her with the waning of the day. The wood snapped and crackled as the flames spread over it, growing taller.

"How did you do it?" Isa yelled.

"Do what? What are you talking about? Where's Mama?" I asked.

"How did you get the tag back on here? I trashed it."

"I didn't do it."

"I know you didn't do it! You can't write like this. So how did you get it back?"

"I didn't," I shrugged. "It just came back."

"It just came back?" she scoffed. "Gift tags don't appear! Just like Santa doesn't come down the chimney."

"You're lying!" I screamed.

"*You're* lying!" She yelled back.

She pitched the present, the small black box with silver snowflakes, into the fire beside her. The box bumbled onto the top log and settled on the disintegrating wood. At contact with the heat, the wrapping paper burst into blue and green flames. The rush of heat radiated against our faces.

"NO! Isa, no!" I cried.

I threw myself on the floor in front of the fireplace, too timid to reach my hands into the fire. I could only watch the blue and green flames swirl and dance as the box crumbled into ash more quickly than it should have.

"No, Isa. Isa, how could you? No! No! No!" I continued to cry.

I curled into a defeated ball in the heat of the fire and continued to wail. Isa stood above me, smirking like she always did, watching my fit like she always did. I felt like she was absorbing my pain, suckling it like a vampire. I wished she would choke on it and her cruelty.

My father heard me first and came storming into the room.

"What the hell is going on here?" he shouted, turning to me then my sister.

Isa said nothing, and I continued to cry.

"I said, what is going on here?" my father said again, planting his hands on his bulging waistband.

"She's having another one of her fits," Isa dismissed.

"No!" I cried, fighting to temper the emotions, struggling to get the words out. "She burned it! She threw my present in the fire!"

"What? What present?" my father glared at Isa, confused.

The blue and green flames had faded, but the vague ashen shape of the box remained scarcely visible. My raged roared up in my chest to replace it. I glared through burning eyes at Isa. She had taken something else from me. She had burned my present just to spite me.

"I don't know what she's talking about," Isa shrugged. "Just look at her. She's crazy."

"Isa! Do not say that," my father growled. "Maria, what are you talking about?"

I felt the emotions throbbing through every inch of my veins. I felt my skin ignite with the tingle of rage. I felt the heavy weight of the tears brimming in my eyes. My throat clogged with my turmoil, and I found myself gagged once again.

"Maria?" my father said, his irritation rising.

I choked down a breath, struggling to stifle my sobs. I did not look at the crumbling ashes of the box or Isa. I forced myself to think of nothing.

One, two, three, four, five...

I collected myself off the floor and stood, head hanging, in front of my father.

"I got a present yesterday," I forced out. "It showed up on the front porch. Isa saw it and tried to steal it. Mama made us put it under the tree. Then she—" A sob strangled me. "She threw it in the fire!"

My composure dissolved beneath me, and the tears returned in a flood.

"She's lying!" Isa began to protest.

"Isa go to your room," my father said.

"But she's—"

"Isa! Your room. Now."

My father's voice was heavy and firm but always calm. If he raised it to shout our names, we knew he was serious. Isa spun around, dramatically flipping her hair over her shoulder, and stomped loudly up to her room. The door slammed behind her; then the awful music blared.

I pulled my knees into my chest and turned to feel the warmth of the fire on my face. All evidence of the box had vanished into the flames. The fire continued to roll over the log as if nothing had happened.

"Maria," my father said. "I want you to go your room too."

"But why?" I turned my tear-stained face up to him.

"Because these fights have to stop. You girls have to figure out how to get along. And these fits of yours, they have to stop, too. You cannot get hysterical about every little thing."

"But she threw my present in the fire!"

"Upstairs. Now, please. I hope you girls can hold it together for Christmas."

"It's not me," I protested.

"Now, Maria."

The tears climbed back into my eyes as I ascended the stairs, calmly this time, though. My sadness rolled gently beneath my chest. The fact that Isa was evil was not my fault. The fits she caused me were not my fault. She was the problem. I should not have to suffer the same punishment as her. She tried to steal my mystery present and threw it in the fire to hurt me.

69

Just thinking of the blue and green flames licking over the wrapping paper brought more tears stinging through my sinuses. I knew it was just one present. I had no idea what it was or who had left it for me. Yet it had been special. It had been my secret surprise. And she had taken it, like she took everything from me.

As I climbed into bed and pulled the blanket up over my head, I promised myself she would not take Christmas from me.

Christmas Eve arrived the next day. I slept in later than normal, wrapped in the weight of my despair. When I finally wrangled my eyes open, my body still felt exhausted. My tongue cleaved to the roof of my mouth from the dehydration into which I had wept myself. I did not feel very festive. I could not stop thinking of my present ablaze the night before.

I shambled down the stairs and began to shuffle toward the kitchen. As I passed the Christmas tree, I saw Isa standing before it. The lights had not yet been plugged in, so the branches looked dormant and mundane. She stood there, unmoving, and just stared below.

"Isa, what are you doing?" I said."

"How?" Isa stammered, still not moving or looking up.

"How what?"

"How did you do it? I burned it. I threw it in the fire. We watched it burn."

"What are you talking about?"

I moved closer to see around Isa. In front of her, my mysterious gift perched neatly upon the red and white packages from Texas. The paper was crisp and completely unsinged and untarnished. I knelt down and reached out to tip the gift tag.

Merry Christmas, Maria.
Do not open until Christmas Eve.

"How?" Isa said again.

"I don't know," I said. "I didn't do anything. Daddy sent me to bed, too. I just woke up."

"You're lying. You have to be lying. That's the same present. Did you have another?"

"No."

Isa turned away slowly, almost cautiously, and crept out of the room with scarcely a footfall. I let my weight fall back and simply sat by the tree, staring at the box. Its ominous return made me not want to touch it, not yet, but I felt the same pleasant captivation at the sight of it. And I felt an unnerving vindication in how its resurrection had deflated Isa. Now, she wanted nothing to do with my gift; now, it was mine again.

Sitting with the black paper, silver snowflakes, shining ribbon, and small card with my name on it, my depression receded. I felt my consciousness levitate out of the weighted darkness and settle back on my shoulders. I even felt my steps float a little when I replayed Isa's quivering voice in my head. I skipped toward the kitchen, ready to enjoy my holiday once more.

After dinner, with the homemade tamales swelling our bellies, we gathered around the tree. We had this brief window for presents before we embarked through the neighborhood on posadas then attended midnight mass. The small lights warmly lit the branches, and the flames from the fire cast shifting reflections over the floor. The room looked like Christmas, every Christmas I had experienced in my short life, and I allowed that familiar, joyful feeling to fully infect me.

Isa seemed to have recovered from her perplexed trance by the tree, yet when she pounced at the pile of presents she did so on the far side, away from my mystery gift. I, instead, sat excitedly right beside it, ecstatic that it was finally Christmas Eve, finally the start of Christmas. Isa and I had been opening doors on our advent calendar all month. Every Sunday, our mother lit another candle on the wreath. Tomorrow morning, she would light the final one. We were finally here.

"Isa, put down the present," my father said gently. "Not until they are all passed out. Then Maria goes first. She's the youngest."

Isa sighed and rolled her eyes, setting the present aside. She crawled under the tree and began distributing gifts. I moved forward and did the same. Since we could read the names on the tags, we were tasked with making the present piles.

Isa and I heaped stacks of gifts from our tias and tios and grandparents. Our mother and father collected a present or two in total.

"OK, Maria," my mother announced, once every present under the tree had been sorted. "You go ahead and start us."

I smiled brightly and snatched up the small box with black paper and a silver bow. I frantically clawed my fingers under the corner of the paper.

"Oh, Maria," my mother interrupted. "Don't start with that one. You don't even know who it's from. Start with one from your tia."

I opened my mouth to object then shrugged and placed the box beside me. I reached for one of the red and white packages and began shredding the paper with abandon. As I tore away sections of wrapping, my mother reached over to gather them up and sweep them immediately into a trash bag at her feet.

The red and white paper, striped to resemble a candy cane, yielded an exquisite doll from my tia's trip to Spain over the summer. The plastic flamenco dancer had hands frozen in a brazen floreo. Her chin jutted up over a proud miniature chest. Her tiny, meticulously layered dress alternated in blue satin and black lace to match the veil pinned to her fake hair.

Blue... Isa's favorite color. I glanced around the tree to see Isa tear open an identical doll in red. She smiled up at our mother. Once my mother turned her eyes to her wine glass, Isa looked at her doll, then over at mine. I could see the intent in her face. My heart sank, knowing where this would be going.

I placed my beautiful little flamenco dancer in blue on the edge of the crimson tree skirt and crawled across the floor to the table. I took a deep sip of my mug of egg nog and reached for the polvorones cookies. My fingertips slipped around the glass surface of the plate, stirring the powdered residue yet unable to locate a cookie. I gaped for a moment then looked over to see Isa grinning wickedly with her lips encrusted with the white sugar.

"I have more in the kitchen, Maria," my mother soothed. "I'll refill the plate after presents."

I felt another degree of weight compress my chest, deflate my joy, but I reminded myself of my own resolve. I would not let her win this year. I would not give her the pleasure of ruining my Christmas. I took another chug of egg nog and returned to my presents.

As I reached my spot, I noticed the flamenco dancer under the tree now donned a red gown.

One, two, three, four, five, six...

"Is that all your presents, girls?" my father asked as the piles dwindled and the trash bag swelled.

"That's all of mine," Isa said, twirling the blue dancer between her hands.

"I still have one," I said, finally lifting the present from the front porch.

"And we are sure that is yours? No more arguments?" my mother asked.

Isa cast her eyes angrily at my doll in her hands, but said nothing.

"Yes, Mama. I—" I hesitated. "I found the tag."

I stood and brought the gift for her inspection. She took the box gently in her hand and examined the tag.

"Merry Christmas, Maria," she read. "Do not open until Christmas Eve. Well, Mija, it is Christmas Eve, so go ahead."

I crouched back down and gathered the present into my lap. The anticipation sizzled on my tongue. I nearly could not stand the culmination of the mystery. My mother and father both set down their wine glasses and leaned forward to watch with actual curiosity rather than the mild interest they feigned during the other gifts. We all wanted to know.

Except Isa. Isa just continued to play with my doll and pretend the little black gift did not exist.

I untied the bow and unwound its length from the box. I wriggled my fingertips under a crease in the thick wrapping paper and tugged until it split.

The underside of the paper was the same shiny silver as the snowflakes, making the tear look like a leaking crack. When I stripped all the paper away, I unearthed a clean, black box.

I spread my hand over the lid and wrapped my fingers around the edges, wiggling and shifting until it slid from the top of the box. My heart pounded now, its echo dragging a ragged edge on my mind. Yet I found myself taking my time, savoring the extra moments, the extra gift just for me—not Isa.

A small card nestled atop perfectly creased and folded evergreen-colored paper. The immaculate script matched the penmanship of the tag.

"What does it say, Maria?" my mother asked almost nervously, perched farther on the edge of her couch cushion.

I held the card, quivering in my fingertips, almost stunned. Holly berries and their accompanying leaves printed in black framed the edge of the card. The short message was scrawled elegantly in the open space.

"Dear Maria," I finally started reading. "In this box is a very special friend. Duende will grant your darkest Christmas wish. No need to tell him. He knows what's in your heart."

"That's it?" my father queried.

I turned the card over. The back was blank. I looked up at my parents.

"Yes," I said. "That's it."

"Who is it from? Does it say?" my mother asked.

"It doesn't say," I answered. "There's no signature. Just a big X."

"What does darkest Christmas wish mean?" Isa asked from around the tree. "What Christmas wishes are dark?"

She brought my doll in her blue dress up to her face as she asked. I felt the rage flicker again, somewhere beneath my new bewilderment.

"Give that card to me," my father demanded. I passed it over and waited.

"Well, what's in the box anyway? What is duende?" Isa persisted

"It means elf," my mother replied.

The excitement had abandoned me, leaving a sort of hollow confusion and nervousness in its wake. My fingers almost trembled as I reached into the box and shifted the dark green paper aside.

Nestled within the evergreen paper, I could make out the shape of a small body, curled into the fetal position. Its slender limbs folded tightly against the narrow body. On top of the impossibly round head, a pointed hat perched above equally pointed ears. The small eyes lay closed.

"What is it?" my father nearly yelled, practically kneeling on the floor in front of the couch.

"It's—it's an elf," I stammered. "I don't know. It kind of looks like those Elf on a Shelf things. But different. Darker, I guess."

"Who would send you something like that?" my mother wondered aloud.

My parents both stood and cautiously moved toward me. They stood behind me, peering over my shoulders into the box at the unnerving figure. Isa refused to move and instead began playing with my doll more blatantly, attempting to recapture the attention. Yet we were all too enthralled with the strange gift in my lap.

The three of us leaned in slowly, none daring to reach into the box. Then the tiny elf's eyes snapped open.

I flinched hard, dropping the box to the floor in front of us. Both of my parents jerked back. My father's hand pressed protectively over my chest, holding me back against his legs. The box managed to land flat with the opening still facing the ceiling. We all huddled together, arching away from the unwrapped gift, for a long and heavy moment.

Nothing happened.

My father's hand gradually loosened from around me. Once we all started to breathe again, he stepped toward the small elf. Isa sat across the room, staring at us dumbfounded like we had all gone mad.

My father took slow and cautious steps toward the box. He approached it the way he would a wounded dog. Just a small, festive doll folded up in a black box. Just a tiny little elf. He crouched down toward it, and as he extended his fingers to gather up the box, the paper rustled. My father snatched his hand back to his chest in a startling flash and materialized back beside me and my mother.

The four of us sat frozen—my mother and father encircling me with their arms, Isa clutching my new doll beside the tree—as the box rocked side to side subtly. The crinkling of the paper grew louder before falling still. A tiny, spindly arm shot up from the present, then wrapped around the rim of the box. Then the other arm mirrored the movement. Both miniature hands gripped the green paper as the red point of the hat began to ascend into our living room.

"Dios ayudanos," my mother breathed into my hair. *God help us.*

I could see my father's jaw drop from the edge of my vision. I could not move my eyes from the small elf crawling out of my mystery gift. Isa looked exactly like our father, as she always did, with her mouth dangling in shock. She pressed my doll into her chest, and I could see she was trembling.

The elf, Duende, popped out from the box in one final, swift motion, like a deranged jack-in-the-box. All at once, its hat, head, and small body leaped into the light. Once it was standing, it fell still again for a long series of seconds. None of us moved; none of us breathed. Then, suddenly, it reanimated again, moving in alarming and jerking movements, like a marionette dancing to a stuttering beat.

My body thickened with fear. The pulsating sensation saturated me. I could feel it prickling at my toes and carving lines all the way up into my brain. Panic erased my mind, leaving me at the mercy of confused impulses and immature instincts. I could only cling to my mother's arm and wait for my parents' cues for what to do.

Duende hopped from the box and landed dramatically, casting its stick-like arms to the side and bowing gravely. It snapped its head back up and faced us. It had two beady black eyes that shined unnervingly as they reflected all the light in the room. Below a sharp nose, the thin, red line of its mouth curved up in a grotesque smile. The four of us uttered a collective gasp, and Duende's smile only seemed to carve deeper into its face.

Duende took shaky, twitching steps towards us, painfully slow and deliberate. It moved awkwardly, as if it was learning its own body. Its torso folded forward oddly and arms splayed haphazardly around its sides. The jerky cadence was more alarming than the fact that the dark elf moved closer to me.

My father stood slowly again and began side-stepping gradually behind us, moving toward the fireplace. As Duende approached my knees, my father leaned down to gather up the fire poker. Duende stopped and reached its miniature hands towards me.

"Don't you touch her," my mother shouted, shooing at the elf with her hand. Her arm tightened around my shoulders.

Duende snapped its head toward my mother and released a piercing hiss. The sound shredded through the air and forced us all to wince and reach for our ears. As my mother cradled her head,

Duende jerked its face back to me. The vile, thin smile returned to its lips.

The tiny elf, with its wretched face, in a small, red hat and plain green clothes, climbed onto my knees. I stopped breathing. I could not even quiver with fear, I was so paralyzed. As Duende moved closer to my face, I saw my father move up behind him, the fire poker raised and ready to strike.

Perched on my thighs, Duende took my face between its two tiny, pointy hands. Its touch was cold, its skin inhuman, more like wood. I could see my fearful face reflected fully in its large, black eyes. It allowed me to see myself, naked in all my terror, through its eyes; then it leaned forward and pressed its little forehead against mine. I felt a strange heat spread from the contact.

Somehow, that heat sedated me. It felt clear, focused. At some point, my eyes had fallen shut. When Duende dismounted my lap, I opened them again. The fear had receded, and I felt a calm like before the tantrums ever started.

As Duende began to toddle over the floor again, my father pounced. He leaped into the centre of the room and swung the fire poker like a golf club at the small elf. The poker whistled through the air yet never found its target. Duende snapped to attention then launched at the wall. It landed on a picture frame with its limbs splayed out like a spider and began skittering over the wall. It moved in frantic patterns nearly too fast to see, scampering up by the ceiling then flitting around the back of the tree. With each movement, its pointed hands made a dreadful scratch against the plaster walls.

Another communal gasp escaped us as we huddled together, eyes frantically searching for a flash of the tiny creature. For a lethargic second, it seemed as if it had fallen silent.

"Maybe you scared it off," my mother breathed to my father.

At the sound of her voice, Duende emerged from the branches high in the tree. Ornaments rustled against the needles at its movement. Its pointy hat jutted from the boughs; then the figure dove straight onto Isa. Isa shrieked as the elf burrowed into her hair, winding its spindled limbs into her tight curls. Duende released that horrendous hiss again to drown out Isa's cries.

My parents released me and rushed over to Isa. Isa thrashed over the floor, groping and clawing into her own hair as the elf continued to move in a tangling frenzy. Her face contorted in sheer terror, eyes bulging wide and desperate. Her brown skin, always darker than mine, managed to bleed into a deep red. I could hear the follicles tearing away from her scalp amidst Duende's unrelenting hiss. Tufts of her black curls drifted softly to her frantic feet.

Again, that eerie calm rose up in me, that same alluring heat that spread over my forehead when Duende put its head to mine. I felt myself stand slowly. In the struggle, Isa had finally released my Spanish doll in the exquisite blue dress. I gathered her up into my hands and gently moved to the couch. I sat myself behind my parents' abandoned wine glasses. I felt like I was floating without the weight of thoughts in my head. My mind felt as blank as the elf's glassy black eyes.

My family continued to tumble and move in a cloud of limbs in front of me. Ornaments shattered as they were shaken from the branches and collided with the hardwood below. My father managed to get behind Isa and plunge his hands into the thrashing mess of her hair. Instantly, he went flying through the air and collided with the tree, taking it down in a shower of brittle glass and flickering lights. His body collapsed, unmoving, on top of the branches.

My mother clung tightly to Isa's hands, trying to pull her away from Duende's force. She had regressed into speaking in Spanish. We only heard her fully speak in her parents' tongue on the phone to distant relatives, when we had made her livid, or if she had too many glasses of wine. I thought she might be praying.

From deep within the tresses, Duende yanked Isa to her feet. My mother was dragged along by her hands. The evil little creature began to spin Isa by her hair, lobbing her in large circles. My mother clutched and groped at her hands as she twirled along with her. They revolved faster and faster until my mother lost her battle against the force of the circle and flew off into the wall. She skidded down the paint as the picture frames rained down upon her. Like my father, she crumbled immobile on the floor.

With my parents unconscious and witnesses effectively removed, the chaos ceased. Isa dropped to her knees, panting and sobbing. Tears soaked her face, and spittle dribbled from her trembling lips. I smoothed my fingers along my doll's black veil and calmly watched her. Duende popped from the nest of Isa's hair but remained perched on top of her head. It looked at me and cocked its head slowly and continually to the side until its pointed hat met its shoulder.

I knew the question without a word.

I let my sight fall from the black orbs in Duende's ghastly face to Isa. Her crazed eyes pulsated in their sockets. I scarcely recognized her without her trademark smirk or aggressive condescension. Crushed beneath her fear, she appeared so small, so frail, so childlike. She almost did not look like the monster who tormented me daily.

Almost.

Duende began rolling its head in the other direction, slow and almost creaking. When the red hat reached the opposite shoulder, I closed my eyes and gave my answer.

The elf smiled.

With the grin carved deep into its face, Duende twirled back into Isa's mane. She let out a shriek that echoed in fear, disappointment, and pain. The elf yanked her back to her feet. Then, in one swift movement, almost too fast to see, it dragged her up the chimney. They passed so quickly there was not even an odor of singed hair, cloth, or flesh. They were just gone.

Feeling calm and warm and more satisfied than my young brain knew how to process, I curled up on the couch and fell asleep.

When my parents regained consciousness and shook me violently awake, I feigned no knowledge of an evil elf who attacked my sister.

"There was just a little elf doll in the box," I maintained. "Creepy, but just a doll."

My father gaped at me incredulously, lost for words. He stomped over to the shambles of the tree and snatched up the black box. Nestled in the evergreen paper, a dark elf doll curled, immobile. He ripped Duende from the box and shook its limp body in disbelief.

"It was alive," he muttered. "It attacked your sister. Isa! Where is Isa?"

My mother brought her thumb to her lips and slowly crumpled to the floor in front of the fireplace, beside one of Isa's shoes lost in her rapid ascent past the flames.

***

Duende perches lifeless on the mantle in my small home. After my father chucked it into the trash in a fit of rage and tears, I snuck out and hid the elf under my mattress until I moved out. Twenty years later, it appears entirely unaged, identical to when I first tore the black snowflake wrapping paper and moved the dark evergreen paper. The large, glassy eyes are closed, hiding the darkness inside, yet the small mouth remains carved into a mischievous smile— a smile with a wicked secret.

My parents searched for Isa for years, though they never could quite explain to the police what happened that Christmas Eve. My mother continues to light an extra candle for Isa each Christmas Eve after dinner, though we no longer open presents until Christmas morning. Christmas Eve became something else, more of an unspoken memorial of that night with Duende.

I should have been more helpful to my parents. I should have felt more upset at the loss of my sister, felt guilty at all for somehow releasing the evil creature onto her. I knew these things in a distant sort of observation. Yet, even as the small elf fell dormant, that warm, infectious calm it had bestowed on my forehead persisted. I never experienced another fit, never felt suffocated and choked by emotions again.

I feel only that calm... a strange and perverted peace.

The End

Kevin J. Kennedy Presents

A Noel in Black
By
Matthew Brockmeyer

The doors to the homeless shelter shut in ten minutes, but Caleb needed another drink. It was Christmas Eve 1970, and he was wandering the streets of Eureka, California in a tattered and filthy Santa suit, crimson hat perched atop his head, dirty beard pulled down around his neck, a streak of vomit running down his left leg.

When the Salvation Army gave him the costume, days ago—how many now? Three? Four?—it had been brand new and shiny clean, but he had gone AWOL as soon as he had begged up enough money for a good drunk. He couldn't believe how easy it was to get money begging in a Santa Suit during the holidays, especially when people thought they were giving to the Salvation Army. Too bad, he thought, that the racket had to end tonight. Fuck it, he was headed to the nearest bar and had a pocket full of money.

Bells on bob-tail ring, making spirits bright. Oh what fun it is to sing a sleighing song tonight.

Finally managing to make eye contact with the simian faced bartender who was absent-mindedly pushing a dishtowel up and down a pint glass, Caleb waved a fiver in the air, a wry smile of *what the fuck?* on his face. Red and green Christmas tree lights flickered over the bottles and mirrors and off in the corner the Ghost of Christmas Past grinned its horrid smile. The bartender nodded acknowledgment and strutted over.

"Yeah? Whaddya want?"

"Beer and a whiskey."

"What kinda beer? What kinda whiskey?"

"The cheapest."

The bartender got him his drinks, took the twenty, and left his change in front of him on the bar.

Sipping the bitter medicine, Caleb noticed a woman a few stools down trying to draw his attention, a jet of blue smoke issuing from her cherry-red lips as she raised and lowered her thickly-penciled eyebrows. He could tell she had done her best to look good tonight: lots of eye makeup, newer, hipper-looking clothes, but he could see the age in her face, recognized her need like a bad smell. Battered, needy women gave off a stink of desperation he'd learned to recognize over the years. Those years since he'd been back from the war. He'd had his fair share of these types. Always good for a warm bed and a hot meal, but too crazy to spend any real time with.

"Hey there, Santa. Buy a girl a drink?"

"Sure thing, honey." Caleb glanced at the barkeep. "Give the lady what she wants."

She slid down next to him as the grim faced bartender mixed a rum and coke, speared a lime with a tiny sword and dropped it in the glass. "I've always had a thing for Santa," she whispered. "Coming in late at night to punish the naughty and reward the nice."

"Yeah, and what are you, darling? Naughty or nice?"

"I've always thought I was a little of both."

"Ha. What's your name, baby?"

"Sandra. They call me Sandy around here. But I think of myself as Sandra."

"All right, Sandra. What's your story?"

"Just a local girl, been in the same place too long. What about you, Santa? Don't you gotta lot of work to do tonight?"

Caleb laughed, that deep, reassuring laugh he'd mastered over the years, to put people— women especially—at ease. They talked for a while. Then Caleb ordered a pitcher of beer and a couple more shots and they moved to a corner booth. Sandra talked on and on, chain smoking Salems while he drank his beer and sipped his whiskey, watching as the room began to spin in slow, psychedelic and nauseating circles.

"You're awful quiet."

"I've been told that before."

"How'd you get them scars on your neck?"

Caleb put his hand to his neck, let it drift down to the dirty fake beard, and pulled the knotted grey and black mess of hair over to cover his throat. And that wicked Ghost of Christmas Past with sunken eyes and yellow teeth whispered, "Tell her." And so Caleb did.

"In the war."

"You were over in 'Nam, huh?"

"Yeah, two tours."

"And then what? You come back to have these damn hippies spiting at you? I feel for you, sweetie. My daddy died in France fighting Nazis. Now my brother is in the Navy while this country goes to shit. You got these bastards like that dirty Abbey Hoffman saying to steal everything. And this Charlie Manson Family killing movie stars." She laughed, shook her head and sipped her drink. "It's enough to make you sick."

They grew quiet. "So, you going to tell me about those scars, or what?"

"Well, I was a Kootchie Kootie. A tunnel rat. You know what that is?"

"Oh, yeah. You were one of those guys that go down in those gook holes?"

"Sure was. Infantry. 1st Reconnaissance Squadron." He sighed, not wanting to get into it, but once he started it was hard to stop. "I was working three clicks west of Duc Pho in the Quang Ngai province. I was down in a tunnel. Just me, my .45 and a flash light. Looking out for booby traps and rats and spiders, and this animal. . . it came out of nowhere. Fucking attacked me. Just latched onto my shoulder and wouldn't let go."

"Oh, baby. You was attacked by an animal down in one of those tunnels?"

"Yeah. But when I killed it, when I shot it... " He couldn't tell her the rest. He couldn't tell her how after he had shot that thing, the muzzle blast a blinding light, the report deafening, after he had filled that monster full of holes and watched it drop, it had looked just like a little girl. Just a tiny, raven-haired girl, all shot up and bloody, when moments ago it had been a beast: a mess of lurching fangs and drool.

His mouth moved up and down silently. He couldn't say anything. Then, with an incredible effort, what he had managed to say was, "I think I brought something back with me. I... I... I don't know."

"You brought something back with you? You mean like that Agent Orange stuff, honey?"

"No, something different. Something, something. . ."

"What? In your head?"

He wanted to say, no, something in my blood: I brought back something in my blood that makes me a monster; but instead, he just nodded yes, his face a knot, visibly fighting to not break down in tears.

"Oh, baby, oh, baby, I understand."

The room was twirling now at a breakneck speed. He was going to be sick. He pulled away from her and vomited on the floor.

"Son of a bitch!" the bartender shouted. "Who's going to clean that up?"

Caleb hung over the edge of the booth, retching and dry heaving.

"Fuck you, Sam. He's a veteran! He fought for this country, got attacked down in one of them gook holes. What the fuck you ever done?"

"I don't care if he was on the beach at Normandy. Get him the fuck out of here!"

"You're a piece of work. A real piece of work, know that, Sam? Where's your sense of Christmas spirit?"

The bartender stomped up to her, eyes bulging, an accusing finger extended. "Get your cheap-whore ass out of here, bitch, and take your Santa Claus friend with you. Got me?" he grabbed her face in his hand and jerked her chin up so that he could look her in the eye. "This bar ain't no place for you any more, Sandy. You make my customers sick. Everyone who's wanted to has fucked you, and none of them's too proud of it either. You'se don't belong here. Find some other place to haunt, you cheap skank." With that he tossed her head aside and stormed back behind the bar.

We wish you a merry Christmas. We wish you a merry Christmas. We wish you a merry Christmas and a happy New Year.

Sandra walked Caleb back to the motel room she rented by the month, holding him up the whole way while he leaned against her mumbling and pointing to ghosts she could not see. Once they were back at her room she helped him out of his Santa outfit and got him into the tub. In the heat of the steamy water he regained a semblance of consciousness, came back to himself. When he looked up he saw her through the mist, leaning in the doorway, staring at him. She had changed and was now wearing nothing but a silk kimono. He had to admit she didn't look that bad.

"How you feeling, Santa?"

"Good. I feel . . ." he paused, unsure what to say, how he actually felt. "Good."

She knelt down beside the tub, ran her finger over the surface of the water. "Thirsty?" she asked, holding up a tumbler of Scotch and water.

"As a matter of fact, I am."

Taking the glass into his hands, he took a sip. Handing it back to her she gave him a penetrating stare that he found hard to decipher and then leaned in to kiss him. She tasted of whiskey, cigarettes and peppermint. But it was good, the way she gently ran her tongue over his upper lip before she pulled away, and Caleb felt himself growing aroused.

"Now that you're all cleaned up, why don't we get you to bed."

"Sounds good, baby."

"Dry yourself off. I'll be waiting." With that she disappeared out the door.

He got up from the tub and dried himself the best he could with the cheap, tiny towels the motel provided. When he entered the room she was already on the bed, prone on her back and naked. She may have had a butter face but her body was to die for, and she knew how to flaunt it. He started towards her but she held up her hand, palm out toward him, and exclaimed, "Stop right there, mister. The Santa suit. Put it on."

He gave her a questioning half grimace and then smiled. "You serious?"

"I told you: I gotta thing for Santa."

Smirking, he pulled on the dirty jacket and set the conical hat atop his head. "Better?"

"Oh, yeah, baby. I've been so naughty. I need to be punished."

With that she burst out in playful laughter, turned over onto all fours, and stuck her ass into the air, whispering over her shoulder, "Come and get it, Santa."

He approached the bed and, still standing, he pulled himself into her. She let out a deep moan and he began to move, slowly. He was still drunk as hell and the room was spinning slightly but he could feel that primal urge within to rock and rotate. He began to lunge faster, and faster, and then, suddenly, it was happening again.

Fuck. No. No. No. It was happening *again*. He could feel himself beginning to change as he thrust against her. A part of him wanted to run away, to bolt through the door and into the night so that he wouldn't hurt her. But another part of him wanted this. It felt good. It felt *so fucking good* to let go and let the animal inside him take over. Still pounding, Sandra moaning beneath him, he watched in wonder as his fingers—tightly gripping her bony hips—became claws and a thick mat of fur began to weave itself up his arms. Thrusting against her with all his might he lifted his face and began to howl as his mouth filled with sharp, gleaming fangs.

Here comes Santa Claus, here comes Santa Claus, right down Santa Claus lane!

Margaret Ashton was the manager of the Lone Pine motel. She had been across the street visiting with her daughter and grandson in their two-story, cookie-cutter house, and she was just walking back to the motel office when she heard the screaming in room 308. It was that cheap-tramp Sandy's room.

Margaret had been waiting for an excuse to evict her and marched up to the door, ready to throw her out, Christmas Eve or not. But as she grew closer and heard the urgency to the screams, the gut-wrenching terror of the squeals, she grew hesitant and stopped. Suddenly, without warning, the window shattered, showering her with glass and splintered wood. She fell back and slipped to the ground, watching in utter disbelief as the craziest thing she had ever seen in her life of fifty-six years came tumbling down atop her. It was a wolf. A huge monster of a wolf, with a snarling mouth of fangs dripping blood and drool. And it was wearing a red coat lined in white fur with a Santa cap perched atop its head.

From his bedroom window her grandson Tommy watched the entire thing.

Later that night homicide detectives would interview the little boy. Tearfully he would relate how he had seen his grandmother ripped to shreds by some kind of beast in a Santa suit. One of the uniformed officers standing idly in the background would then turn to his partner and whisper under his breath, "Looks like grandma got run over by a werewolf, walking home from his house Christmas Eve."

God, the Easter Bunny, and the Ghost of Christmas Present watched as two-year-old Annabelle toddled out the door of her street-level apartment and onto the sidewalk, a thumb stuck in her mouth and dragging a Barbie doll along by the hair. God looked like the guy from the Dos Equis commercials: an incredibly good looking older gentleman with white hair, perfectly coifed, and a nicely trimmed beard, in a tuxedo. The Ghost of Christmas Present looked extremely bored and kept yawning. The Easter Bunny was an out-of-work writer who needed a shave, dressed in a pink bunny outfit.

"Cute kid," the Easter Bunny commented.

"I wouldn't get too attached," the Ghost of Christmas Present replied, disinterestedly stifling a yawn.

Annabelle's parents were fighting again and they could all hear their voices echoing out from the apartment.

"Just how many Quaaludes did you take? You can't even look at me. Jesus, wake up, bitch, I'm talking to you."

"Fuck off, Henry. You always were a bore."

"You dumb cunt. I oughta slap the stupid right offa your face."

When the wolf came galloping down the middle of the street in its blood-soaked Santa suit the Easter Bunny turned to God and said, "You gotta be putting me on, man."

God rolled his eyes.

The wolf grabbed the baby in its mouth and threw the child upward into the night sky where she hung suspended in the moonlight for a moment, tiny arms and legs kicking, and then tumbled down, landing on the street with a thud. The beast leapt at her, sinking its fangs into her neck and thrashing its head side to side until the tiny figure ceased to struggle and lay limp in its mouth.

"It's probably for the best," the Ghost of Christmas Past said.

"What? Why?" the Easter Bunny asked, scratching at the stubble on his face.

"You want to tell him, God? Or should I?"

God gestured with his hands, as if to say, "Go ahead. It's all you."

"If she had lived, her life would have been nothing but a short burst of agony and suffering. I'll spare you the details, but trust me when I say, her life taken like this, quickly and mercifully, is a blessing, a thing of joy. A Christmas miracle."

"Is this true?" the Easter Bunny asked God.

God grinned and nodded.

"You don't say much, do you?" the Easter Bunny asked God.

God just shrugged.

Deck the halls with boughs of holly, fa la la la la la la la la. 'Tis the season to be jolly, fa la la la la la la la la.

Father Mulligan was cleaning up after midnight mass when he heard the click-clack of claws on the wooden floor. He paused, chalice in one hand, ciborium in the other, and listened.

"Hello?" he called out, his voice echoing throughout the empty chapel. "Who's there?"

Beneath the pounding of blood in his ears he distinctly heard panting, like that of a large animal. "Hello?"

Deep in the dark recess of the hall something stirred, moved, and then came slinking out of the shadows: a large creature walking on all fours, its eyes alight and flickering like yellow flames. The beast came forward slowly down the aisle, Santa hat drooping down one side of its head, a dead baby hung limply in its mouth. The wolf approached the altar and came so close that the priest could smell it, a feral odor of blood and musk. It spit the baby to the floor where it landed with a horrible smack.

But the priest didn't run. He stood his ground, murmuring prayers beneath his breath. He knew why the beast was there, why this spawn of evil had come. It was here to punish him. Punish him for the things he had done to all those little boys. So many. First in Ireland when he had just been doing what had been done to him when he was an altar boy. Then, after coming to America, in Philadelphia, where for years the urban darkness of poverty and city life had let him run rampant. Not yet here in California, where he had been sent quickly by the diocese so as not to cause a scandal. But he had his eyes on a few of the boys in his congregation. Some of the poorer ones who he thought wouldn't tell.

Seeing the monster here was a blessing and death would be a mercy. He fell to his knees, kissed his stole, and lifted his neck to the beast. But instead of taking him by the throat, the beast spun him around by the shoulders so that the priest fell face first to the floor. With one quick jerking motion the monster shredded the priest's pants and mounted him. The priest cried out in pain and surprise as the wolf forcibly entered him and warm blood began to trickle down his leg.

God, the Easter Bunny and the Ghost of Christmas Present stood at the back of the chapel watching. The Easter Bunny had taken off his hood of rabbit ears and was puffing on an e-cigarette and furiously tapping away on an iPad mini. "Been blogging about this whole thing, and, yeah, a lot of people see that as offensive. I mean, what the fuck? You got a werewolf dressed like Santa Claus raping a child molesting priest on Christmas Eve?"

The Ghost of Christmas Present laughed heartily. "Well, I hate to say I told you so, but . . ."

"You got nothing to say about this, God?" the Easter Bunny asked, momentarily looking away from his iPad.

God tilted his head to the left, his thin lips bending into a sad frown, and, raising his eyebrows in an, "Oh, well," manner, shrugged again.

Joy to the world, the Lord has come. Let Earth receive her king!

Gravy Brain Jane was out of her mind on LSD and had nowhere to go. She had a thousand tabs of purple sunshine on her but the connect had never shown and wasn't answering the phone. Exasperated and befuddled, her vision a swirling cyclone of light and darkness, she stumbled from the Greyhound Station to a small clearing in a copse of woods. She sat leaning against a tree, the branches dripping and melting around her, the sky a miasma of spiraling stars and galaxies. She giggled and mumbled, "No sense makes sense," to herself.

Charlie had sent a message from prison that she should deliver the acid here. If Charlie said it would work out, it would work out. She was sure of that. She had thought the other passengers on the bus would have been startled and scared by the X that Sandy and Squeaky had helped her burn into her forehead with hot bobby pins, but no one had noticed at all.

The Easter Bunny, who wasn't even wearing his rabbit outfit anymore, and was now just dressed in his usual black jeans and t-shirt, was pacing back and forth irritably. He turned to the Ghost of Christmas Present and asked, slightly argumentatively, "Well, where's God?"

"Oh, he couldn't make it. Had a concert to catch."

"A concert? What are you talking about?"

"Well, it was Skynard and you know how he loves Free Bird."

"Typical."

Gravy Brain Jane giggled when she saw the beast slowly creeping towards her. She had been taught to love coyotes when the family was in the desert of Death Valley. Back on the ranch Charlie had taught them to break down the final walls society imposed on them by having them fellate the stray dogs.

"Hey there, beautiful," she said. The wolf just stared at her with its unblinking yellow eyes.

From their glimmer and spark she knew just what the creature wanted. It wanted what all men want and she had been taught the ways of a free love society. Giggling she squirmed from her panties and lifted her skirt with a vacant grin. She knew that in love there is no wrong. That submission is a gift and that you should never learn not to love. Charlie had taught her well.

She spread her legs, exposing herself, and the beast crept up to her and lowered its snout to her and began to lap at her in quick, greedy, licks. She gripped his ears tight, her head thrown back, and thought about how groovy and sexy it was to be pleasured by the beast, to have death and life so close, to lay your hands upon the monster and be free in love. As she bucked and lurched and felt herself climax she thought about how the Son of Man had taught her that death is only another orgasm, that everything in the universe is in and out and in and out in a cosmic orgy, babies coming out, galaxies sinking into black holes, knives plunging in, blood pouring out. Wow! Talk about the Big Bang!

The beast crawled atop her and slipped itself into her. When it shuddered and released itself inside her she knew within her heart that she would be with child. This was a happy moment. A glorious moment in time. Another Christmas miracle. Oh, joyous night. She would name this child Stewart, Stewart Kirby, after her grandfather.

Afterwards, the beast lay against her, spent. She stroked its fur with her nails and gently kissed its blood drenched snout. In this way the beast kept the girl warm through the coldest hours of the night.

Silent Night. Holy Night. All is calm. All is bright.

Free in the moonlight as snow began to fall, bathed in the stink of congealing human blood, the taste of flesh and woman fresh on its lips and tongue, the lycanthrope ran, the stars above him a smear of spilled milk, the moon a cataract eye aglow in malignancy.

On the First Day of Christmas my true love gave to me. . .

Caleb awoke in the morning naked and freezing, enveloped in the scent of the Douglas fir and redwood. He shivered and looked about. Snow was falling heavily, blanketing the earth in white. Beside him lay his tattered Santa costume, by some miracle the hat still clung to his head.

He glanced above the towering tree tops to the shelter of the sky and saw there a light both majestic and bizarre. Seemingly fake, like a bad special effect from a cheap television show. And in that glaring gleam of white, he saw a black figure descend: The Ghost of Christmas Future who spoke in a deep and sultry voice while extending out a hand, "Do you wish to come with me?"

In his mind all he could hear was Bing Crosby crooning *I'm Dreaming of a White Christmas*, and a million worlds passed before his eyes. Birthday cakes with only a few candles to blow out. His mother's smile as she tugged on thread, sewing patches on a Cub Scout sash. Playing catch with his dad who bought him that special glove for little league and would oil it with him in the falling sun of the suburban evening. Watching Kennedy's skull explode on television, Jackie screeching and trying desperately to crawl away. The Howdy Doodie show. Lee Harvey Oswald grimacing in pain and turning as Ruby put a bullet in his side. That gnarled old apple tree in the backyard, how that ancient tree would fill with tiny white blossoms in the spring so that you could not tell how old and bent it really was, its age hidden in its blooming. How those tiny petals fell in early summer, glistening in the amber light, a shimmering rain of flowers cascading down and lying white as snow on the ground. Sweat streaming down his brow as he pushed a lawnmower, that smell of fresh-cut grass, such a vibrant green it made his head hurt. Behind the baseball dugout with Betty Connors on a warm summer night: his first kiss. How she had moved away soon after and he had never seen her again. His draft card: that plain and innocuous envelope of a pale yellow color that they'd all dreaded and all expected. Telling his father, "Guess I'm going to war, pops." And his father just nodding back stoically. His gal Sally, with her beehive hairdo, who wouldn't let him fuck her no matter how hard he begged and pleaded, telling her he didn't want to go to war a virgin. The ancient apple tree in autumn, loaded with ripe fruit. The bumpy ride over the Pacific in a military transport plane. The Vietnamese whore who spread her legs for a single American dollar. Paddy fields burned and incinerated so that no water stood within them and the rice stalks withered. January 1968. Tet: The New Year, a time to worship ancestors. An intricate barrage of hellfire. Medivac choppers stuffed with bloody men and boys. Fire fights, flares illuminating the night, the thunder of mortars and sparks of muzzle flash. A landscape of smoke and exploding ordinances. Those mornings when the bombers flew in and the ground shook like jelly. Seeing men he knew dancing and screaming in flames. Splintered, broken trees, smoke billowing in the distance. The Pickle Switch and canisters of napalm. VC bodies dressed in black lying in horrible piles. A rifle on the ground with a stream of ammunition dripping out of it. "I dare you to pick up that dead man's gun." "Yeah, right." The tunnels. And the idea of winter, just the concept of it in that hot, hot land where all is hidden from you, taken, and there is nothing to believe in or hope for, but you imagine that tree back home nonetheless, barren and without leaves and fruit, draped in snow and frozen. The way the men whispered when they found a dead body, till all you hear is whispers of body, body, body. Then the beast appears who is really only a little girl. How could you have thought that a little girl was a monster? There was no monster, just a little girl, you made everything else up. But now there is a monster, just as sure as there are ghosts, an Easter Bunny and a God. It's you. You're the monster. You're the beast. And you think to yourself, *"What have I done? What did I do?"* Then, as you face this ultimate truth, the cold takes you. And when would spring come again? Certainly not in this lifetime, and not on this earth. So, "Yes," you say to the cold and the winter. To the Ghost of Christmas Future who holds nothing forth but death. "Yes. Take me. Just take me away and let me be free." An affirmation to end the rest of your negations.

And you let go of that aching, awful, agonizing pain of being a man of flesh and blood, the cold slowing down your heart, and give in to death.

And as you slip away, into the embrace of the Ghost of Christmas Future, you wonder, "Was it real? Was any of it real at all?"

And in the heavens a laughing God finally breaks his silence and answers: "There is no such thing as real. It's all just a dream within a dream."

The End

The Mall Santa
By
Christopher Motz

The parking lot of the Elmview Mall was a madhouse.

Mason Harrison promised himself he'd stay home for the holidays, but like clockwork, he arrived at the mall every year, drawn to the sights and sounds like one of Pavlov's dogs salivating at the ringing of the dinner bell. Mason didn't have relatives to shower with gifts, nor did he particularly care for the sound of Christmas music piped into the mall's audio system. Still, he was drawn here, year after year, with an empty wallet and an even emptier heart.

Look at these sheep, he thought as he parked his car near the edge of the lot. He always parked there. All the good spaces were taken by noon, occupied by mini-vans full of screaming children and adoring parents with pocketfuls of money. Every holiday was another lesson in consumerism and another chance to see how far adults would go to bribe their children into behaving like future pillars of society. He often wondered what would happen if, instead of parking his car, he used it as a two-ton, wake-up call; just drive right through the front door and give these people a good scare. Except then Mason would spend Christmas in jail, and as much as he despised the holiday, he was positive spending it behind bars wouldn't alter his perception.

He locked the car, pulled his jacket tighter around his neck, and sloshed through half-frozen puddles as he made his way across the lot. The sky was gray and overcast; flurries drifted from low-lying clouds and tickled the skin on his cheeks. Nearby, a chubby little girl dressed in a gaudy sweater bedecked with multi-colored reindeer, jumped up and down, squealing delightfully as she caught snowflakes on her tongue. Her parents giggled and beamed proudly as they jammed their vehicle with their day's purchases.

All Mason could hope for was that their Christmas tree was dead when they got home... dead or on fire.

"Mister, Mister," a teenage girl called, shaking a small bell in her hand. "Would you like to donate to The Salvation Army?"

"Not a chance," Mason rumbled. "Give my hard-earned money away to a stranger? You're wasting your time, and you're certainly wasting mine."

The girl backed away slowly, squinting in irritation. "Okay, Scrooge," she whispered.

Mason was just glad she'd stopped ringing that damn bell.

This shit should be illegal, he thought. *They're no better than beggars in the street looking for a handout.*

He shouldered his way past the girl, eying her red kettle distastefully. He hadn't even stepped one foot in the mall, and already he was growing agitated. The front door slid open with a musical chime as he entered the vestibule. The tinny overhead speaker blared Nat King Cole over the chatter of a dozen shoppers trying to exit the building. Their bags collided, their bodies jostled for position, their fake smiles and cordial nods belied a greater need to escape and tend to their nicotine addictions.

Mason hoped someone would start a fight, or

fall... or both. Something to spice things up a bit. Unfortunately, the vestibule emptied without incident. Nat King Cole gave way to Mariah Carey's version of 'Silent Night.' He wanted to puke. Once inside, it only got worse.

Colored lights hung from every available space; store windows were decorated with tacky fake snow and hideous plastic trees; loose tinsel drifted across the linoleum floor like shiny tumbleweeds. Mason couldn't understand everyone's attraction to cheap decorations and sappy carols sung by out-of-key children. In a world where fads are so fleeting, why the hell hadn't Christmas gone the way of disco?

In the center of the mall, beneath a giant skylight, stood a cheesy Christmas village of gingerbread houses and candy cane trees. A crowd milled about, gawking at a mock-up of Santa's sleigh pulled by emaciated papier mâché reindeer. A line of fidgety adolescents hopped around impatiently, wiping snotty noses on their sleeves, awaiting their chance to sit on the lap of a fat man in a fake beard. The time-honored tradition of dumping your kid into the waiting arms of an imposter with gin on his breath was alive and well.

"Were you a good girl this year?" the Santa-man asked.

The brat nodded stupidly, apparently too star-struck to string a sentence together.

What's she going to say? Mason mused. *I pissed in my sister's cereal? I punched the cat? I spied on daddy making out with the loud-mouthed weirdo next door?* Of course not. *Every* kid is good at Christmas, and they're paid handsomely for their failed efforts. Barbie dolls and video game consoles, smart phones and vats of chocolate to keep their mouths busy with anything besides complaining about what Santa *didn't* leave under the tree.

After a few seconds of wide-eyed adoration, the girl jumped down and ran to her waiting parents, who had already posted seven hundred photos on Facebook of little Suzie sitting on Santa's lap. Nothing says 'unwanted social media bombardment' like a news feed full of other people's children wearing crooked grins and covered in drool. Mason only used his laptop for one thing... and he was certain he'd make Santa's 'naughty list' for the images stored on its hard drive.

He came here to watch this ritual every year. Not to find some long-forgotten holiday spirit, but to remind himself exactly why he hated the season in the first place: consumer stupidity, corporate greed, and the widespread brainwashing of the country's youth. Do good things and be rewarded with shiny trinkets. The same kids grew up to be corrupt assholes, fighting one another for the better Christmas bonus and the shinier sports car. Santa's magical village was a training ground for future CEOs, a place where children came to reap rewards for their deceit.

With a grunt, Mason turned and fought his way through the crowd. It had only taken fifteen minutes for him to prove to himself that he was right all along. Christmas is for fools.

By the time he'd returned to the parking lot, it had gotten dark, and the temperature had plummeted. The thin layer of snow beneath his shoes had frozen, turning the asphalt into an ice skating rink. The folks from The Salvation Army were gone, and the lot appeared to have emptied out quite a bit since he'd arrived. He looked at his watch, noticing it was only a few minutes past five. Usually the mall was packed for several more hours.

"You beating the storm, too?" a man asked, as he dumped his bags into the trunk of his car.

"There's a storm coming?"

"Sure as hell is," he replied. "Calling for up to a foot of snow tonight."

Mason nodded and continued walking. His only plans were to stop at the liquor store for a bottle of Jim Beam and get drunk in front of the television. He didn't give a shit if it snowed the rest of week. He bagged groceries at a local, family-owned market. The owners closed shop the last two weeks of the year to vacation in Florida. They had some misguided belief that by giving their employees two weeks off, they were somehow rewarding them, but the time off wasn't paid, and they didn't believe in holiday bonuses. So instead of a relaxing and carefree holiday, it meant the employees would have to make their paychecks last even longer. By staying in the house, Mason only had to worry about getting enough booze to carry him through the rest of December. His only worry was having to dodge shitty Christmas movie marathons, which he usually accomplished by putting 'Die Hard' on repeat. It was as close to a Christmas film as he'd ever get.

"At least we'll have a white Christmas," the man shouted cheerfully.

Mason raised one fist in the air and flipped him the middle finger.

Stick your white Christmas up your white ass.

He angrily jammed the key in the door lock and jumped into the driver's seat, slamming the door behind him. He turned the key in the ignition as his Beretta's engine roared to life. He turned the radio on and waited for the heater to do its job. The damn car was older than him; it took a while to get going in the cold.

He sat quietly, humming along to Radiohead and rubbing his hands together to fight the numbness that had crept into his fingertips. He thought maybe he'd skip the liquor store; he had plenty of booze for tonight, and he had suddenly grown sleepy as the interior of the car filled with warm air from the Beretta's vents.

Just a few more minutes, he thought.

The engine's vibration lulled him to sleep.

***

Mason opened his eyes and shivered.

The car's interior was freezing, and the engine had stopped running. Through the cloudy windows, he saw the parking lot was nearly empty.

"How the hell did I fall asleep?" He looked at his watch and saw that it was almost ten o'clock. He'd been out for over four hours. He wiped his face, blew a warm breath into his cupped hands, and turned the ignition. Nothing. He tried a second time, listening to the weak click of the solenoid.

"The battery can't be dead," he groaned. "The fucking car was *running*."

He tried again with the same result. The Beretta wasn't going anywhere.

He opened the door and stepped outside. He had enough change in the console to make a few quick calls if only he could find a pay phone.

Do pay phones still exist? He instantly regretted not having a cell phone.

"You need some help?" a voice boomed from behind. Mason jumped and pressed himself against the car.

"You've got to be kidding me," he blurted.

Standing well over six feet, a man approached as his polished black boots crunched in the accumulating snow. His large stomach tested the fur-lined fabric of his red top, and beads of condensation clung to his tangled, white beard. Mason found it hard to imagine any greater irony than being saved by the mascot that stoked his ire.

"Looks like you're in a bit of trouble, friend."

"Uh, yeah, I guess I am."

"Dead battery?"

"That'd be my guess."

"Well, I wouldn't be a very good Santa if I

didn't help a man in distress."

"I saw you... in the mall."

"You caught me," Santa laughed. Not only did he laugh, but he placed his hands on his protruding gut and 'ho-ho-ho'd' his way a few steps closer. Mason rolled his eyes and hung his head.

"Listen, pal, I appreciate your help, but you don't need to stay in character for my sake."

"Aw, come on! There's nothing wrong with spreading some holiday cheer."

"If it's all the same to you, I'd rather forgo the merriment and get to the part where my car starts and I drive home."

"Maybe you should've asked Santa for a new car," he chuckled.

"No offense, but I'm not sitting in your lap."

Santa closed the distance between them and scowled. Mason thought it would have been the perfect time for a photograph.

See, kids! This is the man behind the mask. A pissed off, middle-aged phony playing dress-up.

"Mason, you're going to wind up on the naughty list if you keep thinking like that."

"What? What the fuck? How do you know my name?"

"Santa knows everyone's name."

"Okay, knock it off, it isn't funny anymore."

Santa laid his gloved hand on the hood of Mason's Beretta and tapped his fingers. The engine turned over once before sputtering to life; the headlights cut a swath of yellow light across the snowy ground as the radio blared 'Santa Claus Is Coming To Town' by Bruce Springsteen. Mason stared at Santa, mouth agape, no longer shivering just from the cold.

"What... what did you do?"

"Worked a little magic," Santa explained. "It's a Christmas miracle."

Mason's miracle ended when his knees buckled and he collapsed to the icy ground. Springsteen's voice followed him down into the darkness.

***

Mason opened his eyes and grunted. His mouth tasted of fabric softener from the sock that had been crudely crammed between his lips. He tried to stand and found that he'd been tied to one of his kitchen chairs by several strings of blinking Christmas lights.

How'd I get here? he thought. *How'd he know where I live?*

"I can take the sock out of your mouth if you promise to stay quiet," Santa said, approaching from behind. Mason nodded rapidly as small bells jangled from the hat that had been jammed over his head. His abductor stood in front of the chair, smiling down at him through his thick, white beard. He pulled the bunched-up sock from Mason's mouth and held it in his gloved hand, waiting to see if Mason would hold up his end of the deal. Mason spit and sputtered, but otherwise remained silent.

"Why'd you do this?" he questioned. "And how

did you know where I live? Have you been following me?"

"You don't get it, do you? Santa knows where all the boys and girls live."

He's bat-shit crazy, Mason thought.

"Just let me go," he pleaded. "Take whatever you want. I won't say anything to anyone."

Santa chuckled merrily. "It doesn't work like that, Mason. You don't believe in the spirit of Christmas, and I can't have that. The world is such an angry place, and for just one day, people put their differences aside and celebrate something... magical."

"Whatever you say, okay? I don't want any trouble. Just take what you want and leave."

Santa smiled and dropped the sock on the floor. When he moved aside, Mason saw a large, densely decorated Christmas tree standing in the corner of the room. Beneath its fragrant branches sat a dozen expertly wrapped gifts, the smallest easily big enough to conceal a mini-fridge. Lights were strung around the edges of the ceiling, and the windows had a variety of different holiday staples: icicle lights, tinsel, plastic reindeer, and images of the man himself. Santa appeared pleased.

"Why are you doing this? Not everyone celebrates Christmas. You're not going to change my mind, no matter how many angels you hang from the ceiling."

"I do it for the children, Mason. To see their eyes light up on Christmas morning; to hear their laughter as they notice their plates of cookies have been eaten and glasses of milk emptied. Flying around the world in a single night is thirsty work."

"For the children?" Mason scoffed. "Do you kidnap *all* the kids who don't believe in you?"

"Of course not," Santa said, feigning disgust. "Children are innocent. They don't know any better, but they soon come to realize there's no other explanation for the treasures that magically appear in their stockings while they sleep."

"You're mad," Mason replied. "Everyone grows out of believing in Santa. You don't fly around in a sleigh pulled by reindeer; you don't squeeze your fat ass down chimneys and silently drop wishes beneath the tree. None of that is real, and the smart kids figure that shit out at the same time they stop believing in the Easter Bunny and the Tooth Fairy. Now let me go and get the hell out of my house!"

Santa stepped closer and smacked Mason across the face with one gloved hand. The fabric dulled the sting, but Mason was shocked nonetheless. He fought against his restraints to no avail, crying out of anger more than fear.

"I'll make a believer out of you, yet," Santa grumbled.

"Damn you!" Mason thundered. "This won't change anything! Don't you get it?"

"Because of your father."

"Because of... what? How do you know anything about my father? That son of a bitch has been dead for twenty years."

"Yes, but he was the one who ruined your Christmas spirit, wasn't he? He's the reason you behave this way."

"It has nothing to do with him."

"Tell me about 1992, Mason. Tell me what happened."

"You know everything, right? Why don't you tell me?"

Santa dragged another chair across the floor and placed it in front of Mason. When he sat, their faces were only a few feet apart.

"You wanted G.I. Joe toys that year. You were a little too old to still be playing with them, but it was your little secret, one you kept from your friends so they wouldn't make fun of you. It was also your first Christmas without your mother, wasn't it?"

"Who cares? I didn't need her around, anyway."

"Every boy needs his mother, Mason, but yours didn't even call you that day, did she? After she left your father, she found a new family."

"They're welcome to her," he cried. "She was a coward."

"After your father lost his job, he started drinking, isn't that right? Morning, noon, and night until your mother had enough. Can you blame her?"

"I wasn't the one drinking! I wasn't the one making her life a living hell. That didn't stop her from leaving me behind with that alcoholic monster."

"On Christmas morning, there weren't any presents under the tree..."

"That's because there wasn't a tree," he mumbled. "No tree, no family, no Christmas dinner—nothing. Just my dad sitting in front of the television in his underwear, getting drunk on a brand new bottle of brandy."

"You blame him for everything, don't you? Didn't he try his best? Didn't he keep a roof over your head?"

"I split when I was sixteen. I couldn't stand watching him walk around in piss-stained boxers, blaming the world for being such a useless dick. If you want to know why I don't believe in Christmas, go ask him. He's buried up in Shady Oaks

Cemetery." Mason stopped to catch his breath and fight the tears that suddenly sprung from his eyes. Santa watched him without emotion, waiting for him to continue. "Do you know what he got me that last Christmas? Do you? A bottle of cheap booze, a carton of cigarettes, and a porno magazine. I was fifteen years old. He wanted me to be a degenerate just like him."

"Poor, sad, Mason," Santa mocked.

"Fuck you!" he spat. "Where were you, huh? Mr. High-and-Mighty Santa Claus! Tell me about your magic now. Tell me about being a kid and having to clean puke out of the living room carpet instead of playing with your friends. I guess you must have missed my house for a few years."

"Consider it a valuable life lesson."

"Life lesson? You're telling me I deserved it? You're no better than my father."

"Did he make you steal toys from your friends? Did he ask you to break into your neighbor's house and ransack Bobby Miller's bedroom looking for the baseball cards he'd gotten for Christmas that year?"

"How do you know about that?" Mason fought to break free, straining against his bonds. "I don't have to listen to this from a fucking mall-Santa, do you hear me? Untie me right now, before I get pissed off."

Santa hit him again, this time with a closed fist. When he pulled his hand away, the glove was spattered with bright drops of red. Mason spit a gob of bloody mucus on the floor and glared at Santa angrily.

"I'll kill you."

Santa answered with his trademark laugh and leaned back in the chair, holding his prodigious gut. "No you won't, Mason."

"If you were the real Santa, you'd never do this."

"Everything has a balance; the good with the bad. I'm here to balance the scales."

"To punish me for something I did decades ago? To torture me for stealing a few baseball cards? You're a lunatic. I don't know how you know these things, but you're not going to get away with this."

"*You're* not going to get away with this," Santa replied. "For someone who didn't believe in Christmas, it never stopped you from taking what wasn't yours. Toys, money, lives..."

"Now, wait a minute. I never took a life—never! I'm not a killer."

"After you left your father's house, you had nowhere to go, isn't that right? You broke into old lady Finney's cellar and stayed there for weeks, eating her food, taking money from her purse, all while hiding unnoticed in the basement. Poor old girl thought she was going crazy. Furniture was moved, things were going missing. Then one day, she heard you down there, scratching around like a rat in the wall..."

"Just stop... please."

"Mrs. Finney was... what... ninety years old? She couldn't navigate the basement stairs anymore—not at her age and with her vision failing. Do you remember the sound she made when she tumbled down the steps, Mason? Do you remember the blood that pooled on the concrete when her head split open?"

"Stop, it wasn't my fault..."

Something rustled behind Santa's back... the familiar sound of crinkling paper. *Wrapping* paper.

"She was already dead when she reached the bottom, so there was nothing you could do, right? Did you call the police? Let someone know? Of course you didn't. You were too worried about being caught. Instead, you took the rest of the money from her purse, rummaged through her jewelry box, and left the house with pocketfuls of stolen goodies."

Mason heard the soft 'thump' of one of the Christmas presents toppling over onto the carpet.

"What is that?" he moaned. "What's back there?"

"Mrs. Finney's family didn't have Christmas that year, either," Santa continued. "They were too busy making funeral arrangements. It was a closed casket, of course. She'd been lying on the floor for a week when her grandson finally found her. She had eight grandchildren, did you know that? Seventeen great-grandchildren, and three great-great-grandchildren she never had a chance to meet. No Christmas dinner that year; no presents for grandma or pictures around the Christmas tree. Do you know what a human body looks like after a week of lying on the ground? The skin begins to slough from your bones like taffy... not to mention the damage done by her hungry cats..."

"STOP!" Mason shrieked. "I get it, okay? I'm sorry!"

"Sorry isn't going to bring back Mrs. Finney, or the many more years she may have enjoyed with her family during the holidays."

"She was ninety-fucking-years old! She already had one foot in the grave."

"And it was you that shovelled in the last pile of dirt."

Mason sobbed uncontrollably. He no longer fought against his bonds, but resigned himself to whatever punishment was coming. Another gift fell over with a thud; the tree shook as ornaments bounced to the carpet. The room filled with a sickish-sweet aroma as wrapping paper crackled and tore behind Santa's back.

"What is that?" he whined. Something mewled wetly from several feet away, but Mason couldn't see around Santa's hefty girth.

"Punishment, Mason. No bad deed goes unseen. Time to make amends for what you've done."

"You're related to her, aren't you? You're here to punish me for something I didn't even do."

"I'm not doing anything you don't deserve."

"What are you?" he screamed. "A maniac? An avenging angel? The Ghost of Christmas-Fucking-Past?"

"I'm none of those things, Mason. Haven't you been paying attention?" He stood from the chair and kicked it aside, giving Mason his first glimpse of the horrors emerging from the shredded packages. "I'm motherfucking Santa Claus, bitch."

Mason couldn't hear the Santa-man's words over his own terrified screams. One of the colorful packages bulged before falling over, dumping its contents onto the floor in a steaming heap. A naked, pink abomination dragged itself across a layer of slime by tiny, jagged fingernails that resembled claws. Its eyes were tiny, black globes, sunk deep in its deformed skull. The thing opened its mouth, displaying a row of sharp, pointed teeth - not unlike a piranha - set into glistening gums the color of a full-bodied Cabernet. It mewed weakly like a new-born kitten.

Mason screamed until his throat ached and black spots swam across his field of vision. The wrinkled monsters squirmed across the floor, leaving snotty trails of fluid behind them. They chattered back and forth to one another, flapping their gaping mouths like fish out of water, flopping ever-closer to Mason's position. Fine, white hairs poked through the mottled flesh of the creatures' jaws and chin, as one after another, they struggled to their feet.

"What... are... they?" Mason rasped.

"Elves, of course," Santa explained, "or at least they will be... after they feed."

The closest of the new-born atrocities wrapped its thin arms around Mason's leg and bit into the soft flesh of his calf. His jeans were no match for the creature's needle-like teeth. Blood soaked through the fabric and created a small, warm pool at his feet. The *elves* cried out in unison, nostrils flaring, as they inhaled their victim's sweet scent. They surged forward - squeaking like mice - and lapped at the fresh stream of blood trickling from the cuff of Mason's pants. They swarmed around his legs like frenzied anchovies, shredding his clothing and peeling flesh away in dripping strips.

White-hot pain gave way to pleasant warmth as Mason watched Santa open his front door and walk into the snowy yard. He was greeted by sleigh bells and the soft chuff of winded reindeer. Mason watched him mount his sleigh, and with a jolly *ho, ho, ho,* he disappeared into the night.

Mason continued watching until Santa's elves plucked his eyes from his skull and feasted hungrily.

Making toys for all the good girls and boys was hungry work.

With serpentine tongues, they licked Mason's bones clean, leaving behind a skeleton wrapped in multi-colored, blinking lights.

It was the closest Mason had ever come to a Christmas miracle.

***

The Elmview Mall was a hive of activity as last-minute shoppers picked the shelves clean and filled their shopping carts with assorted stocking-stuffers. The overhead speakers played Christmas carols and holiday favorites-same as every year. Children pulled at their parents' arms, eyes aglow with storefronts packed with shiny new toys - same as every year. The mall-Santa sat in his usual place, surrounded by fake snow and papier mâché reindeer - same as every year.

The line of excited, screaming children was longer than usual, but the mall-Santa wasn't complaining. For hours, children piled into his lap, tugged at his beard, and bashfully whispered their secret desires. Santa's little helpers stood to either side, keeping the line moving, so that everyone got a turn.

Santa looked up as a man stormed through the center of the line, grumbling under his breath and knocking a screaming little girl to the floor. He turned to look at her, cursing under his breath, and muttering something dark and unpleasant to her mother before jostling through the crowd. He looked over his shoulder and stared directly into Santa's eyes as he extended his middle finger and mouthed the appropriate words. The mall-Santa frowned and mumbled a single word: naughty.

It was going to be a very busy night, but Santa could always make one more stop.

Sometimes milk and cookies just wouldn't do.

The End

The Yuletide Butcher
By
Mike Duke

December 23, 12:00 pm

"This is *Aaangry* Al," the radio DJ announced in a loud, growling voice, "the man with the *red right hand* of doom, bringing you the heaviest old and new rock during this *far* from blissful holiday season. I'm here for *you*, ladies and gentlemen. I'm the man with the plan to accomplish *one* objective, and that is to make you forget *all* the things you hate: the things you *don't* have and *can't* afford, the people you desperately *don't* want to see, but know you're gonna have to suck it up anyway and do it, the people you love and miss, whose absence has left a *big black hole* in your heart, the existential *angst* and bleak *meaninglessness* of this nihilistic reality we all call life, and *last* but *not least*, I'm here to help you forget how *utterly, freaking depressing* this time of year is for many of us. So, if you're gonna *tie* one on with us this week, make sure it's a *heck of a good time* with lots of alcohol... and *not* a noose, or some other means of ending your *wretched* existence. And remember, Angry Al *cares* and I'm here for you. Also, as a friendly reminder from our *local police gestapo*, be sure to *stay on your toes*! The Yuletide Butcher will no doubt be *prowling* the streets Christmas night, looking for his annual victim. If you've been good, you *might* have a chance, but if you've been a *naughty* boy or girl, I'd stay inside... like me. Now, let's tell all these greedy, half-wit CEO clowns what we think about their *commercialization* of the Christmas season with the Rolling Stones. Let's "Paint It Black" everyone!"

The music kicked in — a frenzy-inducing drumbeat careening along, pounding and resounding through the Randall's minivan at high volume. Jack Randall loved listening to Angry Al on his satellite radio. Their musical tastes were often a perfect match. And right now, he needed a little mental holiday, an escape from his wife, Cheryl, and his teenage kids, Nicolas and Jacqueline.

"What the hell, Jack?" Cheryl groaned. "Do we have to listen to that idiot DJ and rock music? Christmas is two days away." She held up two fingers for emphasis. "It's snowing and we're going shopping for gifts. Is it too much to ask for some goddamned Christmas music and a little holiday cheer?"

She sat, head turned, staring a hole through Jack's right ear as he drove along snow-covered roads, trying hard not to let her distract him from remaining cautious. The local mall was their destination. Jack was sure it would be as busy as a one-legged man in an ass kicking contest, but, on the bright side, that would make it easier to lose Cheryl and the kids. Then he'd be free to decompress from their shit for a little bit, because once they left the mall he'd be stuck with them at home *all* afternoon and evening.

"Did you hear me?" Cheryl raised her voice above the music.

The bitch spoke again, Jack thought to himself. Ignoring her wasn't going to work today. In fact, sucking it up and ignoring how he felt wasn't going to work today. Something inside him felt like it had snapped after years of relentless pressure. He decided a different plan of action was called for... a bold approach. He opened his mouth to speak what was *truly* on his mind this time— for the first time, in fact, in their entire marriage.

"I heard you just fine," Jack answered, his tone like a blunt object upside her face. Cheryl's chin jerked back and down in surprise at his words. Despite being caught off guard, she continued to glare at Jack, expressing her anger with him.

"But I'm with Angry Al," Jack continued. "I don't see any goddamned Christmas spirt or Yuletide cheer from y'all or anyone else. All I see is material greed. Christmas has become one, big, hypocritical shit show of middle class... little, greedy fuckers financing richer, bigger greedy fuckers. Nobody really gives a damn about people or any 'Christmas Spirit' anymore."

Jack made bunny ear quotation marks with his right index and middle fingers, never looking at Cheryl once during his brutally honest diatribe.

"Everyone is out for themselves. The rest of the species can drown as far as they care. Just look at Black Friday sales in big stores all over the country a month ago. It's pathetic, and morally reprehensible... if you happen to have any real morals left. People are cynical, materialistic dicks. I wish most of them would die."

Cheryl's jaw was now wide open in shock, her real chin buried in her double chin. She wanted to speak yet found herself at a loss. The sagging skin at her neck quivered and jiggled as she tried to find words. Cheryl stuttered, struggling to enunciate a response.

"Uh, uh, um, are, are you trying to say that you wish *we,*" Cheryl traced a circle in the air with her finger indicating her and the kids, *"your family,* would *die?"*

Her slack face, vacant eyes and an almost undetectable shaking back and forth of her head as she spoke screamed disbelief. She was incredulous at Jack's rant. Cheryl had never heard him speak this way before, to anybody, much less her in almost twenty-five years of marriage. This was unheard of.

"*Well*?" she blurted, demanding a response from Jack, eyes opening bigger the longer it took for him to answer.

"Weeellll," he mocked her. "Maybe..." He paused, pursing his lips, then relaxed them. *Fuck it*, he thought. *It's on like Donkey Kong.* That's when he let the 'truth missile' launch.

"Actually, there's no maybe about it, Cheryl. Yes. Abso-fucking-lutely YES. There are times where I do wish you all would just die. In fact, it's always right at Christmas when I feel that way. Y'all drive me nuts. I'm lucky to escape Christmas each year with my sanity intact."

Jack gripped the wheel with both hands, knuckles turning white and growled through his clenched teeth.

"God alone knows how I do it."

He wrung his hands around the wheel like he was twisting a chicken's neck off or... *maybe it was supposed to be hers*, Cheryl thought.

"What the fuck, Jack?" she exclaimed. "How can you say that about me, much less your own children? What the hell is wrong with you? Where did this even come from?"

Jack looked at her with distant, indifferent eyes. Like a honey badger, he didn't give a fuck.

"What's wrong with me?" he parroted her question, his tone dripping sarcasm. "What's wrong with me is that I have greedy, disrespectful little fuckers for a wife and children, who only care about my paycheck and what it can do for them, but don't give a *flying* fuck about me. Add to that, I'm forced to put up with in-laws who think their shit doesn't stink. They talk down to anyone however they want, including me. I am sick of the shit. Over it. You can't figure out where this came from? I'll tell ya. It's an accumulation of the last twenty years of our marriage. Today's just the day the straw that broke the camel's back happened to fall and, *oh fucking snap*, the shit is gonna hit the fan now, 'cause I can't take it anymore."

Jack pulled into the mall, right up to the main entrance, stopped and hit the unlock button on the doors.

"Enjoy shopping with my money," Jack grumbled. "You know how much I love to slave away at work just so y'all can get whatever you want, while I stay miserable."

Jack fixed Cheryl with a look that screamed smartass, lips pursed, eye brow cocked. His gaze challenged her to say it wasn't true.

"Now, hurry along before the other gluttonous ingrates cherry-pick the best buys and you miss out."

Cheryl glared at Jack, brow furrowed, upper lip curled back in disgust. Nick and Jackie both crossed their arms, regarding him with hateful eyes and high chins, looking down their noses in judgement at him. But they remained silent. They didn't care what he said or thought, so long as they got his money and could buy what they wanted.

"All right. Scoot now. Out. Scram. Skedaddle. Move along. I have to decompress before I lose *all* my shit."

It was Jack's turn to stare, demanding a response. Cheryl was almost too mad to talk, but, more importantly, didn't want to make a big scene in front of everyone entering and leaving the mall. It wasn't that big of a city that people wouldn't recognize them. A former city councilman and the biggest contributor to 'Toys for Tots' every Christmas, Jack was well known in the community.

When Cheryl didn't move, Jack motioned with four fingers, waving her to leave. Cheryl bit her tongue then released her seat belt.

"All right, kids, let's leave this stranger here on his own. Maybe he can go to the doctor's office; get some Prozac or something, then bring your real father back in time for Christmas."

Cheryl and the kids exited. Before she could shut the door or say another word, Jack gave a mock salute then sped off.

Cheryl and the children were left staring after Jack as he drove away like a man with his hair on fire, trying to figure out what in the hell lit his tinderbox today.

*****

December 23, 8:07 pm

Detective Rick Allen sat at the conference room table, files, reports and photos all spread out. It was a collage of chaos; however, Allen's trained eye saw the order it contained. He was pouring over the documents, examining every detail they had on the Yuletide Butcher—from twenty years ago all the way up to last year's homicide. This wasn't the first time he'd scrutinized the evidence. He did this every year, hoping there was some hidden element of the crimes he might have overlooked, some tiny piece of minutiae that might provide a clue and help catch the killer before he struck again.

It wasn't the first time he felt the weight of futility, either. Year after year of failure to figure the puzzle out, to find, read and assemble the clues in a way that made sense, demoralized a man, even a good man. It made him question his ability to perform his duties, made him suspect his intellect wasn't up to the challenge. He laughed out loud... he had to. If he didn't laugh at himself on a regular basis for being such a persistent and stubborn bastard, he'd have sucked a barrel by now, with a 'come to Jesus' surprise inside.

Music poured through the speakers above him, the radio station playing nothing but Christmas music. He heard a man's deep voice singing "It's beginning to look a lot like Christmas..." and he chuckled. His reality and the average person's paradigm of life were far from similar. Those words carried quite a different meaning for him after almost 20 years of pursuing the Yuletide Butcher.

Halloween, Thanksgiving, cold weather, snow flurries, Christmas lights and decorations, pine, fir and spruce trees outside the grocery stores for sale... it all made him think of the Yuletide Butcher - of his failure to solve the case, of the ticking clock robbing him, one second at a time, of any opportunity to stop the killer this year – no matter how hard he tried. His efforts were futile. A dreadful, meaningless struggle to catch a killer the Universe did not seem to care about one bit. When the proverbial 365th day of sand passed through one end of the hourglass into the other, there would be no more time to stop a murder. Someone would be dead by then. The metaphorical reset button would be pushed, and he then would look for evidence and begin the countdown for preventing the *next* murder from happening.

Detective Allen downed his fourth cup of coffee and rubbed his eyes. The cases blurred together, coalescing into one large mass of useless information - nothing new under the sun... no epiphany or revelatory insights. These murders were well-planned. The Yuletide Butcher was no slouch; he didn't leave *any* incriminating evidence. After nineteen murders over as many years, there weren't even any viable leads for them to follow. The fact that this serial killer limited himself to striking just once a year made it very difficult for law enforcement to solve anything.

Tomorrow, someone from the FBI would arrive to assist. Just one agent, though. A single agent was all his city was allotted. The FBI had bigger fish to catch, fish that were hungry, like piranhas, and killing far more often. One homicide a year wasn't too bad as far as serial killers go. The FBI had thrown a lot of manpower at catching the Yuletide Butcher in the fourth, fifth and sixth years after Allen figured out that they were, indeed, dealing with a genuine, bona fide serial killer. After the sixth year, though, when not a scrap of evidence or a single lead that panned out, had been gathered, the FBI dropped the level of committed resources each year to one agent, and nothing more.

Detective Allen thought through the specifics of each case again; looking for some pattern of dots he might connect to reveal a bigger picture, a web and the spider who sat at its center. He had asked himself on many an occasion, "What makes this killer to be such a difficult puzzle to understand? To locate? After all these years, it seemed it was a simple answer, but unfortunately, one he could exercise no control over, himself.

The key to the Yuletide Butcher's success was the level of control that he was able to exercise over himself and his victims. He never broke down, becoming sloppy like everyone swore he would, like most serial killers do at some point. No. The Yuletide Butcher was not just controlled. He was methodical, deceptive. His kills at the beginning should have been a clue. They didn't even realize he *was* a serial killer until the third kill.

The first victim was found early morning, the day after Christmas. Strangled with a garotte of some sort, her mouth had been bashed in - lips split and bruised, as well as several of her teeth knocked out. An amateurish outburst of violence, and nothing more, it seemed.

The next year was the same MO, but the killer left his calling card - a handful of holly leaves shoved inside the girl's mouth, damn near down her throat. No one connected the two murders: however, due to the lengthy time frame between them the presence of the holly leaves in the second one.

The third year, he strangled the victim like the ones before, except that time he used barbed wire, which he left embedded in her neck. In addition, he cut out her tongue before filling her mouth with holly leaves. That was when Det. Allen realized they were dealing with a serial killer and called in the FBI to profile the man. When the local news got ahold of the story, some reporter coined the name 'the Yuletide Strangler'. It was appropriate at the time.

The fourth year, though, he made a major change to his MO. He killed a man, then gutted him like a deer, skinned him and used some sort of electric saw to vivisection the man's whole body like a cow being readied for the grocery store. He wrapped each portion in Saran Wrap, put them all inside a generic set of luggage that appeared to have never been used, then left them outside the bus station in a spot the surveillance cameras didn't cover. They wouldn't have known it was the same killer if not for the holly leaves shoved in his mouth. After this murder, the news reporter changed the name to 'The Yuletide Butcher' and, no matter what manner of death he chose to employ, since then, the killer has always been known by that moniker.

The fifth year he went back to a female victim, stabbing her eyes out and removing her tongue before slitting her throat. He then stabbed her lower abdomen and genitalia dozens of times— post-mortem, the coroner had determined. Most notable, though, was the change in location of the holly leaves. He stuffed the woman's womb and vaginal canal full of them, like some Thanksgiving turkey.

Each year, there was no way to know what the police might expect to find the morning after Christmas. It was like kids waiting weeks to unwrap gifts. They might guess, but they had no real idea what might be in store for them beneath the tree.

For law enforcement, over the subsequent years their 'gifts' from the Yuletide Butcher ran the gamut. There were brutal bludgeoning's, leaving the victims mauled far beyond facial recognition. One year he dumped six rounds from a .44 Magnum revolver into a man's chest and face, in that order, as fast as he could pull the trigger then just walked away. Once he even stripped a woman down, wrapped her in plastic wrap, doused her with kerosene, then burned her in an unknown location. They found her body in a sitting position on a park bench overlooking a duck pond, a brown bag filled with bread pieces placed next to her.

The killer left a man swinging naked from a tree in that same park the following year. His neck was broken, his penis cut off, blood crystallized from the cold on his groin and inner legs all the way down to his ankles. They searched the area for his missing member, to no avail. When they cut the man down they found it jammed in his mouth. Holly leaves were rammed up the man's anus with a broom handle. Or at least that's what forensics thought, based on the splinters recovered from inside his rectum.

The FBI tried to profile the Butcher, but with him changing his MO each year, it made it quite challenging. What they assumed or deduced one year would often be contradicted by the killer's methods and victim selection the following year.

In fact, the only aspects that stayed consistent were the holly leaves being placed inside some orifice and the time frame of the deaths. Officers always found the bodies sometime after midnight on the morning after Christmas.

Detective Allen had developed a hypothesis after the last murder. However, he decided to abandon it since it was all circumstantial conjecture. There was no evidence to support it. And the possible suspects were not the type of people you came at without some serious probable cause. It seemed a pointless endeavor at the time, something his boss would not approve of him pursuing. He considered it again this year, but soon concluded it was still uncorroborated gut feelings and not where he should focus his efforts.

Allen stood, walked over to the coffee pot, poured himself a fifth cup and sat back down, prepared to stare at the files until he went blind, if necessary.

*****

December 23, 9:30 pm

Jack Randall did not go back to the mall to pick up his family. He was sick of being nothing but a resource — a means to their ends. He decided it was time he looked out for himself... again.

He drove around for a time before stopping in a bookstore to browse and relax. He thumbed through numerous magazines, including the most recent Playboy, then moseyed along each aisle in the fiction and science fiction sections. Seeing nothing that struck his fancy, he wandered over to the history section. There he found a book on World War II U-boat warfare that caught his interest. After purchasing it, he walked back out to his car. Sitting down, he stared out the windshield, focusing as far away from where he sat as he could. He tried to see a different life, imagined a reality in which he was happy, what that might look like. He thought of the Playboy issue; the smooth flesh of youth— fit, toned, tan. That always made him feel better, even if only for a little while.

Jack decided to escape his life, if only for a day, or two, maybe. He refused to go home that night. Instead, he checked into a local Super 8 motel and watched porn on the pay-per-view channels until his frustration levels peaked.

"Fuck it!" he said out loud, having made up his mind. "I'm not spanking any monkey tonight, he thought. "I've deserved better.

He would get a prostitute, he decided. *My go to gal.*

His favorite prostitute was a lady he had employed on several occasions in the past. She was something special... they had a connection. Bringing up the contacts field in his smart phone, he found the one labelled Vickie, then, without hesitation, pressed call. After two rings she answered. She recognized his voice right away. Jack offered her a substantial chunk of change to stay with him until

Christmas morning. Vickie jumped on the employment offer, promising to come right over.

Jack popped two Viagra ahead of time. He wanted to last for more than one round and give an Olympic- level performance.

Vickie brought some Ecstasy with her and they both took one. With Jack adequately medicated, Vickie proceeded to please him. The drug made their flesh sing with sensations, the volume button on every nerve cranked wide open. It worked in their brains as well, chemical compounds helping to bring two disconnected people together, breaking down emotional barriers and distrust so they felt closer to each other then than they ever did to other human beings.

Jack clenched Vickie's hair in his left hand, fist tight, and pulled, just the way she liked it. His arm trembled from the suppressed anger he felt for Cheryl, but he didn't manhandle Vickie in an abusive way. He would never do that. *This is heaven* Jack thought. A cathartic release, eliminating feelings of neglect from his system. The tension within him eased, the frustrations of the holiday season with family draining from him the longer he made love to Vickie.

After climaxing, Jack lay in bed next to Vickie. This was, hands down, the best sex he'd experienced since the last time he met with Vickie. Sex with his wife wasn't anything worth getting hot and bothered about anymore, much less worth talking about with the guys at work. But Vickie... Vickie knew how to please Jack — knew when to be sexy, sassy, submissive, or dominant. She also liked it a little rough sometimes, able to give as good as she got.

Cheryl called numerous times while he and Vickie were engaged in their secret coital collusion. She left multiple messages for Jack. He ignored them all, smiling instead, as Vickie stroked him into being rigid again and climbed aboard. Jack watched Vickie ride atop him, hair hanging down over her shoulders in spiral ringlets, a rich, bright blonde that looked touched by the sun itself. Jack embraced the moment for what it seemed to be, not questioning whether her moans and groans were a fake performance for him or genuine. The frenetic pace with which Vickie's hips rose and fell pushed Jack to climax again. Vickie was close, he could tell. He was glad the Viagra kept him hard. He wanted her to come, too.

Vickie ground her pelvis against him. Pushing herself over the edge, she gripped his chest, crying out as she dug her nails into him. Her whole body went rigid, flesh glistening with a thin sheen of sweat, head thrown back, mouth agape, eyes rolling up before they closed, like a shark biting its prey. She savored every sensation for as long as it could last.

Jack laid his fingertips over the trimmed landing strip of hair where her pubic bone pressed out, swollen. He caressed her with a light touch, tracing a path down to her clitoris.

It made her shiver, squirm and giggle all at once. She bent down and kissed him, a passionate and unusually personal act for a hooker. But Jack was a long-time regular. What they had was more than just a hooker-and-John dynamic.

She slid off him and lay, conformed to his side, one leg thrown over his groin, her calf and foot intertwining with his legs. They stayed like that for some time, enthralled with each other's presence, aware of every inch of skin in contact with one another, every breath of air, the rise and fall of chest and breasts. *Peace and happiness,* Jack thought to himself, *comfort and rest. This is what it's like for normal people with a loving relationship.*

"Vickie." Jack broke the silence.

"Yeah, babe?" She lifted her head from his chest and looked at him.

Jack took a deep breath before speaking what was burning in his heart and mind.

"Would you come with me if I left my wife? I mean, just disappear. Cash out my investments and move to some other country like Costa Rica or an island and leave all the shit behind that our lives hand us every day. Would you do that?"

Vickie's eyes swelled wide with hope and tears.

"You better believe I would! You just say the word and I'm there."

Vickie stretched upward and kissed him.

"You hear me, Jack? You say the fucking word and I'm there. No questions. You respect me, care about me, not just yourself. And even though that bitch of a wife ties your guts up in knots, you've never taken it out on me, like some guys do. I've always been your escape, a delightful respite from the things you hate."

She gave him a coy, sexy look, fluttering her eye lashes for a moment.

"I purge the negative; provide a place for you to rest and recharge. And you, Jack... you treat me like I'm important, like I'm more than flesh and sex. I think about you a lot when you don't call for a while. I miss you when we're not together."

Jack smiled, love in his eyes.

"All right, then. It's a done deal. I'm gonna cash out, shift the funds into an offshore account and day after Christmas we're out. How's that sound to ya?"

"Like fucking heaven, baby. Like fucking heaven on earth."

Vickie hugged him tight, nestling her head into his neck. Jack felt the wetness of her tears and knew he was doing the right thing.

*****

December 24th, 12:10 am

Det. Allen woke, a kink in his neck from where he fell asleep, head lolled off to one side, chin tucked into his left shoulder. Drool left a slug's trail from the corner of his mouth to his shirt. He grabbed a napkin leftover from the Chinese takeout he ordered for dinner earlier and wiped the saliva away. Sitting upright, he stretched, bending his head side to side, from one shoulder to the next, then up and down multiple times, trying to loosen things up.

Managing to stand erect, he walked to the coffee pot, picked it up.

"Empty," he spoke out loud to the Universe, his tone expressing utter contempt for its providential failure. "Dammit."

He put it back down with a malicious thud, deciding he'd rather stop at a gas station on his way home than brew another pot here. He grabbed his coat and headed for the elevator.

*****

December 24, 0700

Agent Michelle Hawks arrived at the police department an hour before the agreed upon meeting time. Still, she was annoyed that Detective Allen wasn't already there waiting for her. The desk sergeant on duty showed her up to the second-floor conference room where Allen had all the files laid out and started a pot of coffee brewing for her. She grabbed a cup and sat down to peruse everything while she waited for Allen. It didn't take long to figure out that there was nothing here she hadn't looked over yesterday in her office before getting on her flight. The same reports, pictures, witness statements, everything – it was all in her briefcase, sitting next to her feet.

She hated that she drew the short straw for this assignment. It was a waste of time and could do nothing besides tarnish her good, case clearance rate. She stood to get another cup of coffee just in time to see Detective Allen walk through the doorway.

She looked at the clock on the wall. It was 7:45 am.

"You're early," he remarked to her.

"If you're not early, you're late, Detective Allen."

Her comment hit him wrong. Not a productive way to start off their day of working together.

"Well," Allen paused and tried to take the higher ground. "I'm sorry I kept you waiting, Agent..." He trailed off with a questioning tone.

"Agent Hawks. Michelle Hawks."

Allen extended his hand.

"Allen. Detective Rick Allen. Nice to meet you."

Agent Hawks looked at Allen's hand with visible disdain, shaking it only after some internal debate. Allen released her hand and walked over to the table, scanning it in quick fashion.

"So, I see you've looked over the files," Allen stated with an optimistic tone. "Is there anything you might have to share with me that I don't possess already? Any new potential profiles, maybe?"

It was Agent Hawks' turn to feel uncomfortable. For all her high fallutin' FBI prestige, the truth was, she had nothing. The Bureau's best minds had done all they could with what they had, and no new insights were pending from them or from Agent Hawks.

"Uuumm…" was all Hawks could say at first. Before she could go any further, Allen read her expressions, determining she didn't have anything.

"Well, that's about what I expected," he confided to her, his words a blunt hammer now that the shoe was on the other foot. "Guess we should get at it, anyhow. There's a couple of leads I thought of while going over the files *late* last night."

Allen placed significant emphasis on the word "late."

"We can follow up on them."

Agent Hawks sat down and kept her mouth shut as Allen got a cup of coffee, then joined her at the table to tell her what he had in mind.

*****

December 24, 1:00 pm

Jack and Vickie spent most of the day in bed frolicking like teenagers, having fun. In between rounds of gratuitous sex, Jack made calls to his accountant and told him what he wanted done. They arranged a meeting at the man's office at 3 pm for Jack to sign and finalize everything. After that, it would only take minutes to transfer the funds.

Jack went out to his car and retrieved his briefcase. As a rule, he didn't take it in the house, so, as luck would have it, it was in his car when he left for the mall yesterday. He brought the briefcase in, took out his laptop computer, then opened the internet while they talked about where they would go.

"It's got to be somewhere that has no extradition agreement with the US. I'll be guilty of abandonment and not providing any child support or alimony. She could come after me if she wanted to."

"I don't care where we go, honey. As long as I'm with you." Vickie rubbed his back while looking over his shoulder at the screen.

"All right, let's see what the options are."

Jack did a quick search and after looking up some of the places he wasn't familiar with, he settled on what he felt were their two best options.

"Ok. First choice. There's this little place between Hawaii and the Philippines called the Marshall Islands. It's got a small population and has plenty of ocean around it. On the downside, it uses the dollar as its economic currency, which means it won't be any cheaper to live there."

Jack clicked a tab, bringing up another page.

"Second choice. Cambodia. It's beautiful, has lots of incredible sites to see and would be quite cheap for us to live there with the funds I have available while we figure out a way to bring in some more money. What do you think?"

"Cambodia!" Vickie said, her excitement apparent. "I've always wanted to go see those temples. The one's like you see in that movie *Tomb Raider*. They're gorgeous. Let's do it! Can we?"

"You bet your pretty ass we can!" Jack wrapped his arm around her naked waist, pulled Vickie into his lap and kissed her, lips pressing together, tongues wrestling in earnest competition.

"Alrighty, then. Let's book some plane tickets to get out of the States as soon as possible on the 26th. Later today we can do some shopping. Get you some clothes, luggage and anything else you might need. Tomorrow evening I'll go home to pack some clothes and essential items. I'll tell Cheryl I'm leaving her and moving out. Then we'll disappear together. She'll never know where we went! Sound like a plan?"

Vickie nodded her head vigorously up and down, eyes wide, lips pressed tight, her joy too great to hide.

"I'm so excited, Vickie. I haven't felt this good in almost twenty years. It's like a weight has been lifted, knowing what we have planned…. knowing that there's a real hope for us to be happy."

"I know," she exclaimed. "I feel the same way." She kissed him on the forehead, nose and lips, soft and deliberate. "Now, how bout some shower sex before you have to get ready to leave and meet the accountant?"

"Damn, woman. I like the way you think," Jack replied, a mischievous grin spreading across his face.

Jack scooped Vickie up, carrying her to the bathroom, his forty-eight-year-old body still fit and strong enough for the task.

*****

December 24, 4:00 pm

"Well, that's two leads run down and nothing to show," Agent Hawks stated for the record, seizing the opportunity to take a jab at Detective Allen. "What now, Sherlock?"

Allen tried not to glare at her, but wasn't quite successful. Hawks half- grinned at him, knowing she was getting under his skin.

"Well, I have one more idea that I haven't shared with anyone, yet. It's a gut feeling. I can't really justify it with evidence. I mean there are some patterns I've recognized, plus a few other details... but it's all circumstantial at best."

Hawks cocked her head, at first, ready to deride him. Thinking better of it, she decided maybe his idea was worth listening to. Her gut had lead *her* in the right direction before, when there was no good evidence to go on. And her gut was telling her right now that she should hear Allen's out.

"Ok. I don't dismiss my gut instincts when I'm working a case. Let's hear it."

Her genuine interest was a pleasant surprise for Allen. He expected to catch more flak from Agent Hawks.

"All right." Allen's brain shifted gears, preparing his thoughts to build his gut- instinct case for Hawks. "So, I was looking at where all the victims lived as well as where their bodies were left for us to find. I established the comfort zone for the killer. Based on that, I did a cross reference search of men who have lived here during the entire twenty-year period of the killings. Then I took out anyone who was younger than twenty or older than thirty when the murders started. That left me with a pool of about a hundred men. Out of those, half of them don't appear to have the resources necessary to own a house or secondary location with the privacy required to take his time and do the things he's done to the bodies. Out of those who do, another ten of them are disabled. Another five had surgeries right before Christmas during various years, the kind that require extensive rehab and recovery."

"Wow. Alright. We're down to 35 candidates, but that's still a lot to investigate."

"Well, I applied all of the profiles your people have come up with over the years. There's only ten guys who fit any one of them. Just five that fit the most recent profile put together."

"Holy shit, Allen! Why didn't you tell me this earlier?"

"Because, all ten of those men are pillars of the community. To go after any one of them, I'd have to have some serious evidence… not to mention, both our chief and the mayor are on the list."

"The FBI doesn't give a fuck about their community status, or if they're law enforcement, Allen. Let's go back to the office. We need to take a closer look at these guys, see if we can narrow it down some more. Maybe bring in some extra officers to do some surveillance on all of them in the meantime."

"Also, I think we need to look at each of these ten men," Allen continued, "and ask ourselves, what kind of motivation would be at work for a man to limit himself to committing murder once a year, and nothing more, for almost 20 years? Why not more often? Why *only* at Christmas? We need to see if there is anything in any of these men's lives that would fit that bill."

"Agreed," Hawks said, smiling big at Allen, then she clapped him on the shoulder. "That's some good, god damn police work, Detective Allen. I'm impressed."

Allen blushed a little, looking down as they headed for the car. "Thanks, Agent Hawks."

*****

December 24, 4:30 pm

Jack and Vickie were sitting high on the hog now. The transfers were complete. Jack had withdrawn enough money to use cash for all transactions until they were out of the country. He rented a car and bought a burner phone.

Jack pulled into a Walmart parking lot about two thirds of the way toward the back of the lot, got out and popped his trunk. He leaned down, pulling aside the felt lining then inserted a key into a lock of some sort. Twisting it, the small box embedded in the plastic opened. Jack retrieved a Ziploc plastic bag.

"What's that honey?"

"This," Jack replied, "is how we don't get tracked. It's a fake ID and credit card under the same name. I had them made for myself awhile back."

"What for?" Vickie sounded a bit perplexed.

Jack hesitated for a moment.

"Well, um, I've been thinking about leaving Cheryl for some time now. I just never had the guts to follow through on it. But I planned for it. I don't want that bitch getting a dime from me. So, I have to disappear. Go completely off the grid with a new name. That also means buying the plane ticket in a name other than my own."

"Gotcha!" Vickie had no problem with it, if it meant they would be free and clear to live their lives together, undisturbed.

Jack tossed his smart phone on the passenger seat along with all his ID's, credit and debit cards that were in Jack Randall's name.

They left in the rental car— next stop, shopping for Vickie. Jack spoiled her with some new clothes. Brand names of a quality she was not accustomed to purchasing. When they were done he took Vickie to the airport to purchase their tickets to Cambodia, paying in cash. They had two tickets for a 5:30 am flight out, the morning after Christmas.

Jack and Vickie headed back to the hotel, packed up then checked out.

"We'll check into a new one using my alter identity," Jack advised her. "All spy- like, so my wife can't track us down." Jack tried to give her a suave, secret- agent- man look, one eyebrow raised, chin down, eyes fixed on her with a confident disinterest.

Vickie giggled and smacked his arm.

"You're so silly. But I love it when you're like that."

Jack gave her a big kiss, then another secret-agent- man look before getting in the rental car. Vickie laughed, shaking her head. She slid inside, shutting the door. Jack started it up and drove away, leaving the Super 8 behind them.

*****

December 24, 4:45 pm

When Detective Allen and Agent Hawks walked into the lobby there was an officer speaking with a woman. An elderly couple sat in chairs, observing the exchange with more than a hint of distaste. Allen couldn't help overhearing the exchange.

"So, let me get this right," Officer Wren clarified with the heavyset lady with too much makeup. "Your husband, Jack Randall, dumped you and your two kids off at the mall yesterday, pissed off, then sped away, and, as of now, you haven't seen or heard from him since? Is that right?"

Detective Allen froze in his tracks the second he heard the name Jack Randall, touching Agent Hawks' shoulder to indicate she should stop as well. He focused all his attention on this interchange. Hawks didn't understand why, but waited, listening as well.

The lady appeared annoyed at the officer for repeating back what she had communicated to him moments ago.

"Yes! That's what I *just* said." She rolled her eyes at Officer Wren as if he were too daft to understand what was going on.

Allen took a step forward, clearing his throat.

"Excuse me, Officer Wren, Jack Randall is a potential person of interest in something we're working on. I can take this one off your hands."

Wren looked at Allen as if he were a savior. He nodded, said "Thank you," then walked out the door to go back on patrol.

"Mrs. Randall, I presume? I'm Detective Allen. This is Agent Hawks. Why don't you come inside? We'll fill out a missing person report. I'd also like to ask you a few questions. Your parents, I assume, can wait out here. It won't take very long."

Allen opened the office door. Holding his hand palm up, he invited her in.

As they made their way through the squad room, Dispatcher Donna poked her head out.

"Detective Allen, FYI, those officers you requested to come in for that assignment are on their way now."

Allen thanked her, then walked over to a cabinet to grab the necessary paperwork along with a bottled water before joining Hawks and Cheryl Randall in the interview room. He offered the water to Cheryl. She declined, turning up her nose at the inferior brand name. After completing the forms that would be entered into the system, listing Jack Randall as a missing person, Allen got down to business.

"Mrs. Randall." Allen leaned forward in his seat, fingers interlaced, resting on the table. "Is this out of character for Jack? Has he ever done something like this before?"

"Heaven's no! He's never talked to us like that or left us stranded anywhere before. I don't know what came over him. I've heard people can act quite strange and out of character when they have a brain tumor. I'm afraid that might be what it is." She expressed her idea more like gossip she wouldn't want others to know, rather than genuine concern for her husband's well-being. "I can't think of anything else that would explain this behavior."

"Well, I'm no doctor, Mrs. Randall, but I do know a thing or two about behavior. Let me ask you this. Does Jack enjoy the Christmas holiday, or does he get annoyed more easily this time of the year? I mean, does he get distant, perhaps? On edge? Does he retreat from family and friends to spend more time by himself? Has he ever disappeared before without being angry, for any amount of time?"

Allen paused to let Cheryl mull over the questions he asked. He could see her brain working, eyes turned to the left as she searched her brain for memories.

"Well," she began at last, "he does seem to be more on edge during the Christmas season. He gets pretty stressed out while the kids are out of school.

Plus, he doesn't get along with my parents at all. They stay with us for a couple of weeks every year at Christmas. But he's never expressed any hostile feelings toward the kids before, like he did yesterday. He does like to be by himself this time of year. I always ride him about not having any Christmas spirit, but he doesn't care what I think as long as his public image is good."

Cheryl leaned forward and lowered her voice, as she gave them a brief backstage pass into Jack Randall's life.

"He gives to that 'Toys for Tots' program to hide how much of a Scrooge he is. It's all for show. I don't think he even likes Christmas." She settled back into her seat and continued. "He'll lock himself in his basement man- cave when he gets home from work or on weekends and not come out for hours. The rest of the year he's pretty normal, though, as far as how much time he spends in there."

Allen squinted, pursing his lips before asking the next question.

"Mrs. Randall, exactly when does Jack tend to revert back to his normal self?"

"Oh, that's easy," Cheryl blurted out. "The day after Christmas; it's like a boulder is lifted off his shoulders and he's right as rain."

Allen looked over at Agent Hawks, their eyes exchanging an agreed upon mutual suspicion that Jack Randall just might be their man. Allen looked back at Mrs. Randall.

" Ma'am, to help us find your husband, we're going to need permission to check his credit and debit card activity, as well as any phone calls he's made."

"Oh. Ok," Cheryl responded. "No problem. If it will help find him, of course."

"Wonderful," Allen said. "Well, I've got your name and number. You can go back home. I'll contact you later. If he comes home or you hear from him, call me right away." Allen handed Cheryl a business card.

Agent Hawks interjected.

"Mrs. Randall, you mentioned your husband having a mancave in your basement. Is there any chance we could look inside there? See if there's anything that might give us a clue as to what's going on with Jack, why he's acting this way and where he might be?"

"Well, agent, I'd love to, except Jack keeps that place locked up like Fort Knox and he's the only one with the keys. I'm not allowed to go in there. Ever. The one time I tried he had a right proper conniption fit."

Allen and Hawks looked at one another again. They both sensed that the hunt for the Yuletide Butcher was active. They had the scent of their quarry... now they needed to run him to ground.

"Ok," Agent Hawks replied. "I appreciate that. Please make sure you let us know if he comes home or contacts you like Detective Allen said."

They all shook hands, then Allen escorted Cheryl to the lobby. He hurried back to the interview room to speak with Hawks. When he walked through the door, she was energized.

"Holy shit, man! Did you hear all that? I think you've cracked this thing wide open!" She clapped his shoulder. "This dude hates his wife, kids and in-laws, making Christmas time one, big, fucking torture session for him. He can't handle it when everything that stresses him out comes together for a couple of weeks. He has to vent his pent-up rage somewhere else, so he doesn't kill his family. We never even thought of that before in any of our profiles."

Allen felt a wave of pride come over him. They had the potential to accomplish something no one else had been able to do in twenty years now. It was like a puzzle you just couldn't figure out and then, one day, something clicks, a part of your brain unlocks, the stars align or some bullshit like that and then suddenly you see. For the first time, you see what's been right in front of you the whole time.

"All right," Allen started. "First, I'll get dispatch to distribute a picture of Jack's driver's license to all our guys, along with his vehicle description, then we put out a BOLO on his car for a stop and welfare check. You and I will run down his credit, debit purchases since yesterday; see if we can locate him that way. I'm not sure we'll be able to get full access to his phone account at this time of night on Christmas Eve, but we need to try."

"Agreed," said Hawks. "And, if we can manage to piece together enough evidence, maybe we can get a search warrant for his basement."

"Damn, Skippy," Allen agreed. "Let's have an officer sit on his house, too. I don't like relying on the wife to call us."

Hawks nodded. She felt the same way.

December 24, 8:22 pm

Allen and Hawks rolled up on the local Super 8 with two backup units. They had found activity on Jack's cards showing he had checked into the motel yesterday, paying through Christmas Eve.

Hawks went straight to the front desk, flashed her badge and demanded to know which room Jack Randall was staying in.

The hotel desk jockey looked nonplussed at both her badge and big shot demeanor.

"Sorry, lady. That guy checked out a couple hours ago. Had some blonde lady friend with him. Lady of the night, that is." The guy puffed on his cigar, the 'No Smoking' sign displayed in front of him.

"We tracked his credit card to here. It says he paid through tonight." Hawks was annoyed.

"Yup. He did pay through tonight. But he decided to check out; for what reason, I know not. Sorry for your luck."

Hawks turned around and looked at Allen. They both seemed to deflate.

"Fuck!" Hawks walked back outside, her frustration at this setback twisting her gut into knots, anxiety replacing hope.

Allen followed her out.

"What the fuck can we do now, Allen? This guy's got some girl who might be his next victim for all we know, and we don't have anything else to work with."

Allen thought for a second, then answered.

"We need to commit every officer we can to finding Jack Randall's car. I say we take everyone we brought in to surveil our potential suspects and put them out there looking for that car. What do you think?"

Hawks breathed in deep, then blew out hard, eyes fixed somewhere a thousand yards away while she thought about it. After a few seconds, she nodded her head.

"Yeah. I think you're right. He's our best suspect. We *need* to find him. Let's do it."

*****

December 24, 9:30 pm

Jack and Vickie finished their meal at a local seafood restaurant, then found another hotel to check into in the next city over, about a thirty-minute drive away. They unpacked a few clothes, then set out the two gifts they had purchased earlier at the mall while shopping. A little surprise for each other in the morning.

Once settled in, they had a nightcap, followed by celebratory sex before pulling up the covers and falling asleep, intertwined, not a care in the world.

December 24, 11:45 pm

"113 to 101," Officer Wren called Detective Allen on the radio. Allen picked up the mic and responded.

"101, go ahead."

"101, I've got your suspect car over here in the Walmart parking lot."

Allen looked at Hawks.

"Hot damn!" he exclaimed, excitement spreading across his face, eyes lighting up.

"113, we'll be there in ten minutes. Standby."

Allen paused, then keyed the mic again.

"Dispatch, send any available units to Walmart. We need to search inside the business for our missing person."

"Copy that 101."

When Allen and Hawks arrived on the scene, Officer Wren directed them to the front passenger door that stood ajar.

"You're gonna want to see this, sir." Wren pointed inside to the front seat.

Allen bent down, shining his flashlight on the items laying there together. Several cards with Jack Randall's name on them, plus a smart phone.

"Son of a bitch," Allen swore, putting two and two together. "It's all his credit cards, driver's license, etc. along with his phone. That bastard is preparing to run. Why, I don't know, It doesn't make sense, but that's what it looks like."

"You think he realizes we're on to him?" Hawks asked.

Allen shook his head.

"I don't see how he could know. He started down this path before we even locked in on him. It doesn't make sense that he could know we're looking at him."

Allen took a long pause, running his fingers through his hair as he paced around.

"What if he's actually planning on leaving with this blonde-haired hooker? What if that's his game? Is it possible he's nothing more than a normal guy who finally got fed- the- fuck- up with his old lady and kids and decided to run off with some young piece of ass? Could we have it all wrong? Maybe he's just bugging out and taking precautions, so his wife won't have a clue where to find him. He probably wants to avoid child support, alimony and jail time."

Adams turned, extending his hand out palm up to Hawks.

"What do you think?"

"Fuck, I don't know," she declared, admitting defeat... that they couldn't be sure of anything at all. "I suppose it's possible. You're right, he can't know we're on to him, so, if he is the Yuletide

Butcher, there would have to be some good reason for him to pick up and go on the run after almost 20 years of staying in one place and eluding law enforcement with absolute success. Fuck, I don't know."

Now it was Hawks' turn to pace and think. She snapped her fingers.

"I tell you what!. Since we have the manpower here, let's search the store, then check any security camera footage. After that, we'll send the officers back to surveil the other nine guys and call it a night unless someone locates Randall."

Allen nodded in agreement.

"Sounds like a reasonable plan," he concurred.

An hour later, their search having yielded nothing, hopelessness had seeped into Allen and Hawk's bones again. There was also no footage of Jack Randall inside the store. They had the manager pull up footage from the parking lot as well. It turned out the cameras were mounted to give a clear shot of the front few rows of cars. Everything else was too far away, including Randall's vehicle. The quality of the video feed wasn't good enough, when zoomed in, to make out the exact make and model of the car that he and the blonde-haired lady left in, much less the license plate.

"Dammit," Allen blurted out. "We're about three hours behind him. No telling where they went after this...or even if he's our man. I think you're right, Hawks. It's a wrap. Send the officers back on their surveillance duty. We'll dive back into this in the morning if nothing suspicious pops up before then."

*****

December 25, 11:15 am

Jack and Vickie woke up rested. He went down, grabbed some food for them off the continental breakfast bar, along with coffee, and brought it back upstairs. They exchanged gifts, sipped their coffee then made love.

This was the most blissful Christmas Jack had experienced since his early childhood.

He was going to enjoy it for as long as he could. Later this evening he would go home and pack some important items he didn't want to leave behind.

December 25, 1:00 pm

Allen and Hawks were feeling the weight of futility crushing their every effort to solve this case. There was no aberrant behavior to report on any of the other nine men they placed under surveillance. No one had seen a glimpse of Jack Randall, either. Even his wife hadn't received a single text, much less a call from him.

They were back to square one. Hell, it felt like square zero…. square 'we don't have a fucking clue'. Once again, it appeared that law enforcement would be able to do nothing more than wait for another body to drop, unable to catch the Yuletide Butcher.

*****

December 25, 8:00 pm

Jack left Vickie at the hotel while he drove into the city to his home.

He thought about how it could possibly play out on the way over. Would she try to call the police while he was there? Would her parents? Should he risk it?. Could he not risk it? There were things he *had* to pick up. The more he thought about it, the more he realized he hadn't given enough consideration to just what was necessary to tie up loose ends to prevent anyone from tracking him down. His brain kicked into puzzle- solving mode. He was good at puzzles. Hell, he was damn near a genius when it came to puzzles.

"You can do this, Jack," he told himself. "You can make this happen. Cover your tracks. Leave everyone confused and unsure as to what is the true status of Jack-fucking-Randall."

He had it figured out. Jack had a plan.

*****

December 25, 8:35 pm

Jack Randall spotted the unmarked police car sitting across the street from his house. It was a black Dodge Charger with tinted windows and too many antennas. Typical cop car nowadays. He turned down a side street and circled back around to travel down a parallel street. He parked around the corner from the police officer, killing his lights. He reached in his pocket and pulled out the folding knife he kept with him all the time. He opened it, then gripped the handle with the knife tip pointing down. Hiding the blade along his forearm, he hooked his thumb in his pocket and relaxed his arm and wrist, creating a non-threatening posture.

Deception would be the key.

He walked along the sidewalk, then out into the middle of the street, approaching the police car in his left blind spot until he was mere feet away. Jack stepped forward, even with the driver's windows and knocked on it. The officer was in the middle of eating a sandwich, nearly choking on it as he startled and looked out the window. The man was in plain clothes with a badge on a chain hung about his neck. He tossed the sandwich in the passenger seat, clicked the button to roll down the window and retrieved a flashlight.

Jack noticed the man's right hand sliding back out of sight. To his gun, Jack assumed.

"Can I help you?" the officer said, a light shining up into Jack's face. Jack lifted his free hand to shield his eyes.

"Actually, Officer, I just came over here to see if you needed anything." Jack might as well have been George Bailey from It's a Wonderful Life, his demeanor so genuinely congenial it was disarming. "I live right around the corner. The wife's got some homemade hot cocoa and marshmallows. Even got some whipped cream if you'd rather have that than the marshmallows. Could I offer you some? It's pretty chilly out here tonight."

"You know, that sounds pretty tempting right about now," the officer confided.

Jack watched as the officer let his guard down some, buying the persona Jack had sold him. The man's right hand came back into view to rest on top of the steering wheel as he turned his body more towards Jack. He lowered the flashlight some and Jack dropped his hand back down to his side.

It was then the officer squinted and leaned his head out the window. His eyes searched Jack's face in the dark to place him.

"I'm Officer Wilson," he offered, extending his right hand, "and you are?"

Jack seized the opportunity, grabbing Wilson's hand to shake it with his left hand instead of the right. Wilson looked at him a little strange, noticing Jack's right hand didn't appear disabled or in any condition that would prevent him from shaking properly.

"Nice to meet you Wilson. You can call me Jack."

Jack gripped Wilson's right hand like a vise then jerked his arm out the door as he brought the blade up and jammed it into Wilson's throat, ratcheting it back and forth. Wilson tried to pull his right hand free as he gasped, spitting blood up at once. Jack felt him struggle, trying to free his arm and get to his gun. It was a dead man's desperate attempt to live, fighting futility. Jack leaned inside the window, forcing the blade through the man's trachea and carotid artery, cutting out to stab the officer in his side behind his right upper arm. Jack held the blade inside Wilson, trapping his right arm and stealing any hope the man had of getting to his gun. Blood sprayed across Jack's shoulder and head. He didn't like getting drenched, but he had to control the man while he bled out. Jack listened to the ragged, guttural attempts at breathing turned to gurgles mixed with weak, wheezing noises, his ear almost touching the officer's mouth.

When Wilson stopped moving a minute later, Jack released the man, then opened the door, rolled the window back up, hit the lock button and closed it. No one would see in with the windows tinted that dark. Not until tomorrow morning, anyway.

Jack closed the knife, dropping it back in his pocket, then proceeded to walk through the shadows to reach his side yard. He went to the old-style, double basement doors that were secured by two heavy duty dead bolts with padlocks to match. He opened them, lifted the doors, the hinges he kept oiled so they remained silent as they moved.

Once inside, he shut the doors behind him and turned on the overhead light. It was an older house with a basement that ran almost the entire width and length of the building—pretty much a third floor. He had tool sets, power tools, tables, saws, numerous cabinets with a multitude of drawers from tiny to large, two huge freezers and an assortment of wood, including several 4x4 posts propped up in one corner with a pair of hole diggers. Some of them were eight- feet long while others had been cut to about five feet in length.

He first picked up a rag and wiped the blood off his body as best he could, still leaving smear streaks of crimson across his right cheek and neck, as well as in his hair. Once he cleaned up as good as he could get, he walked over to a large cabinet, unlocked it and began looking through the contents. There were knives, scalpels, hammers, a short sword, a tomahawk, a garotte made of piano wire, hatchets, a noose, a .22 cal. pistol with silencer and many other weapons or items that could be used for improvised weapons. His eyes came to rest on the cordless nail gun.

Intimidating. Quiet. Efficient.

Jack grabbed the battery pack and slammed it home. ~~Then~~ He then topped it off with fresh nails and clicked it shut. Once he turned it on, he squeezed the trigger at a piece of wood. The nail flew straight, making an audible 'thunk' as it stuck in a board next to where a fresh wreath of holly leaves hung.

Jack felt a tingle in his nether regions, an excitement that he had never felt before. He had decided on his course of action. His heart sang, feeling liberated and exhilarated at the same time. Intoxicated, even. He hefted the nail gun, then headed upstairs into the house where he knew his family would be lounging about. His wife and in-laws would be watching TV. Nick would be gaming online, headphones on. Jackie would be on the phone talking to a friend or have her earbuds in, blaring music while she texted back and forth with one of her BFF's in between cruising social media.

This was going to be a cakewalk, Jack thought. He almost wished he had planned it out ahead of time, so he could take everything slow, enjoy it more, but he couldn't allow himself the indulgence. He needed to take care of business in an efficient manner, not wax poetic and risk something going wrong. With this many people, he had to move with silent efficiency, expediting each execution. If he didn't overwhelm them in quick fashion, there might be some opportunity for one of them to call the police before he could kill them all.

He moved through the door into the kitchen. He could hear the TV blaring. He walked into the living room like a boss... a man on a mission.

"Hi, Cheryl," Jack waived with his free hand, distracting them from the nail gun held down behind his right leg.

"Jack!" she exclaimed in surprise. "Where in the hell have you been?" Then she noticed the bright red stains covering his right side. "Are you hurt?" she asked, consternation written across her face. "Is that blood?"

Her voice grated on every nerve Jack Randall possessed. His neck muscles spasmed at the sound of her voice, twisting his head and causing it to tremble for a moment. He shook it to take control back, then looked her in the eye, happiness filling him as he began to act.

"Oh, I'm fine. Just wanted to stop in for a quick chat, let you know..." Jack paused, turned the corners of his mouth down while rocking his head side to side, then finished his thought. "You know. What's going on."

Jack's voice was stoic, monotone almost. His jaw moved in a mechanical manner, straight up and down, his lips mashing together, then opening stiffly. "I've found another woman, Cheryl. I'm leaving your ass... dead."

He raised the nail gun as he stepped forward, stitching three nails into her face. Two of them went right through the cartilage at the bridge of her nose, straight into her brain, the heads protruding above her makeup- caked skin. The third one went right through an eye and disappeared. Her body twitched a few times, then fell still. She never had a chance to move her fat ass from the chair she loved to lounge in so much.

Cheryl's parents sat staring at their daughter's corpse in horror, hysteria an instant from taking over their faculties. Jack could see them gasp, breathing in to scream. He never gave them a chance. Before they could get out any cries of "oh my god" or the like he let loose a hail of nails, pulling the trigger rapid fire. Jack laughed, "Joy to the World" playing in his head while he watched one nail after another pierce their torso's. This was his kind of Christmas spirit. Mom and Dad grunted from the impacts. He rushed on them, contact shooting each one in the larynx, making sure they couldn't scream, then he pumped a few nails into each one's heart, leaving them to bleed out as he proceeded upstairs to the kids' rooms.

Nick never saw it coming, engrossed in his video game. Jack walked up behind him and let five nails rip into the top of his skull. Burying themselves down into the gray matter, they shut down brain activity in quick fashion. Nick's head lolled back over the edge of his chair.

Jack pivoted and moved across the hall to Jackie's room. He opened the door and strode in without any false pretence. She didn't even look up from her phone until he was damn near next to her. Music blasted so loud from the earbuds, Jack could hear it himself. Exactly as he predicted, she was quite oblivious. She was also the last of them, which allowed him the luxury of being a little more creative. There was no one else he had to worry about alerting. And since Jackie was always so disrespectful towards him, Jack thought she deserved something special.

Jack surprised Jackie. His left hand shot down, pinning her throat to the bed where she lay. He looked into her wide, terrified eyes, witnessing her confusion as he placed the nail gun on her forehead.

"It's night, night time Jackie," he whispered, then pulled the trigger. He shifted and pulled the trigger again, continuing till he had given her a crown of thorns made of nails. Her flailing arms and attempts at screaming stopped long before the last nail drove into her skull.

Jack's breathing was rapid, the adrenaline ramping his body up. He stood there looking at Jackie, admiring his work. This was pretty much what he had planned for some poor stranger this year. A crown of nails, a wound through the side. If he had done things proper, he would have taken a cat o' nine tails to her back before killing whatever girl he selected. Now, he'd have to improvise to add a little flourish to things. He couldn't go into retirement with a whimper. No sir, the Yuletide Butcher had to leave his mark on this city. A mark they would never forget for many, many Christmases to come.

*****

December 26, 3:00 am

Dispatch rang Allen's office, waking him and Agent Hawks where they had fallen asleep, him at his desk, her on the couch. Allen woke with a start, scrambling to pick up the phone.

"Yeah, Donna. What is it?" He was talking before he could think straight.

"Hey, Allen. Wanted to give you a heads-up. Thought you'd want to know. I just dispatched the fire department to Jack Randall's house. A neighbor called, said the place is fully engulfed."

"Fuck me," was all Allen said, then hung up.

"Hawks!" he barked. "Up and at 'em!"

Hawks sprang bolt upright, eyes scanning, but not quite seeing everything yet. She managed to focus on Allen, remembering where she was. Hawks rubbed her eyes.

"What is it, Allen?"

"C'mon. We gotta go. Fire at Jack Randall's house. It's burning to the ground as we speak."

Her mouth dropped open, then clamped shut.

"You gotta be fucking kidding me."

She stood, and grabbed her jacket before heading out the door with Allen.

"For fuck's sake!" she yelled out in frustration. "I can't believe this is happening."

As they hopped into their vehicle, Hawks asked Allen, "So, who called it in?"

"Dispatch said it was a neighbor," Allen responded.

"A neighbor?" Hawks asked, her voice deepening, yet full of concern. "Why wasn't an officer? We have one surveilling the place. He should have seen anything well before a neighbor."

Allen's head snapped right to lock eyes with Hawks.

"Oh, God, no!," he blurted. "Why didn't I think of that?"

Allen scooped up his radio mic. "101 to Dispatch."

"Go ahead 101," Donna answered.

"Can you try to raise Officer Wilson?"

"10-4." Donna heard the panic in Allen's voice and realized what the problem was. Her voice echoed his concern as she tried to raise Wilson on the radio, multiple times. Allen and Hawks' stomachs sank further with each attempt.

"Dispatch to 101. That's negative. I can't reach Officer Wilson."

When Allen and Hawks arrived, they spotted Wilson's unmarked car right away. Pulling up in front of it, with headlights on high beams, Allen turned on the spotlight and directed it towards the driver's seat.

"Oh, fuck me," he whispered, a lump in his throat he could not force down.

They could see Officer Wilson, head lolled to one side, blood soaking his neck and upper torso clothing. Hawks jumped out of the car and sprinted for the driver's side, yanking up on the door handle.

"It's fucking locked," she screamed, then reached for the expandable baton and scabbard attached to her belt behind her gun. She swung down in a sharp motion, opening it then delivered a backhand swing towards the bottom corner. The window shattered. Hawks reached in, unlocking the door and throwing it open.

As soon as she touched Wilson's flesh she knew he was dead, but she checked for a pulse anyway. Nothing.

Hawks turned away, hands grabbing her hair.

"Goddammit!" she yelled in frustration, then looked at Allen. "I'm so sorry Allen. I'm just... so sorry."

Allen keyed his portable radio.

"101 Dispatch. We have an officer down at the Randall house. I repeat we have an officer down at the Randall house. Get me rescue and dispatch additional units to secure the scene."

Within a minute he heard police sirens, even as he watched rescue workers rushing over on foot to their location. Another minute later he saw the blue lights of fellow officers swarming towards the scene.

He informed the first officer to arrive what was going on, even as EMS confirmed Hawks' own observations. Wilson was dead. Then he directed him to set up a crime scene perimeter with tape and watch it till he could check on the Randall house and come back.

Allen and Hawks walked over to the blazing residence. The fire department was at work trying to get it under control, with little success. The house was burning at a furious rate. The Deputy Fire Chief, a guy named Owens, came over and talked to Allen, telling him there was no doubt in his mind that a lot of accelerant, of some type, had been used to make the house burn down this quickly .

Allen resigned himself to a long, painful process of digging through the remains of this burned house to find corpses of family members that would have to be identified, likely, by dental records. Right then a fire fighter came running from the backyard, right up to Allen and Deputy Chief Owens. He was breathing hard, yet white as a sheet. He started to speak, then bent over, his stomach heaving twice before he brought it under control without vomiting.

"You have to see what's in the backyard. Mary, Mother of God!" That's all he could get out before his stomach started to heave again. Allen, Hawks and Owens rushed to see what the man was so disturbed by.

Allen rounded the corner first, swinging wide to keep his distance, the blazing heat emanating from the house, a boundary he did not want to cross. The flames still burned bright, illuminating the ghastly sight more than enough to see every detail.

There were five crosses made from 4x4 lumber buried in the backyard, all in a row. Cheryl, her parents and both teenage kids were all hung on them, numerous nails piercing each limb to attach it to the wood.

The scene was overwhelming. Multiple horrors vying for the brain's attention, eyes flitting from one sick feature to another. Their lower abdomens drew Allen's scrutiny first. Each of them was laid open at the waistline, intestines drooping down over their groin and upper thighs. Then he raised his eyes. Allen couldn't believe what he saw. All of them had a crown of nails driven in the top of their foreheads, circling all the way around the skull. A mockery of Christ's crown of thorns, no doubt. As he walked toward them for a closer look, Allen realized they all had ball gags stuffed in their mouths, secured about their heads with leather straps.

"God have mercy on us," Allen whispered, then keyed his radio. "Dispatch. I'm going to need more detectives on scene."

They waited the next few hours in a state of abject defeat, as forensics arrived, setting about to process the scene and collect evidence. Both Allen and Hawks dreaded the media storm to come. When forensics was finished with the periphery, they took down the bodies. Allen requested that they remove the ball gags first to inspect the mouths. He had a gut feeling what they were for. He stood looking down at the body of the wife, laid out upon the ground, as the forensics investigator pried her mouth open, reaching inside with a pair of tweezers.

Time seemed to slow down for Allen... the lady investigator's hand moving in slow motion, retracting in smaller and smaller increments till he thought the suspense would, indeed, kill him. But then, he saw it crest the lips. In that moment the world returned to normal. The first holly leaf retrieved, the investigator bagged it and reached back in for the rest of them.

"The fucking Yuletide Butcher," Hawks declared with disgust. Disgust with the killer and herself, her part in this failure to prevent multiple murders.

"Yeah. This sucks." Allen stated the obvious. "You know, even if we think we're absolutely sure that Jack Randall is the Yuletide Butcher, any evidence we might have found to prove it has been reduced to smoldering ashes in the basement by now. We won't even be able to say with any amount of certainty whether Jack Randall is still alive after this. For all we know, and can prove, he could have been a victim. We got nothing. Not a damn thing."

Hawks shook her head in frustration. Allen was right. They didn't have jack shit.

*****

December 26, 5:30 am

Jack and Vickie held hands, sitting side by side as their airplane got up to speed and lifted off the runway. It soared into the sky above, carrying them towards their own little paradise. A clean slate. A fresh start. A chance to be someone different, free of the past.

Or, so Jack hoped, despite the photo album he packed in his luggage, the one containing news articles documenting each of the Yuletide Butcher's Christmas murders along with a polaroid of each scene, including one with five crosses.

The End

The Ghost of Christmas Office Party Past
By
C.S Anderson

Kevin leaned against the wall and closed his eyes for a moment, his head was spinning. He cursed himself for being stupid enough to drink too much at the office Christmas party. Snow was falling steadily outside of the window behind his desk. In the background Elvis crooned the song, Blue Christmas, and he could hear the babble of conversation amongst his office mates.

He could hear their laughter.

Bah, what the hell did they have to laugh about? They were all poor enough, after all. The management prissily had announced that, sadly, there would be no holiday bonus this year, times were just too hard for that.

Still, they had scraped together enough for a staff party and the booze had flowed rather generously.

The laughter turned abruptly to screams as gun shots rang out; he dropped the drink he had been clutching in shock and froze in place.

Nancy, the girl from accounting that he rather fancied stumbled by him, with the front of her shirt soaked in blood. She collapsed at his feet, with each breathe escaping her mouth in bubbles of blood.

The music kept playing.

More gun shots followed, then more screams rang out.

A figure dressed all in black with a ski mask on, came walking through the doorway of the office he was in. The masked man calmly shot Nancy three more times, then turned and left.

Kevin closed his eyes and screamed.

When he opened them again, he was sitting at a desk in a different office and a beautiful, dark haired, pale-skinned woman, dressed in a loose-fitting, white fur robe, was sitting across from him.

"Hello, Kevin," she greeted him calmly, as she shuffled absently through a pile of papers on the desk.

"What the hell just happened?" he demanded stridently, his panicked eyes trying to look everywhere at once.

"Relax, Kevin, I am sorry if I scared you. Would you say that I scared the Dickens out of you? Never mind, that is something of a private joke. Let me try to explain, you are, for want of a better term, a lost soul. You are stuck in a loop of sorts, reliving something that happened last year about this time. I am here to help you move on from this place, to where you belong," she told him, not bothering to look up from her papers.

He reached over and swatted the damn things out of her hand.

"Temper, temper, Kevin," she admonished him, with a somewhat mocking waggle of a finger.

"Answer me, damn it! What the hell is going on?" he demanded standing up and looming over her.

She winked at him... and vanished.

He found himself back leaning against the wall again, drink in hand. Blue Christmas was still playing in the background, but he couldn't hear any laughter or conversation.

Nancy was still lying on the floor, in a pool of blood.

The drink fell from his hand again, to shatter against the floor. He rubbed his eyes and prayed that he was dreaming, but when he looked again, she was still there.

Whimpering a little, he backed away from her and scooted along the wall to the doorway. He slowly walked toward the sound of the music playing.

The first body he came across was of his boss, Stuart White. At least, he was pretty sure it was Stuart. Most of the man's head had been blown off, but the corpse was wearing the same stupid, ugly holiday sweater that his boss had been wearing all day. Odds were good it was him.

Nobody else would have been caught dead in it.

As he wove through the room of office cubicles, it was like some twisted, ghastly game of hide and seek... and he was 'it'.

One by one, he found all of his office mates: some had died standing up, at least two had tried to crawl under their desks, but the gunman had shot them right through the cheap fiberboard.

Blood was everywhere.

Gwen, the office flirt, was lying by the water cooler, a single scorched-looking hole right between her baby- blue eyes and a slowly-spreading puddle of blood under her head.

He closed his eyes and started screaming.

When he opened them again, he was back sitting across from the dark-haired woman.

"Ready to listen this time, Kevin?" she asked him with a hint of a smirk on her face.

Terror was suddenly shoved into the back seat by rage and he made a lunging grab at her. Once again, she vanished before he could touch her.

He cowered away from the gunman as he strode by, never looking at Kevin twice. As Kevin watched, he pistol-whipped Gary, from accounting, to the floor and then shot him twice in the head.

Gary had probably been the closest thing to a friend that he had had in the office; they had gone for a pint a time or two after work. The guy had been a fiend for soccer, it had been nearly all he had wanted to talk about. Gary had been smart, easily the biggest brain he knew.

Now those brains were splattered all over the floor.

"No!" he screamed, as he watched the gunman walk down the hallway hunting for more victims.

He closed his eyes and prayed for whatever was happening here to stop.

When he opened them, the woman in the white fur robe was staring at him patiently from across the desk again.

"You, Kevin, are seriously one slow learner. Please understand, I am here as I stated to help you move on from here to where you need to go. You cannot touch me, unless I allow you to, let alone harm me. The sooner you work that bit out, the sooner we can get down to business. Do we have an understanding?" she asked him, quirking one eyebrow again.

He stared blankly at her for a second, his head spinning as he tried to understand what the hell was happening to him. Struggling, he pushed his anger down. He had always struggled with his temper, and tended to react with his fists. His own father had often told him, that it would be the death of him.

"Sorry, I will try to listen. Who are you? Please tell me what is going on," he asked her as contritely as he could manage.

She didn't look impressed.

"I have a lot of names; I have been called many things, by many people. None of those names are pertinent just now. Let us focus on your situation. As I said Kevin, you are a lost soul. Terrible things happened last year at the Christmas office party; you were part of that, and somehow you became stuck there. You have been reliving what happened, instead of moving on to where you need to go. I am only here to help you with that," she told him quietly as she leaned back in her chair, watching him intently.

A terrible thought crossed his mind.

"Lost soul? Are you telling me that I am..."

"Dead? Yes, dead as a doornail I am afraid. Kicked the bucket, passed on, given up the ghost and all that. Which sucks, of course, but it is what it is. Our job now is to work through what happened and send you on your way," she told him brightly.

He hung his head and let that particular information soak in... it had the simple ring of truth to it.

"Tell me what you remember about what happened," she urged him, reaching across to touch his hand lightly.

Her hands were very cold.

"Not much, I was very drunk. Hell, I think we all were. The booze had been flowing pretty steady all night. I, well... I drank a little more than I had planned on, I am afraid. Things hadn't been going well for me lately. I think the boss was getting ready to can me. That bitch, Nancy, turned me down when I invited her for a drink once, telling me some lie about not seeing people from work. Then, not even a month later, she was engaged to that twat in merchandising." He heard the old anger in his voice, but also, sadness.

He was better equipped to deal with one, better than the other.

"And then what?" she asked him, leaning back in her chair again as she stared at him.

"And then what? What the fuck do you think, lady? And then some bastard came and shot up the place, that's what! Some fuck came and splattered my work mates all over the walls and floors, that's what!" he shouted at her, as he shot to his feet with his fists clenched.

She sighed and gave him a pointed look, pointing one long, pale finger at his chair, sternly.

He took a deep breath and nodded at her as he sat back down; once again he tried to look contrite.

Once again, she didn't look impressed.

"Do you remember being shot?" she asked him, her tone oddly gentle for as strict as she had been with him.

He thought about it for a long moment, his memories seemed to be printed on a deck of cards. A long time ago, he used to play a card game called 'Fifty-two Card Pick up' with his shit-of-an-older brother. End result would be all the damn cards tossed up into the air and his brother would make him pick them all up.

It was a lot like that now, trying to shuffle through his memories.

Try as he might, he couldn't seem to find that particular card.

He shook his head at her.

"Well then, let us go look for it, shall we?" she asked him as she stood up and held out her hand.

Kevin stared at the floor for a moment. He wasn't really sure he wanted to go find that particular card, and confront that memory. She stood before him, radiant in her pristine, white fur robe, holding out her hand to him… just standing there waiting, like she had all the damn time in the world.

Which, he supposed, all things considered, she did.

So, he slowly stood up and took her hand, she smiled at him and he saw things in that smile he couldn't identify, but they too failed to give him a warm fuzzy feeling about things in general.

Still, he was dead after all, how much worse could things possibly get.

Like she had heard the thought, the woman holding his hand, gave him a broad wink and a quick smile.

Yeah, that didn't give him a warm fuzzy feeling, either.

"Walk with me," she told him.

She ignored the open door to their left and started to glide towards the far wall, pulling him along with her.

"Um…that's a wall." Kevin pointed out to her, feeling like an idiot for doing so, but old habits die hard as the expression goes.

"Bear but a touch of my hand and you shall be upheld in far more than this." She quoted grandly.

"What?" he asked in confusion.

She sighed heavily and gave him a scathing look.

"Doesn't anyone read the damn classics anymore? Never mind, just walk with me. Walls and doors mean nothing here."

Together they stepped through the wall, like the ghosts he supposed that they must be.

He found himself back in the main part of the office, the maze of cubicles where he had wasted so much of his life. Blood splattered the walls, ceiling and floors all around him. The metallic stench of it appalled him. The bodies of his co-workers lay sprawled all around, some on the floor, some slumped over their desks and some under them. Elvis was still crooning Blue Christmas, oddly that was one of the most disturbing things about the scene before him.

"Why are we here? Why are we looking at this? Everybody is fucking dead! Damn you! Everyone died, so why the hell are we looking at this? What purpose does it serve?" he demanded, his temper flaring once more.

She shook a finger at him again, like a small town junior high school librarian, shushing an unruly student. Her face was unreadable as she stood watching him.

A low moan behind him chilled his blood. He turned slowly and saw Melody, the boss's secretary, crawling painfully across the floor towards her desk. She was badly hurt, her life's blood pumping out of two gunshot wounds to her chest as she moved. She was dying, an inch at a time as she crawled, but there was a sort of nobility in her continued effort that moved him a little.

Tough old bat.

He wanted to shout a warning to her as the gun man walked into the room, but he found that he had no voice and could only watch.

The prick shot her again in the leg and laughed as he watched her still try to crawl away from him.

She screamed, but she kept on scrambling away from the killer, so determinably, that Kevin came to realize that she wasn't trying to escape the killer.

Melody was crawling towards something.

One had to wonder what it might be.

She pulled her purse off the top of her desk and it tumbled its contents across her bloody lap; wallet, lipstick, cellphone, car keys, tampons and gun.

She picked up the gun in her blood- slicked hands and before the gun man could react, she pulled the trigger.

The first shot went wide left and missed him entirely.

The second shot grazed his shoulder, making the bastard squeal like a stuck pig and drop his own weapon.

The next shot went right through the murderous prick's heart and he dropped to the floor, dead before he even hit it.

"Fuck... you," Melody gasped as she fell over, sending the small revolver spinning away across the blood- drenched floor.

Kevin stood there, staring at the carnage with his head down for a moment; he didn't remember any of this. He didn't understand how what he had just witnessed, brought him any closer to knowing how he had died. He did remember Melody being keen on target shooting, but he didn't think he knew she carried a gun in her damn purse.

"Didn't you used to fancy the girl from accounting? Nancy, that was her name, wasn't it?" The woman in fur asked him casually, but with sly tones in her voice that disturbed him.

"What difference does that make now, damn you?" He growled at her, his anger pushing up through his shaky control, yet again.

"But she didn't fancy you, now did she? Took up with some bloke from merchandising, didn't she? How did that make you feel, Kevin?" she asked him, and there was no mistaking the mocking tone in her voice now.

"Shut it, bitch!" he snarled at her.

"Made you angry, didn't it, Kevin? Maybe made you just a little bit jealous and crazy? Not idle questions really, just trying to do my job. Just trying to move you past here and towards where you need to be." She told him with a predatory grin.

He was suddenly very afraid.

"Yeah, I was jealous, so fucking what? Any man would be. Still, she didn't bloody deserve to be shot dead by some whack job now, did she? None of these people deserved what happened to them, but what of it? What the hell do you want from me?" He demanded as he took a couple steps towards her.

Her smile stopped him in his tracks.

"I want you to take his mask off Kevin, that's all. Then we can resolve all this lost soul nonsense and send you off to where you need to be." She told him calmly as she pointed at the fallen gunman.

"Fine, bitch, let's do that." he growled at her, as he stomped over to where the black-clad figure lay on the floor. To vent some of his rage, he gave him several savage kicks to the ribs, to make sure that the murderer was truly down for the bloody count.

He could hear ribs shatter, as he continued to kick long after necessity or even sanity called for him to do so.

She leaned against the far wall and watched him, without comment.

Leaning down, he ripped the mask off the killer in one angry yank, only to stare down at his own face.

The shock hit him hard, as the true memories of that night flooded back into him, in one unforgiving wave.

"No!" he whispered to her, as she came walking up to him.

She changed as she advanced, the pale skin reddened, the white robe was gone, and her eyes took on a heated glow. Horns curled out from the sides of her face and the smile she had trained on him, was now full of very sharp teeth. Leathery, black, bat- like wings, opened up behind her shoulders.

"Not a lost soul any more then, now are we Kevin?" she asked mockingly, as she picked him up effortlessly by one hand and gave him a little shake.

"Now what?" he spat down on her as she choked him with her free hand.

"Now what? Well, just what I promised you, Kevin. You escape this loop of experience and we take you to where you need to be," she hissed at him.

"Go to hell!" he screamed at her, slapping at her feebly with his dwindling strength.

She gave him a truly awful smile.

"Our very next stop, Kevin, our very next stop."

The floor beneath their feet all of a sudden gave way, revealing the fiery pits far below them.

Her laughter—and his wails—trailed behind them, as they fell.

The End

Kevin J. Kennedy Presents

Twas the Night Before Christmas
By
Matt Hickman

24th December 2016

Paula opened the oven door, and inhaled deeply as the enticing aroma of roasting turkey tickled at her nostrils and wafted out into the kitchen. She had always insisted on cooking the Christmas turkey on the evening before the big day. This was mainly due to a hiccup a few years ago, when she had attempted to clean the oven and damaged the sensor that regulated the temperature, leading to them having to dine out on Christmas day.

Not a cheap option - not that it was a problem, it was more of an inconvenience finding somewhere with such short notice. They were an extremely wealthy family. Paula had been born into money, and inherited a fortune when she had lost her parents in a boating accident nearly ten years ago. Her husband, Ray, who also came from a privileged background, worked as a chief executive for a large construction company. The holidays were a lucrative period for him, since it was when his company paid out their annual dividend to the shareholders, which often ran into tens of thousands of pounds.

The couple had been together eight years after meeting at a charity function that had been organised by some mutual friends. Paula had caught Ray's eagle eye when she had made an elaborate bid for a dodgy-looking vase. An item that now took pride of place in their entrance hallway. They had gotten chatting and realised immediately that they had a great deal in common. Neither party had seemed too worried about the other's interest in each other's fortunes as they were equally affluent.

They had married within the first twelve months, and had held a lavish reception for hundreds of their friends and hangers-on, followed by a month long, coast-to-coast tour of the southern states of America. Everything in their lives was luxurious, from Paula's chic wardrobe and collection of designer shoes, to their fleet of prestige cars and Ray's motorbikes.

They could be considered an attractive couple. Paula had a slim face with petite, refined features. She had stunning blue eyes, and a perfect set of pearly whites, hidden behind a set of slender, pink lips. Her long blonde hair draped just below her lithe shoulder blades and hung perfectly over her surgically-enhanced breasts—a gift she had received from her husband for her thirtieth birthday. Her waist was slim, and tapered down to long, slender legs. Ray was tall and athletic, the result of his two hour, daily sessions at his exclusive health club and gym. He had wide, muscular shoulders, and defined arms and chest. He always wore his dark brown hair in a short style, combed to one side. He had a strong jaw, usually adorned with a couple of days' worth of fresh stubble and piercing green eyes.

Five years ago had seen the arrival of their identical twin girls, Sasha and Heidi. The children hadn't been part of their original life plan - not that it had mattered. Heidi was the eldest of the two by mere minutes. Both girls were slim and tall for their age. They both had long, curly blonde hair and brown eyes. The children were typically spoilt by their wealthy parents and wanted for nothing material. Their parents often over-compensated for their lack of personal time and attention by the girls with extravagant gifts.

Using her expensive, designer oven gloves, Paula removed the turkey from the oven and carefully placed the red-hot baking tray upon the kitchen surface. She admired her handy work as she slowly basted the bird's crispy golden skin. She jumped at Ray's touch as he placed his thick arm around her waist and kissed her on the nape of her neck.

"That smells fantastic."

"What, me or the turkey?"

"You know I can't resist the smell of your..."

Paula slapped his hand away as his palm slid playfully down towards her waist.

"Knock it off, will you? I'm trying to cook, and the girls are in the other room."

"I know, but maybe I can get my Christmas treat tomorrow night when you see what Santa brings you from me."

She smiled and turned around, softly pushing him away, and placed a gentle kiss upon his cheek. "How could you ever top what you brought for *me* last year?"

"You'll just have to wait and see, won't you?"

"Go and check on the girls, will you, while I finish up in here? Its half-past seven, and I want them to be in bed by eight, so we can start sorting the presents from under the tree."

"Isn't Sarah going to tuck them in tonight?"

"It's Christmas eve. I gave her the evening off. Besides, she'll be looking after them over New Year while we're skiing."

"I have to do everything around here, there's no point in hiring the help," he joked.

She handed Ray a metal key. "Don't worry, she's left them this, and sorted out some stuff for them to leave for *Santa*."

Ray turned and crossed the kitchen towards the living room. Both girls were sitting side-by-side on the leather sofa dressed in their elf pyjamas, watching *The Grinch* cartoon on the massive television set that hung from the wall. Both girls were clutching a piece of paper, and a pencil.

"What are you doing, girls?"

"We're writing a letter to Santa Claus," they replied in unison.

"Another one?"

"This one is to thank him for all the presents he's going to leave for us. It's awfully kind of him."

Ray fought back the urge to spit out it wasn't actually Santa who paid for the items; it was the result of his hard work and effort, but figured Christmas Eve probably wasn't the best time to get into this particular conversation with a pair of inquisitive four-year-olds.

"So, girls, what are we going to be leaving for Santa for when he comes later tonight?"

"We want to leave some cookies and a glass of milk," replied Sasha.

"And a carrot for the reindeers," added Heidi.

"That's no problem, but how is Santa going to get in here? We don't have a chimney."

Both girls chuckled. "He will be using the magic key of course, Silly-Billy."

Ray smiled and produced the key from his back pocket. A piece of red and green ribbon threaded through a hole in the centre of the bow. Attached to the ribbon was a plastic label that read *Santa's magic key*.

Both girls looked at each other and yelped in delight.

"Right then, girls. I want you to finish up your letters and we can start getting you ready for bed. He pulled his smart phone from his pocket, and loaded the app that supposedly tracked the fat man's journey from the North Pole. He turned the screen around to show them.

"He's just flying over America, so he won't be too long. We have to make sure you two are tucked up in bed, ready for when he arrives. And you must brush your teeth. Santa doesn't visit children with filthy choppers."

Both girls leapt from the sofa and ran towards the kitchen, screaming in excitement, their feet slipping and sliding over the surface of the perfectly polished wooden floor.

"Mommy, mommy, he's on his way, he's flying over America! Can we have the cookies and milk so we can leave them out for him?"

"And the carrots," added Heidi.

Paula grabbed the bottle, and a fresh glass, and filled it to the brim. She placed a saucer beside the glass and tipped out the cookies that had been left by the nanny along with a couple of fresh carrots from the salad box.

"There we go, girls. Now give me a big hug. You need to get yourself off to bed and to sleep as soon as you can."

The two children melted into a rare embrace with their mother, who gave them a tight squeeze and placed a kiss upon their foreheads.

"Goodnight, girls."

"Goodnight, mommy."

"Right then, you'd best go with daddy and sort out the special key. If he can't get in the house, he can't leave any gifts."

The girls excitedly followed their father's lead towards the front door.

"Girls, before you..."

His statement was interrupted as he opened the door and spotted a young figure standing before him on the doorstep. The boy appeared about ten years old, had a skinny, gaunt face and his features were sunken into his pale visage. He wore a tatty, white button-down shirt with no overcoat, a pair of dark trousers, complete with an old pair of black boots. Over his shoulder, he carried a scuffed, brown leather holdall.

"I'm sorry, son, can I help you?"

"Yes, sir. I'm sorry to intrude, but I'm from the local church. Every year, we have a fund-raising event for charity, where we try to raise money by selling seasonal items to members of the local community."

Reaching into his bag, he produced a handful of tatty-looking Christmas tree decorations. They had been moulded into the shape of elves, choir singers and animals from the classic nativity scene. He held them up towards Ray.

"These have all been hand-crafted by children down at the local orphanage. They are all hand-made. As you can see they are individually themed."

He held out an item that had been crafted into the shape of a boy. It was a garish-looking sprite with enormous eyes, and a halo fashioned from a bent up pipe cleaner. On its back was a pair of glued-on angel wings. Around its wrist, a small cardboard tag had been tied, displaying the name *Michael*.

Ray winced at the ugly-looking thing.

"I'm sorry; you've caught us at a really bad time. It's Christmas Eve; I was just putting my little girls to bed."

"I apologise, sir, but Christmas is a time for charity. Could you *please* consider giving something to the needy?"

A sudden surge of annoyance spiked through Ray. "Look, I've told you once. You've caught us at a really bad time. In fact, do you have any identification? How do I know you're from the local church? You could be one of those kids off the Roseland estate, just down here to make an easy few pounds, preying on people's generosity."

"Sir, could you please con…"

Ray's patience snapped and he screamed at the boy. "Get off my property! Get off my property now, before I call the authorities."

The boy didn't respond, he simply held up the scruffy-looking decoration in an attempt to plead once more to the man's better nature.

"Girls, get inside. I'm going to call the police."

"There will be no need," the boy replied calmly.

Ray and the girls watched as the boys facial features turned malevolent. The intensity in his eyes scorched as he stared into Ray's, the vehemence dripped from his contorting facial features and he lashed out and snatched him by the wrist. Ray felt the temperature of his blood drop immediately, despite the burning sensation emanating from the boy's vice-like grip against the flesh of his wrist. A feeling of lethargy washed over him as his world started to blur and his thoughts became increasingly confused and chaotic. The haziness continued to increase as he glanced down towards the blurred silhouette of his two daughters.

Then there was darkness.

24th December 2017

Sarah stood in the doorway, listening intently as the Christmas carol sung by the group of youngsters floated through her open door. The music warmed her heart, despite the few flakes of snow that had started to fall and gather upon the front lawn. It had been the first real flurry she had experienced for about six years, back when she was still with Jessica's father. Before he had gotten a sniff of loose knicker elastic from the barmaid down at his local drinking hole, and they had both disappeared together one evening without a trace.

Christmas had always been her favourite time of year, but since the disappearance of her partner, she had always struggled to properly make ends meet. She had taken on two part-time jobs; just enough to cover the outgoings, and put enough food on the table, but Christmas was a time when she wished she could afford to give her daughter that little bit more.

Not that Jessica ever complained. She was a good kid, and the love she held for her mother was unconditional. They were best friends in addition to being mother and daughter. She often helped where possible with the limited tasks she could perform around the house, and was progressing well in her first year at school. The extra holiday shifts Sarah had taken on this year had allowed her to splash out a little more than the usual shopping budget, and to fund the purchase of Jessica's first bicycle.

Sarah continued to watch as the group of carol singers changed song, into their rendition of *Good King Wenceslas*, one of her all-time favourites. Sarah adjusted the coat she had wrapped around Jessica's shoulders to keep the cold at bay, ensuring she was covered properly, as she was only wearing her nightgown beneath.

She kissed her daughter on the top of her head; Jessica turned around to look at her and smiled without uttering a reply. The singers finished up the song and they both gave a cheerful round of applause. Sarah rooted through the meagre contents of her purse, scratching around for some money.

She held out a tatty five pound note to the young boy at the front of the group who appeared to be in charge. "I'm sorry, I don't have much to offer."

"No, that's fine, thank you," replied the boy, genuinely. "Merry Christmas."

"Merry Christmas," Sarah and Jessica replied, and continued to wave as the group moved on across the road to the next house.

Sarah stood on the doorstep for a moment, watching as the thick snowflakes continued to descend and spiral in flurries. The snowfall was getting thicker and a layer was beginning to settle upon the footpaths and roads. Sarah quietly longed for a white Christmas.

"Mommy, will we be able to make a snowman?"

"Not tonight, sweetheart, but if the snow sticks, I'm sure we'll be able to tomorrow. Now we'd better get inside before we both catch a chill."

She ushered Jessica inside, and hung up her jacket, tossing her purse next to the disconnected phone upon the table, another small sacrifice made in the name of a better holiday.

"Let's get you by the fire for a minute, and get you warm, ready for bed."

Sarah and Jessica cuddled up in front of the open fire, watching the flames as they flickered and danced, and the acrid smoke as it spiralled up into the chimney.

"Do you think Santa will be coming tonight?"

Sarah pulled the child in closer, and gave her a kiss. "I'm sure of it my sweetheart."

"Where do you think he is right now?"

"Nobody knows, that's his magic. We'd best put the fire out once you've gone up to bed. How will he get down the chimney otherwise? Let's go and put the stuff out, ready for him."

They bounced excitedly towards the kitchen. Sarah flicked down the switch on the kettle in order to prepare a hot water bottle, grabbed the cookies from the overhead cupboard and the milk from the fridge. She gestured towards Jessica. "You want one?"

She shook her head firmly. "No, they're for Santa."

"I'm sure he wouldn't mind you taking just one."

She shook her head again, insistent.

"Then let's get you up the wooden hills," she said. "Race you!"

Sarah led the charge through the living room, with her daughter at her heels, giggling away. They ascended the stairs, taking two and three steps at a time until they reached the landing, the bare floorboards creaked beneath the slippers on their feet. Sarah had made a promise to herself that she would get the new carpet fitted following her first pay cheque after the holidays.

"Come on sweetie, brush your teeth and jump into bed; it's cold up here tonight."

"Okay, Mommy."

Sarah headed across the landing to Jessica's bedroom and switched on the night-light. She threw back the bed covers and slid the hot water bottle down into the fold. She grabbed the pillows and fluffed them, frowning as a piece of paper slipped out from beneath them and spiralled gently to the threadbare carpet. She picked it up; it was a note, written in Jessica's scrawl:

Mommy

Donte be sadd if you couldent get me any Christmas presents

Im sure Santa will do his best for me

Love Jessica xx

Sarah fought back the urge to spill tears, as pride threatened to burst through her rib-cage and make a sticky mess of her pyjama top. She slipped the note back under the pillow as she heard the tap stop running from inside the bathroom. Seconds later, Jessica came running into the room on her tiptoes and dived onto the bed. She slid between the covers, and Sarah pulled them up tightly around her chin, tucking her in.

"Are you excited, little girl?"

She nodded, without reply. Sarah leaned forwards and placed a gentle kiss upon her soft cheek.

"Goodnight, sweetie."

"Goodnight, Mommy. And merry Christmas."

"Merry Christmas," she replied. "Now straight to sleep."

Jessica scrunched up her eyes tightly, and Sarah clicked the switch on the night light to minimum, something that she had done ever since the child slept in her own room. Carefully closing the bedroom door behind her, she made her way down the stairs, as light on her feet as she could manage.

Immediately heading into the kitchen, she grabbed the plate containing the cookies and the glass of milk. She took a bite from one of the cookies, and took a large swig from the glass, before placing the plate on the hearth, next to where she had hung a small stocking.

She slumped down onto the sofa, a cloud of dust flying out as she landed. Wrapping a thick blanket around her shoulders, she pulled her knees up to her chest as she watched the last embers of the fire burning out. She glanced up at the clock—it was nearly nine—and decided she would leave it another half an hour to ensure Jessica was properly asleep before wheeling in her bike from the pantry. It had been hidden in there for the past two weeks, covered in blankets.

She jumped at a sudden banging noise – a knock at the front door. She hopped up to the window, glancing through. She couldn't make out a thing through the falling snow outside. Making her way through to the hallway, she hooked on the security chain and opened the front door.

Standing alone, in the midst of the falling snow, was a young girl. She couldn't have been any older than about twelve. She wore a light brown dress with no coat; her ragged, unkempt mousy hair was tied back in a loose pony-tail. Draped over her shoulder was a black bag, made from thick linen.

Sarah immediately unlatched the door and held it open, gesturing the child inside. "Please, come inside, you'll freeze to death out there, you poor thing."

"I'm fine, thank you," the girl replied impassively.

"Can I get you a cup of hot chocolate or something?"

"No, I'm fine, really; you are my last call of the evening."

"Call? Are you on your own?"

"Yes, I'm sorry to intrude, but I'm from the local church. Every year, we have a fund-raising event where we try to raise money by selling seasonal items to the local community."

The girl reached into her bag and produced a handful of tatty-looking Christmas tree decorations. "They are all hand-made by the children down at the local orphanage. All proceeds go to giving them a Christmas dinner."

Sarah looked at the items and nearly burst out laughing at the crude quality of the craftsmanship.

"I'm sorry; I don't have much money."

"That's fine," replied the girl. "Christmas is a time for giving."

Sarah smiled and grabbed her purse. She poked through the change compartment with her fingertip, barely managing to salvage a few pounds in silver coins and coppers.

"I'm sorry, this is all I have."

The girl smiled, enhancing her beautiful young features. "That's fine. It's more than generous."

She held out the open bag, Sarah inspected the contents closely. Just as she was about to select the figure of an elf, dressed in a green velvet costume, the girl held out two different items.

"Here, may I suggest you take these? They are a pair of angels, they will bring you luck."

"Two? Are you sure?"

"It's fine. I need to be on my way now. Merry Christmas."

"Merry Christmas. Are you sure you'll be okay out there?"

"I'll be fine, I don't have far to walk."

Sarah watched as the girl ambled to the end of the driveway and turned left. The girl glanced back over her shoulder and smiled before disappearing into the flurry of snow up ahead. Closing the door, Sarah returned to the living room and headed over to the Christmas tree, ready to hang her newest accompaniments.

She held them up and inspected the detail. They were a pair of angels, carved from wood. Both figures had yellow string glued to the head to represent blonde hair, macabre, crooked smiles, and wide eyes had been drawn on in marker pen. For a brief moment, Sarah could have sworn that one of them winked at her. Each of the angels had a name tag secured to its wrist with a name written crudely in biro. Sarah read the names aloud, *"Sasha* and *Heidi."*

The End

The Kringle
By
Peter Oliver Wonder

The smell of burnt cookies wafted from the kitchen, masking the smell of cordite which hung thick in the air. The cops swarmed the room like angry hornets, flowing through it like water as they made their way around the neat room. The first man through the door made a hand gesture, signaling another group to make their way up the stairs.

Men in heavy gray armor branched out through every corner of the house, searching every nook and cranny. "Second floor is clear," a voice came in through his earpiece. "Officer Castleman is knocked out up here. No sight of anyone else."

"Our status is the same down here. There's no way they could have gotten out of here without someone noticing. Is the craft still on the roof?"

Another voice came through the radio. "Negative. It's... it's gone. It just vanished into thin air. There's no trace of it anywhere, sir."

***

Search lights from below pointed up at the sky. The enforcers were all quite keen to be remembered as the ones that took down Santa, but the man in red had different plans.

He had always known this day would come; hell, they'd already tried it at least a dozen times or so since he had first arrived on this planet. He'd poised as many things before finding just the right form—an aquatic mammal in a dark lagoon, a furry beast in the woods, even a stint of flying around in his saucer with no cloak at all—it always resulted in him being hunted by those to whom he wanted to spread joy. Who would have thought that an obese old man living all alone in a frozen desert that flew a magic sleigh with reindeer at the helm would be what they would never question?

Not until this New World Order took power had he had to fear for his life once more. They were adamant about capturing the Kringle and imprisoning him—likely indefinitely—for no reason other than their own fear, uncertainty, and doubt.

Santa wouldn't let this stand in the way of his only mission. He would absolutely deliver these gifts to the children of the world. No guns, rockets, gas, or anything else would be a match for the Kringle technology—faster-than-light travel was only one of the many tricks up his sleeve.

His purpose was to give hope to a new generation of humans, year after year. He wanted the youth of this world to know that there was magic and joy out in the universe, but the powers that be wished to control every aspect of the world's population. Christmas had been outlawed. Every business was to be open at regular hours in the morning, but the Kringle took to the skies—his ship once again cloaked as a reindeer-driven sleigh. In the seat beside him was his Nibirian sack of toys—though it wasn't quite bottomless, it was much, much bigger on the inside.

The ship darted around the spotlights. Above the great city skies hovered several blimps—the eyes in the sky, watching over every aspect of daily goings-on. On this night, all their numerous cameras and lights were focused up at the night sky while troops on foot watched every dark alley and avenue. There was every type of equipment one could imagine watching for what was considered one of the greatest threats to mankind, including cameras that detected every color in the spectrum. Men at podiums spat out twisted facts about the technology he used and said how easily it could be used to harm men, women, and children when they were at their most vulnerable as they slept peacefully in their beds.

Now, as we all know, the Kringle—better known as Santa—is the kindest, most peaceful, and loving sentient being in the Milkyway Galaxy. What we haven't been made aware of is that he is part of an ancient, immortal species and came from a planet orbiting Betelgeuse and has made Earth his home. His jolly, human exterior is merely an illusion, as is his sleigh. In truth, Kringles are stony beings that can pass into the ether, but they can take any form they wish at will. The sleigh is a ship capable of a whole host of things that seem magical to all terrestrial beings.

For the Kringle, this would be his greatest challenge to date and—though he wasn't quick to admit it—he was actually rather glad for it.

Centuries had passed with the reward of love from all the people of the world without question. Now, he felt like a villain in some alternate reality. After hundreds of years of being the good guy, this was something new, though his goals remained the exact same; to deliver gifts to all the good boys and girls of the world. It didn't matter what the opinion of the establishment was; only what Santa knew he had to do.

Dashing through the clouds, he and his sleigh started to move from the industrial sector of the city below, toward the residential zone. He knew there was a worldwide curfew in effect, which meant everyone out on the streets below would be actively hunting him down. He took his left hand off the reigns and reached toward his head to press a button on the side of his hat. After half a beat, the apparatus transformed into shiny, whirling disk. The saucer had a diameter of nearly five feet and was only around three feet from top to bottom. The whole thing seemed to spin in both directions at the same time.

In the dark night sky, it could nearly be seen by the naked eye, but once one of the lights from below shone on it, the metallic surface reflected back down the image of the stars that were beyond it, rendering it nearly totally invisible.

His jolly red cheeks inflated as his lips curled around his dull, yellowish teeth. The craft's altitude dropped suddenly in a way that would have utterly confused the physicists of Earth. It rapidly decelerated until it was merely hovering over a large apartment building—it was one of many beige, tubular structures that were all nearly identical, and not a single chimney was in sight.

The top dome of the vessel retracted and the Kringle leapt out, landing on the snow-covered roof. A stuffed, red bag was draped over his shoulder as he raced toward the roof access door. With a snap of his fingers, the door burst open and closed shut again—just a fraction of a second after his ass had passed the threshold, letting scarcely a gust of cold air in.

Inside, he found doors running along a sloping, spiralling walkway that continued all the way down to the ground floor. After examining the place while running his fingers through his grey beard, he plunged a hand inside a small, red pouch which dangled from his belt. From within, he pulled out a tiny seed. With a jovial "Ho, ho, ho!" he hurled it over the railing and watched as it plummeted like a stone before a narrow trunk sprung from the top at unfathomable speeds. All at once, as the small seed fell, the trunk rose, leaving the peak of the tree level with the Kringle's eyes, and the trunk itself sprouted branches toward each door.

Every single one of the branches sprouted their own colorful bulbs, tinsel, lights, and green needles. As they extended away from the trunk, the tips of the branches became bulbous, colored, and engorged. By the time they reached their respective doors, the tips took on whatever their final shape would be—most of them were more or less cubical—and fell from the tree at the foot of each door.

Before the final gift landed with a thud, Santa had already gotten back in his ship and sailed across the sky to the next apartment building. Despite the intense security, the Kringle was able to continue on, without being noticed, throughout the entire residential district. The real challenge, however, lay ahead. In the financial district, everything was going to be much more difficult, yet it was absolutely imperative that he do so. The little boys and girls that resided there were perfectly innocent, despite the lifestyle they had been born into. If they were shunned by Santa, what would that say about him?

***

The tall buildings tapered off, revealing a river on the horizon. Across from it was the political district, with large and lavish homes speckling the beautiful green landscape that had a sparling creek system lacing around the roads. While it all looked quiet, Santa knew that the greenery and waterways were swarming with patrols with itchy trigger fingers.

He was no stranger to incoming fire. During many wars, Santa had delivered gifts through swarms of gunfire and artillery rounds. Enormous damage had been incurred, but the Kringle craft managed to self-heal and allow Christmas night to go on as planned. Every house in this zone looked like its own little castle, speckled along the fairytale-esque landscape.

On the seat beside him, the list of all the naughty and nice children sat. Year after year, there were more people on the planet, yet Santa's job got easier and easier as children moved away from the nice list and toward the naughty list. The saddest part for the Kringle wasn't that the children were inherently bad or being malicious on purpose . . . it was the way in which they were being raised. Many of the children here were taught to strive for the stars and to not let anything stand in their way. There was no challenge too great, no problem too difficult, and no person too important to be stepped on to get what they desired most—a big fancy house, brand new cars, and heaps and heaps of money.

Most of the children here were being raised by the sick and depraved and they weren't even worthy of stopping to drop coal in their stockings, for they wouldn't learn the lesson. Being good to their fellow man was such a foreign concept that, perhaps, they were too far gone. They lived in fear of living life as a poor 'nothing' when they grew up and there wasn't anything that would stop them from attaining the top rung of the ladder. A little black lump plucked from the Earth would mean nothing to them.

Of course, not every child conformed to their sociopathic peers. Every day on the playgrounds of the schools, there would be children who would stand up for others, those that would share their toys and lunch, those that would assist the teachers, and so on. These were the boys and girls with whom Santa was concerned. These children were to be rewarded handsomely, for they made these choices despite what they were shown by their parents, teachers, and peers.

The first name on the list was located just on the other side of the river. Elaine Jones was a little seven-years-old girl. The day before, she had gone to school with the rest of her classmates—December 24th, was no longer a day worthy of celebration, much less the 25th. However, it just so happened that yesterday had been a Friday. It was a day when her friend—classmate would be a much better descriptor, but Elaine considered everyone to be her friend—Robin showed up without a lunch.

Her house servant had been placed under arrest after attending a protest, and so a lunch had not been provided for her. Elaine had no hesitation at all in sharing half of everything she had with the girl sitting next to her, much to the chagrin of the other children, as well as the adults charged with the care of the children. For this, she was sent home early and chastised by her parents. Her older brother even spat on her for her actions, calling her a weakling.

***

The camouflaged craft came to a silent landing atop the snow-covered roof right beside the chimney. On the ground below, he heard the police force patrolling the streets as they had for the past few years. There were foot patrols with dogs, spot lights illuminating the sky, and snipers posted atop select structures. After grabbing his sack full of goodies, Santa sprang from his seat and peered down into the chimney. No smoke rose, but he could feel heat radiating from inside.

Deciding not to risk it, he reached inside the cloth pouch affixed to his belt and withdrew another seed. This one did not yield a tree once he dropped it on a clean roof tile. Instead, it expanded, leaving a hole in the middle as the snow and roof material disappeared—a perfectly round portal straight down into the family's living room was left, and the Kringle jumped through it.

As he descended toward the floor, his eyes fell upon the fireplace, which had a roaring fire in it. Beside it was a wrapper for a clean-burning, faux-wood log. Parents using the same old tricks year after year to try to keep an allegedly fictitious character from entering their homes always managed to put a smile on his old face.

There was no tree to behold. There were no stockings hung to be stuffed with goodies. No fresh baked treats to entice an old man to leave treasures behind—just a fire left in hopes of burning an alleged foe to death. Needless to say, in all their years on this planet, humans hadn't learned the lessons given by lumps of coal. The only thing he did find that had to do with Christmas was a note resting on the counter. He walked over to it, seeing that it was done in a child's hand and was quite colorful. The message was, "Please, go away. We don't need what you got. Mommy and Daddy say they can give me anything I want, so I don't need you. Love, Arron."

"Oh, Arron! It's a shame your big sister hasn't taught you better, yet," he lamented, stuffing the note into his belt pouch. Then, he hefted the large, red sack he carried on his shoulder and stuffed his hand inside. At the very bottom of the bag, he found the gift for which he was searching. Wrapped in green and topped with a big, red bow, the Kringle placed the parcel on the counter top where the letter had sat. The tag read: *To Elaine, a good friend to those in need.*

And at that, he was finished in this place. He walked back into the living room, looked up at the hole in the ceiling, and sprang through it as though he was rocket powered. As he passed through the opening, he spread his legs—one landing on either side of it—before stooping over to collect the ring. He placed his hands at opposite ends of it and collapsed it in on itself, leaving the roof below it intact and undamaged. The hoop shrank back into a seed and was deposited back into the small sack as he closed the distance to his craft.

The next name on his list was that of a boy whose father was part of the police force. The year before, the man had almost caught Santa in a trap. As the Kringle barely escaped with his freedom, the man shouted after him if he was ever to return, it would be the last thing he ever did. Needless to say, he man's son was a good kid again this year, much to the disappointment of his oppressive father.

Ryan Castleman, age eleven, was an athletically gifted youngster. He ran track at school and, rather than being a bad winner, he always did his best to lift the spirits of his teammates, as well as his opponents. At their last race, Ryan was neck and neck with his biggest competition—Bluto Raspman of their top rival school. Just before the finish line, Bluto turned to spit in Ryan's eyes, blinding him, but instead missed a small rock on the track just ahead of him. The spit missed its target completely as Bluto momentarily flew before sliding, face down in the dirt. Rather than kicking dirt into his eyes and mocking him, Ryan helped the other boy to his feet as several others ran past to finish the race. Ryan went so far as to walk the injured, bloodied boy across the line together. Not so much as a "Thank you" was uttered, but it didn't matter to Ryan. He did what he had to do and had no regrets about it.

Now, Ryan slept soundly in his bed. He didn't care whether or not some kind-hearted mysterious individual came to his home and delivered this or that trinket. Yet, there was the Kringle, landing on his roof as he slept peacefully.

Officer Castleman, on the other hand, was not asleep. Rather, he was dressed in full riot gear, wiping down his disassembled rifle with his service pistol by his side. He knew his boy had acted in a manner that would bring Santa by and he was almost glad for this. He had commanded additional cameras to be installed in the area and insisted upon extra foot patrols around the neighborhood for the night. He felt if the jolly, fat man was to be caught, his house would be the best place for it to happen.

***

Year after year, Ryan begged his parents to bake cookies to leave for Santa and every year, his father said no. Earlier this night, Ryan decided he was old enough that his father couldn't tell him no anymore. To avoid confrontation, he snuck down stairs as the old man sat with his back turned, scrubbing away at the rifle's chamber. As stealthily as possible, he whipped together the ingredients and tossed a pan full of sugar cookies into the oven with a proud smile on his face. *Old Saint Nick will really love these,* he thought as he ran upstairs to wait patiently in his bedroom.

He was lying on his bed with his nose in a physics book when his father entered the room unexpectedly. "I know we don't celebrate Christmas the way you think we ought to," he began, arms behind his back, "but I want you to know that it's not because I don't love you." He brought his hands to the front, a plain brown box in his right. "This is for you, son. You're a great athlete and I think you have a lot of potential to be a good man when you're a little bit older."

Ryan took the brown box—which was much heavier than he was anticipating—and opened it up. Inside was a brand-new handgun. "I don't understand," the boy said, furrowing his brow.

"Go ahead and pick it up." The boy did as his father said, still quite confused. "You're getting to be about that age where you should be able to protect yourself from whatever may come at you. I was about your age when my own father gave me this same gun. I used to believe in Santa Clause, too, when I was younger. Now that I'm older, I've seen news reports of the awful things he does to people when they're at their most vulnerable. I'm not going to let those things happen to you, son. I love you."

Tears welled up in the boy's eyes. His father rarely showed him any signs of affection, much less said that he loved him. He gave a nod as his father clapped him on the shoulder and turned away. The fire alarm sounded, scaring them both. "I'm, so sorry, dad!" he shouted as he bolted past him and down the stairwell. He grabbed an oven mitt and yanked the nearly black, smoldering balls of sugar from the oven and dumped them into the sink before swatting at the smoke in the air.

***

Now, that same pistol was tucked beneath Ryan's pillow as he slept.

He was not in trouble for the cookie incident, he was only asked to make better choices in the future. His mind was racing a million miles an hour in all directions as he clenched his eyes shut, wishing for sleep to wash over him. He was no longer certain what was right and what was wrong. Maybe he had been wrong about the world and people were just showing each other tough love rather than those with the power pushing around those without. Even though he thought he heard a *thud* in the room that was just barely audible, he chalked it up to his imagination trying to keep him from sleeping.

Santa looked down at the boy, noting the image of pain that was painted across his face. That was a sloppy landing, no doubt about it. Santa waved his fingers around in the air, particles of light appearing out of the ether. Once his squeezed his fingers together, the gold dust rushed over to the boy, filling his nostrils and ears. The pained expression melted away from his face as he sank into a deep sleep.

The Kringle turned, and with the snap of his fingers, the door ahead of him opened silently. The rest of the house was still well lit, meaning he had his work cut out for him. He remembered this house and the booby traps that had nearly worked in the past.

Cautiously, he stepped through the door frame and looked to his left.

"Surprise, freak!" Officer Castleman was directly behind him with the rifle fully assembled. The muscles in his trigger finger contracted and, for the Kringle, time slowed down. He watched as the trigger hit resistance, the hammer fell, smoke burst forth from the chamber and barrel. Before the round even began to make its way down the barrel of the weapon, the Kringle split down the middle from the top of his head to his groin as though he were two halves of an Oreo. Each half hopped around the firing officer, as he was frozen in both space and time, before reforming on the other side—each half of his face met and sealed together with no trace of a seam.

"I'm the one that delivers the surprises," Santa declared from behind the very confused man. Then, before Officer Castleman had a chance to turn around, the Kringle delivered a punch directly to the back of his skull. It wasn't often he had a chance to express his anger and frustrations in such a way and he'd be damned if he didn't enjoy it just a little bit.

He rushed downstairs and heard the officer's radio barking static. One of his uniformed buddies on the street heard the shot and was shouting that backup was on the way. The eye in the sky had spotted-lighted something indescribable on the roof.

Hefting the big red sack from his shoulder, Santa quickly plunged his hand inside and withdrew a small package and placed it on the counter before running back upstairs. The buzzing of helicopter blades could be heard outside overhead. It was so loud it shook the whole house.

After stepping over Officer Castleman, he was unpleasantly greeted by a rather anxious looking Ryan. Sweat was pouring from his forehead as he glanced back and forth from the scene outside the window—officers bathed in the light provided from an overhead drone—and the red suited so-called *man* before him. Between him and the Kringle was the gift he had received earlier. The boy's unsure finger was wrapped around the trigger—Santa saw that the weapon's safety was flipped to the off position.

Directly above the pair was the seed ring, through which snowflakes were falling silently. "You could pull the trigger," Santa began, "but it won't do anything good for you."

The gun was waving around in the air as Ryan gasped for air. Tears began to stream down his cheeks. "Is it true what they say? Are you... an extra-terrestrial?"

Santa was genuinely surprised by the question. "That's hard to say. You see, I've been here on this world for longer than homo sapiens have been in existence. I'm not an invader. I pose no threat to anyone not looking for it." As he spoke, he stared down the barrel of the gun. "Don't make the same mistake your father did, boy-o."

A loud *BANG!* rang throughout the house as the front door was smashed in. Immediately after, Ryan's body tensed, causing his finger to squeeze the trigger.

Santa's lips curled into an evil smile as time once more froze around him. Calmly, he stepped around the plume of smoke that escaped the barrel just ahead of the projectile. He pulled the red sack from his shoulder—it now appeared as empty as could be—and put it over the boy. The weapon with the round still in the barrel was also trapped inside the magic bag as it continued its way to the floor.

With his bag once more slung behind him, he leapt through the hole and got into his craft. The rotors of the helicopter above could be seen just barely moving as the Kringle flipped switches on the control panel before buzzing off into the atmosphere.

The ship tore through the storm clouds and zoomed toward the stars. Once it reached the edge of Earth's atmosphere, the ship stopped and Santa turned to his passenger. "Do you know the last time I had a meal as good as you?" The face of the Kringle morphed from that of a jolly fat man to that of a young, stone-faced man. His cheeks and chin were covered with a beard that appeared to be made of braided blocks of rock. His eyes appeared to swirl with ink before turning completely black. "It's only those who lost their way on such a special night that I'll allow myself to feed upon. There are those that know what they believe in, and there are cowards like you who just can't seem to figure it out. The taste of ignorance is the best of spices."

The sound of stones grinding echoed about the craft as the Kringle's jaws separated. His powerful arms wrapped around the petrified boy and forced his screaming head down into his mouth. As the blood dribbled down the corners of his mouth, tentacles from his suit reached up and soaked in the hot liquid. Not knowing just when his next meal might be, he enjoyed every last bit of the boy before shape shifting back into loveable old Saint Nick. There was work yet to be done.

The End

Ho Ho Hollow
By
Mark Cassell

"Mum," Kitt said from behind her, "I've got a stomach ache."

Rachel peered over a shoulder.

From her chair at the dining-room table, she saw her son looking at her. Lanky for a ten-year old, he stood framed in the doorway with sleeves halfway up his skinny forearms. Perhaps they should've bought him a new coat rather than all those presents. A glance into the lounge reminded her of the mess to clear up: wrapping paper and toys everywhere. Her and James's gifts were neatly stacked beside the sofa from which they'd earlier watched the chaos unfold.

"You're dripping snow on the carpet," she told him. "Take off your coat."

His face, rosy from the cold, didn't change as he slunk back into the kitchen. The sound of his shuffling feet was almost in time with James's vegetable chopping.

"At least you took off your boots," she called after him.

Coloured Lego bricks of varying shapes and sizes covered the table, several obscuring the instruction booklet and surrounding the half-complete model. Indeed, much like the toys scattered in the other room, this was another present he'd played with for not even five minutes. Most, after tearing open the wrapping paper, he'd simply given a once-over; some, barely a cursory glance. Every year, it was the same. Flo seemed to be following in his ways. As it was, she often copied him, a trait Rachel knew was common in all younger siblings.

She found the Lego brick she'd been searching for, attached it to the part Kitt had already completed, and glanced at the photo on the box. What she had so far in her hands, she guessed, would be a section of car engine. She recalled the 70s when Lego models were basic vehicles. But now, they were impressive, intricate, and with so many moving parts. Back then, it was pretty much only the wheels that moved. As a kid, she'd marvelled at how her older brother would construct them. She wondered if she had copied him as much as Flo copied Kitt.

In just a few hours, her brother and his children would come crashing through their front door, presents in hand... more chaos... more wrapping paper to tidy later. And, besides... all that packaging – seriously, was all that packaging necessary?

Tea. She wanted a cup of tea, but as she stepped into the kitchen, the smell of brandy and cinnamon warmed her nostrils. When she saw the saucepan of mulled wine steaming on the stove, she knew she had no intention of putting the kettle on to make a cuppa.

Yeah, she wanted some mulled wine.

James didn't look round as he said, "I'm looking forward to this."

He dragged a bunch of carrots across the work surface, and with nimble fingers, he began chopping them into even slices. She often marvelled at how he never cut himself. He was a fine cook – indeed, modesty aside, she wasn't too bad herself – and he seemed to enjoy it more than she did.

"Kitt…" He still hadn't removed his jacket. "Where's your sister?"

"Out in the Hollow."

The Hollow, as they'd named it after moving to their country house during the summer, was a bomb crater in the woodland which backed onto their garden. It was one of many overgrown scars from the Second World War. Rachel had once been trapped in a conversation with a local elderly woman who insisted some German pilots hadn't wanted to reach London and so deliberately dropped their payloads onto empty countryside. She was unsure how much faith to have in the woman's knowledge, but it was admirable to be positive about a piece of history that was otherwise devastating.

Positivity, however, was at a low level in Rachel's reserve and she was, sadly, dreading her brother's troops invading her home.

She placed the red Lego brick she hadn't realised she still held onto the worktop. "Why don't you both come in now?"

"I'm in," Kitt said. He'd unzipped his coat and was now rubbing his stomach.

"Yes, but your sister's not." She reached up and opened the cupboard for some glasses. "Besides, your cousins'll be here soon."

"I don't feel well." In truth, the boy didn't look himself. Maybe he'd caught a chill. After all, it was cold out there: the sky was white, and the snow was coming down in impressive flurries. However, ever since he'd turned ten he'd become a bit of a whinge-bag.

"Okay." She took two glasses from the shelf and placed them down on the counter. "I'll make some hot chocolate while you go get Flo, and by the time you're back, it'll be ready to drink."

James glanced at her. "Mulled wine for me." He looked at the glasses in front of her and grinned. "Good call."

She watched Kitt continue to rub his stomach. Perhaps he really was ill. "What do you say, sweetie?"

He shrugged.

"Deal?" she prodded.

His eyes drifted from her, to the window and beyond, to where his sister was probably still playing in the den.

"Seriously, Kitt, go get your—"

His face slackened, a whiteness – no, a *blueness* – tinted his cheeks. Traceries of veins raced beneath his skin. His eyes, the whites themselves, turned a cold blue. Ice formed across his cheeks, crackling, and spreading fast to cover his whole face. Even his hair suddenly frosted. Clothes, too: they whitened as though he'd been stuffed in a freezer for days.

The sound of crackling intensified.

Rachel staggered forwards, knocking the Lego brick onto the floor. It skittered across the tiles.

James had now turned, eyes wide, knuckles whitening as they gripped the knife.

"Kitt…" she whispered.

His body stiffened. More crackling, sharp, from inside his body like fracturing ice. His skin, his hands, his face, white as the sky, cracked in places. A deep crevice zigzagged upwards from beneath his collar, shooting along his jaw and up his cheek and across his brow.

He stood there. Frozen.

Fragile as glass, he shattered. Exploded.

Hundreds of multi-coloured ice crystals, twinkling in the kitchen light, shot in every direction. It sounded like a dozen windows cracking at once. In whites and crimsons and purples and blues, their son's body vanished in an icy haze. It was like a bomb had gone off in the middle of an iceberg. Several shards stung Rachel's cheeks.

Her scream filled the kitchen as Kitt became nothing more than hundreds of ice crystals scattered around the kitchen.

Still clutching the knife, James backed off, retched and spewed. It spattered the worktop, and as it dribbled down the apron she'd bought him for Christmas, she noticed she'd not removed the price tag.

A hundred thoughts collided in her suddenly small brain. Dizziness pressed down on her. What was left of Kitt absurdly made her think of the time she'd dropped the ice cube tray and the cubes had scattered across the tiles.

James stepped forward and reached out for where Kitt had stood. He then backed up… his foot shot out in front of him. Vomit flicked in the air, and for a crazy second, it was as though he ran on the spot.

He fell – face down – onto the knife he still held.

Blood pumped from his chest as he scrambled sideways, then slumped, and kicked the glinting ice crystals. They made the same sound as the Lego brick a moment ago.

"James!" She leapt towards him and dropped to her knees beside his shuddering body.

His moans, strong at first, weakened... softening, quietening. He jerked and a slice of carrot shot across the floor, bounced off a crystal, and skidded through a small heap of snow to rest against one of Kitt's boots. One more twitch, another... then he stopped. His head flopped to the side.

She pulled him into her arms, stroking his face. His dead eyes stared past her head. A dark pool soaked her trousers, warm, now spreading beneath them both. She screamed and her agony tore through the house. A glance out through the glass of the back door, into the relentless snow and out to the bottom of their garden, she remembered Flo. The Hollow.

Tears prickled her eyes as much as darkness crept into her periphery. Somehow... somehow she pushed both aside.

Flo. She had to get Flo.

* * *

On her feet, not realising she'd stood, she glanced down at James. His blood had now spread to blend in with the crystals that had once been their son. With one boot on, one off, she reached for the backdoor, gripping it with slippery fingers.

James couldn't be dead, could he? Can't be possible. And Kitt. What happened to Kitt? She staggered back towards her husband, refusing to believe any of this. The sole of her Wellington boot squeaked, slipping in the blood, and she stumbled into the dishwasher, causing it to rattle.

Leaving red handprints up the front of the appliance, she put on her boots properly.

Flo.

Back to the door, after fumbling the handle, she was soon outside, the air freezing her lungs. A quick look over her shoulder brought into view James's legs amid the glinting crystals, and she considered going back to get a coat.

But... the Hollow – she had to get to the Hollow.

Already, Kitt's footprints had vanished.

Snow filled the sky, coming down in flurries. It stung her face as she started to run up the pathway, every footfall crunching. In what felt like hours, she made it to the gate at the bottom of their garden – the one James had purposefully cut into the fence to allow access to the woodland behind, so the kids could play in the Hollow. Acres spread out behind their property, where even the Estate Agents couldn't tell them who owned it. All of it so remote, it was never to be a problem.

Something red flashed up ahead, someone darting between tree trunks and winter-dead foliage... then nothing. Perhaps she hadn't seen anyone. But, then again, no... she *knew* she saw him – yet it was ridiculous *who* she saw. This wasn't happening! And it was at that moment, despite the freezing snow buffeting her, she knew she was dreaming... she had to be... surely.

Father Christmas. Or at least someone dressed like him.

A sickness rose in her throat... James, Kitt. Dear God, what was happening? She bit down on her lip and fought the urge to collapse to her knees, to cry, to let the snow take her, freeze her. She remained upright, managing to sprint into the woodland. The snow on the ground thinned the deeper into the woods she went. As she ran, she searched for Father Christmas – for Santa... for the man she'd seen... This was such madness. Kitt had... had exploded! Whatever the cause, she wondered if that man in the red suit had anything to do with it. Kitt had said he felt ill. Poison? Had the imitation Father Christmas poisoned him? Insane. The man—

Rachel interrupted her own thoughts. Flo! He'd better not harm her.

With those thoughts, she sprinted through crispy leaves and snow, kicking it up. Already, she felt damp through her trousers, and James's blood was freezing her skin. The trees were sparser here, and so the snow was thicker, in the sky as well as on the ground. Finally, she saw where the woodland floor dipped slightly. That was where the crater began – the Hollow.

Where had the man gone? There were no footprints. She could've sworn he ran this way. It was snowing heavily, certainly, but not enough to cover his tracks that quickly. Everywhere was a mix of white and subtle streaks of brown where tree trunks and foliage had so far avoided the heavy snow. Her breath clouded the air in front of her and she regretted not getting a coat.

She held up an arm as a feeble shield from the stinging snow.

At the rim of the Hollow, her breath cold and sharp in her throat, she looked down. Below her, in the centre of the crater, was the kids' den. In the shape of something between a cabin and a tepee, built with James's carpentry skills, it was a sturdy weave of branches and pallet boards. Snow covered the roof and heaped the sides in drifts.

Still, she saw no sign of Father Christmas.

A short laugh escaped her, and she refused another as it seemed to get lost in the snow. She worried that would bring on a madness she felt was close to overwhelming her, just like the darkness she felt at the edge of her vision. She stumbled down the slope, almost tripping, but snagged herself on the winter skeleton of a tree. Beside her, a startled robin redbreast took flight. The branch it had been standing on wobbled in the wake of its lift-off.

Flo *had* to be down there... she hoped... she prayed.

Down the embankment she went, taking sideways steps between branches and tangled brambles. The snow was untouched here, too. Again, she wondered about the man she'd seen. *Had* she even seen him? Whoever he was, and indeed if she'd even seen him, couldn't be in the den. No footprints, she thought with relief.

But she knew her daughter was in there. She couldn't be anywhere else.

Rachel slowed her pace, her lungs burning with a strange, cold fire, and her breath plumed about her in great clouds.

"Flo?" Her voice sounded close to hysterical, and, again, she somehow pushed it aside. She reached the paving that hid beneath the smooth snow. "Honey?"

No answer.

Closer to the door, she saw colours between the snow-coated boards and branches; bright yellow, too. Was that Flo's coat? Yes, thank God. There she was, sitting inside.

"It's Mummy, I'm coming in." Rachel pulled open the door, and it made an arc in the snow. "Flo, honey..."

Her daughter sat cross-legged on the blanket the kids used as a carpet. For a moment, Rachel couldn't understand what she saw. Food. So many paper plates, piled with food, surrounded her daughter. She wondered at which point during the day her children had taken all the food from the kitchen. Had it been today? Yesterday? Then Rachel realised none of the food was theirs. She didn't recognise any of it. There was a Christmas pudding and gingerbread men, mince pies, iced biscuits, tree cookies, and a perfectly-made Yule log. The chocolate looked *divine*.

Flo turned towards her. There was a headless gingerbread man in her pudgy fingers, and through a mouthful, she said, "Mummy, I told Kitt not to eat it."

A flash of memory: Kitt rubbing his stomach, turning to ice, exploding... She wanted to laugh, to cry, to tell Flo to stop eating, and... she wanted some of that chocolate log. Kitt, James... a shiver ran up her spine, and she crouched to step through the doorway.

She slapped the gingerbread from the girl's hand.

"Don't eat anything!" Tears again threatened to overcome her. She bit her lip, feeling her chin quiver.

Shocked, Flo cradled her hand in the other, and declared, "It tastes fine."

"Kitt—" Her boy's name caught in her throat.

"He shouldn't have eaten any of *that*." Flo pointed to a plate Rachel hadn't noticed tucked between the Yule log and Christmas pudding. It was a pie with a smiling elf's face made from chunks of lumpy pastry. Crudely made, and entirely unappetising. There was a piece missing, and the filling oozed a deep red onto the plate. It glistened, reflecting Flo's yellow coat.

Again, she thought of Kitt's exploding body. Again, she bit her lip. This was not the time to lose her cool.

Wind howled, and through the gap in the branches and boards, snow drifted in. Several flakes landed on the elf pie to instantly dissolve into the pastry and filling.

Rachel's lip hurt, and the copper taste of blood teased her tongue. Perhaps it even trickled down her chin. A shuffle forwards, and she could finally wrap her arms around Flo. Tight. An embrace. Mother and daughter. A life-thread... Family. Her only family now. Tears welled, blurred her vision. It was like water filled the den, brimming to drown them both. As though that was precisely what was happening, she began to choke and gasp. But they were sobs.

"He's outside again," Flo whispered.

Rachel gulped, held back the next sob, and mumbled into the girl's hair, "Who?"

"I'm scared, mummy."

With reluctance, she held Flo at arm's length. "Who are you talking about?" Rachel knew. Of course she knew.

Flo's eyes widened.

Outside, the sounds of twigs breaking and snow crunching beneath boots made them squeeze one another tighter.

The air froze in Rachel's throat.

In a roar of snapping wood, exploding splinters and screeching nails, the roof and walls of the den were suddenly ripped away. . A blanket that had been bunched in the corner was swept up into the air. Wind and snow buffeted them, and they both squinted into the whiteness.

Through the swirling snow, the toothy grin of a pockmarked and bearded face bore down on them. The rotund man was dressed in a tatty Father Christmas costume. Frost clung to the grubby fibres. A long, arthritic hand jerked towards Flo, one finger extended. The dirt beneath the fingernail hovering in front of the girl's nose was black.

"You!" His voice was sharp. "I told you... to... eat!"

Flo's bottom lip quivered.

Rachel shoved her away from him, and stood up straight. Flo cried out amid scattered plates and crumbled food, as Rachel tilted her head back. The man – if she could, in fact, call him that – had to be over eight-feet tall. He reeked of a mixture of cinnamon and sewage.

"Who are you?" she shrieked, her hands shaking. Adrenaline buzzed in her head.

When he grinned, his teeth appeared to lengthen, each as sharp as a pine needle and just as green. His red face was cratered, deeply scarred, oozed pus. He wore the floppy, red and white hat of an average Father Christmas, and his bulky coat was of the same shade of red, its buttons tarnished, rusted. A cold, cobalt blue fire burned in his stare – the same coldness that was in Kitt's eyes... just before... before he...

"What have you *done*?" Her shrill voice echoed around the Hollow. Yet again, she realised how close a personal darkness was to taking her away, but she had to stay strong for Flo. It was all about Flo now. They had to get out of there – now!

Breath steamed from gaping nostrils as he stepped back, gloating. As he did so, a plate flicked up crumbs over his tatty leather boot and a tree cookie crumbled into the blanket. He shifted the sack she'd not noticed he held. Covered in frost, just like the rest of him, it was crudely stitched in a patchwork effort that was confusing, and not entirely Christmassy. Each section was different: snowmen, love hearts, candy canes, shamrocks, skulls, pumpkins, eggs, rabbits; there was even a baby in a crib. Those were all she glimpsed, but there were more.

A grey-green filth oozed from in between the stitches, dripping onto the ground. It hissed, dissolving the snow and singeing the twigs. It smouldered when it spattered the blanket. An acrid curl of smoke wafted upwards, only to be snatched up by a sudden snow flurry.

"Flo, honey…" Rachel said, fighting the urge to cower before the gruesome creature. "Come here." Her hands shook so much more than from the cold that rooted her.

Flo reached up, and with a cold and clammy grip, grabbed Rachel's hand.

The man's blue eyes, with a hint of red, locked onto Rachel. Unable to look away, she felt Flo yank her sleeve.

"Mummy!"

One more step back, and the fake Father Christmas shrugged off the sack. It slumped to the ground between them with a thump.

"What have I done, you ask?" Incredibly, his grin widened still, seeming to split his head in two. Those craters in his skin now leaked a greenish muck.

Rachel moved slightly, and a branch snapped beneath her heel. She felt as though the ground had frozen up and around her boots.

In one movement, his veiny hands untied the frayed rope that fastened the sack. It gaped for a second then fell sideways. Dozens of coloured crystals scattered... and James's body flopped out.

Her heart corkscrewed into her throat and she cried out.

"Daddy!" Flo's grip crushed Rachel's fingers.

Most of the crystals and the majority of her husband's body remained in the sack. Those icy shards of her son twinkled.

"What have I done, indeed!" He laughed and it was more a shriek of delight, the sick bastard.

Flo pulled against Rachel's hand, but she wouldn't let her rush to her dad. No way.

"And..." The man booted James's lifeless body. "I even have a bonus."

James's dead eyes stared up to the sky as though watching the drifting flakes. A bitterness rose in Rachel's throat, choking her, and her mind reeled and warped her vision.

This man, this *monster*, reached down and picked up one of the crystals. He squinted into it, rolling it between thumb and forefinger. "Beautiful," he muttered and flicked it back into the sack. That tinkling sound sent nausea flushing through her. Still crouched, he picked up the elf pie. Its filling now bubbled.

Rachel willed her feet to move, and, finally, they shuffled backwards – inches at a time – slowly dragging Flo with her. As before, a dizziness threatened to take her down.

Balancing the plate on his upturned hand, he stood and offered it to Flo.

"Now, eat!"

She shook her head, clamping her lips tight; they turned as white as her cheeks and her tiny nostrils flared.

"I only need one more of you, then I can leave this ridiculous season."

"Get away from her!" Rachel yelled. One hand squeezed Flo's hand, while the other dug fingernails into her own palm to force away the darkness.

"Only one more mouth to feed, then I am out of here, away from this selfish season of gift-sharing-loveless-family-nonsense."

"One more?" Rachel murmured. The dizziness was strengthening, but she had to get Flo away from there.

"Yes." His eyes shone a deeper red amid the blue.

"Just one more?" she repeated, her voice shaking as much as the rest of her. "Then you'll leave us?"

"Yes." He took the plate away from Flo, and tilted his head to look at Rachel.

She straightened her back, lifting her head high. "I'll eat it," she whispered.

"Mummy, no," Flo cried.

Holding that monster's cold gaze, Rachel hardened her next words.

"If you promise to leave my daughter alone, I'll—"

Without waiting for her to finish, he rammed the pie towards her. His grin seemed to fill her whole vision.

Without hesitation, she snatched the plate from him and brought the pie to her mouth. It tasted of cinnamon, rotten vegetables, and off-meat. She gobbled, chewed, swallowed, then choked. Tears came, and then body-wracking sobs followed along with the image of James, of Kitt, of Flo... of a Christmas morning that began so normal.

She released Flo and used both hands to shovel the foul stuff into her mouth.

The man in the red suit chuckled.

"The more you eat," he whispered, "the quicker it'll be."

Gagging, she managed to swallow more. Some slopped onto her boots. Most of it went down her throat.

"Mummy." Flo had backed away and was almost sitting on the splintered remains of the den. A tiny crease had formed in her forehead, and her bottom lip quivered.

Rachel dropped the empty plate. The back of her hands whitened as they frosted. Her lungs filled with freezing air. Then feeling as though her organs had chilled to burning cold, her stomach swelled. A dizziness swept into her blurred vision, a whiteness leaking into her periphery.

So cold! she thought, numbed. *But no pain...*

As she watched ice crystals form over her sleeve and across her jumper, the freezing sensation intensified. . The sound of cracking came from somewhere inside her.

Her skin began to split.

From inside to out, that coldness surged through every inch of her, and perhaps... perhaps she heard Flo call out before a darkness replaced the blinding whiteness... and Rachael shattered into hundreds of ice crystals.

The girl cowered against the splintered remains of the den, her arm covering her face. Wind roared and snow stung her forehead. When she looked around, through a tornado of red and white and multi-coloured ice, she saw the pretend Father Christmas. He flew around her, swooping up and down, circling.

It was like she was trapped in a storm, and it made her dizzy. Her throat hurt from screaming, but she couldn't hear herself over the shrieking wind.

The man's ugly patchwork sack gaped open to scoop the crystals. Soon, the colours dissolved into the whorl of snow, and even his red suit blended with the white. She could barely see him now.

Although the man had vanished, his laughter remained close.

"Better go indoors, little girl..." His words shrieked, then faded with a dying wind, "or you'll freeze to death."

The End

How the Witch Stole Yuletide

By

James Matthew Byers

Every Dane down in Daneland liked Yuletide
a bunch...

But the witch off the mainland, to give you a hunch,

So despised Yuletide splendor, the whole Yuletide
feel!

Now, just don't ask me why, no one quite knows
her deal.

It could be the noises from parties each night.

It could be her leathery boots fit too tight.

But believe me, whatever the reason might be,

You might say Grendel's mother drew hatred from
glee.

No matter her purpose; no rhyme for her pains,

She plotted on Yuletide Eve, loathing the Danes.

Sending out from her waters to lend her a hand

Came her beastly son, Grendel, who crept through the land.

For she knew every Dane down in Daneland below,

Was now actively kissing beneath mistletoe.

"And they're drinking their spice ale!" she grumbled with grit,

"Tomorrow is Yuletide! I must make it quit!"

Then she thought about Grendel who she had sent slumming,

"Perhaps he and I can keep Yuletide from coming!"

In the morning, she knew, every Dane, wall to wall,

Would arise bright and early in King Hrothgar's hall!

And then! Oh, the din! Oh, the din! Din! Din! Din!

That's one thing she hated! The din! Din! Din! Din!

Then the Danes, young and old, would gather and dine.

And they'd dine! And they'd dine! And they'd dine! Dine! Dine! Dine!

They would dine on their beef, cheese, and drink nude or clothed.

And you know, this the witch did not like, no, she loathed!

And THEN they did something she loathed most all!

Every Dane down in Daneland, the small and the tall,

Would lean in together, with ale mugs a clinging.

They'd raise a glass high. And the Danes would start singing!

They'd croon! And they'd croon! And they'd croon! Croon! Croon! Croon!

And the more the witch thought of the Dane's Yuletide Tune,

The more the witch thought, "It will end with my goon!"

"Why, for hundreds of years I've endured this vile day!"

"I'll stop this year's Yuletide! I'll have my own way!"

Then she got a notion! A horrible notion!

THE WITCH GOT A WRETCHED AND HORRIBLE NOTION!

"I now have just the plan!" the witch started to gloat.

And she sent up a spell through the muck and the moat.

And she cackled, and laughed, "This will aid Grendel's case!"

"With those words I shall change him to have Odin's face!"

"All he needs is a Sleipnir ... " The witch glanced aware.

That, since horses were tasty, she would find none there.

Did this halt the old witch? Nay! The witch simply spoke.

"If there aren't any horses, I'll craft one from smoke!"

So she called on the dragon. Its scales were all red,

And she conjured eight legs and a rein for its head.

She filled up some sacks on an old rotting wagon,

And tethered them tightly around her pet dragon.

Then the witch said, "Get going!" The wagon would crawl,

To the Danes down in Daneland asleep in their hall.

Here the dragon met Grendel. The scene was all set.

All the Danes were all snoring without any fret.

When he entered the hall, he would bring them regret.

"Here we are at our stop," the false Allfather jeered,

And he moved to the roof, knowing he would be feared.

Then he found a slat open. A hiccupping glitch.

But the squeeze didn't bother him, thanks to the witch.

He maneuvered down slowly, and made it alone.

Then he pushed through headfirst there upon the hearthstone.

Where the tiny Danes' spits all turned round from below.

"These boar spits," he sneered, "I will eat nice and slow!"

Then he changed up his shape, and he ate some roast pheasant,

And silently slinked, munching on thane and peasant!

Small ones! And tall ones! And plump ones as well!

Skinny ones! Mini ones! None gave a yell!

And he crammed them in sacks. Then he pushed them up duly,

Crammed all the sacks in the hearth opened newly.

Then he sneaked to the next pile. He took the Danes there!

He took all the bald ones! He took those with hair!

He snatched up those sleeping in quite a mad dash.

Why, then Grendel decided he'd mince and he'd smash!

Then he crammed all those Danes up the hole with a grin.

"And NEXT!" Grendel smirked, "I will cram up more men!"

And he snatched up more men, and he started to fill,

When he caught a light laugh, someone else he would kill.

He shifted his gaze, and it fell on a man!

Tiny Beowulf, standing to thwart the fiend's plan.

Grendel Odin was found by this Geatland son,

Who feigned to be sleeping while vile deeds were done.

He glared hard at Grendel, and said, "Odin, stop,"

"Stop all this snatching the men here, now! STOP!"

But, you see, Grendel Odin had quick witted guile,

He told quite a story; he spoke with a smile!

"Why, my wee, tiny man," Grendel Odin there said,

"These poor men need my magic, but they are not dead."

"So I'm bringing them home to my cavern, you see."

"I'll make them brand new. That's a promise from me."

But his lie didn't work. Then the man gave him fight,

And the two had a tussle that long winter night.

Then when Beowulf finished, he held up an arm,

And Grendel was bleeding and fled fast in harm!

He lost his false face and climbed higher and higher!

Then he went through the open hearth, singed by the fire.

On the roof he went screaming back home through the mire.

And though many a Dane was left dead on the floor,

Brave Beowulf had stopped him from killing some more.

Then he raced on the wagon all across forest floors

Exiting with the dragon who took him through the moors!

It was just getting light ... All the Danes, yet to wake,

All the Danes, still asleep or those he didn't take,

In his wagon crammed tightly! The bodies! The feeding!

The pain at his shoulder! The horror! The bleeding!

Two hundred feet down! Down to his mother's cavern,

He pushed with the dragon beyond the hall's tavern!

"Harrumph to the Danes!" he let out his mother.

"I messed up their Yuletide you soon will discover!"

"They'll all arise soon! Mother, now I must die!"

"Their hearts have been broken, I gave my best try,

Then the Danes down in Daneland will let out a cry!"

"That's a sound," hissed the witch, "that I need in MY ears!"

Grendel died. And the witch listened out for their jeers.

And she did hear a noise rising out of the hall.

It came as a hoot. Then it bounced wall to wall.

But the sound wasn't sorrowful! Why, how could this be!

It drove the witch madder! The foul joy there! The glee!

She listened to Daneland! The witch let a yell!

Then she screamed! Her son, Grendel, had given them Hell!

Every Dane down in Daneland, the small and the tall,

Was crooning and toasting! Alive in that hall!

He HADN'T made Yuletide stop! IT STILL ARRIVED!

Those Danes celebrated; those who survived!

And the witch, with her dragon beneath her cool lake,

Grew angrier: "This is just too much to take!"

"It came without roast boar! It came without bread!"

"It came, still the same, although many are dead!"

And she wondered for hours, till she wondered no
more.

Then the witch thought she simply must even the
score.

"This Yuletide," she pondered, "I will break down
their door."

"This Yuletide ... all Daneland ... will be smattered in
gore!"

And what happened next? Well ... in Daneland they
tell,

That the witch's full wrath came among them to
dwell!

And the moment her hands tore through wood to
get in,

She ripped up the bodies and shredded the skin,

Of the Danes she brought back! Hrothgar trembled
with dread!

SHE TOOK HIS ADVISOR and ripped off his head!

The End

Kevin J. Kennedy Presents

Sugar Vision
By
Sara Tantlinger

"You're fired." Santa's face was blooming into the same deep shade of red as the blood on Sugar Plum's hands.

"Excuse me?" She clutched the butcher knife and dropped the half-skinned rabbit into the marble sink of her workshop. The light lilac of her wings morphed into a burnt indigo shade. The tips twitched as she stepped closer to Santa, the knife still in her hand.

The large, jolly bastard shifted from foot to foot, his thin lips frowned between the white cloud of his beard. Beady eyes flickered to the knife and back to her face. "I know what you've been doing. How could you? To innocent children!"

She snorted and tossed the knife down. After inhaling a deep breath, she crossed her arms and relaxed. The dark purple of her wings and veins faded back to a friendly lilac. The once-sparkling tulle of her tutu was already covered in dirt, so the smeared blood from her hands on it didn't bother her. She had a million of these dresses.

"All I've done is to merely punish those on your naughty list properly. What lesson does coal teach besides resentment? I teach fear."

"Christmas shouldn't be about fear," Santa pleaded, his grubby hands folded together like he was praying to her, or for her to understand, at least.

Sugar Plum leaned against the counter and sighed. All she had wanted to do was cook her dinner of rabbit in peace and then get back to work. Her experiments sat piled around the workshop in heaps of unwrapped candy and new ingredients she wanted to try. Children kept having the same dreams about the same types of sweets they would find on Christmas morning in their stockings, and she longed to give them something new. Something exciting. "I've done nothing wrong."

Santa pounded a fist against the counter near her and she jumped. The cherry lump of a man rarely, if ever, got angry.

"What you have done goes beyond any humane punishment. You cannot live at the North Pole and hurt children."

"It's not like I killed anyone! I just took little pricks of blood for some experiments. I mean, that one horrible girl tried to drown the family puppy and you think giving her coal is going to fix that? And don't even get me started about the brat who shit in his neighbor's swimming pool."

Santa stormed past her to where a large, oak cabinet sat with a black cloth askance over half of it. His hand lingered on a drawer's handle, but he did not pull it open.

"That's my property," Sugar Plum declared between gritted teeth. Her lilac deepened into a near black shade. Fury pumped hot tendrils through her blood and wrapped around her bones with a burning sizzle.

Santa shook his head. When she stomped over to him, he raised a hand and must have tapped into his greater powers because as hard as she tried, she could not move from the spot where he froze her. His round eyes filled with sadness as he yanked the drawer open.

Vials of blood sat neatly organized in the first drawer, and the second drawer, and the third drawer that he opened. His chubby hands lightly touched the vials, and the color drained from his cheeks.

"What have you done, Sugar Plum?"

"I didn't kill them!"

Santa jerked the first drawer out completely and tossed it across the workshop. Vials of blood flew out like glass cardinals, smashing against the concrete walls and floor, splattering red smears everywhere.

"Stop!" Sugar Plum tried to leap in front of Santa and get to the vials, but the magic held her rooted.

"Whatever you were planning to do with the blood of children will not happen under my watch," Santa avowed. He removed the next two drawers in the same way and made sure every last vial was obliterated until nothing but glass shards and stains of crimson littered the floor.

Rage sent trembles throughout Sugar Plum's body. It had taken her years to collect that blood from enough children since she really only did pinprick their sleeping fingers and take such small amounts away from them.

"You might not have killed any children yet, but I have no doubt you would have." Santa unfroze her and walked quietly to the door.

"You are banished from the North Pole. You are banished from coming anywhere near children, and if you do, I will know." He tapped at the side of his head. "I will see you, and I will lock you away into the Pole's cellars, which I should do now, but..."

Sugar Plum shivered. The prison of the North Pole was a hellish place that existed deep into the freezing earth. Only darkness and ice resided there, along with the reindeer that had gone mad, but Santa hadn't the heart to put them down. Just like he didn't have the heart to lock her away down there, at least not yet.

"Fine!" She stomped through the glass and the shards turned to pieces of glass dust. She didn't need Santa or the North Pole or any of this. Santa disappeared from her workshop without another word.

Sugar Plum retreated into her room, which was adjoined to the workshop, and stuffed the few belongings she needed into a big, mauve duffel bag. Everything else she needed would have to be recreated. Let that red-suited, kiddie-loving, freak of a man try to stop her from what she started. She'd just start over. She'd find a way; she always did.

She was the very symbol of holiday splendor and joy, after all. A sparkling delicacy with sugar-sweet promises and a smile of hope, at least to everyone on the outside who needed to see her that way. But still! If she couldn't represent children's Christmas dreams and joy, then Santa Claus sure as hell wasn't going to.

She finished packing and left. She would rebuild both her workshop and the candy village she used to lull children to her. And her final masterpiece... she would create it all away from the prying eyes of the North Pole and Santa's loyalists. She could make the village she was really destined to create with her talents that Santa had wasted.

#

Somewhere in the darkness of the north-eastern United States, Sugar Plum was aching with hunger. In her nearly six years away from the North Pole, she had not missed the place or its ever-watching eyes at all, but she did miss the easy access she once had to children—to their blood. She had accomplished, for the most, what she had set out to do, but the toll it took on her was undeniably going to kill her if she didn't provide herself with the proper sustenance. She had *tried,* but everything she really needed and wanted had been used to appease the gods who had granted her enough magic to recreate her true village again. It was there she could at last bring children and collect their blood without the paranoia of who might be watching. All in the name of Christmas cheer.

Just little pinpricks of blood, she told herself as her stomach grumbled. All of her materials had gone to village, and so little of it was saved for her. Yet still, determination beat a steady drum in her mind, and she would find a way to regain strength, especially since she had, at last, been sneaking her way back into the minds of sleeping children.

Santa had tried to keep her away from the kiddies, and he'd set magic in place to keep her physically away, but her power over dreams was stronger than Santa's. The children dreaming of Christmas went to bed with visions of sugarplums dancing in their heads, after all. They dreamt and called, so she came.

The most recent dreamer, the one she'd decided to take to regain her strength, was a lovely little boy with big green eyes. Sugar Plum couldn't wait to give this blessed child a gift to remember.

When Christmas Eve arrived, she said her prayers to the gods of her village and set out to meet the boy in his dreams. His mind was saturated with shiny red bows and unwrapped gift boxes, striped candy canes and piles and piles of sweets everywhere. The little brat constantly dreamt of the candy he often hoarded and gobbled down after mommy and daddy went to bed. His love of sweets was perfect for what needed to happen, though. Lately, the dreams Sugar Plum observed from the boy were filled with mice kings and chocolate pudding, of ballet dancers and fairies.

She grinned and traced the outline of his dream with her fingertips. She eased herself into his mind like a shadow.

Sugar Plum came to him with her music-box voice, a melody children followed as if hypnotized. The shine of her tiara caught his attention right away, and the dream-version of the boy walked slowly closer to her. On the outside, she appeared to him as a beautiful, lilac-dusted princess with curled hair and plum-colored lips. She smiled, and the boy's eyes, big and green like succulent gumdrops, lit up with joy at her presence.

"Hello," she greeted and conjured up a throne made entirely of white chocolate. She sat down and arranged the sparkling tulle of her new dress. The outer covering was a deep, royal purple, with glimpses of rainbow beneath it. She crossed her legs and the pointed satin of her shoes reflected the glittering lights dancing around the dream- like fireflies.

The darling boy tilted his head and looked at her, bewilderment apparent on his face, but also that look of enchantment Sugar Plum loved. Enchantment and trust melted into each other so well.

She held out a dainty hand and summoned up little, sugary bits of blue candies. "Would you like one?"

The boy poked his tongue out for a moment. "What are they?"

"Something I invented, but I'm not sure what to call them. Could you help me name them? I hear you're the candy expert around these parts." She winked.

His eyes lit up. "Yeah!" He smiled shyly and grabbed two of the candies out of her palm. He chewed them up and swallowed the sugary residue down.

"Wow," he remarked and grinned.

"What do they taste like to you?" This was one of her favorite parts. Every child tasted something different.

The little bugger really thought about it, his tongue darting around his mouth as if to sweep across all the flavors. "Like, a mountain. Fresh like a mountain's water, you know? Kind of minty. A minty mountain!" he declared.

"Oh," she said and chuckled. "A little poet, you are!"

She had never eaten a poet before.

He giggled and looked a bit dazed.

"What's your name, poet?"

"Gabriel."

A poet named after an angel. Great.

"Gabriel, would you like to come with me to my candy village?"

He nodded so eagerly she thought his head might lop right off.

Sugar Plum took his hand and shifted the boy's dream away. They exited his subconscious and the world around them morphed into something new.

The effect of the candy was still glistening in Gabriel's eyes. Sugar Tunnel Vision, she called it.

"Welcome!" Sugar Plum gestured toward the village, a wonderland where the small houses were perfect sizes for young children. Each home was like a gingerbread house come to life. The powdered sugar dusted through the air like snow and piled up on roofs and in the streets. Gumdrop doorknobs, peppermint walkways, graham cracker walls, jellybean decorations, pixie dust paint, and stretched-out toffee windows came together in a kaleidoscope of candied color.

The cinnamon chimneys puffed out tufts of flavored air. Edible pebbles lined the pathways between the houses and glass-candy icicles dripped down from the roofs.

The main road between the lined up houses led to the village square. Gabriel clutched tight to Sugar Plum's hand and she grinned in delight at seeing his young face glow with wonder. He reached out a tiny hand and watched the powdered sugar gather on his palm before gleefully licking it away.

"There's more," Sugar Plum whispered.

"More?" His saccharine eyes widened. She wondered if they tasted more like limes or green apples. She longed to scoop them out and use the bulbs to sweeten her tea or suck on one like a hard peppermint candy.

Instead she pointed ahead and Gabriel followed the direction of her gesture. He walked in front of her, slowly making his way into the village square.

Twizzling lampposts encircled the center of the village where beautifully carved chocolate fountains bubbled out even more chocolate delight. A basin of rock candy stood in the middle of the square, gurgling out frothy syrup. A small moat of fluffy whipped cream circled the basin. Butterscotch permeated the air as the chocolate fountains changed their flavors.

"Magic," Gabriel murmured.

Sugar Plum smiled. The real magic was about to begin.

She knelt down and looked Gabriel in the eyes. "What do you want for Christmas, my dear?"

"I want to stay here! This is way cooler than home." He darted away and stuck his face beneath the waterfall of syrup from the basin. The kid must have inherited amazing metabolism to be so small yet so full of sugar and junk. She was surprised he'd want to stay here since while yes, the place was seemingly full of all his candied dreams, there were no other forms of life in sight. No other visible people, no small animals for him to toss rocks at. No little sister for him to try and choke.

"Yes, I think you should stay here," Sugar Plum agreed quietly. "Gabriel, do you know what happens to bad kids at Christmas time?"

The boy extracted his syrup-smeared face away from the fountain and grinned. His teeth were stained dark brown from his gluttony. "They get coal!"

She sighed. "No, I mean, the children who have gone missing over the past few years just before Christmas?"

"Oh." He frowned and looked away, locking his gaze on the creamy moat that surrounded him instead. "Momma says I shouldn't talk about that because it's sad and they never found the guy that took those kids."

Gabriel stuck his mouth back under the fountain, his perturbed thought only short-lived. Sugar Plum grumbled in slight annoyance that her hard work would forever be credited as "some guy" who stole kids, but whatever. She would know the truth.

The magic of the blue candies was beginning to fade away. The village wavered like a mirage in the distance, but Gabriel kept his face in the syrup fountain. Well, until the syrup turned to blood.

He gagged and stumbled away, frantically spitting out the liquid and wiping at his face until the blood was spread across his mouth and cheeks. The initial look of wonderment was replaced with horror. His mouth opened, but only confused whimpers came out.

"You see, Gabriel, a long time ago I used to take the naughty boys and girls of the world, bleed them just a *tiny* bit, and try to see what I could use their blood for because these kids just didn't deserve to be walking around with all that life-giving juice inside them. My gods told me to build a village with that blood where I could store those bad children, keep them away from good kids, and sacrifice them to the gods in order to keep the spirit of Christmas alive."

She paced around the child and could feel her lilac wings turning to something darker and burnt. "But you see, that is what dear, old Santa Claus didn't understand! He thinks all his magic, all he rules over at the North Pole is just his inherent right and good fortune, but in reality, everything he has was given to him by *my* gods, all in exchange for those bad, bad children. But no one ever told Santa this. I should have. I almost did when he banished me, but I guess I'm a softie after all, and just couldn't stand to see the old man hurt."

She walked over to Gabriel and knelt down beside him again. Her thumb wiped at the blood on his mouth. "I've been rebuilding the village all these years and it's the only thing that has kept Santa and Christmas alive. The gods are pleased, but see, now I am hungry. I've worked so hard, never taking anything for myself so that the gods would make sure Santa and Christmas were saved. And now I'm just *starving*."

The boy's eyes shifted from her face to something behind her. She grinned and sat beside him, throwing an arm around him to make sure he didn't run off.

The warm scent of butterscotch that had drifted through the air grew into something heavier. The weight of a copper aroma replaced the sweetness. The gurgling fountains all shifted from spewing out chocolate and syrup into frothing out thick streams of dark gore, vital pools of sweet scarlet nectar.

The rock candy basin morphed into one made entirely of small skulls. "Those," Sugar Plum said and pointed, "were all the naughty children who dared to dream of me, their Sugar Plum princess that they didn't deserve. Children are capable of such brutality, aren't they Gabriel?"

The boy remained silent, but shook violently. She hoped he didn't urinate himself like some of the others had.

The rest of the sugary village morphed into what Sugar Plum had been building all this time. The gingerbread homes turned into small huts held up by a structure of bones. The walls were stretched out chunks of flesh, dried and attached to the bones. Instead of gumdrop doorknobs or jellybean decorations, everything was ornamented with various, small organs. Hearts for doorknobs, sets of lungs lining the roofs, livers smashed and cobbled together into the pathways between the homes. Finger bones had been carved into wind chimes where nerves with eyes still hanging from them served as decoration between the bones. Hair was stuffed into the fleshy walls of the huts like insulation.

Some of the bones had been charred to make black lampposts. Blood flowed freely in the moat where small chunks of scalp and brain floated.

Every part of the children Sugar Plum had collected had been used to create the new village.

"Bad things happen to bad children, Gabriel. They must be punished."

"I...I," he stammered. "I'm not bad."

She smiled and cupped his face in her hands. "I think your sister and kitty cat would feel differently about that, wouldn't they?"

He stammered again, but she had grown too hungry to keep playing with her food.

"Dear gods who have helped me create this village, keep the spirit of Christmas alive with my sacrifices to you. I will keep myself alive with this sacrifice that I take for myself."

"Please," the little boy pleaded as he tried to squirm away. "I'm sorry."

"Shh, I'll make it quick."

Her lilac wings quivered in excitement as her belly rumbled. Her jaw unlatched and the sweet smile was replaced with a hundred teeth, sharp as candy canes that have been sucked into dangerously pointed tips. The boy's eyes widened and she thought the beautiful green of them looked just like Christmas lights.

She'd save them for last.

The End

The Dance of the Sugarplum Fairy

By

Steven Stacy

1941 – One Year into the German Occupancy of France

Everything seemed absurdly calm. Ariella Becker sat on the floorboards next to her grandfather as he quietly read his book. She tried to read over his shoulder but he read much faster than her, doodling along the margins as he went with his fountain pen. Her mother was asleep in the small attic above them, sharing a mattress with her sister, Blondelle; they mostly stayed in the church crawl space, but Ariella was slight, and, at the age of seventeen, she could move about quickly and soundlessly. Her grandfather draped a warm arm around her shoulders, and she leaned in closer to read alongside him.

Suddenly, the sounds of whispered voices came from the room on the other side of the organ.

Ariella's grandfather dropped his book to his lap and looked up.

"Go to your hiding places, go to your hiding places!" voices whispered. Ariella saw the fear on her grandfather's face and heard him answer in a hushed tone. "Okay, okay, thankyou!"

Ariella spun around and looked out the nave of the church. Her eyes bulged with horror as she saw the French Nazi police searching the church. "What are they saying?" she asked quietly.

"They say, someone has accused the church of hiding guns."

Ariella inhaled sharply. "They're searching the *church!*?" she squeaked "Grandpapa, I'm scared."

"Quickly!, Go to your hiding place," Grandpapa whispered urgently. He brought her in for a hug, and underneath the thick, static smell of dust, there was the scent of the rich tobacco smoke he sometimes smoked in the nights. Into her hand he pushed his fountain pen. She looked at it, wide eyed.

"What's this for?" she breathed, holding the heavy pen up to her eyes. Navy blue with gold trim.

"It's for good luck!" he called softly over his shoulder as he rushed to the ladder at the end of the room and crawled up.

"I want to come with you!" she implored tearfully.

"Go! You have the best hiding space – use it!" Grand Papa urged in a hushed tone as he reached the top of the ladder. "Hurry!" he insisted as he drew the ladder up, not daring to pull it because it would grate along the side and make too much noise. He blew his granddaughter a kiss and quietly closed the trap door. Ariella could hear the police getting closer. She squeezed into the small gap around the cold metal of the organ pipes and manoeuvred herself behind the crawl space. She escaped into the adjoining room, just as the Nazis entered; her grandpapa's book left in the dust. Her father was waiting for her on the other side with her younger brother, Frank. They moved silently down into a cramped space underneath the floorboards.

Ariella heard raised voices in the adjacent room. She put her lips to her father's ear and whispered, "What are they saying?" Her father spoke German, as well as French, English and

Yiddish; he was well educated, and a former lecturer at the state university.

"They are asking about a book..." He looked at her reassuringly and shrugged as if this was nothing. She felt his hand grasp hers and squeeze. All at once, horror struck her, loosening her bowels and shivering up her spine. She tucked her grandfather's pen into her cardigan pocket.

"Papa, Grandpapa left his book in the room," she murmured. Her blue eyes glittered with unshed tears in the murk of the crawl space. Suddenly, and shockingly, gunfire rained in the room next door. Her father crawled over her body. Ariella tried not to groan under the weight of her father's bulk. She could feel he was trembling. He spread his legs to cover his son. Frank's hand pushed through the limbs and grasped his father's free hand. The three of them became conjoined in terror.

Ariella closed her eyes and prayed – *'they won't come in this room, they won't.'* Abruptly the door to the room flew open and Ariella looked up through the floorboards. Leather boots stomped above her. There were three men with the priest— a Nazi officer and two younger Nazi soldiers. Ariella held her breath, afraid to make even the smallest sound.

The priest spoke in French, a language that Ariella had been brought up to speak, read and write. "Please, I beg you. This is a holy place. These people sought sanctuary," the priest begged, his hands up in the air. Then he burst into ragged sobs and fell to his knees. "I beg you!"

"Are you hiding enemies of the State? If you do not tell me where, I will not only shoot to pieces your entire church... I will also shoot you!" The Nazi officer tapped the priest right in the middle of his forehead, the leather of his glove creaking. "However, if you tell me you are hiding more enemies of the State, I will leave your beautiful church intact, as well as your wrinkly forehead." The priest's tears slowed to a steady flow as he nodded his head. "Point out where. . ."

Ariella's father released the trap-door underneath her body and it soundlessly fell away. She fell through the gap, making no sound, as her father grabbed her forearms and, slowly, using all the sinewy strength he could muster, lowered her to the ground below. Just like their practices, it went perfectly. He smiled weakly all too well.

"Shoot!" he screamed. Suddenly, the church lit up with gun fire, pummelling its way into the floorboards where the Becker family lay; smoke, splinters, dust, bullet casings and blood flew through the air, one bullet hitting the organ. The sound of death echoed throughout the small church. Her father's dead body hung above her, limply. She hesitated a moment and then she ran. "Get downstairs, one of you to each exit!" the Nazi commanded. The soldiers ran out of the room. The colonel looked at the priest with a wry smile. "A trapdoor? Very clever." Silence hung in the air as the dust settled. Then the colonel raised his gun and shot the priest in the gut, before racing out of the room and down the stairway.

Ariella sobbed as she raced through the church, her bare feet smacking against the stone. She forced herself to run beyond her limits; her heart racing and begging for oxygen. She threw herself against the secret door at the back of the church; it flew open and she sucked the sweet country air into her lungs. "Arret!" she heard screamed from behind her. She came to an abrupt stop, hair falling into her face. It was one of the German soldiers pointed at her head, she saw at a glance. She turned to him, defiantly, her chest heaving, up and down, in her torn white blouse and filthy cardigan. The Star of David hung between her small breasts. She held her head high, but looked down.

Officer Nardo Vogel looked at her in astonishment. The girl was about sixteen, and extremely pretty. She didn't look like one of *them*. Her long hair was fair— almost golden— and it fell around her chest. Her face was a rosebud. Large, blue eyes, a small, straight nose and rosebud lips. Rosebud, rosebud, rosebud, the word repeated in his mind.

She burst into a sprint again... filthy feet against dew-sleek grass. It reminded him of the time he had seen one of the most beautiful deer in the forest. He had been hunting with his father and it had come out from behind a huge tangle of brambles and stopped in front of him. That same look of panic and fear had been in its eyes... that same need for desperate escape.

He raced after her, grabbing her by her long hair. "Wait! Wait!" he implored in a hushed tone. He then hurriedly checked over his shoulder as she turned to look also. "You won't make it to the woods in time! Hide behind this door." Her brows knotted in confusion. "Do it quickly," he commanded. She ran behind the door, and found herself back inside the church, and he quickly shut it behind her. She took out her grandfather's pen and held it tightly in her fist. *Would it penetrate a human eyeball? Was she strong enough, accurate enough?*

"What are you doing!? Where is it!" his colonel screamed, emerging from around the front of the building. Jerking him and the girl from their individual thoughts. "Where–is–it?"

"It ran off into the woods, it was a young girl. Around sixteen, sir."

"Why didn't you shoot her?"

I was unable to shoot such a beautiful creature, he wanted to say.

The colonel approached the young officer, his leather boots and trench coat creaking against the weight of his body. "Why did you just allow an enemy of the State to escape?"

"I... I would have missed, colonel," Nardo stuttered.

The colonel smiled at the young officer. "Was this young girl pretty?"

Nardo felt the hair on the back of his neck prickle up. He could not speak, and so he nodded. "You couldn't bring yourself to shoot a pretty young girl in the back? Am I correct?"

"Yes, sir..."

The colonel grinned, his teeth strong and white in his pink gums. "You dirty dog." He wrapped a friendly arm around Nardo's shoulder. "You like the Jewish pussy, no?" He laughed loudly. "Why not, eh?" His arm squeezed tightly around Nardo's neck. "You did the right thing,' he said gently, his breath tickling Nardo's ear. "To put a bullet in the back of a young girl would be... cowardly." The colonel slapped Nardo's chest affectionately and then reached out and snatched his balls, squeezing hard. Nardo groaned and his eyes immediately started watering.

"I should twist them off," snarled the colonel, "and then we will see how popular you are with the little Jewish whores." He squeezed tighter. "You want to be a eunuch?"

Nardo shook his head, his face turning bright red. The colonel twisted his balls a little more—and then abruptly released them.

"No matter!" he said, brightly. "She is hardly a danger—after news spreads of what happened here today, no farmer or holy man will take her in. She has no family to turn to-she is completely alone in the world... and you made that happen. Shooting her in the back, might have been kinder, actually. Remember that."

Nardo looked down from his colonel's face, to the floor and then to his gun.

Ariella listened, her back to the cold stone of the Church.

She heard the men walk away, their voices and footsteps gradually fading to silence, and burst into silent tears. Then, holding on tightly to her Grandfather's pen, she sprinted off into the forest.

Four Years Later - Paris, France

Margot Lagière took her standing ovation as one of the top dancers at 'The Bel Tabarin' with her dancing partner, Louis Bisset, at the end of their performance of 'The Nutcracker.' Dancers dressed as different sweets, fairies and snowflakes all stood in a row. During her performance, one-time Nazi officer, Nardo Vogel, had been watching from the balcony; a celebratory night for him, since he had recently been made a Corporal - *Corporal Nardo Vogel*. He had been studying Margot Lagière for two reasons. The first was that she was extremely beautiful and a magnificent dancer... especially in her role as the sugarplum fairy. The second, was that she reminded him of a young Jewess whose life he had saved when he was a boy. Of course, it was difficult to tell positively, due to the woman's powdered face and white-blonde hair. He turned again to one of the soldiers – "What do you think?" he asked.

The soldier blew out air from his cheeks. "Incredible, sir, *incredible*. I would give away a month's rations to kiss just one of her breasts. Sir."

Nardo nodded dreamily, his eyes fixed on the smiling woman.

Margot and Louis waited for the curtain to drop and ran backstage. A mixture of noise and laughter blended with the audience's applause. They were greeted by the producer of their show, Elias, who kissed Margot on both cheeks and then leaned in for a more loving kiss, on the lips, to Louis. Margot, weary from the performance, started to walk away to her dressing room. "Wait!" Elias said sternly.

"Oui?" Margot asked, turning. "What is it now?"

"We are being joined tonight by certain decorated members of the S.S." Both Margot's and Louis' faces dropped as they looked at each other. "Before either of you protest, it is obviously not something that I am relishing the thought of, either. I had no choice in the matter – one of them has been made a corporal– I know, I know, but to them it is a big deal. He is a great fan of yours, darling." He took Margot's hand and kissed it. "Put on your most dazzling frock, my delicious little sugarplum. And Louis - put on a fresh suit. One which shows off your beautiful derriere." He slapped his lover on the backside and shrieked in laughter.

Margot and Louis didn't even try to argue. "As you wish," Margot said, and the dancers walked hand in hand back towards their dressing rooms. A nervous knot had started to tie itself inside her stomach. She closed her eyes, and as always in situations such as these, her mind threw up a single, stark image: an open book laying on dusty floorboards. Doodles in the margins. "I think I'm going to be sick," she declared, before snatching a bucket away from a passing cleaner and throwing up in it. Louis placed a warm hand between her shoulder-blades.

"Don't worry, it'll be fine. We've had to deal with them plenty of times. We've done three P.O.W camps in the last three months. What's wrong with you?" He studied her face with his dark eyes.

"I don't like surprises," Margot said, standing up and smoothing her hair back under her tiara. "What if they know about the letters?"

"Don't think like that, my dear. Stay strong." He hugged her tightly, her tutu pushing against his thighs. He smelled of rose water and fresh perspiration, a sweet scent inside the musky interiors of the ballet house.

"I'll try," she mumbled, her head nestled into his strong neck.

"It'll be a piece of cake. See you in fifteen," Louis said and kissed her. He ran off, leaving Margot to stand with one hand against the wall, breathing deeply. Her feet ached from the performance and her saliva tasted like bile. "Merde!" she hissed to herself. Her mind raced with anxieties. She needed to draw no further attention to herself; she needed to get to her dressing room.

Margot sat in front of her vanity mirror and started to do her make-up for the evening. *Hide in plain sight,* her adoptive mother, and head of a very lucrative and famous French ballet school for children had once said. *And peroxide your damn hair – it is still too dark.* Madam Phi-Phi was a very wise woman. Margot drew on her lip-liner, a deep scarlet, then dabbed rouge on the apples of her cheeks and started to blend it as she sucked a mint. She styled her long, fair tresses in the peek-a-boo style of Veronica Lake; she felt safer if she could hide behind her hair. To the left of her reflection, she stared at one of her suitcases. Her eyes closing in on the one that held hundreds of illegal prisoner of war letters, from prisoners to their families. On seeing the horrific ways the prisoners were being treated by the Nazis, she and Louis had agreed to help. Margot had a way of talking men around to her way of thinking, even homosexuals like Louis. She had to help in as many ways as possible.

Her dressing room door was knocked upon…, *rat-a-tat-tat-tat.* "Just a minute!" she called out.

Elias called through the door, speaking French in his terrible German accent. "Some of the officers would like to speak to you about your performance," Elias said. *'Performance'* was their insider word for fans that had chocolates, praise, flowers and bullshit.

She ran to the back of her door and grabbed a white silk robe and relaxed into her seat, lighting a cigarette on the end of her ivory holder. "Come in!" she called, draping one hand over the dressing table; trying to look as relaxed, sultry, and self-assured as she could. The door opened and two S.S. soldiers came in with bouquets of flowers.

"You were sublime tonight!"

"Simply fantastique!"

She smiled demurely and accepted the flowers. "Merci beaucoup. Please stop, you're going to give a girl a big head." She laughed, her hand fluttering to her breast. Then she signed her black and white headshot with the pen her grandfather had given her; before finishing it with a kiss of her bright red lipstick.

Then another figure walked into her room, alongside Elias.

Him. The young soldier who had –

She quickly looked away and focused on smoking her cigarette. Stomach like a ball of molten iron, heart clanging. Him. It was really him. Finally, she managed a smile.

"Margot Lagière, this is Corporal Nardo Vogel, he has seen the show several times and is a huge fan of yours," Elias explained. She lifted her chin, defiantly. The German's blue eyes examined her face. She quickly crossed her legs and let the material from her gown reveal her bare thigh, which drew his attention away from her face. She swallowed anxiously.

"I recognise you," the corporal said, wagging a finger, a smile touching his lips.

"I should hope so," Margot replied, before inhaling from her cigarette holder. "I've danced for you German devils on more than one occasion." The two soldiers laughed. Corporal Nardo simply smirked with his ever-watchful eyes back on her face. Margot grabbed her grandpapa's pen and started pushing the nib up and down, anxiously. She hid this within her dressing gown sleeve.

"May I speak to Fräulein Margot Lagière alone please, gentleman?" Nardo asked, placing his gloved hands together. The two soldiers glanced at their Corporal, and Elias looked up, immediately concerned. The soldiers thanked her once more and excused themselves. Margot looked at Elias desperately. She was finding it difficult to breathe.

"I do hope there is nothing wrong, Corporal Vogel?"

"Are you questioning an S.S officer?" Nardo said officiously. Elias fell silent, but fear blanketed his face. "Do not fret, my dancing friend," Nardo said, "I am simply a very big fan and would like to speak to the young lady alone." Smiling graciously, he ushered a flustered Elias out of the door.

Margot took the opportunity to glance worriedly at herself in the mirror, and then at the suitcase of letters near the door. "Are you *sure* that we have never met?" Corporal Vogel asked for a second time, his back to her. The long leather of his black coat creaked in the now quiet dressing room.

"Oui, quite sure," she said, firmly. Her fear was turning to anger. He turned back to her and smiled, taking off his hat. "Do you wish to see my papers?" she asked him, moving toward the top drawer of the dresser.

"No, no! I'm quite sure they are excellent. You reminded me of a girl I once saw in a church."

"Church?How fascinating... It couldn't be me, though." Standing, she allowed her hair to conceal half her face. "I never go to church. I'm a good girl, and God is in my heart." His eagle eyes assessed her, taking in every iota of her body and visage. She pulled her robe together.

"I am sorry if I stare, it's just you are so beautiful... but no church?"

She shook her head, glaring at him.

"Well then, you won't be doing anything tomorrow on Christmas Eve?" He smiled, his eyes exhibiting no emotion.

"Pardonez-moi?" *Did he truly not know her?*

"You remember how we used to celebrate Christmas, non? With Jesus being a Jew, it created... problems. So, now we simply celebrate in other ways. Christmas Eve is now the night that Odin brings good little boys and girls toys. Have you been a good little girl, I wonder?" He flashed another shark-toothed smile. "But I digress, Fräulein. I would like very much to take you out to dinner tomorrow night. Many people still celebrate the holiday even with a swastika on top of their Christmas tree. How traditions change, huh?"

She crossed her arms and lifted the cigarette holder to her dry mouth, remembering her own Jewish traditions that she shared when she was a little girl at home with her family, back when her name had been Ariella. There was never Christmas, then. Her eyes glazed over as smoke travelled in two twin vapours from her nostrils. She nodded sentimentally.

"So, whether it is a star or a swastika on top of the tree," continued Vogel, "as long as I am with you, you will make my Christmas a very happy one. So, what do you say?"

She really had no choice. Anxiety danced along her spine, cruel and relenting. If he knew, the bastard had control of her, and she could see with his greedy eyes that he wanted more than just her friendship. That young soldier who had let her live had disappeared in the horrors of war. He had probably died a slow death. One saw the cruelty every day, the murder and torture of innocent people – just because of the beds they were born in. He was carved in granite now, all the softness chipped away by bullets. *How many had he killed?* she wondered.

Margot sighed and prepared to do some of her best acting; she was quite sure her life depended on it. She smiled broadly, embraced him, and kissed him twice; once on either side of his face. "I'd love to," she lied.

"From the moment I saw you, I *knew*..." He raised a shrewd brow. Up close he stunk of cigars and whiskey.

"Ah, you charmer – can't you leave a girl be for a moment?" She lowered her lashes flirtatiously. "If you don't mind, I have to get changed for the party."

"I shall see you later, then." He took Margot's hand, kissed it, and then left, shutting the door behind him. She hurried to it, turned the lock and immediately burst into tears. Afraid that someone would hear her crying, she turned on the radio. *'My Funny Valentine'* was playing. The faces of her father, her mother, her siblings and her grandfather appeared to her... She fell to the floor weeping, holding her stomach, her heart pounding against the cold stone. Her sinuses closed and she gasped for air. She clambered to her feet and turned out the lights. Outside, the wind picked up, howling against the building. She walked up to the large art deco window. It was snowing outside, the flurries thick and white in the dark, louring sky. Her tears took her make-up with them in rivers of black down her porcelain face; she tried desperately to wipe them away, but some tears stained.

She was almost certain Nardo knew who she was. He would use this knowledge to his full advantage until he grew tired of her, if that were the case. He had once had the opportunity to kill her and had, for some reason, not been able to do so. So, she owed him something. She lit another cigarette and started smoking, long deep drags. She grabbed her grandpapa's pen. Nardo's would be a quick death, she decided. She could offer him nothing more. She pushed in the retractable pen slowly, and let go. 'Pop!'

Christmas Eve

Margot waited for him at the bottom of the stairs to her apartment building, wearing one of her most stunning tailored suits – black pin-stripe with a large collar and a white mink fur stole she had been given by an admirer. Corporal Nardo Vogel was late, and in her paranoid mind, she wondered if this was all just a twisted game he was playing with her. Perhaps tonight he would take her to one of the concentration camps – an early Christmas present. Yet, there was something in his eyes when he looked at her. Love? Or a strange facsimile of love? *Could a Nazi really love?*

Her neighbours walked past, pulling her out of her reverie

"Merci," she smiled. "You, too! Do you have a cigarette?"

"Oui," the male neighbour replied. He lit her cigarette and she looked up to see Nardo walk through the door to her building. Her hand moved to her grandpapa's pen in her breast pocket. The couple left, and they were alone.

"Fräulein Margot Lagière, you look more stunning than ever," Nardo said. Margot turned her head, acting coy. He came to a halt just in front of her. He was wearing his highly decorated Nazi uniform and a long fur coat. He took his hat off and ran his hand through his cropped blond hair. "Are you ready?"

"Oui," she answered. He held his arm out for her, elbow bent. She forced herself to link arms with him as they left her building and entered the cold night. He had a car pulled up outside, which pleased her, because the winter air hit her like a slap in the face, tightening her pores. Snow fell softly and, despite the curfew and the controversy surrounding Christmas in France, there were a lot of fairy lights in the windows, alongside the flashing swastika lights that sparkled hesitantly around the black street. It was difficult to believe this nightmare was a reality.

"I have booked us a table at a restaurant," he smiled, lighting a cigar, when they were both sat in the backseat of the vehicle. "Are you hungry?"

"Oui," she smiled back. *No*, she thought — *I want to vomit*. She turned her head to the window and looked at the Christmas lights and the falling snow. "Beautiful night," she commented nonchalantly. When she looked back at him, she did a double take because he was, yet again, ogling her. "I wish you would stop staring at me, Corporal Nardo."

"Call me Nardo, Fraulein. And please forgive me."

She rolled her eyes. The sound of the windscreen wipers swishing away the snow would be soothing in other circumstances. The Strasbourg

Christmas market was in full swing... it looked beautiful, and the choir singing outside the cathedral, though muted through the car windows, sounded glorious. Margot could almost smell the chestnuts roasting.

"I've heard that the Réveillon dinner can continue for up to six hours, is this true?" he asked.

"Oui, when I was a little girl my mother would..."

"Would what?" he asked

"Oh! uh, it doesn't matter," she sighed and forced herself to turn to him. "What do German families do at Christmas?"

"Uh, uh, uh, you're trying to project the question back onto me. Please, tell me what was Christmas like for you as a little girl?"

She made a stone of her heart and held her head up high – there would be no repeat performance of last night. Tracing her fingertip lazily through the window's condensation, she recalled Madam Phi-Phi's memories and stories of Christmas as a French girl. "Very quaint," she replied. "We would all decorate the tree and eat together. My mother had many children as you probably know." He indicated that he did with a nod. "And we would all eat and feel fat, then put our shoes in front of the fireplace for our presents from Pére Noel." She shrugged, *nothing more to hear.*

"What did you used to eat?"

"You sound like an interrogator," she whispered with nervous laughter.

"I am, so you had better do a good job!" he yelled, causing her to jump and widen her eyes with terror. "I'm just teasing you." His hard shell cracked and he smiled sincerely, but for a moment he had looked monstrous. She forced a smile. "I hope I didn't startle you," he commented. "Please continue."

"Je ne sais quoi, we would...." She folded her arms and sighed heavily. "We would eat salmon and foie gras, with goose or turkey stuffed with chestnuts. Satisfied?" He nodded slowly. "Of course, that was before the war. . ."

He started clapping, which made her jolt again, and then laugh at her own embarrassment. He continued to clap slowly. Again, her hand went to the pen in her breast pocket.

"That doesn't look like snow," she stated, looking outside.

"Oh, that!" he muttered with annoyance. "That is the burning of the Jews."

"The w-what?" she stuttered. Coils of white ash blew in the wind. She shuddered.

"Orders from the top, I'm afraid. Try not to look if it unsettles you, it is not nice."

She turned away, trying to control her breathing. She felt sick and light-headed. She wanted to ask more, but didn't. Knew she should ask more, but couldn't.

"Ah! Look - we are at the restaurant," he declared, delighted. With a broad smile he took her hand and helped her across the back seat. She looked out through the window and up at the ashes swirling amongst the snow flurries.

"Do you have an umbrella?"

"Of course," he responded, and took one out from the car, beside her. He pushed the umbrella up and then dusted ashes off his coat as if they were a few inconvenient flakes of dandruff. She stepped out and clung to his side. He laughed mercilessly. "Sensitive little thing," he remarked, pulling her close.

The restaurant was rustic, with a huge fire and pretty candles dotted around the tables. The tables and chairs were of thick, well- made wood, and the cutlery and crockery were spotless. It was run by a French family, and though her accent was near perfect, Margot tried not to speak much around them. They sat through three courses of rich, gourmet food, with him studying her the entire time. Salmon, Foie Gras, Caviar, all served beautifully. Of course, Ariella had only heard of these foods, but now, Margot had to love them. She did as best she could, considering the types of food and their richness. After each course she would excuse herself, go to the bathroom and vomit. At the start of the fourth course, guests joined the table – mostly Germans in uniform, but there was also a girl with dark hair, a fair complexion and wearing a beautiful, black sequinned gown. Margot approached the table, her make-up disguising her nausea. She sat in the only free seat, opposite the brunette. Nardo introduced everyone. They all spoke their greetings in French and then promptly returned to their German. Margot sat smoking a cigarette and politely smiling. They could be plotting her death and she wouldn't know it. The brunette suddenly craned her neck towards Margot. "Do you have a cigarette by any chance? You *are* French? Nardo said you were."

"Oui, and Oui. When was Nardo discussing me?" Margot asked, handing the girl a cigarette. The girl took it and lit it from one of the many white candles dotted around the restaurant.

"He *never* stops talking about you. He has taken us to see you dance *so* many times! It's so nice to see him in love... My name is Bettie by the way, and I'm French too, just so you don't feel alone." Bettie smiled; she was very attractive – *no doubt one of the Germans' whores*. The smoke made the entire restaurant seem dream-like. As Margot drank, her eyes become heavy and her nerves dissipated. The Christmas lights in the restaurant were bright white and flickered on and off through the foggy haze. She learnt that Bettie was dating one of the SS soldiers. *Traitorous slut*, she thought, nodding and smiling. "I know a lot of people would say that dating a German soldier was nothing to be proud of," Bettie admitted under her breath. "Of course, they wouldn't say it to my face."

"Only for fear of being shot," Margot mocked, forgetting herself. Bettie's eyes widened with hurt and surprise. Margot made herself laugh, loud and brashly. "I'm just fucking with you," she joked, placing a warm hand on Bettie's shoulder. Bettie smiled unsurely before giggling lightly. She had caught the look that Margot had given her—a judgemental one. Trying to change the subject, Margot asked if she was dating Tom. Bettie took a sip of her wine and groaned.

"He is trying to woo me," Bettie whispered, her face full of disdain. *Tom must be the SS soldier she is dating.* "Sometimes a woman does things that she is not proud of. That she wouldn't normally." And with those words Margot knew what Bette was trying to convey.. She didn't want to be dating Tom, but for whatever reason she was, perhaps under duress, like in her own situation.

Margot risked looking over at Tom, and saw that her glance had been met with a flirtatious smile. She didn't smile back, merely turned her head back to face Bettie. "Our choices are always harder and that is why we must stick together. If I offended you tonight, then please accept my apologies." Bette giggled gently.

"It takes more than that to offend me! The burning of the Jews offends me — I find it repulsive," Bette stated, twisting her cigarette out angrily.

"What is this? What are you talking about?" Nardo interrupted. Tom told him in German. Nardo laughed. "Let us not talk about such ugly things on Christmas Eve. I want my beautiful Margot to enjoy Christmas, just as she did as a young girl." He then spoke to the band in German and the music started playing a Christmas hymn. Most of the people in the tavern joined in. People clapped. The mood in the inn was happy. Next, the band played the English version of 'Silent Night.' Everyone started to sing along together. "Silent night, holy night, all is calm, all is bright..." Margot mouthed the words, glancing at the red, drunk faces around her. She had never craved her family more.

Later that night, when most were drunk and passed out, Nardo approached Margot and whispered into her ear, "Merry Christmas." She looked at the clock and saw it was gone midnight. "I think it is time I took you home," he said.

Margot smiled at Bettie, who had Tom's head resting on her shoulder. She nudged him awake, saying, "They're going."

"It was so lovely to meet you both,' said Margot. 'Joyeux Noel!"

"I am going to walk Margot home. I shall see you tomorrow, Tom," Nardo said in a gentle voice.

"Nice to meet you, merry Christmas!" Tom stood up, causing Bettie to moan in annoyance. He took Margot's hand and lowered his voice to a deep, gravelly tone.

"Fräulein Margot Lagière, it has been an honour to meet you this evening. I hope that your feelings for Corporal Nardo run as deep as his for you."

"Merci," Margot managed, with a forced smile.

They left the tavern and walked past the pretty little houses decorated with lights and candles. A thin layer of snow had sugar coated the entire town, making it look like something out of a storybook... one in which an entire race of people had been edited out. Margot shivered. She felt so alone.

They reached her apartment block and Nardo walked her inside. He held onto her hand and placed little kisses on her neck while humming 'Silent Night' in his off-tune, German accent.

Margot tried to break away, but he pulled her closer again; both his hands moving along her shoulders and up her neck.

"Enough! Please Nardo, I'm tired." She tried to pull away but he gripped her wrist hard, and pulled her back against his body.

"I know who you are," he whispered in a sing-song voice.

She glared up at him. "You're hurting me!"

"Ariella..." he whispered. Shock registered in her haunted eyes, which stared up at him. She felt the air knocked out of her. "Ariella..." he repeated, smiling. He forced his mouth onto hers, his mouth sucking her lips – it couldn't be called a kiss. It *could* be called revolting.

She squirmed and pulled her face away from his sucking kisses. He seized her head firmly, gazing coolly into her eyes. "Oh, my pretty Fräulein, don't be angry with me. How could I ever forget you; the prettiest Jew I never shot." He grinned at her, his lips stretching over his strong teeth. "But no matter. We German soldiers, we have ways of heating up the little Jewish girls...no?"

Her blue eyes glowered up at him. *Monster*, she thought. He'd played her like a fool all night.

Making her wonder and question his trustworthiness. Monster, monster, monster.... the word sang in her head, like a siren's song.

"Oh, come now, Ariella," he whispered. "I only make these little jokes to see you smile. But you don't smile. It breaks my heart."

Ariella doubted he had a heart. She needed to buy herself time. "We will have to go to your apartment," she blurted, desperately. "There are no men allowed upstairs after six."

He glanced up at the building and, then slowly nodded. "If those are the rules..." He grasped her wrist and dragged her back towards his car. "We must abide by them." The snow swirled and chilled her skin, and the wind tossed her hair back from her face. As the car drove to his place, silence fell over the small town.

Ariella stood in his apartment, her back to the front door as he locked it. The place was neat, sparsely decorated and very minimal. A clay bust of Hitler sat atop the mantelpiece, scowling intolerantly over proceedings. "Seems like I have quite the Christmas present, hmm, Ariella?" He spoke more to himself than her. She despised the way he said her name, like a pet's.

Nardo smiled and sat on his bed, taking his jacket off and folding it neatly. "Take off your clothes," he said gently, unbuttoning his shirt. She stood by the door, forcing herself to breathe calmly. "I know about your queer friends,' he said. "The dancers. I know about the letters too. I searched your room *personally* when you were performing. It's okay, you can relax. No-one knows except me." He took off his cufflinks and tossed them onto a dressing table. "What do I care if you give a few of your people hope? We will still..." he searched for the word. "...exterminate them."

Fiery tears burned, turning her eyes glassy. How could this be the same man who let her live only four years earlier?

"I'm joking," he whispered, laughing. "So sensitive! Don't you know I love you, Fräulein? I will keep your secrets if you are a good girl..." He rubbed his crotch and the fabric stretched as he hardened. Then he clapped his hands together abruptly. "TAKE OFF YOUR CLOTHES!" he demanded.

"Why don't you take them off for me?" she suggested, pushing her hair away from her face. She raised an eye-brow seductively, and Nardo was upon her in seconds. He grabbed her by her suit jacket and started to unbutton it. She closed her eyes. It would be rape. Of course it would be rape. He kissed her dancer's neck, pulling her jacket over her shoulders and exposing her black lace bra. He cupped her breasts, gazing at them hungrily. She gritted her teeth as her jacket fell to the floor. He placed both arms above her, so that she was trapped between his shoulders. His muscular arms leading down to a mass of dark underarm hair and his pale chest.

"Get on your knees, Ariella," he whispered. "Now it is time to be a good girl."

Breathing shakily through her nose, she lowered herself down to her knees, her nose mere inches from his bulging crotch. Her jacket lay sprawled around her feet. She noticed something glistening inside the silky fabric of the inside pocket – her grandfather's pen! With one hand she ran a hand up the inside of his thigh, eliciting a low, animalistic moan from him, and with the other she quickly reached out and snatched the pen.

"Take it out and put it in your mouth," he urged.

She smiled, remembering one of her grandfather's favourite sayings: *The pen is mightier than the sword.* It was time to test this theory out. She thumbed off the lid – a small sound, like a blade 'snick' bouncing free of a flick knife – and rammed her grandfather's pen into Nardo's groin, just where genitals met thigh. She yanked it out – with a spurt of blood – and jammed it back in again. Nardo screamed in agony and shock. He backed away from her, clutching himself, his eyes screwed up. Ariella kicked her shoes off, grabbed one of her heels and jumped on his back. They stumbled forward, like some hulking beast, and all the hatred and rage that had been bubbling inside Ariella was finally released. She hit him repeatedly over the head with her high heel, breaking his nose (which exploded with blood) and cracking one of his cheek bones.

He roared in pain and determination, then bent and reached, and grabbed her by her neck and hair; forcing her over his head and onto the bed with a bounce. She dropped the heel. Through his uninjured eye, he saw her crawling towards it, and quickly struck her across the face; her bottom lip split, sending spittle and blood over his expertly-made bed. He reached down to pull the pen out of his groin and as he worked it free, she shot her right foot forward and kicked him straight in the balls. As he recoiled the pen came free and blood cascaded out, running down his leg, soaking his trousers. He bent over, screaming, the cords of his neck sticking out like thick cables.

She looked around with frantic eyes and saw the Hitler bust. She picked it up (it was unbelievably heavy) and with all her might and all her fury, she smashed it down on the back of his head. He fell to his knees, head and shoulders coated in exploded clay dust. She still held the marble base of the bust – it was the heaviest part. She raised it up and ploughed it into his face, making his bulging nose jerk harshly to the left. Blood and snot exploded across his messed up face. He fell backwards with a thud onto the floorboards of his apartment.

Ariella sat on the bed, panting heavily. She touched her swollen lip with tentative fingers and looked down at the unconscious man. "I bet you've always wanted your Fuhrer to give you head," she snarled. Then she laughed hysterically, her head snapped back and her mouth throbbing, but soon the laughter turned to shuddering, hopeless crying for her family, for her people, for the fucked- up world. She fell asleep, her sinuses closed and her eyes throbbing. And then... a cool silence.

When Nardo came around, he found he could only breathe through his mouth, and only see out of one eye. His entire head throbbed repetitively, giving him waves of vertigo. Moaning, he tried to move, but found he was tied to one of his dining chairs. He regarded Ariella with disdainful admiration. She was sat in front of him, her legs crossed, with one of her bloody high heels going up and down with impatience. She had put her suit jacket had re-done her make-up. He'd been out for a good few hours.

"Nar-do!" she uttered gently in a sing- song voice.

His mouth hung open; drool dripping down his chin and onto his chest. He tried to speak but all that came out was a long series of deep moans. "I already know what you're attempting to say," said Ariella. She imitated his German accent and low male voice: "But I let you live, Fräulein! I am a nice guy really!" She sneered at him. "Was what you did the right thing to do? Of course!" She laughed gently, then stopped abruptly. "But hadn't you just taken part in murdering my entire family?"

He shook his head resolutely.

"No?" She paused for thought, then shrugged... "All the same, Corporal Nardo – you are complicit. And the way you have blackmailed me tonight? Was that a nice thing to do?"

He shook his head, then vomited down his chin.

"No! It was not nice! Hiding behind your disgusting jokes as if it wasn't blackmail. We both know where the power lies." She held her grandfather's pen in her hand. Pushing the mechanism down over and over. "Anyway, I digress. When you spared my life, you did what any human being should have done. You should not be rewarded for it. You do not win a medal for it. You have murdered hundreds of people. You are a worthless piece of Nazi shit."

She stood up and went to the kitchen, grabbing two bottles of whiskey. She unscrewed the lid of the first and poured it over Corporal Nardo's squirming head. "You'll be just an idiotic soldier who fell asleep smoking." Ariella lit a cigarette. She poured the second whiskey bottle in a trail around the chair, as she performed a short segment from her dance as The Sugar Plum Fairy. She stopped her pirouette and leaned over. "I owe you only *this* much,' she whispered in his ear. "Frohe Weihnachten und einen guten Rutsch." Then she jammed her grandfather's pen into his throat and watched the dark, hot blood pump out. He gasped and gurgled, phlegm and blood dangling from his bottom lip, and bucked around wildly. As the blood left him, so did his strength. His head slumped first, and then his shoulders. She undid his hands which were tied behind his back. The fire would destroy all signs of the violence.

Ariella walked slowly to the doorway, unlocked it and pulled it open. She took one last drag of the cigarette, breathing it out through her nostrils, her chin tilted, and then she flicked the butt towards Nardo's body. It spun through the air, in circles of smoke, before it hit the alcohol and exploded into flames. Ariella quickly walked out of the apartment block and through the deserted streets. She hummed 'Silent Night' all the way.

On Christmas Day, hundreds of Jews heard about their loved ones who had been captured. Louis had posted the letters the night before from

Ariella's suitcase – and that was the best gift she could have given.

The End

Kevin J. Kennedy Presents

Something in the Stocking
By
P. Mattern

There was no better thrill than a thrill kill, he was sure of it.

It was better than sex, better than chocolate cake on his birthday, better than puffing on a cigar soaked in cognac.

She had been taking a shortcut through the park just after the shops, open late for the holiday season, had finally closed. Her arms were full of packages as she walked across the street, and a light snow had begun to fall. He pulled over into a vacant parking space, watching her hesitate and then elect to head through the park. He'd figured she must be making her way to the Coventry Arms apartments.

He'd given her a head start before he put the car in park and got out, looking around. Above his head twinkling multi colored holiday lights swung gently back and forth in the wind, and he pulled up his collar, partly to obscure his face.

The rush of adrenalin that flowed through him was energizing, and so he took off.

At first, he thought she'd somehow veered off in another direction, but, rounding a corner of the well-lit pathway through the deserted part, his heart quickened as he caught sight of her: red hat with one of those ridiculously oversized pom poms on top, a dark coat, and a matching scarf that furled out behind her whenever the breeze picked up.

There was enough snow on the ground that he was making footprints, and he frowned, then decided that he could grab a tree branch and obliterate his tracks on the way back to the car if the snow didn't fall fast enough to cover them first.

He had always been a careful killer.

He quickened his pace, light on his feet so as not to make any discernible sound as he closed the distance between them. When they were about halfway through to the other side of the park and he was within three feet he noticed a detail that had escaped him... she was wearing ear buds.

Perfect.

He grabbed her hair and jerked her head back, his knife going to her throat. The packages she was carrying scattered and bounced, sliding across the path as her hands instinctively flew up to her throat.

"Not a word," he cautioned her, hissing close to her ear, "Not a word!"

He glanced around again to make sure he was safe and dragged her off the path and into the thick, tangled growth at the base of the trees. He was huffing with the effort of containing her as she struggled to be released from his grasp, and as soon as he had an opportunity to kick her legs out from under her and throw her down he did, hitting her in the head a few times with a billy-club he'd picked up at the community swap meet in order to slow her down. She groaned, her head lolling to one side, as he sat on her chest. She was a pretty girl, nice white teeth, decent tits, but none of that figured into his plans for her.

He was sitting there dreamily gazing at her face, watching a bluish gray lump rise on one side of her forehead when he clasped his broad hands around her throat. He had had a steady, decently paying job for the last nine years. He didn't mind being a blue-collar worker. He had worked with his hands his entire life, and they were strong.

Some instinct prompted the young woman out of her fugue, and again her hands went up to her throat. She scratched at his gloves with her long manicured nails, breaking two of them in her efforts to lessen the pressure, but it was to no avail.

He was in the driver's seat now, watching her eyes. In them he saw fear, panic and incredulity that this should be happening to her. It became his fevered mission to convince her that what was happening was indeed real, so he increased the pressure, holding back just a little. He didn't want to lose her.

Not yet, anyway.

Just when he noticed the whites of her eyes flipping up, he stopped.

She began sputtering and coughing in an attempt to get her breath back. She turned her head to the side and something that was the color of a partially digested latte spurted out. Her chest heaved hard against his undercarriage, and he had the thought that somewhere underneath her coat her heart was beating like a frantic, trapped bird.

He lost track of time as he watched her. She tried to speak and made a coarse squawking sound.

"Don't try to speak," he told her gently. There was nothing in her eyes but fear now. She was perhaps getting ready to bargain with him for her life. He had heard it all before, in the early days.

"Take my purse! Take everything! I won't tell anybody!"

Those pleas had always fallen on deaf ears, because he knew they were lying. She was lying in the same way humans always lied and tried to bargain at the eleventh hour before their deaths in a last ditch attempt to preserve the same miserable lives they always complained about.

Her eyes were filling with tears, and he thought she might be about to tell him she had a child at home, or maybe children. She was thinking what a shit Christmas they were going to have if he killed her.

Well, he didn't want to hear it, and so he tightened his grip around her throat once more.

He brought her back one more time before he finally squeezed her neck so intensely it made a noise. The resistance of her flesh against his hands and the feeling as he overcame that resistance, was nothing short of orgasmic.

But he had promises to keep. He had run out of time to play with his prey. Emma would be wondering about the groceries she'd sent him out to fetch.

He stood with difficulty, one of his legs having fallen asleep. He stood over her, then thought for a moment before he dragged her motionless body further into the woods to a specific spot. The snow picked up, and he thought it might take them awhile to find her.

He had grabbed a large branch to use as a broom to wipe away his tracks but ended up tossing it. The snow had already obliterated any evidence that he, or even his victim, had ever come through the park.

All good then. At the last minute he reached down and grabbed a keychain that had fallen out of her coat pocket. He always took a souvenir.

It was a four leaf clover, green and bejewelled around the edges, with "LUCKY" written across the center.

"There's a blank spot on the tree near the bottom, and another one top left!" Emma said, holding her eyeglasses in her hand as she leaned forward squinting "Can you add another string of lights, Reece?"

"Sure thing," he said agreeably, but he was, in fact, bored out of his skull. His only hobby, following himself on media, hadn't delivered any thrills lately, especially since they hadn't yet discovered the body of his latest victim.

The fact that they'd had record snowfall, the most in 50 years hadn't helped the dull- witted detectives in our town close the missing person's case of one Melanie Janzen, mother of three, whose fiancé was currently mentioned as 'a person of interest'.

Police suspected 'foul play'. Every time he heard that phrase it conjured up images of chickens running around a barnyard cackling in some sort of chicken tag game.

"Wait Em... maybe I can just move some over. I'll try that and you can tell me if we still have bare spots!" he reassured his wife of nearly 20 years.

They had never had children, so they babied each other, making a big deal out of birthdays and holidays, especially Christmas. Emma was an excellent cook, and devoted at least two days each season making a dozen different cookies and tarts. She gifted some to the neighbors.

They also spent a lot of money on presents for each other, buying things they would never think of purchasing for themselves. Christmas, after all, came just once a year. She bought him imported cigars and he bought her high-end fragrances. They always filled a stocking for each other and participated in the Choral Christmastide Walkabout sponsored by their church.

Emma knew how to do up the holidays right. Her mini mince pies were his favorite.

After dinner they watched television with a fire crackling merrily in the fireplace. He wondered what the 'task force' assigned to what they were now calling the Denney Park Murders was doing now. Probably sitting with their thumbs up their asses, spinning around, which was what they'd been doing for the past three years. Thirteen women initially thought kidnapped or missing, twelve of them found in remote areas of the huge preserve known locally as Denney Park.

He knew that they would have a 'War Room' in the basement of the local police station just to make update announcements and compare notes and theories. The task force had been careful not to reveal too many details concerning the murders, or even admit to assuming they were all the work of one man.

But they knew, he was sure of it.

He had a large wall map of Denney Park in the old coal storage room in the back part of his basement, and he imagined that the police had one also with pins with little labels on them indicating where each of the bodies had been found. He had started killing during the Christmas season, his first victim was a nun he happened upon as he was hunting skeet. He'd found her in the most Northern area of the park. From there on a pattern emerged- a literal pattern of where the body of every victim showed up that formed an image, just like in the connect the dots books he'd loved when he was a child.

He kept waiting for the cops to catch on to the image created by where the bodies had been left. If they ever found the latest victim's body, they'd be idiots not to notice that the pattern they created formed the most iconic symbols of the Yuletide season - a Christmas tree. A stylized but recognizable one with a pointed top and three tiers of branches, the shortest at the top and longest at the bottom.

The next day was a slow one. Many of the precinct employees were off on holiday leave. He was wringing out his mop in the huge industrial bucket when he felt a tap on his shoulder. It made him jump, he hadn't heard anyone coming up the hallway because of the piped-in Christmas music they always played over the intercom on the lower floors.

"Didn't mean to startle you, Reece," the friendly, gap-toothed cop (MacKay was his name, Reece remembered) said, smiling when he looked up. "Just wanted to say Merry Christmas!"

The cop was holding out what was obviously a small box of chocolates with a red ribbon tied around it.

Cheapskate.

"Thank you," Reece said, amazed how sincere his voice sounded.

They chatted a bit more. Mostly about the wretched weather, and how the grocery stores were gouging customers for everything that was an essential ingredient for homemade holiday goodies. Sugar alone was up thirty cents a bag. It was outrageous.

It wasn't a surprise that the cop was chatting along just to kill time, even though he was on the clock. In Reece's opinion, all cops were lazy, doughnut- munching buggers, not particularly interested in solving crimes as long as the crime didn't involve the death of a cop.

Eventually, he found the perfect spot in the conversation to lead it to the rash of murders.

"So are there any new leads in the Denny Park murders?" he asked, "Anyone come forward recently with information? Any eye witnesses? Any new leads for the detectives to follow up on?"

MacKay lifted his cap and scratched his head before replacing it. Reece almost snorted. He felt a small swell of pride in realizing he'd created a 'head scratcher' of a crime for the local cops to puzzle over.

"We figured out it must be a local, a lazy fucker who enjoys hunting on home turf," he answered. "Definitely male because of the force required to choke another person. Strong hands, probably has a blue-collar job that requires working with them. Thinks he's smart. But he made a mistake with this last one..."

Reece's heartbeat was suddenly pounding in his ears.

"That so?" he said, trying to keep his voice casual.

"Yeah," the cop grinned again," left a footprint in the mud under the tree where he dragged the body. Size 9. Might be heavyset as well. I guess he thought since it was snowy he didn't need to worry about it, but the wind must have changed direction because it was protected by the lower branches of the pine."

When Reece didn't answer, the cop sighed and slipped the jacket he had slung over his shoulder back on.

"Merry Christmas, then," he told Reece, clapping him on the side of his arm, "in case I don't see you before."

Emma usually took a nap in the late afternoon and was still lying down when Reece arrived home. He carefully removed his work boots, setting them under the coat pegs in the short foyer and climbed the stairs quietly in his sock feet so as not to awaken his wife.

Emma had been less talkative than usual lately. He figured she was preoccupied with the home invasions the neighborhood had experienced that holiday. They had started just before Thanksgiving that year.

For an early Christmas gift, he'd bought her a handgun that he'd gotten off one of the officers who was short for cash because he was going through a divorce. It didn't have to be legal because he'd only gotten it for home defense. It was a .38 special revolver. It was small enough so that Emma could handle it, but powerful enough to stop someone.

She'd seemed to calm down after he took her to a range to get used to it, but that hadn't lasted long. Lately, she seemed strangely on edge again.

The bedroom door squeaked a little as he pushed it open but Emma was gently snoring and didn't stir. He slid the closet door open, bent down and retrieved what he'd been looking for.

They were what he called his 'Sunday boots'. Good leather. Emma had managed to catch them on sale the previous Christmas for his Christmas present.

Now they would have to go in the Goodwill drop box. Or maybe he should burn them hadn't quite decided. He had mixed emotions. On one hand he resented the loss of a perfectly handsome pair of boots. On the other hand, he was appreciative of the heads up MacKay had provided.

That could have turned out badly.

In the end, he went into work a half hour early to throw them down the chute into the basement incinerator. It was an older building so it still had one.

It seemed like a fitting thing to do.

The same evening after a pot roast dinner that he shared with his wife, he retired down into the basement to 'putter', as Emma called it. He had a work bench and tools down there and several ongoing repair projects. He had always been a tinkerer, and he enjoyed repairing old lamps, replacing the legs of an old stool or even the occasional antique piggy bank, the metal kind that moved when a coin was inserted.

This evening was the night he reserved to immerse himself in his favorite hobby, and the padlocked door in the rear of the basement that had been the coal cellar was his 'memory room'.

He strode past the long workbenches with fluorescent lights hanging over them and straight back to his lair. A quick turn of the key in the heavy padlock, a flick of the light switch and he was in.

He didn't have many pictures of them, although if he heard on the news that one had been found he usually rushed off to buy the papers that were carrying the story. There were three large bulletin boards that he had posted the articles on with push pins.

The ones on either side were past kills, and he didn't find them interesting anymore. But the bulletin board in the center was his latest, and it showcased all of the Denney Park victims.

He sighed as he surveyed them with hungry eyes. Looking at their faces brought back all the glorious sensations, and if he focused on any of them individually and closed his eyes, he was right back there again with them, re-experiencing all the smells, sounds, colors and textures of the last moments of their lives. That he had shared their last moments made him more of an intimate than any lover they had ever had. The moment of death was an unsurpassed intimacy, and he alone had shared it.

He was the last man they had ever seen before they died.

It was a privilege and a curse, he decided, as he rummaged with thick fingers through the rectangular plastic container roughly the size of a shoe box. It was his treasure box, much like the one he had had as a kid growing up. Back then, his had contained a robin's egg, several old keys, a small collection of comic books, baseball trading cards and a page out of one of his best buddy's Playboys with a picture of a nude Playmate of the Month.

One by one he took out his trophies. There were key chains and sunglasses, a thong and a pair of panties... He'd never touched them down there, but sometimes he just had to peek.

He fondled a silver cigarette lighter personalized with the letter "L", remembering the platinum blonde he'd followed into the woods.

His oldest victim had been a middle- aged birdwatcher, and he had taken her binoculars as a trophy. He didn't usually take anything that bulky, but they were an expensive brand, and he found that he couldn't just leave them there.

Beyond that, there were hair clips, one a rhinestone butterfly that had belonged to a redhead with really long legs, lipsticks and a couple of handkerchiefs.

He lost time as he reminisced, realizing once more what a sacred mission had been set before him. He decided then and there he would look for an opportunity to add one more victim to his 'Christmas tree' murder pattern.

It would take him further off the trail than he had ever been, but worth the extra effort because It would be the star at the top of the tree.

He heard Emma calling out for him and, hastily returning his trophies to their container, left his private cathedral... Christmas Eve dinner was done and put away. As usual, Emma had outdone herself. The Cornish hens were succulent and roasted to a turn. The asparagus was tender and lemony, the mashed potatoes were buttery and delicious, and he had stuffed himself with her homemade yeast rolls. It was perfect.

Emma hadn't had too much to say, but she'd told him that her doctor had discussed hormone replacement therapy for her occasional 'blues'.

Well, he thought, that's women for you. No accounting for moods, but he was confident she would brighten up when she opened her presents. After an internal debate, he had decided to get her the $350 Coach bag she'd been wanting.

They settled down in front of the fireplace after he'd gotten the fire going, and as she set down a silver-plated tray with Christmas sprinkle cookies and tea on it, she sat down at the opposite end of the couch.

"Stockings first?" he suggested.

"Stockings first," she agreed. Was it his imagination or did she seem to be shaking slightly?

She handed his to him. It was the bigger one, and she had embroidered his name along the length of it.

The first thing he noticed was how heavy it was. And it was filled nearly to the brim with wrapped packages.

"You go first then, Reece," she said.

Reece chuckled and pulled out the package at the top. It was a small square box, wrapped in gold foil and tied with a red ribbon. Slowly, he tore the paper away, carefully placing the velvet ribbon on the arm of the couch.

Before he lifted the lid, he shook it, just to heighten the drama of opening his first present.

"Hmmmmm... cuff links?" he guessed, winking at her.

She didn't answer, she just smiled enigmatically, though her smile seemed strained.

He took the lid off the box and stared. It was a keychain... an enamelled four-leaf clover with rhinestones.

Wordlessly, he ripped through the next few carefully-wrapped packages. There were the sunglasses, and a tube of lipstick labelled "Pink Orchid', and a butterfly- shaped hair ornament. His fingers scrabbled downward of their own volition, and at the bottom of the stocking they encountered an awkwardly-wrapped package that felt like something metallic and weighty.

The bird-watching binoculars... he was sure of it.

Anger exploded from somewhere inside of him, and a red miasma descended over his eyes. Obviously, Emma had been snooping. She had entered his sacred temple to his life's work, corrupted everything he had achieved, ruined the sanctity of his refuge from the world.

Heaving himself up with difficulty, he began emptying the contents of his stocking in the fireplace. He was vaguely aware that he was making awful sounds. The kind animals make when they are mortally wounded.

The kind his victims might have made if he hadn't had his hands clenched so tightly around their tender necks that they were rendered mute witnesses to their own deaths.

When he turned around again, she'd already put the couch between them and was holding the gun he'd gotten her as an early Christmas present out in front of her.

It was aimed directly at him.

"MURDERER!" she shrilled, with the Christmas carol, 'Oh Holy Night', playing in the background, causing the situation to seem even more macabre.

"KILLER!" she choked out. Tears were running down her face, ruining her carefully applied makeup.

"...HOW COULD YOU?"

"Emma!" he said desperately, sweating, "It's not what it looks like. Please can we talk about this? You won't believe the story I have to tell you!"

"Yes, I'm sure!" she spat out, "You've been telling me stories for years, apparently, Reece. I'm not sure I want to hear ANOTHER one!"

Her mind was racing as he stretched out his hands toward her imploringly. For a long moment she stared at them.

They were the same hands that had killed all those women—that decided her.

She knew he would have hated prison. He probably would have died there.

A bullet to his brain was the best present she could give him for Christmas, and so she did.

The End

Kevin J. Kennedy Presents

Black Eye Friday
By
J.C. Michael

Never mind that ridiculous, and largely unwelcome, US import, Black Friday, Black *Eye* Friday is a true British institution. When work finishes on the last Friday before Christmas, it's time to hit the pub, hit the pints, and possibly hit some other inebriated reveller who happens to spill your pint, eye up your girlfriend, or simply look at you in a way you don't appreciate. At least that's the stereotypical view. Sure, there's always plenty of trouble, but there's trouble every Friday, and Saturday, and every other day ending in "y". It's purely a matter of volume – more people out equals more potential for things to get a touch out of hand. Simple maths. Of course, there are other variables to factor in, one of which is that the longer you stay out, the greater the chance some pissed-up wanker will smack you 'round the side of the head for accidentally nudging them while trying to get served at the bar. It's why the four of them had resolved to only grab a quick couple straight after work before heading home.

"Merry fucking Christmas! Here's to another outstanding year of nonsense at Tumman and Turner I.T Solutions." Mike was already slurring slightly, the lunchtime glass of Prosecco in the office helping tip the balance from steady to merry once topped up with the three pints of Fosters—the agreed couple now a hazy memory, and which he'd swiftly poured down his neck since they'd got there half an hour ago.

"TATITS!"

Dave, Mark, and Paul, all jovially shouted the unfortunate acronym of their place of work in such unison you could be forgiven for thinking it had been rehearsed, chinking their own pint glasses against Mike's as they did so. A group of women dressed in a combination of Christmas jumpers and earrings paired with the usual blouses, skirts, and smart trousers of the modern professional woman, looked over with disdain. Their reward was a repeated shout, "TATITS!", Mikes own voice joining that of his friends.

The women looked away, the perceived insult bringing scowls that dissipated into the glasses of gin and cocktails that were soon to their lips. One of them broke ranks and tottered off towards the toilets on heels only an inch or so longer than her skirt. "Receptionist," said Dave. Sexism, alive and well in the twenty-first century, and never more at home than in the pub on Black Eye Friday.

"That or recently divorced," muttered Paul into his pint. His own marital problems never far from the surface.

"Fucking cheer up y' miserable bugger and get that down y'. It's your round next." Mark finished off his own pint, sitting it on the table next to Dave to reinforce his point.

"Thought we were only having a couple?" mentioned Paul, disregarding the fact they were already three in apiece.

"Why? You got somewhere better to be?"

"Yeah, a cold empty house that's nice and quiet without anyone annoying me. Same again?" Paul supped off the dregs of his Stella as Dave and Mike slid their own empty glasses next to Mark's.

"Go on then," said Mike, a broad grin on his face. "That'll do though, fours enough and I'm going to have to bail before we start going round again."

***

Three full pints, sitting on the table. A fourth, slightly less than full due to slight spillage on the perilous journey from the bar, raised in salute. "TATITS!"

The others picked up their glasses, and bumped them together over the centre of the table. "TATITS! Merry Christmas one and all." Each of the men took a drink that half emptied their glasses before raising them once again towards the group of women who had been so easily offended before. Two of the women ignored them, another two shot them daggers, and a fifth, the divorcee/receptionist/possibly both or neither, nudged the guy she'd been chatting to in the ribs and pointed over. Black Eye Friday... this was how trouble started.

"Come on, lads. Let's supp up and away. I can't be arsed getting into any strife tonight and don't fancy a disciplinary meeting on the first day back for bringing the company into disrepute." Paul could always be relied on to see the potential negative in any situation.

Dave smirked, "Becca can haul me into her office for some discipline any time she likes."

Mike sniggered, took a drink, and wiped his mouth with the back of his hand. "You'd be so lucky."

"We can't all be the bosses, pet," said Mark.

"Yeah right." A conversation can quickly turn on its head, particularly on a day like Black Eye Friday. The sniggering was replaced with a sneer and a defensive comment: "Only if by 'pet', you mean the bloke who holds the business together while she swans around coming up with bright ideas the rest of us have to make work."

"She's alright," retorted Paul. "Been good to me this past year with all the shit that's been going on."

"The gentleman doth protest too much," sniggered Dave, a wicked glint of mischief in his eyes. "You'd be more than happy to find her in a pair of Christmas stockings come Christmas morning, Michael."

Mike grinned, the atmosphere amongst the friends flipping once more and the fake sneer packed away, "That I might, but I doubt our lass would be."

***

Fourth drinks down and done, the friends had split. Dave and Mark had headed to another bar saying, "May as well make a night of it now," and Paul and Mike were heading home. They didn't exactly live in the same part of town, but the same side, so the first part of the journey was one they could make together. Paul was in no rush to get home, he had nothing to rush for. Mike, he had other things on his mind.

"Things any better, then?"

Paul was about to try another topic when Mike finally answered with a sigh. "Not really. I mean things are great, usually, well, ok, ish, but when her family's around it's a fucking nightmare."

"Sounds it. You got any coming over for Christmas?"

"Oh yes. As if her brothers weren't bad enough, we've got her fucking mother coming over for a week."

"Fuck me, that's harsh."

"Tell me about it. She'll likely be there when I get home. Think I'll walk the long way."

"Well, any time you want to nip out for a beer give me a shout. I should be able to fit you into my busy schedule."

"Yeah, thanks. You have a good one." They'd reached the point where they would part ways. For Paul, a walk down by the river to the flat he'd had to rent after leaving the family home. For Mike, it was another twenty minutes over the railway bridge and through the estate to the house he shared with the woman he loved, or at least part of him did, but whose family was tearing them apart.

The men parted, and Mike watched as Paul walked along the towpath until out of site. He checked his watch, it was only half-past seven. Taking his phone from his pocket he selected the most recently dialled number. The call was answered on the fourth ring, "Mind if I come 'round?"

**

He should've said it didn't matter, he should've said no, but Becca had convinced him it was ok. She told him her brother knew about them, and would probably be gone by the time he got there anyway. He wasn't. He was sat there in the tastefully decorated living room with a mug of tea and a mince pie. The bedroom door was shut, Becca was in a tracksuit. It wasn't the scene which Mike had hoped to be greeted by as he was ushered in and introduced.

"Becks says you've had an interesting year."

The statement caught him off guard, he'd never considered how much of what he'd told Becca she might have shared with someone else. Had she said much at work? Nobody had said anything but what about the looks he got sometimes? Paul knew some of what'd been going on, it was hard to keep secrets when you shared an office and spent 8 hours a day only 6 feet apart, but he'd trusted Becca and now it turned out she'd said something to her brother. Well, better that than one of his colleagues he supposed.

"She didn't say much. Don't worry." Her brother flashed him a smile as if reading his thoughts and looking to put him at ease. He was handsome and well dressed. Hardly surprising, really, since his sister was stunning—even in her tracksuit and slippers—and was always immaculately turned out when on public display.

"It's fine," said Mark with a smile of his own. "You wouldn't believe the half of it." The booze, barely audible Christmas music, not that godawful yelling but proper, church- type Christmas carol music, and Becca's presence all served to relax him.

"Why don't I get you a whisky and you can tell Pete about it while I get changed."

"Changed?"

"Pete offered to take me out for a meal while you were on your way over. We're booked in at The Grand, so shouldn't get mixed up in any aggravation." The hurt must have shown on Mark's face. "You don't want to be too late back anyway, there's only so much you can blame on Paul and why start the holiday with a row." Not just hurt. Disappointment. "And girls like to spend time with their mothers. I'm sure you'll have enough spare time to call in later in the week." She smiled, clearly pleased to see that his own face had brightened. "There." She'd poured his drink as she spoke, and kissed him lightly on the cheek as she placed it in his hand.

She left the bedroom door at the end of the hall slightly open. Open enough for Mark to be able to glance over as she undressed, and appreciate her figure. He was falling in love with her. Maybe even had already. Her brother, sat as he was beside the Christmas tree, was blissfully unaware of the show his sister was putting on for her guest, her colleague, her lover.

"She doesn't mind, you know."

"Pardon?" said Mark, quickly pulling his thoughts from what he'd been hoping to do when he'd rang and asked if he could drop by.

"Being the other woman. She knows you've got yourself in a bit of a mess."

Mark had taken a liking to Pete, a man he'd only known for ten minutes. He guessed it was probably a genetic thing. He'd been immediately drawn to the guy's sister when she'd interviewed him three years back, so why shouldn't he get on well with her family? Then again, he'd been drawn to Katrin, and look where that had got him. He certainly didn't have any affinity with her siblings.

"A bit of a mess is a bit of an understatement."

Becca had been in a relationship herself when he'd started working for her. They'd grown close, first as colleagues, then as friends. There'd never been anything more, even after she'd split with her boyfriend. It had been his problems with Katrin that had caused them to grow closer, late nights in the office telling her about the latest problems. He could laugh about the absurdity of it all with her. The joking around had drawn them ever closer. Close enough for a one-night stand that had soon become a three-month affair.

"So you met this girl in Iceland, then?"

Pete's comment brought Mike back to reality, so much so that he wondered if he'd actually been dozing off. "Yeah, we were over there for a conference." He'd been there with Becca, she'd turned in early after taking a call from the then boyfriend. It had been February and he'd walked down to the harbour hoping to see the Northern Lights. He hadn't. But he'd met Katrin.

"And she just turned up a week later? Out of the blue? That must've been a shock."

"Too right. Sure, we'd had a nice chat, and I'd bought her a drink, but that was it. She worked at the hotel the conference was at, so I guess I should've found it a bit creepier when she popped up on the doorstep, and I'd never told her where I lived, but hey, what can you do? You wake up one morning, there's a knock at the door, and you're greeted with a stunning blonde who tells you she was in the area and thought she'd look you up."

"And you hooked up just like that?" Was there a hint of judgement in Pete's tone? Mike couldn't tell for sure, he was well on the way to pissed having left merry in the bar an hour or so ago.

"Not at all," slightly defensive, but what the fuck. "We went out for breakfast. Met up again that night. I saw her a few times that week, she went home, we kept in touch, and she came back. Things happen, her flight back got delayed by that damn volcano with the unpronounceable name, and she'd moved in by Easter."

"Whirlwind romance, then."

There were mince pie crumbs down the front of Pete's shirt and Mike was beginning to feel irritable. It'd been a long day and the evening wasn't panning out as planned. On the other hand, his alcohol-loosened lips had decided they weren't as tired as the rest of him and resolved to tell the tale in full.

"You could say that, and things were great. Work was good, Becca's great to work for, you should be proud," (he's her brother, not her dad, said a part of his brain while his mouth continued to run), "and life with Katrin was great, too. For a while. But turns out magically appearing at people's front doors without warning isn't peculiar to her. Oh no. It's a fucking family trait. That's what it is." He sipped his whisky, lubricating his lips before ploughing on.

"Turns out, right, she's got thirteen brothers. Thirteen! There's bloody fourteen in that tribe and she's the only girl, youngest, too. Reckon Mum and Dad decided to just keep on trying till they got a lass, even if it did mean popping a kid out regular as clockwork for a decade and a half."

"There's some long nights that far north, got to find something to keep you occupied."

Mark's brow furrowed as he contemplated the comment, took a drink, and stumbled over to the dresser to pour himself another. He looked down the hall and into the bedroom as he did so. Becca was putting on her make-up and all he wanted to do was walk in there and fuck her, not chat with her damn brother.

"Well, by all accounts her dad's a lazy bastard," stop swearing so much said some sober cells that still resided in some part of his mind, "and barely leaves his bloody rocking chair," there, toned the expletives down a bit, satisfied?, "so, all in all, a surprise there's so many of 'em. Unless they aren't all his, I guess."

"I'd be shattered if I had fourteen kids, I can tell you. My two wear me out."

"Here's hoping they don't grow up to be insane crackpots like Katrin's mob." Mike considered his drink and added another poorly-judged measure.

"You don't get on with her family, then?"

"Don't get on? Are you for real? They're fucking mental." Drink poured, easily a triple, he returned to his armchair. Bedding Becca was a write off for the night, and all he could hope for was a quick fumble with Katrin when he got home, as she was never up for anything with family in the house. And there always seemed to be family in the house.

"Yeah, well, so Easter was great. Bit of time off with the Bank Holidays, spring in the air, blah b-blah." Pete smiled, and Mike continued, hitting his stride, "But May Day, that's when things started to go wrong. That's when she says, 'Do you mind if my brother's visit?'. I said we'd talk about it. Next morning, there's a twat right there. Right there on my doorstep, large as life."

"And that's the guy who got involved with the police?"

"No, not him, we'll get to them bastards. This one—don't ask me his name, I get them all jumbled up—this one, he'd come because the eldest brother, get this, was in some sort of trouble for bothering sheep, and his bad legs were playing up."

"Bothering sheep?"

"Exactly. I don't know what it means either, rustling hopefully, but anyway, he didn't come, never met him, and don't want to, but the one who did visit, barely been there two days when I get woken up to a load of shouting and bawling in the street because he'd been caught peeping in through the next door neighbour's bathroom window while their daughter was having a shower and then, when her old man shot outside to have a gentle word, he'd half inched the milk off their step and done a runner. So he was shouting after him, the daughter was wrapped in a towel, crying in their doorway, mum was banging on our front door, Katrin was shouting in Icelandic. It was mayhem."

"So what did you do?"

"What any man does when the shit hits the fan at home. Got dressed and went to work."

"You two ok in here?" Becca was stood in the doorway and looked beautiful, her radiant smile bringing a pair of reciprocal smiles from both of the men in the room.

"Fine."

"Yeah, fine."

Her presence helped Mike focus, he hadn't realised just how drunk he was getting. Becca obviously did. She put the whisky away in the cupboard. "I'm nearly done, just need to fix my hair." Her hair looked perfect. But what do men know about women's hair?

"Never saw him again," said Mike, "but it wasn't long before our next visitors turned up... two of 'em this time."

"Double the trouble?" Pete had found a box of Quality Streets and was tucking in. He offered the box to Mike who waved it away; he wasn't a big fan of chocolate.

"Exactly. A right pair they were, one was about 4ft tall, the other nearly 7ft and thin as a rake. Pan Thief and Spoon Thief I call them two. Found a duffel bag full of pans and spoons hidden in the garden shed a few days after they arrived. God only knows where they got them from, but there was something dodgy going on."

"I guess all of this put a lot of strain on your relationship."

"Exactly. That first month we'd barely argued, now it seemed we did little but. If you loved me, you'd love my family she'd say. Like that makes any sense whatsoever. Things are different in Iceland she'd say. Well obviously, but we don't live in bloody Iceland, do we?" His glass was empty, but Mike didn't need any more; he was in the zone, and, for some reason, wanted to finish his tale before Becca had finished trying to make her long black hair straighter than straight can be. "Anyway's a little holiday, I thought, that'll help. So off we trot for a week away on a cheap deal just before the kids break up and prices rocket. And we had a good time. Until we got home. The place was a sodding pigsty, dirty plates in the living room, stains on the carpet, pots and pans piled up in the kitchen, and there on the fridge, a selfie of one of her brothers licking a bowl clean as if he hadn't eaten in a month. And what does she say? Oh, I thought he was coming next week, such a shame to miss him! A shame, a shame he came at all. He'd eaten us out of house and home, not a scrap of food left in the damn house. Twelve hours we'd been travelling that day and what do I end up doing? Heading off to Asda to do a shop. All the rest and relaxation gone. Poof. Just like that."

"That must've been a blow."

"Exactly. Things did settle down a touch, and our next guest, mid summer this was, he wasn't too bad. Granted, he had a weak bladder and you'd hear him going to the toilet and slamming doors all night but he was only with us a couple of days. However, by September things were mental again. Another double visit, pair of 'em always pissed and then I get knocked up at 3 in the bloody morning by the police. Dragged down to the station with Katrin crying her eyes out because her brothers had broken into the Co-Op and stolen a crate of yoghurts and a dozen packs of sausages. You know the Co-Op's a client of ours? I had to pay for all the damage and pull in all the favours I had to make sure charges weren't pressed. That's when I had to tell Becca what was going on and, well, I needed someone to talk to and hadn't realised just how much until that point. Only good thing that's happened to me this year."

Mike felt Becca's hand on the back of his neck, hadn't even realised she was back in the room as he'd ranted on, his eyes fixed on the bottom of an empty glass. "We'll lose our table if we don't go now, but we could always cancel if..."

"No, you go on out." Mike reached up and put his hand over hers. "I've intruded enough." He was starting to sober up and felt a bit rough, and a bit silly. "Your brother's a good listener, and probably thinks I'm a right dick."

"Don't worry, Mike," said Becca, her touch settling him. "He's heard worse I'm sure."

"I doubt that."

"Well if you'd let him get a word in edgeways he might have had a chance to tell you."

"Tell me what?"

She leant in close, her perfume arousing a desire in him he subconsciously covered with a hand over his lap. She mock-whispered, loud enough for her brother to hear, "He's a therapist."

Pete laughed, he was standing now, putting on his jacket, but it wasn't a cruel laugh, and Mike decided that he really did like the guy, and wished Katrin's family could be so normal. "If I'd have told him, then I'd have had to charge him for the session. Union rules." The smile was genuine as they shook hands.

"You can stay a while if you like Mike, have a coffee, sober up before heading home? Tell Katrin you had to walk Paul home after he'd had a skin full or something." The way Becca would advise him to lie to Katrin sometimes hurt him, it made her even more complicit in his betrayal than she already was, but in reality, there was little left of his relationship with Katrin to betray. They shared a home, and a bed, but little more. They touched, at times, but were no longer connected. He wondered why she even stuck around, although perhaps the alternative, a life at home with all her family, all at once, all the time, would be just too much. He could understand that. "Mike?"

He snapped out of it. "No, it's cool. It isn't that late and the walk'll set me right. You guys have fun." He shook Pete's hand again and kissed Becca on the cheek. "I'll call you, and as for you," he patted Pete on the shoulder like he'd known him for years, the alcohol still breeding a familiarity beyond that normally afforded to a man you'd met just that evening, "I'll tell you the rest some other time."

***

"Jesus, Becks, you know how to pick 'em."

Pete was driving. He was smiling, but Becca knew he wasn't entirely happy with the situation.

"He's going through a rough patch, that's all."

"And you can do without getting dragged into it. I mean, what is this? A rebound thing? Something genuine? Where do you see this ending up?"

"Is this my brother talking? Or my therapist?" A hint of irritation, but nothing more.

"Your brother. Just be careful. I'm sure he's a nice guy, but if half of what he says about his girlfriend and her family's true, you need to be as mindful of them as you are of him."

"Fair point. How much did he tell you anyway?" She was looking out of the window as she spoke, the shops with the Christmas displays, lights over the street... and a young girl throwing up in a doorway, as her friend held her hair back and a guy crouched next to her groped her arse.

"As far as you two hooking up after the breaking and entering debacle, you told me about.

443

That's what I'm getting at... not only you getting dragged into it, but your business getting dragged into it, for Christ's sake."

"And he was devastated about that, and did all he could to put it right. This isn't his fault, Pete. Nor is the fact that not a week later, another brother turned up that got caught peeping into the neighbour's house, or the one who visited for a week around Halloween and spent all his time standing in doorways, sniffing and rubbing his nose."

"Seriously?"

"Seriously. Mike thought it was drugs and I sent him away on a project for a few days just to get him out of the house. He was close to cracking and, feelings aside, he's a damn good member of staff, and a friend."

"Ok, I get it. Things are tough and he's pretty much trapped until he either kicks her out..."

"Easier said than done."

"... or, he walks out himself."

"Again, easier said than done when he's mortgaged to the hilt, and it's his home, not hers. She's the cuckoo."

They pulled into the hotel car park. A big tree decked in white lights dominated one corner, and an LED reindeer pulled an LED sleigh over the porch roof of the hotel. Frost was starting to form on the ground. "Let's drop it, then," offered Pete. "A nice meal and, hopefully, no Black Eye Friday bother to contend with."

"Not here, not at these prices," his sister remarked, flashing him her best 1,000-watt smile as she got out of the car. The hotel door opened and they heard laughter and music before it closed and became muffled once more. "But, before we close the topic, I should really finish off the tale of Katrin and her thirteen lunatic brothers."

"Really? There's more?" They walked arm in arm across the car park.

"Of course, we haven't got to the part where another one of them gets caught by the police with a garden cane with a hook on the end, trying to fish meat through the letterbox of the butcher's on the

High Street, or the one Katrin took to visit Castle Howard all decked out for Christmas, and when Mike got home, he'd found out he'd stolen a pair of antique candlesticks and was busy eating the candles."

"That's it, Becks, you're making this shit up now. The pair of you've been pulling my leg all night and now you've gone too far." He opened the door for her and looked deep into her eyes as she passed him.

"'Fraid not big bro', it's all true. And this week he's got to contend with her mother."

Her eyes told him she was telling him the truth. "Christ, Becks, you really do pick 'em."

***

The walk home took longer than anticipated, a plethora of flashing blue lights, shouts, and a multi-limbed brawl in the centre of the street necessitating a detour. Fucking Black Eye Friday. All he wanted to do was get home like Michael Douglas in Falling Down, even though part of him could've contradictorily stayed away forever. It gave Mike time to sober up in the cold night air. Gave him time to think. Katrin's family were obviously some kind of Icelandic hillbillies, short on both cash and social graces. He could see why she'd run away and latched on to him. And he cared about her, there was no denying that, and she him, but he'd never asked for any of this, and certainly hadn't signed up for all the grief and baggage she'd walked into his calm and steady life. If her folks were that poor, he told himself he'd rather send them a cheque each month than have them come to stay—even though no one used cheques these days and he'd never actually do that should that choice be placed before him— why the hell should he? He shivered in the cold night air. He was already supporting Katrin financially, her family weren't his problem. Wasn't it enough that she sent what she earnt from her part-time job cleaning at the local school to them while leaving him to cover the costs of running house and home? And then they used that money to come over and make his life a misery. So what if Iceland was an expensive place to live? Not his problem and they shouldn't be wasting money on airfares.

His thoughts wandered as he himself wandered the streets. Thoughts of Becca and her warm embrace brought a guilt-tainted smile to his face. If anything good came of this, it was the way it had brought them together, forging a relationship from a friendship that may have otherwise never been anything more. Becca was his future, Katrin his past. The overlap an unfortunate, but unavoidable, episode that needed to be brought to a close. This year was a transition, that's what it was. A painful metamorphosis from bachelor to part of a settled, loving couple stimulated by a fair few months of what had seemed like madness and trauma, but which he and Becca would be able to laugh about once it was all over. The greatest gift he could receive for Christmas would be freedom, and it was something he would have to give to himself. He and Katrin needed to part ways; it hadn't worked out, and that was surely the fate of most relationships. To end it wouldn't be unusually cruel. It would be merciful. It was the right thing to do. He would tell her it was over, and if she objected he would tell her he had found someone else. If that didn't send her packing, then he'd leave himself for the night and take things from there. She had no claim on the house, no name on the deeds—he'd kick her out if he had to, but hoped it wouldn't come to that. His drifting mind had allowed the streets to pass like mist and he was at his door. He felt like a stranger, something within him had changed. He'd had enough. Things had come to a head and would end that night. "Happy Black Eye bastard Friday, honey," he muttered as he opened the door. "I'm home."

∗∗∗

The first thing he did as he crossed the threshold was sneeze. "Katrin?" he said, as he rubbed his eyes with one hand whilst reaching for the hallway light switch with the other. "You there?"

No answer, but he could hear someone moving around in the kitchen. "Katrin? Is that you?" Again, no reply. His shoes kicked off he walked into the lounge, the thought "*what the fuck*?" entering his head as soon as he saw the shreds of wrapping paper scattered around the floor, partially unwrapped presents dispersed amongst the mess as though torn open by an over-excitable toddler and then cast aside to move onto the next of Father Christmas' deliveries. The tree was leaning to the left and a sudden thought hit him: *"we've been bloody burgled,"* before a second thought stopped him in his tracks... *"and the bastard's still here."*

His heart began to race and panic started to set in. Should he shout out and hope to scare him—or even worse, them—off? Creep up on them and give them exactly what the arseholes deserved? It could be kids, nothing more, or it could be grown men who'd kick the shit out of him without breaking a sweat. Or it could be Katrin's bloody family. The thought settled him, and then angered him. Of course it was! The curse of the Icelandic idiots strikes again. Well, this time something nasty just might accidentally happen to whichever brother it happened to be. Unlucky number thirteen, that was it... the sheep-bothering clown he hadn't met yet. Had to be. Slowly he moved towards the fireplace to grab the poker, his mind unclear on whether he was going to merely scare the prick in the kitchen or actually batter him - "honest guv, it was self-defence, how was I to know my girlfriend's brother had ransacked the house and then gone to make a herring sandwich?" – as it was, he did neither, as that's when a cat jumped out from behind the tree and knocked him flat on his arse.

The cat hissed, Mike swore and sneezed at the same time which came out as a loud "acuntchoo", and a bellow came from the kitchen. A female bellow. "Is that him? Did he get any clothes?"

Mike had no idea why whoever was in the kitchen wanted to know if he'd got clothes for Christmas— never did, always insisted on buying his own—or who they were asking unless they were asking the cat, but what he did know was that he'd had enough. The poker was still in his hand and he cracked the cat across the back as it stalked toward him, causing it to jump back before growling at him like a tiger and baring its teeth. He could see now that the feline had more in common with a bobcat or a lynx than a regular housecat. It was larger, with fierce green eyes and sharp needle-like teeth. Its fur was brown and yellow, and matted together in clumps. It sat back on its haunches as Mike began to get up, then launched itself at him as he sneezed once more.

To an onlooker, it would've appeared absurd; to Mike it felt like a life and death struggle. The cat had buried its claws into each side of his temple as it took him to the floor and was biting at his right cheek with razor-like teeth so that it resembled a patch of bloody pulled pork. Meanwhile, Marks eyes streamed with the allergic reaction that had plagued him since childhood, and all he could do was sneeze over and over again rather than fight back. Rivulets of blood ran down the side of his head and pooled in his ears until, eventually, the sneezing eased for a second and he grasped at the presence of mind to get his hand between the cat's hissing and spitting face and his own, lacerated cheek. He pushed, but the cat was too strong, too heavy, and as they wrestled, an old bedtime story came to mind about someone who'd tried to lift a cat only to find out it had been a serpent wrapped around the whole of the world. A stupid thought that made no sense at a time like this—not that anything had made much sense for far too long. It was that thought that gave him renewed strength as he lay on the floor amongst shredded gift wrap, a wildcat clinging to his face and biting down into his hand. He brought up his other hand and grabbed the top of the cat's head; the cat responded by clawing at his eyes and all he could do was squeeze them shut, leaving him blind. The hand in the cat's mouth was on fire, so he grabbed the lower jaw and simultaneously found what he was groping for with the fingers of his other hand—the cat's own eyes. Jamming two of his fingers into the sockets, he felt the creature's eyeballs push back into its skull, forcing the animal to finally try to pull away, but he wasn't giving up, nor was he letting go. Something inside had snapped and the frustrations of the year spilt out into one almighty wrench from both of his arms as he pulled the cat's skull up and the jaw down. There was a crack, and hot liquid splashed upon his face, another crack, and he felt the cat's body twitch on his chest, then go still. Slowly, he opened his eyes, and threw the cat off him, before starting to sneeze.

He was doubled over sneezing and trying not to vomit when the kick came to the side of his head. A kick so hard that when he turned around his vision was blurred and his mind scrambled.

Looking up he would have sworn that the figure looking down at him was more troll than woman. Hair grew on her chin and her ears hung down as low as her shoulders. "My cat!" she roared from a mouth that held far too many teeth, all of which were stained charcoal black. She loomed over him, spittle dripping into his face and a sewer-like stench coming from her gaping maw. He blinked, but when he looked again the figure was no more human than before, if anything, the monster was less so and the only possible explanation was that he had gone insane. Behind the woman a number of long cat's tails whipped through the air as though they were part of her, and atop her head were a pair of goat's horns. As he scrambled back and away in total confusion the old woman pointed a long bony finger tipped with a sharp yellow nail straight at him. "You've been a bad boy to my sons, a bad boy to my daughter, and a now a very bad boy with my cat."

Somehow a moment of clarity burst through the jumbled thoughts that rampaged through Mike's mind and he leapt to his feet and dashed towards the kitchen, pushing the monster to one side as he went, but falling to the floor again after slipping on a piece of Elf on the Shelf-adorned wrapping paper. Behind him he could hear shouting in what sounded like Icelandic, and as he crawled toward the kitchen he began to shout himself, yelling for Katrin in the vain hope that she would come to his aid and save him from what could only be her mother, Gryla.

"She's gone out for some potatoes, you pathetic man."

Mike, now scrambled as far as the kitchen, got to his feet and turned. Gryla filled the doorway from the lounge—a filthy old woman dressed in rags. Whatever damage the blow to his head had done wasn't easing off as he was still hallucinating, for behind the old witch was a room filled with red balloons... red balloons that contained the screaming faces of young children. Slowly, he edged back towards the only other available exit as Gryla advanced, her cat's tails swaying behind her and the balloons floating into the room as she came toward him. His back hit the door and he grabbed the handle. Outside was only an inch away. The real world, the world away from all the madness, was only the depth of the door from him... it might as well have been a million miles away. He began to cry, the fight gone out of him as his legs gave way. He sneezed, sniffed, and looked the old hag right in her jet black eye as she drove the poker through his throat and into the door behind him.

***

"I'm glad you could come, Mother," said Katrin as she tucked into her second bowl of meat and potatoes.

"As am I, my sweet," answered Gryla as she stirred the cauldron over the fire. The room was still a mess, but no worse than they were used to back home in Dimmuborgir. At least it smelt like home now with the aroma of her mother's special stew filling the air.

"I'm sorry about Jolakotturinn." Katrin spoke through a mouthful of meat, the cat laying across her lap, softly purring through its broken jaw.

"He'll be fine, he's got a few lives left, yet. You are ready to come home now? Once you have eaten?"

"Yes," said Katrin. "I have missed my family."

"Good," replied Gryla. "They've missed you, too. We'll pick them up on the way back to the airport."

"They're here?"

"Oh yes, only a quick visit, their busiest time of year, of course. They insisted on coming when they heard what was going on. Wouldn't have it any other way. That Miss Tumman, she deserves a visit from my Yule Lads, no doubt about that, no doubt at all," she answered as she stirred the pot. The old crone gave her daughter a lop-sided smile before picking out a piece of meat that looked suspiciously like an ear. "And we wouldn't want her to miss out now, would we?"

The End

Kevin J. Kennedy Presents

Christmas in Hell

By

Kevin J Kennedy

You know, I always hated Christmas. It just wasn't for me. I hated that it had nothing to do with the religious side of it anymore and was basically a retail-run holiday in which everyone felt obligated to spend money they didn't have on shit that they gifted out to people who would never use it. Over the years I received some ridiculous gifts that I can only assume were recycled from the year before. Some of those gifts must have been in circulation for years now. If you didn't already know, lots of people stock-pile the gifts that they get that they consider to be shit, for want of a better word. These items remain in a closet for the next eleven months or so until the current owner decides to rewrap them in some new paper, add a new little name tag and hey, presto, they spent fuck-all but still have a gift for your ass. Everyone is a winner. Well, except you. You then need to hold onto that piece of shit until next year, until you can palm it off on some other unlucky asshole.

Anyway, I digress. 'Christmas is shit' was always my motto. I did enjoy time I spent with loved ones, but I always enjoyed that at any time of year. I enjoyed eating too much but then again, it's not like I'm exactly strict with my diet throughout the year. The time off of work was probably the only bit I really appreciated. I wasn't one of those Grinch-like assholes, though. I didn't spend the season telling others how it was all shit and try to get them to see things my way. People are entitled to do their own thing. Who am I to try and tell them what to enjoy and what to avoid? At the end of the day, I was roped into spending the same cash as everyone else and playing along, otherwise my wife and daughter would have killed me. Living with two women is never easy, but try disappointing them on a special occasion and just see how difficult your life becomes.

I suppose that brings us onto the point of my story. I'm in Hell. Not the 'my life is falling apart and I'm getting all dramatical about it' kind of hell.... like the actual, real Hell. It's not going to be one of those stories where I tell you that I'm not supposed to be here and then go on a mission to find my way out of Hell. Neither is it a story about me defeating some great evil, even though it means I need to stay in Hell forever. It's much less grand than that.

I arrived in October and it's now the twenty-fourth of December. Wherever Hell is, they celebrate Christmas here, too. *Of course they fucking do*, I can almost hear you saying. It's not for the same reasons people on Earth do, and what goes on is very different, but it's called Christmas none the less and it's celebrated on the same date. There is a Santa Claus of sorts and he does leave presents for some. Those are the main similarities. Everything else is a hellish parody of what I once knew and hated.

When I first arrived in Hell, I was sitting in a waiting room. The heating was turned up several times higher than any Earth- bound heating system could have achieved. I imagine the temperatures would have matched that of a furnace and yet there was no fire. The room was being heated by air vents pumping into the reception area. I wasn't sweating; I didn't catch on fire, but the discomfort I felt was insane. There was a desk with a sign above it saying 'Welcome to Hell'. I approached, but as I did the small creature behind the desk held up its paw and abruptly said, "We'll call you, please take a seat," before going back to its newspaper. I moved back to a seat and collapsed into it. My body was in no physical pain but the incredible heat was debilitating. After two hours of sitting around and getting more and more agitated, I approached the desk again. I got an identical response. When I tried to press the matter I was ignored. The small red creature that had been there before had gone and had been replaced by a slightly larger creature completely covered it blue fur. It reminded me of Cousin Itt from the Addams Family TV show. The creature was reading the same newspaper that the last creature had left behind. I went a little mental for a good few minutes, shouting at the new person behind the desk but when it finally sunk in that the creature hadn't as much as raised its head, no security was coming for me and almost no one in seemed to be paying any attention at all, I returned to my seat again.

After somewhere in the neighbourhood of twelve hours, my name was called. I rushed to the desk to be told to go into room six-six-six. Not only was it a cliché... it was the only room. I got into the room and sat in front of me was one of the most gorgeous women I have ever seen—apart from the two extra arms she was sporting—she was a perfect ten.

"Please take a seat," she told me.

I took a seat.

"Can you tell me why I'm here?" I asked her.

"You're here for your work assignment," came her reply.

"No, I mean why am I in Hell? Wait... what? My work assignment?" I asked, confused.

"Yes, your work assignment."

The conversation went nowhere fast.

I could take you over the hours and hours that we went round in circles but it would put you to sleep. What I can tell you is that I learned a few things. Firstly, no one in Hell is going to answer any of your questions. People will often give you pieces of information in general conversation, but never as an answer to a question that you asked. Secondly, time in Hell runs the same as it does on Earth, or at least it feels that way. What I didn't realise until a bit later is that when you aren't progressing with whatever is expected of you in Hell, time just stops completely and waits for you. It moves on when you do. The best example I can give you of this started occurring in noticeable scales when I began my first job.

My first job began directly after the meeting that I spent hours in trying to find out why I had a work assignment in the first place. When I left the little interview room, feeling pretty exasperated, I walked into a much larger room that held a mixture of people and creatures of various assortments that must have been in the thousands. Each sat in front of PC's with headsets on chattering away. A dippy-looking blonde girl with a too-large grin appeared next to me wearing a too-big t-shirt that read, 'welcome to the call centre'. *Typical,* I thought to myself. What else would be my given profession in Hell but a damn Telesales Advisor? I should have known. It turned out that for eight to twelve hours a day, I would be on the phones, cold calling people to try and sell them crap that they didn't need. The extra catch in Hell was that no one ever got a sale. Ever! I tried hanging up on customers that the system had called and put through to my line, hanging onto the call after the customer had hung up and various different techniques that were applied regularly in the call centre industry when you just couldn't be bothered. None of them worked. As I said earlier, if you weren't doing what you were supposed to be doing, time just stopped for you. It didn't seem to effect those around you, so I'm not quite sure of the logistics of it, but, still... time stopped all the same. Now everything was kind of irrelevant since it wasn't like anyone had anything better to do than to work at telesales all day, every day, with no chance of ever having a buying customer; 'tis tough on the mind. Oh, and we don't get weekends off. It's a seven- day- a- week number. We do get paid, though, and while it's Hell, there's no one here whipping and torturing us. As crazy as it sounds, some days I think I'd swap a day in the call centre for a savage whipping.

When I got off work from my first shift I was given a token for twenty hell notes. It was a fifth of my day's salary. Everyone was paid daily in Hell. You got a fifth of your salary and the rest went straight into your Christmas account. The money could only be lifted the week before Christmas and could only be spent on Christmas gifts. You couldn't even buy yourself one. We walked through a doorway that looked like it took you into another room, yet lead, instead, into a park, I ranted loudly that this seemed like bullshit to me. I was informed that there was simply no way around it. The various call centre workers headed in every direction. I wasn't sure where any of the directions took you, so I just stood there looking dumb. After deciding it didn't really matter where I went, I just started walking in a straight line. I came to an edge of the park that was completely surrounded by a twenty-foot- high fence, dripping in barbed wire. There were three doorways with signs above them. They read, 'Halloweenland', 'The Gate' and 'Just Relax'. Obviously, I picked the one marked 'Just Relax' and quickly left the park.

To say it was a mistake would be an understatement. I spent the next fifteen or so hours being tortured before being released to go to work in the morning. I'm sure I died a few times, but each time something serious happened to my body it seemed like I blacked out and would wake up okay again... only for the torture to start all over. I was let go fifteen minutes before my shift began. I decided not to go into work and sat in the park for hours. After wandering around the perimeter of the park a few times and realising every door in the gate had disappeared, apart from the call centre one, I gave in and went to work. I thought maybe I would meet someone that could help me out a little. I was wrong. When I arrived, the shift was just beginning. Time had waited for me. I spent another day calling customers who wouldn't buy anything before leaving into the park again. I repeated this routine daily, every day finding new doors to try but each was as bad, if not worse, than the last. I thought a few times about just staying in the park, yet my mind kept niggling at me, whispering that one never knew if there might exist a good door to be found. When no one will answer any questions, it's difficult what to know about anything.

The weeks went by and I made no progress in discovering anything other than small quirks to Hell; nothing of any real use. They start celebrating Christmas in early November. That's one of the things that was hard to miss. I think it was around the tenth of November when I walked out the usual door at the end of my shift to find the park covered in fake snow with a massive Christmas tree in the middle. It was no different from Christmas trees on Earth in the way it was decorated. The only small difference was it leaked blood instead of sap. Although the actual day was a long way off and the money wasn't released for a while, it became apparent it was just another method of torture. Christmas songs played twenty- four hours a day or rather longer if time stopped for you for any reason. They played through the call centre headsets between calls, from speakers that were positioned everywhere, inside and out, and from the random places that the mystery doors took you to between shifts. Some of the songs I had liked in the beginning, others I'd always hated and some I'm sure had been made up badly on purpose just as an extra measure of pain. Not only did we have to listen to the shit non-stop, but we had to actually sing carols on breaks. The entire call centre had to stand at their desks and sing carols at the top of their voices for both fifteen minute breaks and their lunch as well. Not that any of them had to eat and no one went to the toilet in Hell, but it seemed to make the day even longer. I tried again to just not do it and my fifteen minute break went on and on. I gave up in the end and sung along. Miraculously, in Hell, you will know the words to every single carol in existence, even if you didn't before.

As time passed, I realised that no one made friends in Hell, it was part of the plan. No one tried although I'm sure everyone wanted to. I couldn't work out if the ones who seemed to have a little more control in the call centre were born in Hell or had been here longer. What granted them the privileged role of being able to wander about and occasionally talk to each other, but, really, who knows if they are actual conversations or just another strange goings- on of Hell? Our call scripts that we had to stick to, word- for- word on every call without deviation, suddenly changed. We were calling customers to sell them Christmas products at massively reduced prices. No one bought anything. I wondered if we were calling real people or if it was some kind of simulation that had us believing we were talking to someone. I seemed capable of independent thought. It was everything else that I had no control over. It was almost like I was watching a movie of myself having a shitty life but couldn't exert any control over the situation.

The weeks continued to pass by and it reached the week before Christmas. The eighty percent of our salary that had been kept back was released to us in the form of a card with a Christmas parcel on the front. When I found the gates at the edge of the park on that night, each just said 'Presents' above it. I picked the middle gate for no reason other than I was standing in front of it. It took me to the largest department store I had ever seen. It was the stuff that nightmares are made from. Now some of you may think that sounds like a pretty fun evening, you're wrong. Shopping is an evil pursuit. You are surrounded with morons who pay no attention to where they are going, bump into you then look at you as if it's your fault. All the stores are always too hot, but, to be fair, pretty much everywhere is too hot in Hell. There are people looking for money from you for one thing or another on every corner. The queues are ridiculous, and stale alcohol reeks from those around you. I can't lie... I've never seen the attraction to being surrounded by a large crowd, and shopping often put me in a place where I hated everyone and everything. Now, that was my experience on Earth—in Hell it's so much worse. The shopping centre only plays the one Christmas song on repeat endlessly, so there is that to deal with. We all get a tour guide because the centre is so large. I got my ex-girlfriend. To say that she was an absolute bawbag on Earth would be an understatement, but, in Hell, she talks even more shit. None of what she says makes sense, not that it really ever did. She bursts into tears every twenty minutes or so and irrationally tells me how it's my fault—again, talking mainly gibberish that I'm not sure anyone would understand—and worst of all I couldn't lose her. Every time I tried, I turned around and she was standing next to me.

Each day I'd try a different door in the park and every time I would be back in the same shopping centre with the same ex doing the same shit. This lasted until the day before Christmas, today. The day at work was the same as always. There was no party or games or anything else... just another shift of meaningless labour. As I walked out into the park, I thought something festive might be going on, but other than the tree and lights, it was the same. Everyone made their way to various gates on different sides of the park. I sat around for a while, wondering if I would have to spend the day with my ex again. I reasoned that surely Christmas

Eve wouldn't be more shopping. When I got to the doors they read 'Griswold', 'Kingston Falls', and 'Hill Valley'. I had no idea what any of them meant, so I went into 'Hill Valley', thinking that it at least sounded like a nice place. It didn't so much take me anywhere as much as transport me into the future.

I found myself, on Christmas day, at a dinner with the Devil. The real one: big guy, red all over, horns, disproportionately large upper body with small legs. Yep, that's right, dinner with the Devil. Just him and me. I did wonder if somehow everyone had dinner with the Devil on Christmas day. Time was strange and I'm sure he could have arranged it had he wanted to. I didn't imagine I was special. What I did find a little disconcerting was the Santa Claus costume he wore. It wasn't evil and terrifying, just the normal costume that Santa wore on Earth and it looked high- end. I can't imagine the Devil has money problems.

I just sat there looking at him. I wasn't sure what to say. We sat at either end of a long table. No one else was in the lavishly decorated room. After staring at him for a minute, wondering if I should say something, I realised this was the first time since I came to Hell that I wasn't being roasted. The room temperature was actually comfortable. It would appear that the Devil doesn't like it toasty.

Moments later a large set of doors opened and in came a troop of what looked to be female elves, apart from the fact that they were bright red like the Devil. Each was naked, wearing only sets of multi coloured Christmas lights. They carried trays of food which they placed along the table before disappearing back through the door. The Devil noticed me looking over everything.

"You can eat today, son."

My eyes quickly moved to him. "I thought no one ate in Hell."

"Well, you can eat today."

It wasn't exactly the in depth sort of answer I was looking for but I was getting used to knowing next to nothing in this new life. I grabbed what looked to be a turkey leg and devoured it in a few bites, the juice dripping from my chin.

"Help yourself, boy, for tomorrow you go back to the start."

"What do you mean I go back to the start?" I asked.

"Back to the day you came here. You start all over again," he answered. He didn't eat. He just sat smiling and watching me.

"What the fuck? I need to go through all this shit again? What's even the point to it?" I bellowed, standing up and slamming my fists on the table. Fuck the Devil, right?

I did kind of regret it as soon as I had done it. I was waiting for him to spring across the table and rip my throat out, but he didn't—he didn't even move. He just waited for me to take my seat again. It was all a bit embarrassing if I'm being honest.

"Feel better?" he asked with a knowing smirk.

"A little," I answered honestly. It's always good to blow off a bit of steam, even if you do feel like a fool afterwards.

"Good. Now. I have a proposal for you."

"A proposal? Don't you control everything here?" I blinked in genuine surprise.

"No one controls everything anywhere, son. I'm looking for a replacement demon. One of my seasonal demons was killed and I need to get a replacement for next year. I gave my son a shot at it this year after he wouldn't stop hounding me about it, but he will make a mess of it like he does everything else. The lad is truly evil, but if I said he had shit for brains, I'd be insulting the shit. Anyway... the job. I need a new Krampus. You know who that is, right?"

I did, at this point, wonder if I was having the longest, weirdest dream of my entire life, but it was all too real. The smells and the details weren't dreamlike at all.

"You want me to be Krampus? The anti-Santa. Big blue guy that looks a bit like you and hates Christmas? Are you serious? Why the fuck would I want to do that?"

The whole set up in Hell is weird as shit, but this was next- level crazy.

"I've watched you. You've kept more of your own mind and memories than any of the others. I'm tired of replacing my minions constantly. You know, the saying that you can't get good staff is so true. I'm surrounded by idiots everywhere I go."

I had to remind myself that the Devil wasn't having a heart-to-heart with me. I wondered if he'd had one too many drinks before dinner.

"Why would I want to be one of your minions? No offence, but we aren't exactly well acquainted. Your back story precedes you and by all accounts, they say that you're a bit of an asshole. On top of all that, this place is insane. You're in charge. What about that says 'good boss' material?"

The Devil actually threw his head back and burst into a fit of laughter.

"Son, the way I see it, you can keep going back to the day you arrived and live through our extended Christmas season for eternity or, you can go through the transformation and return to Earth where you will hunt and kill throughout the Christmas season, year after year. Now tell me, which of those two ideas sounds like the most fun?"

I've got to be honest. The moral side of me was screaming at me to tell him where he could shove his job, that I could never take it, but if I'm truly honest with you, I just really hate Christmas.

As I said at the start, there is no great epiphany. I'm not going to spend eternity trying to redeem myself. In actual fact, I'm not all that sure what I did wrong to end up here in the first place. Either way, here I am, back on Earth, leaving my story for someone to find. It may become a new legend that parents tell their children and then pass into myth as time goes on or, maybe no one will ever read it. Who knows? I will tell you one thing, though. The next time I hear a Christmas carol, I'm going to tear everyone in the room to pieces. Merry Krampus.

The End

Kevin J. Kennedy Presents

Santa Claus Comes At Night
By
Andrew Lennon

A green blur sped past the windows as the family car drove along the expressway that led to Norton Valley. Marcus had never seen so many trees. After living in the city for his entire life, he couldn't wait to move into the suburbs. His parents had told him about how all the streets were lined with trees, but he didn't realise that they meant it so literally. The car took the next exit and followed a roundabout to the third exit. A large white sign stood on the side of the road displaying 'Welcome to Norton Valley'. It had a picture of a beautiful white house with three huge trees in its front garden. Marcus pushed himself up on his seat in an attempt to get a better view.

"Dad?" Marcus asked. "I thought all the leaves were supposed to fall off trees in the winter."

"That's correct, son." Frank answered.

"Then why..."

'Why are they all still green here when it's only a week until Christmas?" Frank smiled.

"Yeah." Marcus bounced with excitement. "Are they special trees or something?"

"They're conifers. Also known as evergreens. They're a bit like Christmas trees."

"Wow. So we're going to live in a town full of Christmas trees? It's going to have them all year round?"

"That's right, honey." Jane turned from her front seat to face her son. "And guess what else."

"What?"

"They have pine cones. Which means we can collect them and decorate them. We could spray them gold and silver and put them on our Christmas tree. Does that sound like fun?"

"Yeah, that sounds amazing." Marcus flashed his pearly whites at his mother. "I think I'm going to like it here."

It was a bit of a hectic time for the Reeves family to move, with Christmas only being one week away., They'd decided, however, it would be better to get all this bit out of the way and be settled in time to start the new year in their new house. Besides, Marcus had loved the idea of spending Christmas in his new home. He had a bigger room for a start, which meant he could have more toys.. That meant more presents— at least he hoped so.

"Dad." Marcus said.

"Yes, son."

"How will Santa know where we live now?"

"We left him a note." Frank winked at Jane, who flashed him a smile.

"Where?" Marcus frowned. "I didn't see any note."

"We left it in the fireplace."

"But..." Marcus's forehead creased as his frown grew. "But we don't have, I mean we didn't have a fireplace."

"We left the note in the fireplace in the new house." Jane turned to see Marcus's face.

"What did it say? I don't understand."

"It said *Dear Santa, just a quick note to let you know that this is now the home of Marcus Reeves. He's been on your good list every year so could you please deliver any gifts for him to this house. He's been a very good boy again this year. We'll be sure to leave you lots of milk and cookies. Lots of love. Mrs & Mrs Reeves.*"

"Oh, I'm so excited!" Marcus bounced in his seat. But how will we know if he got it?"

"I guess we'll have to wait and see won't we?"

The car turned right into a long driveway. Two large conifers sat either side of the entrance. Marcus was shaking with excitement when he saw the large, white house they parked alongside. This house looked exactly like the one on the picture.

"Is this it, Mum? Is this really our house?"

"It is," she smiled. "Do you like it?"

"I love it!"

Frank parked the car and Marcus was out of the door like a shot. Before Frank or Julie had even gotten their seatbelts unbuckled, Marcus was stood at the front door jumping on the spot.

'Come on!" he shouted. "I want to see inside!"

His parents laughed and climbed out of the car. Frank stepped in front of Marcus and inserted the key, and with a "snick" the door was unlocked. Marcus pushed it open and ran inside.

"Oh my God!" His shout echoed in the empty room. "It's huge, but where's all our furniture?"

Frank laughed. "That's following us in the delivery vans. Don't worry it'll all be here by the end of the day."

Marcus walked through the first door he saw. It was the living room. His eyes fell upon the fireplace.

"My letter." He sprinted across the solid oak floor to the fireplace and then suddenly came to a halt. He turned to flash his father a look of sadness.

"What's the matter?" Frank asked.

"The letter. It's not here." Marcus sniffed as though he were about to cry.

483

"Well you know what that means, don't you?" Jane asked, as she entered the room.

"What?" Another sniff.

"That means that Santa has already been and collected it, so he knows to bring your presents straight here next week."

Marcus's teeth suddenly filled his mouth as his grin grew wider and wider.

"He has it? He has the letter?"

"He does, sweetheart."

"Yay!" Marcus ran across the room and jumped into his mother's arms and hugged her tightly around her neck. She hugged him back, sniffing the crease between his neck and shoulder. He still faintly had that baby smell that accompanied his soft skin. No one else could smell it, but Jane could, or at least, she thought she could... She knew it wouldn't be long before that smell went away forever, so she held him in her embrace, trying to get enough of it that she'd never forget what it was like. He was already growing up too fast.

"Right, you two." Frank interrupted. "Enough cuddles. We need to go and get the bags from the car. Once we've unloaded we can go and get some dinner."

"But Dad, I haven't seen my room yet." Marcus whined.

"Oh! Yes, that'sright." Frank smiled. "Well, you best go upstairs and see if you can spot which one is yours, hadn't you?"

Marcus turned on his heels and ran up the stairs. It was a huge wooden staircase that rose through the centre of the hallway. The house was almost mansion- like. Something Frank and Jane never thought they'd be able to afford in their lifetimes, but after some recent luck on the lottery, they were able to buy it outright... the home of their dreams.

When Marcus reached the top of the stairs, he saw a door with a sign hanging from it. It read "Marcus's room." He barged through the door and sprinted inside. He almost fell over when he saw his new room. Frank and Jane had ensured that this was the first room to be ready in time for their move. They wanted Marcus to enter this house and have his own space ready for him. It had blue walls with rocket ships painted on them. He had a rocket ship bed, a desk in the corner and loads of space in between to play with his toys. Fitted wardrobes ran the full length to the end of the room, with mirrored sliding doors.

Marcus saw something on the bed glisten in the corner of his eye. He approached it to see what it was. On his pillow lay a shiny, red bauble.

"Mum, Dad." He shouted. "Santa has already been to have a look around."

***

As planned with the delivery drivers, everything had been fitted into place while the Reeves family was out having dinner. The last driver was in the process of posting the keys just as the family pulled back into the driveway.

"Everything okay?" Frank asked.

"Yes sir. All fitted just as we discussed. I've left contact details on a leaflet on top of the fireplace in case you have any problems."

"I'm sure it'll be fine." Frank smiled and shook the man's hand while sliding a twenty into his palm. "Nice little touch with the fireplace by the way." He glanced back over his shoulder to Marcus who sleepily walked up the path to the front door.

"Erm, no problem at all, sir." The delivery driver smiled. "Hope you enjoy your new home."

"I'm sure we will. Thanks again."

The family entered the house and the delivery lorry slowly pulled away.

"Right, little man." Frank announced. "I think it's time for you to go to bed."

"But, Dad."

"Don't 'but Dad' me, and aren't you excited to spend the night in your *new room?*."

"Oh yeah." A grin covered Marcus's face. "I forgot." He ran up the stairs.

"Toilet and teeth before you get into bed, Mr!" Jane shouted.

'Okay, Mum," Marcus called back.

Jane climbed the stairs and passed Marcus on the way to his room.

"I'll leave your pyjamas on your bed for you. You get changed straight into them and then give me a shout when you're ready. I'm going to go and get changed in my room."

"mmmaaay mmmm," Marcus mumbled with his toothbrush in his mouth.

A few minutes later, after Jane had changed into her pyjamas, she heard Marcus call to say he was ready. She walked into his room to kiss him goodnight, Frank following right behind her.

"Can I have a story?"

"I don't know," Frank hesitated. "It's pretty late."

"Please?"

"Okay," his father sighed, relenting.

"Yay!"

"What'll it be, then?"

"Three Billy Goats Gruff."

"Again?"

"Yeah, I love that story."

"Okay," Frank laughed.

"I'll leave you two to it." Jane gave Marcus a kiss goodnight, and Frank a kiss on the cheek and left to unpack her clothes in her room.

A short while later, Frank entered the bedroom where Jane was unpacking. He began to unbutton his shirt.

"He go off okay?" Jane asked.

"Out like a light." Frank took her by the hips and pulled her close to him.

"What are you doing?" she giggled. "We have to unpack."

"It can wait," Frank said and playfully threw her on the bed.

489

***

Marcus woke to the sound of footsteps in his room. The light from his Buzz Lightyear nightlight glowed purple at the end of the room. Coming toward him, he saw a tall shadow walking through the light. He sat upright and prepared himself to sprint out of the room when suddenly, with a "click" his bedside lamp was switched on. Stood before him was a large man with a white beard, wearing a red suit and a red hat. The man looked down on Marcus who still sat, frozen, in his bed.

"Santa,." Marcus whispered.

"That's right." the tall man answered. "And you must be Marcus."

"Yeah." Marcus's eyes opened wide. "Yeah, I am. How did you know that?"

"Ho, ho, ho," Santa laughed. "Don't you know? Santa Claus knows all the little boys and girls. I check my list twice, you know."

"Yeah, like in the song," Marcus laughed.

"That's correct."

"But it's not Christmas yet. How come you're here now?"

"Well, I like to pay a few visits to some of my favourite boys and girls each year and see how they're doing. We sometimes play games and sometimes sing songs. We have such fun."

"Can we play games and sing songs?"

"Of course we can,." Santa whispered. "But we have to make sure we stay quiet. We don't want to wake Mummy and Daddy, do we?"

"Gotcha," Marcus whispered back. "What shall we play first, then?"

"How about this game?" Santa pulled a board game from under Marcus's bed.

"Oh, yeah. I love that game."

"I know, Marcus. I know everything remember."

The pair played the board game for a while, until Marcus began to rub his eyes.

"It looks like you need to get to sleep."

"No, please Santa. Don't go."

"Don't worry. I'll be back tomorrow. Now go to sleep."

Marcus let his head fall to his pillow and he listened to the footsteps of the man leave his bedroom.

***

"Mum, Dad! Guess what! Guess what!" Marcus screeched as he charged into their bedroom and jumped on the bed.

"Woah! What is it?" Frank abruptly sat up.

"Santa came to see me last night!" Marcus bounced up and down.

"What?" Frank exclaimed.

492

"Oh, did he now?" Jane asked.

"He did, he did!" Marcus continued to bounce.

"That sounds brilliant." Jane flashed Frank a sideways glance to tell him to play along.

"What was he doing?" Frank asked.

"He came to play games with me and sing songs."

"Really? We didn't hear anything. You sure were quiet."

"Yeah, because Santa said it wasn't fair to wake you up."

"Well that's very nice of him, isn't it?" Jane smiled. "You head downstairs and I'll be down in a minute to sort your breakfast."

"Okay, thanks Mum." Marcus jumped off the bed and ran out of the room.

"What was all that about?" Frank asked, still in a half- sleep daze.

"I think he's a bit excited for Christmas. It's cute that he's dreaming about Santa."

"Yeah, sure it is. Doesn't have to jump on me to tell me about it, though."

"He's still a baby." Jane slapped Frank on the arm.

"I know, but..." Frank looked embarrassed. "He nearly landed on the boys—you know?"

Jane looked down to where Frank was gesturing and burst out laughing.

"Well don't worry. I'll protect them." She gave him a kiss and then headed downstairs.

***

"Are we going to get our Christmas tree today, Mum?" Marcus asked in between munching on his cereal.

"We sure are." Jane answered. "Would you like to pick it?"

"Yeah, sure." His excitement echoed in the room.

"Okay, as soon as you've finished your breakfast, go and get dressed and then we'll make a move."

"Great." Marcus did as he was told.

It was only a short drive until they reached the garden centre that was selling Christmas trees. Frank parked the car and began giving Marcus instructions on what their tree had to be like. He couldn't go choosing the biggest tree in the place or it wouldn't fit. Of course, Marcus wanted the biggest tree in the place.

"If we were going to get a tree that big, then we may as well use one of the trees from our garden," Frank laughed.

"Ooo, can we? Can we?" Marcus asked.

"Don't be silly." Jane stroked her son's head. "Come on, let's go and see what they have here."

After about fifteen minutes of walking around and looking at trees, the family ended up getting the one that Jane wanted. Of course, she'd managed to convince her son and husband that they'd chosen this tree, but she smiled to herself and knew the truth.

Once home, the tree was up and the family had fun decorating it. The day seemed to fly and by the time they'd finished, after a dinner break, it was Marcus's bedtime. He didn't even question it when he was told he'd have to go straight to sleep, as it had gotten late. He ran straight upstairs, brushed his teeth and then got changed into his pyjamas. By the time his parents reached the bedroom, Marcus was already lying in bed waiting for his kiss goodnight. Once his parents left the room, he turned to his side and closed his eyes tight, hoping to fall asleep quickly so that it wouldn't be as long before his new friend came to visit.

Marcus woke to the sound of footsteps in the darkness. His bedside lamp switched on and he was greeted with the smiling face of Santa Claus.

"You came back," Marcus grinned.

"I told you I would." Santa rubbed his head.

"Did you see our new tree? Do you like it?"

"I do, I think I could fit a lot of presents under that tree."

"What am I getting?" Marcus bounced his bum on the bed.

"Ho, ho, ho!" Santa laughed. "I can't tell you that, Marcus."

"Aww."

"But I can tell you that when you wake on Christmas morning, there will be a present waiting for you on your bed. That way you can play for a little bit without having to wake your parents. How's that sound?"

"That sounds great. Are you coming to play every night? Are you coming to play on Christmas eve?"

"Ho, ho, ho! I can't very well come here on Christmas Eve, can I?" Santa ruffled Marcus's hair. "I'll be busy delivering presents to all the boys and girls around the world."

"Oh yeah," Marcus sighed. "I forgot."

"I'll tell you what… it's three days until Christmas. I'll come here and play games with you for the next two nights."

"Really?"

"Really, but you have to make me a promise."

"Sure, anything."

"Well…" Santa began. "My magic only works on Christmas Eve while all the good boys and girls are sleeping. And you know the song, right?"

"'He knows when you are sleeping, he knows when you're awake'." Marcus sang.

"Ho, ho, ho! That's right. Well, you have to stay in bed and try your best to stay asleep. If you're awake then my magic won't be working properly and I won't be able to make Christmas arrive in time for everyone. Do you think you can do that?"

"Yes I can."

"You promise?"

"I promise." Marcus held out his little finger. Santa linked it with his and they shook on it.

***

Over the next two nights, Santa stayed true to his word. He visited Marcus during the night and they played games and sang songs. Marcus told his parents stories about these games when he woke in the morning. They thought it was cute, and truth be told, these fabulous Christmas dreams were making Marcus sleep in a little bit later in the morning, so they were taking full advantage of that and catching up on much needed sleep themselves.

The night of Christmas Eve, Marcus sat on his father's knee by the fireplace and Frank read "Tw*as The Night Before Christmas*" to him—a tradition they'd started when Marcus was born, and one Frank hoped to keep for as long as he could.

Once the story was finished,. Marcus asked if they could get some milk and cookies for Santa, and of course his parents agreed. He thought about asking if he could put them in his room, seeing as Santa was going to be leaving a present on the end of his bed, but then he remembered that he had to stay asleep,. no matter what. He didn't want to ruin Christmas.

"Night, night my beautiful boy," Jane cooed while kissing her son's forehead.

"Goodnight, little man." Frank kissed him, too.

"Night, Mum. Night, Dad. I love you."

"We love you, too," they replied in unison.

Marcus turned to his side and closed his eyes tight.

"See you on Christmas morning," Jane whispered as she pulled his bedroom door shut.

***

Marcus woke to the sound of footsteps in his room again. He almost sat up to say hello to his friend, but then he remembered his promise. He lay still and kept his eyes shut tight.

He felt the gentle press at the end of the bed as Santa placed his present there, just like he'd said he would.

The footsteps approached the door.

"Merry Christmas, Marcus." Santa whispered, "I hope you remember this one forever."

Then he left the room.

"I will," Marcus whispered and turned over to try and sleep again.

Excitement was fighting him. All he wanted to do was look at the present at the end of his bed, but a promise is a promise. He couldn't ruin Christmas for everyone. He kept his eyes shut, and, after a while, he lost the fight and sleep took over.

When he woke, sunlight was shining through his curtains. Marcus crawled to the end of his bed and retrieved the blue paper wrapped box that had been left for him. He tore the paper away and lifted the top off the box.

Marcus screamed. A bloodied hand lay in the box. It was only now that Marcus noticed the blood had begun to soak through the box and left a wet, red patch on his bed. He dropped the present to the floor. The blood was on his hands.

"Mum, Dad!" he screamed with tears filling his eyes.

He stood, staring at the severed hand on the floor, waiting for his parents to come and see it and tell him it wasn't real. He stood waiting to wake up from this nightmare. They didn't come.

Eventually, Marcus's legs started to work again. He ran to his parent's bedroom. When he entered the room, he went dizzy at the sight before him. His parent's bed sheets were soaking red. They both had thick red lines crossing their necks from where their throats had been slit. His father's arm hung from the side of the bed. It ended at the wrist—just a red, bloodied stump remained.

Marcus ran out of the room, down the stairs and straight out the front door. He'd been running along the street for nearly ten minutes before a car, occupied by a neighbour's family members coming to visit, stopped by him. They began trembling when they saw the bloody hands of the small boy.

After the visitors had taken Marcus to their family's home and calmed him somewhat—he'd stopped screaming for now—they called the police. The police came to talk to Marcus and asked the neighbours if he could stay there while they went to investigate... of course they agreed.

The police quickly arrived on the scene, and after securing the perimeter, they cautiously approached the house. A quick scan told them there was nothing amiss downstairs, so they proceeded on up the stairs where they discovered the bodies of Marcus's parents, and the severed hand of his father; just as Marcus had told them. The rest of the rooms were clear. The only place left to check was the attic.

Slowly, Officer Duncan and Officer Geller climbed the stairs to the last place to investigate, one after the other. When they arrived, they saw that the attic was huge. It covered the full width of the house. In the far corner of the attic something caught their attention.

They approached to see what was hidden up there. Officer Duncan turned to Officer Geller, unsure of what to say. Lying there in the corner of the attic on an old, dirty mattress was a white, elasticated Santa Claus beard, a red hat and a letter. Officer Duncan looked at the first line.

Dear Santa, just a quick note to let you know that this is now the home of Marcus Reeves......

The End

Catching Santa
By
Michael A. Arnzen

I sit in the big, brown La-Z-Boy recliner, listening to the crackling of wood in the fireplace and watching my dad watering the little, red pan under the Christmas tree. He has a plumber's butt-crack showing as he crouches on all fours to reach the bottom of the trunk with his pitcher full of water. A little icicle ornament keeps poking his exposed cheeks, but I can't laugh at him. This is serious business.

"This is a thirsty one," he mutters, and I nod as I size up the Blue Spruce that towers above him. It's a heavy, thick tree and surely needs a lot of water to keep its needles. I smile when I see the hand-carved oak cross at the tippy-top, nearly touching the ceiling -- and then I enjoy the way the antique wooden ornaments he'd gotten from his German great- grandmother catch the light from the red and silver ornaments I'd helped him pick out last week from the local Walmart. It is a warm image, this tree, but a haunting one as well. Our Christmas tree always reminds me how my mother was stolen away from us four years ago.

I was just ten years old then, and still held on to the fantasy that maybe there could be a Santa Claus despite what all my friends had said. My parents had kept the fantasy alive by always marking at least one of my gifts -- usually the biggest -- with an oversized tag they reused every year that simply said, "To: Johnny, From: Santa" in ornate, script lettering. And they always acted as surprised as I was by the contents when I opened the package. I was either innocent or ignorant then, I guess, but what happened that Christmas to my Mom put an end to any innocence I might have had left.

And ignorance? Well, now I know the truth about Christmas better than any of my friends ever will.

The day when Mom died had started like any other Christmas morning back then. I'd get up as early as I could -- if I'd slept at all -- and then sneak down the stairs before my parents got up, intending to catch Jolly Old St. Nick in the act. I secretly hoped he'd adopt me as his little helper and take me for a ride around the world in his sleigh, letting me put presents under trees and rewarding me with a portion of whatever kind of milk and cookies people had left out for him -- sampling different kinds of treats from around the world!

But every time, I'd creep down the stairs to discover that all the gifts were already under the tree, wrapped in colorful paper, and that Santa had already come and gone. I'd missed catching Santa, but I didn't ever *really* expect to see him... and it didn't really matter anyway, because I always loved my presents and it was a happy time with Mom and Dad, who let me play in my pajamas all day long afterwards. Under the tree, though, I'd always find one big, green package with a thick, red ribbon on it—larger than the rest—and that was always Santa's gift. I'd locate it quickly and, before my parents came downstairs, I'd try to guess what was inside by shaking it, pressing my fingertips against the box as if reading Braille, and peeling up the edges of the wrapping paper a little to peek underneath. My mom was a light sleeper and had an uncanny knack for detecting my sneakiness; she would usually arrive around then, creaking her way down the stairs in her plaid bathrobe and funny banana-colored slippers, smiling at me as I tried to play innocent. She'd just smile and shake her head at me and go into the kitchen to make coffee while I perused my other gifts, curious about their contents, but mostly still wondering what Santa had brought me that year in that big, green box.

Mom would sit in the recliner and slurp her coffee while I sat cross-legged under the tree, waiting for the ritual tearing of wrapping paper and the untying of bows. Inevitably, she'd get impatient with me and we'd just argue about whether or not I could open up a present early, with her always insisting that we wait for my father to join us. "Christmas is about family," she used to chide,"... not presents." I'd counter with some tortured logic about how Santa brought the presents early, so I should be able open them as soon as I wanted to, but she'd say something about the birth of Jesus and how that was the gift of a family, not just a surprise package. But I'd ignore all that claptrap until she called me to sit on her lap and wait, even when I was getting way too old for such silly things.

But when I was ten, the last year I ever would sit on my mother's lap and giggle with her over Christmas cookies and secret sips from her coffee mug, Santa surprised us both.

It started with a loud scratching noise somewhere above the fireplace, a deep stone-scraping sound like the house was literally itching itself. Mother's head shot up toward the ceiling as if she could see through it to detect the source of the sound. I hopped off her lap and walked toward the tree, wondering more about the presents than some stupid scuffle, when I noticed the fire was sputtering. And *that* was because something was snuffing it out... sooty dust was dropping down from inside the fireplace, muffling the log that had almost burned down to a little black cinder. I crouched down and tried to peer up the chimney while my mother walked over to join me. "Huh! What's up there?" I wondered aloud.

"I hope it's not those pesky bats again," she grimaced.

And then... Santa's boots dropped down in front of us: calf-high, shiny leather, laced up tight, beneath the red fabric of his pants. They stood stock still in the dwindling flames as I stared in awe.

A man, who could only be St. Nick, contorted and revealed himself as he stepped up and out from our fireplace as my mother stood stunned beside where I was squatting, and leaning back on my hips.

"Merry Christmas!" he chortled, but I quickly realized this was not the jolly fat man from my Christmas fantasies. He was slender, and his outfit was as faded and filthy as a dishrag... missing buttons and stained with pink, smeary clouds of God knows what. I could smell the burnt leather of his shoes, but stronger than that was the cloying odour of rancid meat that hung in the air around him as he looked furtively from me to my mother. I remember just blinking a lot as I gazed up at him, before he relaxed a little and scanned around the room. His face was not hairy with a beard, but gaunt and yellow, and his eyes were as beady as a rat's. Santa had no flowing locks beneath his cap, either; there was some white hair, but it looked more like oily cotton strings pulled down from his hat here and there than anything attached to a scalp.

"Who the hell are you?" Mom finally asked, putting a hand on my shoulder to pull me back a little from the strange Santa.

His head jerked toward her, but he only answered with a smile as his eyes seemed to become solid as porcelain in their sockets. I was a little mesmerized by how amazing those eyes looked until I was distracted by the glint of his teeth reflecting the blinking Christmas tree lights. That glint made them look sharp and as long as a lion's as he towered over me, eyes locked on my mother.

She dropped her coffee mug and it jumbled onto the floorboards and rolled, gurgling itself empty by my foot. I pulled my attention away from Santa's 'fangs' to look at my mother, stunned, as she dropped her robe to the floor and started walking toward him. There before me, in nothing but her underwear, my mother slowly marched toward him as if sleepwalking, and he opened his arms for what looked to me like a loving hug.

"Mom?" I asked softly, but she kept walking and, to my horror, he embraced her, pulling her flesh against his disgusting outfit. I noticed she lifted herself up a little bit on the balls of her feet as he clutched her, his greenish, gangly arms sliding down her waist -- one hand going very low, broken claw-like nails dimpling into the cross-hatched pink underwear she wore -- and then she leaned her head to one side, as if bearing her neck to him.

"Mom!" I shouted, angry and wanting to do *something*, but feeling like I was nailed to the floor as I crouched there on all fours.

The ugly thing that was masquerading as Santa Claus snarled over her shoulder at me, the top half of his mouth all teeth gleaming with wet shine and, while his eyes dared me to speak again, I knew he was getting ready to chomp into her neck... when suddenly I heard Dad's loud footsteps bounding down the stairs.

I turned my head to call out to him, but he was already zooming across the room and tackling 'Santa' before I could even open my mouth.

The two of them fell back into the pile of my gifts, squashing boxes and tearing open packages as their bodies twisted and pummelled at each other. Santa's hat caught on a limb and I saw more of his ugly hair for a quick moment -- just thin, white tufts sprouting from random patches on his scalp, like he'd been losing it in clumps for years. His bulbous head was as lumpy as a rotten potato, and the flesh had that same greenish tinge as his arms. Its arms flailed as it snarled and struggled with my father. Dad threw an elbow under its chin and the thing's flesh made a mud-sliding sound in response, and I watched in terror as they rolled together against the tree. Needles showered down from above them as the glass ornaments rattled and the tree made reedy scratching sounds against our panelling. I heard a crack, and then the tree's top snapped off and tumbled down. A chain light went out, and it got a little darker in the room, as my father yanked the cord from the socket and appeared to be trying to lasso Santa's squirmy hands in front of him.

My mother suddenly slumped to the floor and her head audibly knocked against her fallen coffee cup. I rushed to her, and immediately realized she hadn't just fainted, but it was something much worse. Her body began convulsing on the floor as if someone else were controlling it. Blood was pouring from the place where her neck settled onto her torso... which was now all gore. "Santa" had torn the muscles of her shoulder right off the bone when I had turned away to call my dad. Now there was only torn meat and exposed bone, and blood—so much blood! — spreading and pooling on the floor to mix with her spilled coffee like some horrifying kind of creamer.

Stunned, mouth agape, I looked again toward the tree and saw that my father had somehow gotten his hands on the fallen tree top -- the hand-carved cross that we had always used as the crowning glory of our decorated tree -- and held it aloft over the fiendish imitation of Santa Claus. Its long bottom had been whittled to a sharp point, and frayed twine draped around my father's clutching fist. His other hand had the beast pinned to the floor by the neck, as it writhed beneath his strong grip. Its arms were lashed with a Christmas lights rope, and the green lines were actually steaming into his flesh—to my surprise—as were some of the broken ornaments that jounced around on his body. Then, in a flash, my dad brought the long end of the wooden cross down into the creature's chest. It burst right through his ribs, as easy as a pencil through paper, impaling all the way down to the cross' wide arms. There was more steam, and a black smoke that rose from his wound. The creature went silent and stiff, and it was only in that silent moment, when all I could hear was my father's heavy breathing, the hiss of the steam, and the blood trickling from my mother's throat, that I realized "Santa" had been growling like a wildcat most of the time they'd been wrestling.

The thing stayed stiff as my father let go of the cross and got to his feet, staring down at "not-Santa" and backing toward me. It was too ugly to look at anymore, so I just watched my father and when he met my eyes, I gestured my head towards Mom, hoping he'd know what to do.

But, when he saw my mother, he did not cry or move to save her. We both just stared at her and knew she was gone. He cursed and turned back to the creature and began kicking the dead body mercilessly, and the limbs flopped around like made of fabric. I finally dared to move, reaching over to tug on his swinging pant leg and begged him to stop.

He hugged me then -- perhaps the only time I've really had a long embrace from him -- and as he held me, he kept my head turned away from mother's body. I couldn't help but see the dead ragdoll of a goblin on the floor and found myself asking, "What happened to Santa?"

He crouched down to my level, blocking my view, and slid his fingers up both sides of my head -- gripping my temples a little too tightly -- and said: "I'm sorry you had to see that, Johnny. But the time has come for you to know the truth. There is no such thing as Santa."

"I know that," I said, frowning.

His grip tightened further. "There's no such thing as Santa," he repeated. "But, there *are* such things as vampires."

He took me by the hand then and walked me up the stairs as I looked down at the worst gift array I could ever imagine: torn boxes, bloodied bows, and the dead bodies of my slaughtered mother and this vile stranger -- the disgusting vampire dressed like a homeless Santa Claus with a bloody stake standing up lewdly between the big black buttons that ran crookedly down his coat.

In my bedroom, my dad lifted me up and placed me on my bed like I was much lighter -- and much younger -- than I was, and then he covered me up in my racecar-adorned blanket. He sat beside me, lit a cigarette, and told me more about the vampire. I just listened and nodded, trying to absorb everything that came out of his mouth, hanging on to the words while my head throbbed with the trauma of it all. "You're fourteen -- a teenager, for crying out loud -- so I guess you're old enough now to know the truth," he declared. But I wasn't sure I wanted to hear it.

Between careful puffs on his cigarette, he explained how holidays were literally "holy days," and that these special dates always threatened the vampires. Since Christmas was the holiest of them all, it was the time of the year when vampires were at their weakest. Holy water, garlic, crosses... all of the stuff I'd seen in movies and knew about from stories was only the beginning: during Christmas season, everything that had the whiff of Christianity about it had the power to harm the blood-drinking creatures as much as a crucifix. The vampires — who, to my surprise, apparently walked among us disguised, but in plain sight at night -- were extra careful about their hunt for humans during the holidays, like Thanksgiving and Easter., Since Christmas was so strong and widespread, they would usually hibernate like animals during late December, feeding only on the blood of any animals they may have kept in their crypts or near their coffins, as they cowardly hid from the religious celebrations of mankind.

He surveyed my face after all this, checking to see if I was comprehending it. Seeing the care in his eyes, the strength in his features, made me feel strong enough to ask him, "So why did this one come to our house?"

He turned from me and snuffed his cigarette into a glass of milk I'd left on my nightstand. "Because you summoned him," he stated matter of factly, as he stood up and turned out the light.

I frowned and twisted onto my side. Puzzled, I looked at his silhouette framed by the doorway. "I...what?"

He held the door for a moment. "I should have warned her about all this," he muttered, as if that had answered my question. "And maybe I should have told you sooner, too." He shook his head in the shadows. "You brought him here." He lit another cigarette and his eyeballs glimmered from the flame as he stood in the darkened doorway. "Because you wanted him to come. Vampires must be invited into a home before they can attack their prey. And they have learned that children want Santa Claus to come into their houses so much, it gives them free passage... so they pretend to be him." He puffed and blew smoke that looked black in the faint hallway light. All of this would have sounded ludicrous if his tone hadn't been so serious. "The desperate ones risk coming out during Christmas, lusting after the fresh blood of innocent children." His voice got a little softer then, but his pace picked up, so I could tell he was getting angry. "Kids like you. Kids who believe in Santa more than Jesus. Kids who believe in a man who only comes out in the dead of night and can fly in the air across the world to deliver his gifts. Well, vampires can do those things too... so they pose as him, and their disguises offer them some protection, even. But their gift is death."

It all sounded crazy, but I still believed him. The evidence was on my living room floor. I wanted to ask him how he possibly could know all of this.

But he shut the door before I had the chance. And his rantings tapered into crying as he slowly walked downstairs to tend to my mother.

Miraculously, I managed to fall asleep afterwards, while my mind searched all that I knew about vampires and Santa Claus, and contemplated a whole new realm of terrifying possibilities lurking in the world outside my bedroom. Later that night, I remember waking to the commotion of the police who he'd called to report Mother's murder. I never learned what he did with the vampire, but I'm pretty sure he just burned the body in the fireplace, because the whole house stank of the creature's meaty odour whenever we lit the fire all winter long. It is a smell I will never forget.

It is an odour I sense right now, even as my father crawls from under the tree, plastic pitcher in a fist from watering the tree, his pants nearly falling down to moon me completely as he scooches back.

"Okay, we're all set," he says as he stands up and admires our tree. Multicolored lights glimmer within the needles and branches of the spruce, casting a pomegranate blue tinge on the walls. It is a relaxing moment, but I can't let my guard down for long.

We are waiting for another 'Santa'...the tree is a beacon. My father has brought me into his secret life -- into the world of the holiday vampire hunter -- and our Christmassy living room belies the real purpose of our holiday decor: it is the equivalent of a rat trap, all set up to catch another one, if they dare to take the bait.

And I am that bait.

Dad looks around at the end tables and then pats his loose pants. "Dammit, I'm out of cigarettes," he remarked.

I shake my head. "Quit."

He frowns, pointlessly flicking a lighter. "Someday," he mutters, distractedly searching around the room in hope of a cigarette package. "Shit."

I look at my own packages under the tree. I don't anticipate opening them like I used to. Apparently, Mom had done all the gift shopping. Dad's gifts, aside from the obvious ones I'd begged for, were usually lame ones, like jeans jackets with logos on them I didn't wear, or toys that kids far younger than I was played with.

He stops his search for smokes to size me up. "I'm gonna go down the street and get a carton." He tilts his head. "You gonna be good if I'm gone for a moment? Remember what I told you about the... weapons?"

I don't want him to leave me alone, but I also don't want him to think I am a sissy now that I am a hunter just like he is. I gesture my chin at the ornaments and tree top and the other cross on the wall like I'm a tough guy. "I know, I know. I'm good to go."

He kisses the top of my head. "I'll make it quick."

After I hear him grab his coat and keys, I listen for the door to shut.

Then I sit in the comfy chair where my mother used to cuddle me, smelling of coffee and rubbing my hair. I miss her. I want the vampires to pay for taking her away from me.

With Dad gone, I realize that I am alone with all my presents. There is the big green box, with the funky "From Santa" label on it. It's so big this year, it doesn't quite fit under the tree, but stands against the nearby wall. I dimly wonder if Dad would have saved up enough to get me the remote-controlled monster truck I'd dropped hints about all year, or if he chose something last minute and practical again. I got up to do my ritual shaking of the box, and it was lighter than I'd expected. Maybe he was on to me and it was a trick box. I had to know. And he wasn't as good at checking these things as Mom once was. I carefully peeled back the paper and started to pry at the brown cardboard edges when I hear a muffled clumping noise to my left.

There are feet in the fireplace again. Only this time they aren't Santa's.

They're banana slippers. Mother's.

I am torn between racing to her for her loving embrace or grabbing a fistful of the garlic clove garland that father had wrapped the tree with. But it makes no difference, because in the time it takes for me to decide how to react, she has me locked in a trance with her beautiful eyes—turned alabaster white—and her face freakishly green. This is not my mother, but face looks so similar to it as she shakes her head and smiles and walks past me. I pray that my father returns in time to put a stop to whatever it is she plans to do with me.

She sits down in the recliner. She pats her lap. "Come, Johnny. Sit with me. I want to enjoy this."

She blinks, and I am let go of her trance.

"I'm not going anywhere," I say, as I get my balance and start looking for the best weapon to use on her.

She makes a tsk-tsk gesture and taps her lap again. "Now."

"No. You're not my mother. What are you going to do? Eat my face off?"

She grins, and her teeth are razors between her lips. "No, I am still your mother. And no, I will not eat your face off. That, I might do to your father. But you... no."

I eyeball the pan that Dad filled with water.

She keeps talking. "For you, I have brought a gift. A gift of everlasting life..."

I keep my eyes on the pan. The parched spruce has already slurped a lot of the fresh fill of water into its trunk. I know what I have to do. I dive and swing into the trunk and knock the tree down onto mother's lap.

I want to look away, but I can't. Our tree lands right into her chest and flames flare out from her torso as she grapples with the tree. She tries to fight back as her body sizzles and crisps and flops around under its weight, but the pain has her pinned down in the leather recliner, and she quickly weakens. The wood remains green and wet so it doesn't catch fire as my mother swiftly turns to cinder.

When it's over, I look over at Santa's gift box and don't care really what it holds anymore. Dad's gift to me -- and to my Mom, now finally freed from her torment -- was filling the pan with holy water, feeding our thirsty tree with it, all along.

The End

Christmas Curse
By
Weston Kincade

Ties... I hate ties. Have you ever tried tying one? They're insufferable, despicable... like trying to wrangle a four-foot boa constrictor and fasten it around your neck. What's worse is how it always seems to tangle in my beard. I'm proud of this beard: white, fluffy, with wispy curls. I've had it for millennia and don't plan on changing things now, not for a wedding or a funeral, as is the case today. Sigh... but when it's the funeral of your son... that's different.

The image in the mirror is one of shame, my rotund size framed in red and trimmed in arctic white. It isn't the red that's bothersome; the white, on the other hand... The room's decor is more to my liking; limestone walls, colorful ancient banners hanging high, and the red and black I was known for decorate the bedroom. I harrumph and turn from the mirror, flinging the reindeer tie against my belly. I hate having to kill—wait, revise that. It isn't so much the killing, but family is family.

My wife walks past, knitting a shirt for one of the elves. Her glasses slide down her nose as she peers at me beneath white curls. "Quit pouting, you old coot. This is your fault. Always is." She drifts out of the room.

"Thanks, doll," I mutter sarcastically.

From down the stone hallway, her voice echoes, "If you hadn't pissed in Telemachus' oats so often, you might have avoided the penance. Hell hath no scorn like a displeased child."

Sighing, my shoulders sink and I button the suit jacket. It isn't the penance Telemachus ordered. Very few even know of it today. It is the deaths. It wasn't a car wreck that took my son, like so many of our youths these days. At the North Pole, we don't have many of those. You're more likely to fall prey to a pack of arctic foxes or seals. Hell, you'd have a better chance dying from a hare than an automobile. But it wasn't any of those.

It was... me.

Stepping away from the mirror, I set my jaw and grab my glasses off the dresser. The walk out of the limestone castle is lined with colorful elves.

My sleigh waits at the entrance, a formality everyone has grown used to. Liam wasn't the first.

The ride over is short. When we reach the cemetery, further depression anchors my shoulders to the sleigh. Three lines of chiseled, framed graves cross the graveyard, the ice covering them transparent. Across the top, their names are etched into the surface. The one closest, a few spots short of the cemetery edge, stands open. Seawater sloshes in its depths. At the bottom, Liam's body lies unmoving.

Striding to the foot of his grave, I whisper the Prayer of the Ancients. With a wave of my gnarled staff, frosty snowflakes fall onto the water, freeze, and spread until Liam is encased. His face and body are still visible far below. Turning my gaze to the other graves, I am reminded of the hundreds like him, my progeny.

"Too many," I whisper, louder than I realize.

"Well, if you could keep your pants on long enough to finish your annual run, this wouldn't be such a problem," my wife nags.

"Penelope, give it a rest."

"Really?" she continues. "You don't think I have a say in it? They even have a song now, 'I Saw Mommy Kissing Santa Claus.'"

"Woman, stop!"

"Don't you dare take that tone with me," she retorts.

With distaste, I step into the sleigh and slide in next to her, ignoring whatever else she has to say. Before we begin home, a thunderous crack resonates through the icefield. The crack angles toward where I was standing, breaking the ice block encasing Liam. With a roar, the ice shatters and rains down.

What the...? I step cautiously back onto the ice, withered staff in hand.

Out of the grave, Liam leaps to his feet, broadsword in hand. "Hello, Father," he growls. "Miss me?" Dressed as before, his black torn shirt flutters and camo pants cover his legs.

"This... this is not possible. Hades! Where are you?" Hades, god of the underworld, must be behind this.

A chuckle echoes across the ice. A red-eyed arctic fox wanders out from behind a snowy crag. From it, a familiar voice echoes, "I do not have need of Hades. That lech could not distinguish his ass from a hole in the wall."

I peer at the animal and sneer, "You would dare meddle in my family affairs, Loki?" I glance around, searching for the source of power over the dead.

"Of course, I dare. It is what I do," Loki says with a flick of his white, fluffy tail. "And don't worry about Hel, Odysseus... or should I call you by the name you style yourself with now, St. Nicholas?"

"I didn't pick it, Loki. You know that. I see you are living up to yours, though. You couldn't have done this yourself."

A maniacal cackle rings across the landscape. "The rumors are what only simple minds understand. You should know that. I am no mere mortal. This was just a bit of sleight of hand, sliding one energy down a different path. Easy." He finishes with another laugh, then disappears beneath the snow.

"It doesn't matter how I've come here, Father," Liam interrupts. "We have unfinished business." Hefting his sword, Liam steps forward, his soaked boots and leathers freezing as they drip.

Frustrated, I stamp my staff down once, twice, three times. A funnel of dusted snowflakes and ice spins up around me, pressing against every ounce of fat and muscle within my body. The shift is painful, but not unendurable. At the magic's core, a flicker of icy flame beckons, reminiscent of days of old. I push it aside. I can lose myself in the icy hatred within its depths.

Liam yells, his rage spilling over as he raises his sword and charges. The whipping arctic winds sweep him up before his broadsword can pierce my skin, tossing him fifty yards into the air. Liam skitters over his ancestors' ice-chiseled graves. Propping himself on a knee, my son levers himself back to his feet.

The winds falter and a physical change settles onto my frame. As the currents dwindle, my old form is left, that of the namesake so many across the world know—Odysseus. Toned and muscular, magic even altered the garish suit better than any tailor could. But it still persists. Black boots now adorn my feet, and my beard and staff remain unchanged. For a silent regretful moment, I ache for the longsword of old. However, the penance dealt me requires balance. Telemachus' curse will never allow me to truly become whole. The staff, however, is not too dissimilar from the spears of my youth, and I have spent as many years wielding it. Twirling it with a smile, I level the butt on the ice at my feet. The boy deserves one final chance to change his mind.

"You do not have to do this, Liam," I say, hopeful he will see reason. "You've been given a second life. Take it and leave."

Liam glares. "My purpose is renewed. You left, and when I found you, you did nothing. Nothing! You wouldn't even lift a hand to save her."

"Liam, I can't. Look around you." Raising my hands and staff, I motion at the cemetery surrounding us. "These are your brothers and sisters, Liam. My sons and daughters from ancient Greece and Rome, Pompeii, even America."

After scanning his surroundings, these words enrage him more and he takes a threatening step forward.

"I don't say this as a threat, my son. They were disillusioned with the distorted tales or mortal man. Of Santa Claus. Some came seeking power, some with a childhood naivety I cannot give. They could never understand. Every wound taken here, I have suffered as well. You are my progeny, my children. You have the ability to do so much. I am held with invisible shackles. I can no more tread on the soil of mankind whenever I choose than become who I once was. Stop this infantile behaviour at once and become the man I know you to be."

Liam stutter-steps for a moment. The anger deep within his green eyes reflects thought and intelligence, before being overcome once more. "Rather than help, you killed me. Shoved that staff right through my chest."

He holds out his heavy sword in one hand, pointing directly at my weapon. There is no question whether he is my son. No mortal man could do such a thing so steadily, especially not one of his physical stature. While not sleight, nor musclebound, Liam has a frame that matches my own true form. Toned and muscular, he would no doubt be nimble and strong without my blood coursing through his veins. But as I saw in our fight the previous day, he is no mere mortal. Parts of me still ache from the exertion.

Grumbling, I say, "I have done what I must, my son. I cannot leave the confines of this place. Given that prison, I don't wish to die. What would you have me do?"

Liam laughs. "Prison? You take to the skies every year and visit house after house bearing gifts. And you expect me to think you're a prisoner? It's certainly a gilded cage you've crafted, and quite a tale you've spun. I'm done listening. Prepare yourself."

My eyes widen as he leaps, closing the distance between us in seconds, his sword thrust down to impale me. With a spin of my staff, I deflect his blade and leverage it into the icefield. "Stop, Liam. I don't wish to do this."

"You said that before, Father," he screams, pulling the half-sunk blade free. "I have been in battle. I'm a soldier. You cannot win. Not this time, Santa Claus."

Spinning away, I twirl the staff before us, sending an enormous gust of wind outward. This cannot happen, not on sacred ground. Surprised, Liam is thrown into the air, this time falling miles away. One step and a silent word carries me to his feet in an instant. Beneath Liam's body, a crater of cracked ice threads outward in jagged tendrils that stretch toward the sea. As much as it pains me to drag this fight out, I am happy to find him breathing.

Liam's eyes flutter open and he raises himself to a knee, testing the grip on his sword with one hand. "Father, end this. Our family needs you."

With sad, downcast eyes, I meet his gaze. "I can't. I know your mother's pain. Cancer will do that. It was worse when Hirtia came begging for help. She cried frozen tears. You see, she was from Pompeii, a lone survivor. She pleaded for my help. I could do nothing then, nor could I have helped had she come earlier." The memory of her standing before me in the hall, kneeling, is one of the most tragic memories I have. It eats at me at the mention of her name.

Anger fills Liam's eyes. I was prepared for him to retaliate with his weapon, but as the iron grip of his fingers encompass my neck, the reverie of the sad memory shatters. I can only stare.

"I don't want to kill you, Father."

"I do not wish to kill you either, Liam," I rasp. I consider the possibilities, but my sensibilities tarnish any retribution that comes to mind. Part of me aches for family, part wishes for death after so many years, but Penelope waits. I can't leave her behind.

Liam lifts me a foot from the ground. Our gazes never waver. "No matter what you've done or refuse to do, I just need what's mine. Mother is sick, wasting away. If you can't do anything, then I must. Your time is over."

"Do not do this," I intone. "Death is natural."

His fingers dig into my skin. "Not for us. Give me what's mine."

Liam's intent is clear. Imprisoned, there is no solution, no salvation for either of us. I honestly don't know if my death will give him the power he wants. I can't allow myself to die, but something stops me from raising a hand against this man—my son.

I glimpse a red-eyed fox dashing between craggy outcroppings and know the source. *Playing on my sense of guilt. That's a bit old fashioned, Loki.*

The frosty flame leaps from deep within. Only once have I ever dared touch it, and once was enough. However, the bloodthirsty desire of old tantalizes, so much so that I lick my lips in anticipation. This time I shove myself in, immersing myself in its glory. Icy tendrils course through my veins, dusting my skin with flakes of snow and frost. A scream echoes from outside my mental void. Unsure who it belongs to, I open my eyes. The world appears through a frosty film, but I clearly make out Liam cradling his hand. His entire forearm appears to have frozen.

"I told you to stop," I rumble, the words coming out harsher than I plan. "I am no gift-giving Santa. Not at heart. I told you, it is my prison. Your brother Telemachus cursed me at the bequest of his wife Circe. I am Odysseus, victor of the Trojan War, conqueror of the underworld, and ambassador of truth and vengeance. Now your time is at an end."

The words barely seem to register in Liam's pained eyes. Instead, he hefts his sword and charges. My staff twirls and maneuvers to meet it, each time resounding with metal on frozen wood as hard as steel. The battle rages, my motions automatic like I'm watching through a two-windowed television. Any remorse or guilt I feel does not factor into my motions. The ice beneath our feet tears apart with each heavy blow and impact. I thrust and Liam spins aside, landing his own blow across my thigh. Blood seeps into the red and white suit as my staff crashes down on his injured arm. He bellows and draws away. I stand waiting.

"Just give up, Father... St. Nicholas... whoever you are. I can do what you can't. Let me."

In the same gravelly voice, I reply, "That may be, but not today." I spin and level my staff at Loki's fox form sitting atop an icy mound. "And you need not meddle with things that don't concern you."

The fox cackles and Liam seizes the opportunity to thrust at my exposed back. Somehow aware, I spin and slam the staff across his chest. Liam is flung backward, skittering over the craggy surface until his body is consumed by a snowdrift. Beneath our feet, cracks spiderweb from where he landed. As I stride forward, Liam pulls himself out, scraped and battered.

The fight continues, each of us dodging, striking, and leveraging the other for an opening. The cracks beneath our feet widen, sea water rushing in, but I hardly notice aside from avoiding a misstep. Ducking a violent blow, I sidestep and swing. But something grips my foot, anchoring it to the ice. The staff goes wide and I'm thrown to my knees.

Liam grabs the staff with his frozen hand, relishing the surprise in my eyes. "My turn!" He twists it from my hands and steps back, gazing at the weapon with supreme victory.

"The magic is not in the weapon, my son," I say, struggling to my feet after freeing my boot.

The battle frenzy seems to have dissolved at the shock, leaving me somewhat unsteady. A glance at Loki's cocked head a few yards away answers my question though. He couldn't resist meddling, as is his nature.

"No, not entirely," Liam says. "But it's a start."

Swinging the staff upward, the blow cracks against my chin, sending me over the cracked ice and sliding toward open water. The frosty anger that consumed me moments before returns. My fingers dig into the ice until I come to a stop. I stand. Water laps at my boots, my red and white funeral suit tattered from Liam's blade and our icy surroundings. "Enough!"

Liam quirks an eyebrow as I begin grinding my hands together. An icy longsword grows out of it, inch by inch. "That's your answer?" he asks condescendingly, then shakes his head. Dropping his own sword, he hefts the staff over his head and shouts, "I command the power of the ancients, power over St. Nicholas, Odysseus, and whatever names he has adopted. Imbue me!"

To my surprise, the frosty light I both detest and grew to love streaks down on Liam. The familiar frosty whirlwind I used just minutes ago surrounds him. From its depths steps an enlarged Liam with blue eyes that mimic my own. Now he is muscle-bound, physically enhanced. It is the first thing any warrior seeks out—physical power. It will take years for him to realize his folly. A subtle smile tweaks the edge of my lips, but before I can say anything, a bloodcurdling scream echoes from my snow-covered castle miles away.

Penelope? "No!" I scream.

Liam chortles. "Looks like there's more to this than you thought, Father."

I mutter the small word that has always commanded my magic, "*Oikos.*" Nothing happens. I still stand in front of both men. Astonished, a second later I feel the loss as Penelope disintegrates. "What have you done?" I demand.

Liam smiles, but there is confusion within his gaze. He clearly doesn't know. I turn my attention to Loki, still in his arctic fox form.

"What? Why are you looking at me?" he asks.

"You did this," I growl.

"Did what?"

"You killed Penelope."

"What?" Loki retorts, sounding offended. "I did no such thing. You did."

"The hell I did."

"Odysseus, she was bound to you and your winter magic. Without it, she would have died long ago. The only reason you're still alive is your stubborn ego and innate magic, but that isn't enough to keep her for all eternity."

An insane rage takes hold with more strength than any magic. "Bring her back!"

"Sorry, too late. Besides, wasn't it you who said death is natural?"

Grief and hatred bleed together, and I charge Loki. Before I make it two steps, a thunderous blow rings through the icefield as Liam swings the staff down on the fissure. The crack separating us heaves and the corner of the continent breaks off, rolling. Loki and Liam disappear from view, replaced by sky. My steps take me vertical and soon I'm climbing, grabbing for handholds, pushing forward.

Kill. Kill. Kill, punctuates my thoughts. There is nothing left, no one alive. Only murderers. And their blood is the only way to satiate this thirst. A hunger I haven't felt in millennia.

The world continues to spin before I catch sight of them. My footing gives way. I slip, then fall, until the icy embrace of frigid waters hits me like a sledgehammer. My breath escapes. The cold seeps in, scalding every sensation. My skin freezes like never before and thought slows. Through the turbid water, I watch the tumbling iceberg descend overhead. It crashes down, slamming into me and forcing me deeper. As the world slows and darkness floods in, the final voices I hear are cackles of victory... then one other.

A voice I haven't heard since Telemachus' horrible edict echoes through my mind. "The penance of Santa Claus lives on."

The End

Weihnachtstag
By
Mark Fleming

Christmas Eve, 1914

When the explosion reverberates along the tunnel I roll over, heart hammering. Soil rains in clumps, extinguishing candles; duckboards shudder and split. I grind my fists into the ground, every sinew coiled as I wait for each rumble to be the one that buries us beneath tons of mud. When silence finally falls I spit black filth from my throat and stare into darkness.

My coughs are echoed sporadically. Behind me there is a spark. A candle flickers through the curtains of dust. Deacon is first to make his voice heard, as always. "Fucking artillery," he growls, in-between hacking, "couldn't hit the side of Wipers Cathedral with a twelve-inch, the fucking donkeys."

Further down the chamber more wicks are lit. Shapes resembling bodies in shallow graves judder to life as sappers shake themselves free of muck. Lieutenant Hamilton stoops forward, eyes darting. "Enough, Deacon. Anyone hurt?" A muted chorus agrees the only damage seems to have been to nerves. "As you say, Deacon, fucking artillery. They were supposed to hit a thousand feet further ahead. They can aim their howitzers, but they can't read their maps. Corporal Foster." He glances over at me. "That *is* you Foster?"

"Sir?"

"You look like one of the Froggie colonials."

"I think we probably all do, sir."

His teeth flash against his sooty features. "Get your section forward, Foster. After those fireworks there'll be an infantry attack, keeping Fritz off the scent of this surprise we're cooking for them down here. This tunnel is to be finished over the weekend. It'll be a belated Christmas present for the brass hats."

"Number two section, you heard the officer," I snap, "up to the face again. Get fucking digging."

* * *

I clutch my Princess Mary box, the metal tin engraved with the young princess's profile, surrounded by a laurel wreath. Inside is a miniature treasure trove: a bar of chocolate, cigarettes, tobacco. There's also a postcard with Queen Mary smiling, and a copy of King George V's greeting to his loyal troops.

"May God protect you and bring you safely home," Deacon reads his aloud, his normally uncouth tones dripping with irony. "I'm sure Georgie boy will be thinking about each and every one of us when he tucks into a nice fucking fat turkey in Buck House this afternoon."

"Enough, Deacon," I reprimand. "If you're not happy with your Royal Family's Christmas gifts, feel free to divvy them out to the rest of us."

For once Deacon shuts up, although it's impossible to tell whether his dirt-caked features are betraying remorse or resentment.

"God bless His Majesty, is what I say," adds

Watson, a 15 year-old from Haddington who lied about his age so he could enlist.

"And Merry Christmas to him and his Missus, too," I add, gnawing a corner of chocolate, holding it in my mouth, my tongue roving around the slowly dissolving chunk. After the normal breakfast ration of corned beef and army biscuits, the sweet textures are magical. For moments the only sounds are ungainly biting and chewing. Fags are sparked and lung-rattling coughs add to the human cacophony. After a while these subside. I study the dirt ingrained beneath my nails. Deacon hacks loudly and spits.

"Fuck sake, Deacon," I remark.

"Sorry, Corp. Fucking frog in my throat."

"Isn't that something you dream about, Deacon? Having a Frog in your throat," MacKay goads him. Sniggering, Deacon balls his chocolate's paper wrapping and launches it at him.

"One of their great big fucking Algerian Zouaves," adds MacKay, "with his red pants at his ankles?"

The others guffaw, but Deacon's grin vanishes and he fixes me with a cold stare.

"Take a joke, Deacon."

For a while he says nothing, keeps me targeted.

"Well?"

"*Listen*, Corp … can't you hear it?"

Perhaps having spent so many hours grafting in utter silence my hearing is playing tricks on me, because I can imagine singing. The more I concentrate, the clearer this becomes. "What the fuck is *that*?"

Presently Sergeant McIntosh pokes his head into the dugout. "Corporal Foster?"

"Sir?"

"The Lieutenant says you've all to come and look at this."

Cigarettes poked into the corners of our mouths, we skulk out into the trench. The first thing I notice is the sunrise warming the skies over the

Hun lines. Lieutenant Hamilton is half-way up a ladder, craning into 'No Man's Land.' "You've never seen anything like this, lads."

He clambers back down and hands me the periscope. I climb up and peer through. At first I can't make sense of it. For so many months there's been nothing but a quagmire ahead, pockmarked with foxholes, interspersed with charred tree stumps and criss-crossed with mile-upon-mile of barbed wire. The Huns have placed lanterns along their front line, glowing eerily through the swirling dawn mists. But the most inexplicable aspect is the sound. Across the deathly stillness of those three hundred yards where men are shredded by metal, day upon day, week upon week, a choir is in full voice. *"Stille Nacht... Heilige Nacht..."* I remember Elizabeth and I singing our version to our son Tom last Christmas. A tear trickles down my cheek.

Someone is tugging at the seam of my trousers. "Hurry up, Corp, let me see."

At that moment a baritone voice breaks off from his accompaniment, carrying across the desolated countryside. *"Good morning, Englishmen! Merry Christmas! You no shoot. We no*

550

shoot."

Deacon fills his lungs, stares into the slate grey skies and bawls: *"Merry Christmas, Fritz!"*

* * *

I'm huffing and puffing over the rutted ground, gasping with the unfamiliar exertion but grinning ear-to-ear. Each lungful dispersing in a white cloud is a relief from the dust I'll be inhaling when my shift starts. I gaze at the uniforms — khaki and grey or wrapped in mufflers or encrusted with so much filth it's impossible to identify the tunic colour.

When the muddy football trundles past Watson's despairing hands, I blow the whistle. I jab a thumb towards the Huns in the background who are cheering and playfully goading the Tommies as if they've just entered Paris.

Someone throws the ball towards me. I march to the centre spot; I marked this earlier with a discarded boot, checking there wasn't a ragged foot inside. I peer round the expectant players, coiling for action as if they're awaiting the whistle-blow that will send them up the ladders for a push. Instead I lift the whistle to my lips, toss the ball into the air, then give a sharp blast.

A German wins the ball and sweeps it to the right. Deacon slides in to tackle, relishing the excuse to go for an enemy's legs, but sportingly helping his victim to his feet again. There are curses in various dialects when the ball lodges in a puddle and men jostle, neither side gaining purchase; a stalemate that could be a metaphor for what has been happening between the rival armies for so long. My mind dwells on how surreal this all is.

It started with their carol singing. Our whole line joined in, the 16th Irish and 36th Ulster Divisions adding thousands of strident Irish voices to our right, then the Froggies far to our left. Eventually sentries had climbed over their respective parapets, white rags brandished, meeting around the point where this match kicked off 20 minutes ago; shaking hands, exchanging rations and fags, joking. Hamilton was first to clamber up from our trench and we trailed him into

'No Man's Land', as the infantry follow their officers over the top in less amenable circumstances. We made our way towards men it has been our duty to kill these past months; grasping hands, embracing, laughing at faltering attempts to chatter in broken English and German. The one thing I've missed since being posted on the front line, or rather *under* it, is birdsong. But hearing carols and then laughter rippling over this destroyed landscape has made Christmas Day so far from loved ones easier to bear.

When the Huns produced a football, Hamilton suggested I referee. Since there's nothing at stake here – apart from amassing as much extra time as possible to prolong the inevitable moment when we must face in opposite directions to return to our trenches – my role is merely to restore some order every time the ball gets mired. I need to keep a watchful eye on Deacon; and the other side's loose cannon, a ruddy-haired German sergeant who is as free with his elbows as he undoubtedly is with his bayonet.

At times the match threatens to turn into one of those traditional football games they still play in rural England, where rival villagers meet in a similarly muddy field and form a mass scrum for hours, the ball eventually forgotten in a melee that is less a sport and more a re-enactment of Naseby. So my main function is blowing my whistle to signal the players to step aside whenever the football gets trapped.

I'm already composing the letter I'll send home, although I appreciate the censors will most likely remove all mention of a truce. If any of us ever make it back again, we can make this a Christmas story to be told every year: how a team representing the House of Saxe-Coburg faced the Second Royal Saxon Corps.

One of the Huns I was speaking to, a bespectacled youth named Uwe, who abandoned university to enlist, mentioned how ironic it was that the King and Kaiser are first cousins; that they should've agreed to fight a duel, right here in the middle of 'No Man's Land', to decide the outcome of this war.

I race after a wiry young Saxon who is running rings around our defense, a clay pipe lodged in his mouth. In a war where every day brings fresh ironies, Christmas on the Western Front has trumped them all.

* * *

We crawled into our underground lair late in the afternoon, just as troops were starting to drift back to their respective positions. The remaining hours of Christmas Day, 1914, are spent remorselessly boring into the earth. Hamilton informed us there's to be an artillery barrage at dawn. After the last one on Christmas Eve, a Black Watch battalion went over the top. Half of them made it back. That's why there were hundreds of spare Princess Mary tins to distribute further up the line. But as Lieutenant Hamilton stated, it was important Fritz was made to believe the shells were a creeping barrage covering another push. The aim is to make their sentries jittery, focused on the British trenches ahead... right up to the moment the mines are detonated beneath their noses.

The blisters in my joints are raw from clay-kicking. Lying on the plank, my wrists ache from twisting my spade into the wall. To maintain silence, I have to use my fingers to painstakingly prise out shards of chalk, passing them to Deacon and MacKay to bag. In my peripheral vision I notice Hamilton's shadow studying the brass watch he keeps tugging out and poking back into his tunic. That object is our only connection with the world so far above us; the relentless motion of its tiny hands compelling us nearer our target, measuring these hours burrowing beneath Belgium. By tomorrow, when my mother and sisters will be clocking-in at the munitions factory in Gretna, we should have reached our own destination. The infantry lads, the 'beasts of burden', will have shifted tons of earth back down the tunnel and the engineers will have wired up enough explosives to alter the geography of Messines Ridge forever.

The operation keeps grinding to a halt when Hamilton thinks he hears something. The further we bore, the more frequent these interruptions become. I wonder if the thinning air is playing tricks on his mind? But, as I thrust the spade again, there's a noise ahead of us — a muffled cry. I catch Hamilton's bulging eyes moments before he hisses,

"Stop, Foster!"

I freeze. Hamilton crawls beside me and pokes the geophone tips into his ears, touching the device against the base of the wall. In the light pool, I notice his lips working, as if in prayer. He stabs a thumb downwards. Despite the cramped conditions, everyone moves aside, and there is a spatter of licked fingers snuffing out each tiny flame.

Deacon shuffles forwards with the camouflet pinned to its long iron rod. As he squirms by me, I clamber from the plank and move backwards. I press myself into the wall, my grip tightening around my shovel. Now I hear voices, just yards ahead, below our level. They sound as if they are arguing, their gruff tones snapping, hysterical almost; wild behavior considering stealth is all that stands between the bastards sharing this stale, subterranean air and being blasted to fragments of meat. I hear earth shifting from the floor, as if a fat mole is burrowing closer, a trickle at first, then a deluge. Voices amplify, before stopping dead. A candle winks as the nearest miner excavates a doorway up into our dimension. His white eyes meet Deacon's.

"Sie kommen! Sie kommen!" Fixating on Deacon's khaki uniform, the German lunges into the folds of his tunic. Just as I realise he is tugging out a white rag, Deacon thrusts his charge into the fissure. I wait for the pulverising explosion, the screams, the magnified stench of blood. But the only sound is Deacon cursing, gasping. The flickering light reveals the nearest enemy scrambling through the gap. He lunges for the pole. For desperate seconds the two men writhe on our tunnel floor, like a parody of lovers. During the melee the German shoves the rag into Deacon's face.

"Stopp! Bitte! Die teufel! Sie kommen!"

Another struggles through, clutching a candle, shrieking incomprehensibly. Snapping out of shock, I swing the spade. The candle falls from his grasp. Blood flecks the backs of my hands.

"A light! Need a fucking light!" screeches Deacon. Candles flare behind the melee, spotlighting Deacon as he delves into his belt, then lunges his bayonet into the Hun's neck. When he slumps forward Deacon snatches the white rag and slides his blade through it. "Fucking charge didn't work."

"Just two?" I gasp, staring into the hole.

Deacon slithers forwards, blade before him. "Candle," he snaps.

MacKay materialises from the gloom, pawing into the corpse's belt. "No grenades? Bastard. Theirs are so much easier to throw." He passes a candle to Deacon.

"He did have a white flag, though," I murmur. As the light flickering over his blank features I squint. When I visualise him sucking on a pipe I realise it's the lad who was scoring so many goals a matter of hours ago.

MacKay sees only the grey uniform and spits into the staring face. "Fuck him."

Deacon leans down, shining the candle into the cavity before glancing back. "I can see into their tunnel for about fifty yards, sir. There's the Hun Foster clobbered lying down there, seems to be a fucking goner, like... can't see any more."

The lieutenant squirms forwards, revolver poised as he glares through the hole. I poke the shovel, excavating more soil. The candlelight flickers over sacks and piles of earth.

"If we're quick enough we could use their tunnel to get right under their lines," the lieutenant continues. "Only thing is, looks to have been a lot of caving in after the bombardment. I'm going to do a quick assessment of the damage."

"We'll cover you, sir."

"Yes. Deacon and you, with me, the rest of you wait here. MacKay, if we get over-run in there, seal this point. We can't give the Huns an open invite to our trenches … I suspect the Christmas spirit has died out. Deacon, pass me the light."

The lieutenant scrambles down into the German shaft and we follow. As we pace cautiously along, the light casts a menacing reflection of Deacon's bayonet, while I imagine my shovel is a Viking axe. The first thing that strikes me is the flooding on the enemy level. Dark puddles sluice below their duckboards. Twenty or so feet further an enormous boulder has dislodged from the ceiling and crashed into the planks.

"If our guns had undershot by a fraction yesterday, our tunnel might've been as badly damaged," Hamilton remarks. "Just be careful, lads. From here on, the whole construction is unstable."

I fire Deacon a nervous look but his expression is staring grimly ahead. I switch my attention to the officer, watching him ease around this obstacle. I notice his shocked reaction when he reaches the other side. The lieutenant doubles up, retching into the quagmire. Deacon clambers next to him, his expression foreboding. I join them and gaze down at the horror revealed by the fitful flame. A miner's legs have been crushed beneath the rock. But the portion of the corpse above the impact has been devoured by rats, right to the skeleton, the flayed bones betraying myriad teeth marks.

"I've seen more dead bodies than I care to tally," Hamilton states, drawing his cuff over his chin, "but I'll never get used to it."

"We're used to bayonet wounds, or revolver fire, aren't we, sir?" Deacon sympathises. "Grappling in the dark. Hand to hand. Last thing we wants to come across is a pack of fucking starving rats."

My knuckles whiten around the shovel while I scan the walls and ceiling for beady eyes. Hamilton appears distracted. He steps away from the mutilated German and paces further down, handgun sweeping from side to side. Deacon matches his faltering footsteps along the duckboards. Thirty yards on, the tunnel halts, swallowed by an avalanche of earth. Massive deposits of chalk and stone form an impenetrable barrier.

"Well this has fucking torn it," Hamilton growls. "Our artillery hadn't even planned on obliterating a German counter mine. But they sure as Hell have put the kibosh on our little scheme, haven't they, lads? This landslide can't have happened during the barrage if there were Huns *this* side of it."

"One of the two that bought it. I recognised him from the truce."

Hamilton nods. "Most likely a lot of large rocks got dislodged during the fireworks... but this part of the unstable ceiling collapsed recently."

I banish the thought of tons of Earth shifting at any moment. "Those two Huns," I observe, "couldn't dig their way back to their own lines. If they wanted to avoid being rat fodder their only option was to keep burrowing westwards."

Deacon glances warily around the floor, bayonet poised. "Then they'd have to work their way up into No Man's Land," he adds, "where our snipers would pick them off. Eaten alive or a fucking bullet to the head? I'd have gone with the sniper option, too."

Hamilton lifts the candle. "I feel a draft. It's coming from there." The flame plays over bulging sacks stacked against the wall, quivering nearer the top of this pile. The lieutenant pulls an earth-laden bag aside and peers through. "It's another tunnel."

"It looks as if they tried blocking it," Deacon says. "Maybe that was where the fucking rats came from, like?"

"We'll need to see where it goes, Deacon."

"Maybe the bastards had detected our

tunnel?" I wonder. "They were building the counter mine, but also this second one, to outflank us?"

"Let's unblock it and see." Hamilton pokes the candle onto a ledge.

"Shall I call the rest of the section, sir?"

"No, Foster." Hamilton peers through the fissure, his harsh whisper carrying. "I've told MacKay what to do if Fritz shows. There are more camouflets." He begins working at the sacks, his slender, public schoolboy arms tugging them aside. Deacon and myself pitch in, heaving them free, the draught bringing a terrible stench. When the bags are shifted, Hamilton brandishes the candle again. We gaze into this tunnel in astonishment. Wider than the German shaft, it is clearly much older, its walls defined by intricate but crumbling brickwork. The temperature emanating from the murk seems even icier.

"What the fuck?" mumbles Deacon, stepping into the aperture.

Hamilton foists the candle at him. "Take it, Deacon. What do you see?"

"It runs for... about fifty, sixty feet, like, then starts curving... starts running downhill, too."

"What d'you think, sir?" I ask. "Ruins exposed by the bombardment? Roman or something?"

"I'd say more likely Holy Roman."

"Sir?"

"This ... this is fucking *unbelievable* ... this must be the remains of Touraille Castle."

"What, sir?"

"Before I signed up for this mess, Foster, I was studying Medieval History, at Edinburgh University. There was a castle outside Touraille, at the time of the Holy Roman Empire. See the slits along these walls? They were firing points for archers, then later on, they would have been used by musketeers. This is more of a *passageway* than a tunnel... it would've been part of the castle's outer defenses."

I study the layers of bricks stretching off into the twisting shadows. "When exactly, sir? How old was the castle?"

"It was destroyed in the early seventeenth century, Foster."

Hamilton purses his lips when we reach the curve in the tunnel. The sound of rushing water becomes prominent as we shuffle around the bend. The lieutenant edges further, then halts. "Fucking Hell."

Deacon and I come alongside, gawking at the unexpected panorama. The walkway disappears into a vast cavern. The meager light hints at a decaying structure looming in the shadows: buttresses and ramparts have buckled under the weight of tons of earth.

"How come the ruins are buried like this, so far underground?" I ask. "What happened to this castle, sir?"

"It's actually a terrible story, Foster. You're from Edinburgh, aren't you?"

"Aye, sir."

"You've heard of Mary King's Close?"

"I have, sir. A whole street, with shops and

blocks of flats, was quarantined at the time of the Black Death. People, livestock, the lot, were just sealed in and left to die. They say their houses are still there, hundreds of feet below the High Street, just as they were, with the skeletons of the plague victims."

"Something similar happened right here, Foster, where we are now. During the Thirty Years War."

"Thirty Years War?" my incredulous whisper carries along the dank cavern.

"Yes, Foster. That war, fought three hundred years ago was, in some respects, a precursor to this war."

"Sir?"

"It started as a civil war, between Protestant and Catholic states within the Holy Roman Empire. But it soon drew in half of Europe. On one side, Sweden, Denmark, Saxony, Bohemia, the Dutch, England, Scotland; on the other, the Holy Roman Empire, the Spanish, Austria, Hungary. The Empire covered most of what is now Germany. But it was a pitiless war. Regular armies and mercenaries rampaged the length of Europe. They plundered at will, taking whatever they wanted from any villages that happened to be in their paths. They also brought disease with them. Some of the German states lost over a quarter of their whole populations."

"Hopefully that's how this is all going to go, like," Deacon chimes in.

"No, Deacon. It was a fucking *brutal* war to be waged on civilians like that." Poking his fingers into an arrow slit, he pauses. I can see he's grateful for this respite from the incessant tunneling and listening for counter mining. After so many weeks of living on our nerves, sharing this knowledge is a release. Despite his tender years, the lads all look up to Hamilton. Like most of the junior officers, his courage is unquestionable. We also appreciate he volunteered to join a mole unit rather than regular infantry. This has put him on a particular pedestal. The rest of the men were sappers and railway tunnelers before the war, making this less of a transition. Similarly to my new friend, Uwe, Hamilton abandoned his studies when duty called.

"How did this castle feature in the war?" I query, watching the shadows dance along the ancient bricks.

"The fighting was driven by religious fanaticism, Foster. There was certainly no Christmas spirit in those days, no truces. There were pogroms, whole populations uprooted from villages and towns, massacred. Amidst the battles, the butchery of civilians, the endless looting, burning and rape, witch hunts were rampant."

"Witch hunts?"

"Yes, Foster. Touraille Castle was surrounded during the conflict. Where we are now, Belgium, was part of the United Provinces of the Netherlands. Mercenaries fighting for the Hapsburgs, the Austro-Hungarians, laid siege. They over-ran the stronghold. Hundreds of civilians had taken refuge beyond these walls, hiding in the castle dungeons. They were condemned as heretics and witches, en masse. The Hapsburg soldiers dynamited the castle walls, then spent the following weeks burying the remains until there was no evidence that a castle had ever been there."

"Them fucking Austro-Hungarians have a lot to answer for, haven't they?" Deacon remarks, spitting into the gloom. "Their fallout with Serbia has drawn in half of Europe again."

Somewhere in the murk of this subterranean ruin, a voice carries. Although the words are garbled, they are German. We react, clenching weapons.

"There are Huns along this section," Hamilton snaps. "We'll need reinforcements, after all. Foster, back to our tunnel, rouse the others. Deacon, we'll stall here. If any Huns appear, we'll give them the customary British Engineers' welcome. Take the light, Foster."

I sprint back to the main shaft, heart pounding. Behind, I can make out more German; several voices crying out — silencing abruptly. I stall, wondering if their agitation indicates my comrades have ambushed them, but the officer has given me a direct order. I round the bend. The point where this passage adjoins what was the German counter mine, is directly ahead. Except sacks have been piled high across the gap again. I halt in my tracks, the candlelight flickering over this nonsensical blockage. I squint, crouching to the nearest bags. Where they have been manhandled into position, there are bloodied handprints all over them. The pool of light bathing the water at my feet catches my attention. I hold the candle closer. It is not floodwater at all. The floor is awash with blood.

I jam the candle into a point on the wall to my right. Bowing to the bloodstained sacks, I begin lifting them clear. Laden as they are with refuse from the German sapping, perspiration drenches my tunic. When I heave sacks out from the bottom of the pile, the top of the pile begins receding from the ceiling. I finally judge I have created enough space to wriggle through. I grasp the candle again and squirm towards the crack. But just as I'm clambering up towards it, further sacks appear.

"What the fuck?" I punch at the barrier, but someone is pressing the sacks in place. *"You Hun bastards!"*

Shovel poised, I heave at the closest sack with my free hand. One hundred feet below the surface of the world, a desperate tug-of-war ensues. Eventually, I manage to prise it free from the Fritz's grip. The candlelight exposes a momentary silhouette: eyes glaring malevolently towards me. I get the impression of two soldiers, their faces twisted, rat-like, accompanied by a rank odour. Then a hand flashes through the gap, quicker than a snake strike, its fingernails sharp as talons. They rake across the back of my hand, drawing blood. The shovel falls from my grip. The pile of sacks part like a ruptured dam. I get the impression of figures barging through but I tumble backwards into the ancient passageway. The light vanishes and my head cracks against the ground.

* * *

I become aware of my aching skull and, as consciousness creeps back, the agony rises. I feel blood caked to my face. My eyes waver through darkness, catching a blue glow. Calcite deposits in the cavern's ceiling cast a ghostly hue, reflected by a pool of water below. Trying to move induces further pain. Something is restraining my stiff limbs. My wrists and ankles are bound by rusting chains that converge on a metal pin riveted to the wall. As my vision gathers strength, darker shapes lodged further inside this chamber begin to cohere. There are many others here, all tangled into paralysis, like flies in a web. The last of my senses to return is smell, and, as my eyes dance feverishly, the fetid aroma makes me retch.

Even with the sparse illumination, I recognise some of the prisoners shackled to the rusting rings are actually defiled corpses. The one immediately to my right has had most of its entrails clawed out of its shattered ribs.

"Foster?"

I recognise the lieutenant's thin voice in the gloom. "Sir?" The chains check my attempts to swivel towards him.

"Did you raise the alarm, Foster?"

"There were Huns in the tunnel. They blocked the way."

"Deacon and I were attacked. Didn't see them coming until they were all around us. They dragged us further into the castle ruins, threw us over the edge into this dungeon."

"Who are these other prisoners?" As my eyes grow accustomed, I count over a dozen tethered silhouettes.

"German miners, Foster."

"Germans? Who has captured us all? Has there been a mutiny on the Hun side? Where the fuck are we?"

"We're in Hell, Foster."

"Hell?"

"Hell."

"Where's Deacon?"

"His neck snapped when he was thrown down here. They took his corpse away."

"*Who* did, sir?"

"Remember how I asked you about Mary King's Close?"

"Sir?" Again, I try facing him, but the shackles restrict my movement. There is a manic edge to the lieutenant's voice. I've heard it so many times with the lads on the verge of shell shock, the disciplined calm they use to try and mask the fact they are sinking into despair. "What do you mean, sir?"

Movement below distracts me. Ripples are breaking the serene pool, as if water has dripped from stalactites. But there are shapes slithering just beneath the surface, like large fish.

"*Sie kommen! Die teufel!*" a hysterical German cries from the murk. Gazing in that direction I see a prisoner squirming, his limbs twitching for feeble inches within their constraints. His panicked voice lapses into feeble wails.

"What did that Hun say, sir? When the Huns breached our tunnel, that was what they were shouting at us."

"He said the devils are coming."

"Devils?" I am drawn to the pond. A head rises from shimmering bubbles, closely followed by another. Their hair is long and matted, and the liquid that runs down the lank strands is glutinous. They have emerged from a pool of blood. A slender arm breaks the surface, its spindly digits reaching towards the chamber walls. Shadows obscure the figure but the hand grasping the rock face seems unnaturally strong as it heaves the man upwards. He launches himself up the cavern with cat-like stealth, then vanishes from view. When I search I can see no sign of his companion. Someone screams. I gaze upwards. Reflected by the water's shimmering waves I can see eyes staring down.

"Who are you?" I shriek. My voice echoes in the gloom and when I look into the man's face, I can make out someone else, to his right. I squint, but just as I focus on a naked, hairless frame, he is gone. Scree loosens as the figures leap to another outcrop, spraying the bloody basin. Silence envelopes the prison, broken by whimpering from several directions. I peer back to the water. More shapes are swirling around, paddling to the surface. Then I hear a body scrambling closer. I try to turn but the rusting metal is keeping me restrained.

"Don't look at them, Foster," the lieutenant pleads, voice quavering.

"What?" My attention flits between the pond, and whoever has clambered onto the wall behind me. The stench is overpowering. The breathing rattles like a gassing casualty. Dank air whistles through nostrils.

"This is our fate, Foster, for burrowing into Hell." Hamilton's unhinged voice tapers into a despairing cackle, before he gibbers on: "When those witches were sealed in, Foster, they fucking *survived*... they carried on living — down here. They kept fucking *breeding*, in the darkness, shut off from the world above. Kept alive by air filtering through cracks — for all those years and years, breeding, and *inbreeding*. Inbreeding for food, Foster, *cannibalising* each other to survive, and producing hideous children and grandchildren for generations, until our fucking howitzers opened the door from their world to ours — *we opened the doors to Hell!*"

Claws dig into my shoulder. I gasp as the man heaves me towards him, twisting the chains until they are burning my skin and my gasps echo around this tomb. The face is now feet away. Bathed by the blue glow it scarcely looks human, its sagging checks and pouting lips resembling a fish. Another face materializes just beyond. I think the shadows are deceiving me. They seem to share one body, the torso misshapen and riddled with festering sores, its limbs wiry, but incredibly strong. The smaller head is a deformed parody of its neighbour, a black tongue flicking over its lips, venal eyes blazing above the point where it juts from the shoulders. As it draws me inexorably closer, I fixate on the razor-sharp teeth in the Siamese twin's mouths. I am aware of splashing, of an entire brood of crooked figures emerging from the gore to scramble up the dungeon walls before choosing a prisoner to home in on.

"They want a fresh bloodline!" Hamilton shrieks hysterically. "Look, Foster! These ones all have cunts. They want us to *mate* with them, Foster— before they *feast* on us. *Ha ha ha ha ha ha ha ...*"

When the thing draws its mouth towards mine, its putrid halitosis makes my eyes stream and bile explodes from my guts. Fighting for breath, I feel spindly fingers grasping at my groin, while the twin's tongue slithers around my neck.

I picture Elizabeth rocking Tom by the Christmas tree, singing "Silent Night." I focus on Hamilton's delirious laughter, allowing it to fill my head. But most of all I wish I was an infantryman, waiting for the whistle, ready to march towards the machine guns.

The End

Kevin J. Kennedy Presents

Secret Santa
By
Veronica Smith

It's no secret. I don't do Christmas.

It's not that I'm anti-religious, although I don't go to church. It's not that I hate all the decorations and Christmas music, but I am sick of it already, with still over a week to go. I have no family so I have no need to decorate a tree or wrap gifts. It's just me and has been since this upcoming Christmas for twenty-five years. At forty years old, I'm not a grumpy old man. I just have my reasons.

So when I got the 'Secret Santa' email at work asking me to participate, I politely declined, as I do every year. You'd think they'd stop asking me by now. I've been with this firm for over ten years and everyone knows how I feel about it. Oh, other holidays are okay. Thanksgiving is great. I usually go to one of those massive Thanksgiving buffets at a restaurant or hotel. They're never crowded and the food is amazing, huge selections of everything. I don't even eat turkey; I like to try something new every year. This year was escargot, and it was a lot tastier than I thought it would be. I go alone, as I always do. I'm happy in my solitude and I'm too old to change that now.

Yeah, holidays are generally okay. Just not Christmas. Especially this Christmas.

Anyway, I replied back to the email and I *was* nice about it.

December 20th

I saw a small wrapped present on my desk when I came in this morning.

To Zach from Your Secret Santa

I searched back through my emails and replied again to the Secret Santa request that I really did not want to participate. This time I may have been a little rude. Standing up, I peered over the wall of my cubicle and looked around to see if anyone was watching me. Nothing suspicious up there so I plopped my ass back down in my chair and stared at the present.

It wasn't big, less than four by four inches and wrapped in shiny red paper with a black and red bow. Odd choice of color for a bow at Christmastime. I poked at the box with my finger as if I expected it to explode. I picked it up and shook it like a small child testing packages under the tree, as if I could figure it out by the sound. Just a light *thunk* that could be anything.

I pulled the bow off, one of those self-adhesive kinds, and tossed it aside where it stuck to my cubicle wall. It was wrapped very nice, like those professional wrappers at some expensive store in the mall. I carefully pulled it apart at the taped edges. When I was a child I never just ripped into a present, I've always tried to take the paper off in one piece. My mother used to joke that she could reuse the paper the next year for presents for other people. Other people, because she didn't want to give away the Santa myth back then. I removed the paper and carefully folded it up. I opened up the simple white box and took out the item wrapped in tissue paper. As soon as the prize was visible, I dropped it on my desk. It landed on its side and stared at me. I backed up my chair and caught my breath in my throat.

It couldn't be!

I wheeled closer and picked it up with my thumb and forefinger, its face smiling at me. The half burned Santa candle even smelled as if it had been recently burned. The Santa hat was gone, melted away as well as the forehead and part of the left eye. But there was still enough of that eye to keep my gaze. My face turned white and my vision blurred and I quickly boxed it back up, throwing it into the trash. I followed it up with the wrapping paper and bow just to be safe. Again I stood up and looked to see who might have been watching me open it.

No one.

Personally, I didn't know anyone here who would do such a thing to me, to be so cruel. But then how would they know anyway?

That night I had the first nightmare in at least five years. Nightmare, memory ... for me they're one and the same. One for which I wasn't ready.

School had let out two days earlier for the Christmas holidays. An unpredicted snowstorm had gathered strength and blanketed the city. Conditions were too dangerous for students and staff to get to school, so with only a few school days left, officials started the holiday early. I was enjoying my extra days off but my mother was upset. She still had a few presents to buy and would be unable to get them. I think at least one was for me based on the looks I caught her giving me when she thought I wasn't looking. I wanted to tell her it didn't bother me. Day of or days after, it made no difference to me. It's not like I still believed in Santa. I better not have; I was fifteen this year.

Dad and I shoveled off the walk as often as we could, but each time we went outside it was deeper. The walls of snow surrounding the walk were now taller than us both and the snow was still coming down hard. This time we had just cleared about eight feet of the walk when I saw movement from the corner of my eye.

"Dad!" I yelled, grabbing his arm, pulling him towards me.

He looked up in time to see the snow caving in above him. He dragged the shovel along as we back-pedaled to the front door. As my foot stepped over the threshold, a pile of white covered my dad.

"Mom, help me!" I screamed as I frantically dug, trying to find him. The snow almost filled the doorway.

"Oh my God!" she choked out, reaching us, "Zach, where's your father?"

"Somewhere in here!" I pointed as I dug faster.

We were throwing the snow inside the house but didn't care. How could he just disappear? He'd been standing right there! My hand hit something and as I reached in further I felt his hand encircle my arm.

"Here! He's here!" I yelled.

We both dug more and as I pulled back, my father shakily stood up, his grip on my arm becoming painful. He was covered in snow and looked like a snowman. There was a light poofing sound and I saw that more snow had fallen to cover the rest of the walkway beyond him. Any more and it would start avalanching into the house. Mom and I pulled him inside and shut the door. He shook off the snow like a dog and Mom and I laughed, relieved he was all right.

"I don't think we're going anywhere soon," he said, shivering. "Turn the heat up. I'm freezing."

Once Dad was finally warmed, we sat down to a dinner of Mom's famous pot roast and the lights blinked once, then went out completely.

"No, no," Mom started, "This can't be happening."

"It's okay," Dad comforted her. "I'm surprised it hasn't gone out sooner, as bad as it is out there. We have candles and lanterns. And last night I brought in the firewood from the back porch. It's in the laundry room so we can have a fire. We'll be fine."

"We'll finally get to use my new Santa candle," Mom said, brightly. She light the wick at the top of the hat, the red wax quickly melting, marring the chubby face and beard.

December 21st

The next morning when I came into work there were two boxes on my desk. The red one was neatly wrapped, exactly as yesterday, but now it was joined by an even smaller green wrapped box. It had an identical black and red bow stuck to the top of it. I usually don't eat breakfast and it was a good thing, because I think I would've puked if I had had anything in my stomach. With shaking hands, I aggressively ripped open the red box, and gasped to see the same half-burnt candle. I whirled around to look in my trash can, but it had been emptied by the cleaning crew last night. I began to sweat as I opened the green box, back to my careful extraction method.

Another white box, only smaller. Inside the tissue paper was a small crudely made Christmas bell. I dropped it on my desk, hoping it would break, but it didn't. Ordinarily, it wouldn't take much of a drop to crack it, as it was made of modeling dough, coated in paint and shellac. A Christmas ornament; the kind kids do in kindergarten or early elementary school.

When it hit the surface it bounced and flipped over. Carved into the back was *Dec 1982*. I blinked rapidly, trying to clear the image from my mind, but it was still there. With the back of my hand, I swiped it off my desk. It didn't break when it hit the carpet, but the crunch seemed loud to me as I crushed it with my shoe. The pieces went into my trash, along with the red box and the rest of the green wrappings. I turned my back on my trash can for a moment, then turned right back to it as I pulled up the plastic bag, tying the opening shut. I took it into the break room and stuffed it into the garbage can there. I ignored the strange looks I got from my coworkers gathered in the kitchen, getting their coffee and chatting before the day started. When I got back to my desk, I laid my head down and took several deep breaths to keep from crying.

Who here could have known my past? The ornament brought back the unwelcome memories again.

I tried to push them from head, but failed, once I fell asleep that night. Unfortunately, I remembered more of that Christmas.

I had lost track of the days. There was nothing to do but sleep and read and I was getting headaches despite my love of books. Reading by candlelight is hard on the eyes. Sleeping killed time and was warmer, especially when bundled under two quilts and a comforter. I woke when I got hungry and went into the kitchen. It was so cold in there I didn't worry about opening the fridge and having the food go bad. There was no temperature difference inside or out. After peeling two hard boiled eggs, that were, luckily enough, boiled the day before the power went out, I walked back into the living room and sat on the sofa, immediately wrapping one of the throw blankets around me. Mom and Dad were at the fireplace. Dad had just brought more wood in from the laundry room and was starting a new fire since it went out during the night.

"Did you soak the bottom ones?" Dad asked Mom.

She nodded, shaking from the cold as well. It was freezing in the room and Dad wanted to make a larger fire than before. After he arranged the top layer, he took the bottle from Mom and soaked them as well. He got up to set the bottle safely away from the fire and turned back at the sound of a match being struck. Mom was kneeling only inches from the fire, thoughts of warmth overshadowing any sense of safety.

"Caroline no!" Dad yelled as he tried to run back to her in time.

Whoosh!

The fire flared up the instant the match lit the flammable logs. I watched in horror as the fire jumped from the wood to my mother's face. Both hard boiled eggs fell from my hands, rolling under the sofa.

"Mom!" I screamed as I jumped up.

She fell on her back, slapping herself and screaming, as the flames spread to the top half of her body.

Dad and I had the exact same idea. I handed him the throw that had been around my shoulders and he snatched it out of my hands, dropping it over her. He and I patted the blanket, smothering the flames and her screams slowly stopped.

"Quick! Put out the carpet," Dad told me, pointing to the edge by the fireplace which had caught fire as well.

I picked up another throw and used it to put out those flames, careful not to let any of the blanket get into the fire. I pulled the fire screen in front of the opening quickly, then turned back to my parents.

Dad had removed the throw from Mom and was crying. She was only moaning now, her pain had to be insufferable. The hair had burnt on her head, a melted lump sat across the top as if she wore a night cap. Her clothes were partially burned off and I couldn't stop looking at her body. Blackened from the fire, it didn't look human. Her face caught the worst of it. Her eyes were swollen and black, like the rest of her face. I wondered if she could see if she opened them; if she could even open them. One of her favorite earrings, a pearl set in gold, was melted to her ear lobe. I had gotten her those earrings last Christmas with my own money. Her other lobe was empty. I began crying as I patted the floor around her, desperate to find her missing *earring. It was all I could think to do. I couldn't touch her for fear of hurting her more.*

"What do we do?" I whispered to Dad, still crying.

There was no power, no phones, and we were snowed in. Even our cell phones had already died as we had no way to charge them.

"Go bring a mattress in here," Dad told me, "we can put her on it. Then go see what we have in the medicine cabinet that we can use."

December 22nd

I held my breath as I turned into my cubicle. Just three days now until Christmas. I breathed a sigh of relief when I saw my empty desk, exactly the way I left it last night. The debris from the broken ornament was missing from the carpet and my trash was empty.

It was over!

I started my workday with new vigor and apologized to my confused coworkers about my behavior yesterday. All thoughts of Christmas flew from my mind, even though the start of our holiday would be Christmas Eve, just two days away. For lunch I treated myself to a gourmet burger with a chocolate shake. I was walking back, digging in the bag for a French fry, when I stepped around my cubicle wall. I dropped the bag and caught myself before dropping the shake. I unsteadily set it down as I stared at the *three* boxes that now adorned my desk. The bright red one, looking to be the same as the first gift; the smaller green one, identical to the one I threw away yesterday; and now an even smaller one, jewelry sized, wrapped in silver paper. All three had the trademark black with red bow topping them. Grabbing all three I stepped on my burger bag, squashing it, as I violently threw each into my trash can. I sat down and tried to concentrate on slowing my breath. My heart was beating so fast I thought I might have a heart attack. Tears slowly fell from my eyes as I put my face in my hands. Sobbing as quietly as I could, I pushed back the memory that threatened to overwhelm me.

Not here. Not here.

I had a hard time concentrating after that. I made so many mistakes and took twice as long to get anything done. Just before five I glanced into the trash can that I had been avoiding for four hours. Gritting my teeth, I pulled them back out and ripped all three open, shiny Christmas paper flying everywhere.

How the hell was this possible?

The candle, still half burned, was there.

The ornament was whole and unblemished. I turned it over to see the same *Dec 1982* carved into it.

But this newest present had me shaking even more once I opened it. It was a single earring, a dangling pearl in a simple gold setting— just the one. I knew where the mate to it was. There was a pink piece of paper folded up inside. I bit my lip as I read it.

I found it! And you thought it was gone forever! Your Secret Santa

I scooped it all up and wrapped it in a light jacket I had hanging behind me. I stormed from my cubicle and went downstairs to the large document shredder that was in the back office. We were required to shred anything that had a customer's credit card, birthdate, or any other personal item on it. Our computers were secured but our trash was not. Technically, we weren't supposed to put anything more solid than a CD into it, but I didn't care. I just turned it on, shaking out my jacket, and watched the items get caught up briefly before succumbing to the sharp blades. A few pieces of the ornament spit out back into my face but I wiped them off, wiping the memories away with them, I hoped. The candle, being a soft material, didn't shred or break, but smooshed into a thick ooze, coating the blades until it became thinner and thinner as they turned. The earring was chopped in half immediately before being sucked down into the belly of the beast. After a few more minutes, I turned it off.

If they come back from that, then I'll know I'm losing my mind!

I drove home in a daze, afraid to come back the next day.

That night, before I went to bed I had a beer— well, I had several beers. These past few days had shaken me up and I needed to sleep deeply... the kind of sleep I could only get from booze or sleeping pills. Just one more day until the holidays, and we would be off from Christmas until January second. Quite drunk, I dropped off to sleep almost immediately. And, unfortunately, I dreamed again.

"She's getting worse," I told Dad, as we stood in the doorway to the kitchen, watching her.

We didn't know if Mom could hear us, she spent most of her time unconscious. Another three days or so had gone by. The days blurred into one another and we couldn't even tell when it was day or night. The snow blocked all the windows; it was that high. We'd used up all the gauze and bandages we had and were now using torn up sheets to wrap Mom's burns. I couldn't find any more anti-biotic ointment, once we ran out of the two tubes we had. But I did find three huge jars of petroleum jelly, dated back when I was little. I'm betting, at some point, this stuff had coated my ass within a diaper. There was no medicinal value to the jelly, but it kept the cloth from sticking to the burns so we used it.

"I know," Dad replied, "I've thought of a way to get out. I'm going to do it today."

"What are you going to do?" I asked, fearful of what he might try.

"You know that vent up in the attic? It leads straight outside. It's got to be higher than the snow. I'm going to go and get help. Surely they can come get her in a helicopter or a snowplow or something."

I shook my head. "No, Dad. You don't know how deep the snow is. You'll sink and die out there."

"Well, I did worry about sinking since I can't find my snow shoes. I think your mom sold them in the garage sale a couple years ago." Dad answered. "But I did find some tennis rackets. You see people do that on TV all the time. I'll just tie them to my shoes."

"Dad, that's TV. It doesn't mean it will work."

"What choice do we have?" His eyes filled with tears as I reluctantly nodded.

I woke and glanced at the clock... 3:00 am. I wondered why I was awake until the nausea forced me to run to the bathroom—just what I deserved for drinking that much beer. Work would be miserable today. I was still sitting on the cool, tiled floor, my head bowing to the porcelain god, when I spied something glittering on the floor near the edge of the tub.

"No, please, no," I begged, as I reached for it.

I knew what it would be before I picked it up.

It was the same earring that I had run through the shredder at work.

I shook with fear—fear that I really was going insane. I dropped it back on the floor, it really didn't matter where I left it; it was going to show up on my desk tomorrow, anyway. I got up, and after puking one more time, stumbled to bed.

I lay there, awake, until my alarm went off at 5:30.

December 23rd

I plopped down at my desk, hung over and needing sleep, then I laid my head on my arms. Since I had tomorrow off, I planned to sleep the whole day. I realized, now, that I really needed a cup of coffee to make it through today, so I got up, then suddenly looked back down. There were no presents on my desk! I looked under and around, even inside my desk. Nothing. A feeling of relief washed over me. God I hoped it was over.

I walked to the kitchen with a renewed spring in my step and came back with a steaming cup. I stopped just before my cubicle.

What if they were there?

I peered over the wall and was happy to see my desk just the way it should be. Today would be a good day.

They cut us at noon. Happy employees streamed out into the parking lot wishing each other Merry Christmas and Happy Holidays. Some even forgot and sent me wishes as well. I only nodded thanks to them. I was smiling more than usual as I got in my car.

Out of habit, I checked my mailbox, even though I got home early and didn't think our mailman had delivered yet. I turned the key and opened the little door. I froze when I saw what was inside. The same three red, green, and silver boxes! Luckily, my keys were still hanging in the lock, or I would've dropped them in shock.

How can this be?

I felt a hand land on my shoulder and my neighbor, Kevin, who lives on my floor, greeted me with, "Hey Zach! How's it going? Off for the holidays?"

I whirled around and grabbed the offending hand. Twisting it around so it was being pulled up his back, I forced him forward and slammed his face into the wall.

"What the hell, Zach?" he croaked. "What are you doing?"

"Did you put these in my mailbox?" I yelled at him hysterically. "Why are you doing this to me?"

"I don't have a clue what you're talking about," he answered, using his free hand to push off the wall. "What's in your mailbox?"

I let go of his arm and he turned around. When I saw his face I knew I'd made a mistake. What the hell did I just do? Running my hand over my face and through my hair, I began crying.

"Oh, shit! I am so sorry, Kevin," I told him, bending over and putting my hands on my thighs.

I thought I might faint. Tears fell from my face to lightly splatter on the floor below me. I couldn't believe I almost hurt someone.

I stood up and put my hands out apologetically. "I didn't hurt you, did I? I don't know what came over me. It's the holidays;. I always get stressed out this time of year. I am really so sorry."

Kevin rubbed his nose, which was red, but not bleeding. "I'm fine. But what's bothering you? You act like you've seen a ghost."

I quietly gathered the boxes from my mailbox and locked it back up. As I turned to leave I replied, "Maybe I have."

I locked my door behind me as soon as I reached my apartment. I stood with my back against the door, breathing heavily. The weight of the three small packages seemed heavy in my arms and I wanted to be rid of them, permanently. I set them on the coffee table; throwing them away wouldn't work. Then I went straight into the kitchen and got myself a glass of whiskey. Despite what the beer had done to me last night, I really needed something stronger. Stepping out of the kitchen, I dropped the glass, spilling the whiskey all over the carpet and my shoes, before I'd even gotten a sip of it.

There was a small Christmas tree in the corner of the room. The decorations looked old and very familiar. These were some of the same decorations we had on our tree when I was a child. Beneath the lowest branches was a small box, wrapped in bright blue paper with a black and red bow on it. The bow didn't match the color of the box, but it was identical to the other three bows I already had. I dropped to my knees, right in the whiskey-soaked carpet, not even noticing it seeping through the cloth. I wanted to run away, but I knew it was useless. I crawled to the tree and picked up the present. There was a tag on it.

To Zach Love Mom.

I simply held it in one hand for a few minutes while I covered my face with the other. I was crying again. It seems I'd been crying more in the past couple days than I had in many years... twenty-five years, for sure. I swiped my eyes with the back of my hand and unwrapped the present, taking care not to tear the wrapping paper. Me and my habits.

It was a Nintendo 64 game—Mario Kart 64, to be exact. I'd wanted this game so badly when I was fifteen. Even though I didn't write to Santa, I'd written out a list of what I wanted and taped it to the fridge so my parents would see it. I set the game on the coffee table with the other three unwrapped gifts and stared at them. I began laughing manically; I didn't even own a Nintendo 64 system anymore.

Leaving the carpet wet, I went into the kitchen and refilled the glass. I downed it in one gulp and topped it off again to sip. I spent the rest of the evening watching movies in my DVR, sipping my drink, often glancing at the gifts on the table. I fell asleep on the sofa halfway through my third movie.

I stood in the hall, watching my father climb the pull-down attic ladder. He used one hand to steady himself. Under his other arm, he had tucked two tennis rackets and a roll of twine. He'd tossed a thick, hooded coat to the attic floor in before ascending. I really didn't want him to go; I feared I'd never see him again. He looked down at me, squatting at the top.

"I'd tell you to close this to keep the heat in, but there is none anyway," his vain attempt at humor was failing. "Honestly, I'll be fine. It might take a few hours to get to someone, but I will be back."

He sat down and tied the tennis racquets to his boots. I had serious doubts that they would work. Once he stood, precariously balancing his footing with the ungainly additions, he put on the coat and removed his gloves from the pockets.

"I did forget something," he called down sheepishly. "I forgot a hammer to break open the vent."

"I'll get it," I offered, wanting to do anything but.

I ran into the kitchen and pulled open our hardware drawer. It didn't have much but a hammer, several screwdrivers, and some picture hangers. There were a couple small boxes of nails and screws inside as well. I ran back with the hammer in my hand, stopping next to Mom for a moment. I was hoping she might wake and ask what I was doing. Then I could tell her and she could make me stop this foolishness. But she was still unconscious. Her breathing was even slower than before and worry slammed into me.

She really doesn't have any more time. Dad really does need to do this. But I'm younger, though. Maybe he'll let me do it.

I ran back to the hallway and held onto the ladder as I proclaimed my suggestion.

"Sorry, son," he replied, holding his hand out for the hammer. "I'm already up here and dressed. Besides, what kind of father would that make me if I let you go out in this?"

Reluctantly, I handed up the hammer and waited as he walked out of my view. I could hear hammering and banging as he broke open the vent. Finally, I heard the high- pitched whistling of the wind and could see snowdrifts floating above me after the last loud noise. He'd done it.

"See you soon, Zach!" he called out to me, and then he was gone.

The storm sounded even worse with an opening in the house. And I just let him go out in that.

So what kind of son did that make me?

December 24th – Christmas Eve

When I woke, I was still on the sofa and my head was killing me. My TV had gone into sleep mode automatically when it was inactive for too long. I glanced at the clock and saw it was ten am.

Oh, shit! I'm late for work!

I jumped up to get ready when it hit me that it was Christmas Eve and we were on holiday until after New Year's Day. My head pounded and throbbed with each step I took. As if in a bad dream, I turned to look at the coffee table and sighed when I saw it empty. I changed direction from the bedroom to the kitchen and made myself some scrambled eggs with hot sauce. For some reason this always got rid of my hangovers.

Once I felt better, I steeled myself to go toss the Christmas tree out my patio door. Maybe someone else would want it; surely not me. As I came around the sofa, I could see under the tree and froze.

I should've known.

A fifth present was sitting amid the other four. This time it wasn't a box but a gold envelope with a tiny black and red bow. Of course, the Mario Cart game was wrapped back up as before. I wanted to ignore it but I knew if I did, it would pop up everywhere until I opened it.

With shaking hands, I picked it up and felt it. Whatever was inside the envelope was thick but flexible. I slipped my thumb under the flap and slid it to break the gummed seal, hissing, as a papercut appeared on my knuckle. I turned it over and let the contents fall to the floor.

Confusion was the first emotion, then a nagging, plucking thought, like something forgotten.

It sat on the carpet. A slim piece of plastic, the printing facing up at me.

ZACHARY FRANKLIN   DOB 10-06-77

DR. GAUBERT   MIDHAVEN PSYCHIATRIC HOSPTIAL

It was a hospital ID bracelet. *My* hospital ID bracelet? When did I have one?

I slid to the floor and picked it up. The clasp was open and ready for me to lock it to my wrist.

My mind felt loose, jarred; and then dizziness hit me hard until I passed out.

Several days after Dad left for help, Mom took a turn for the worse. We had run out of firewood and I was now burning the furniture. The lacquered wood burning in the fireplace gave off a chemical scent that I'm sure was bad for us to be breathing, but the alternative was freezing to death. I first broke down the dining room chairs and table. I'd already burned the first end table and was about to ready another for the fire when I heard my name softly called.

I turned and saw my mother looking at me. This was the first time in days she'd been awake. I ran to her and reached to take her hand but pulled back, realizing how much that would hurt her.

"Zach, where's your father?" she asked, her voice hoarse from the damaged vocal chords.

I shook my head, tears falling from my face. "He went out to get help."

"When?"

"A couple days ago," I answered, wiping my face.

She sighed and lifted her hand from the mattress. It hovered in the air before she placed it lightly on my cheek. Her charred hand felt like bark on a tree.

"Mom, I don't know what to do."

"Yes, you do," she whispered. "You just have to find the strength to do it."

I looked quizzically at her and she smiled. Her blackened face cracked and red, raw flesh peeked out within the crevasses'.

Black and red... her face seemed striped with it.

"I'm in pain," she whimpered. "...so much pain. I feel like I'm still on fire. I need you to help me end it."

I backed up quickly, slamming my back into the sofa.

"No!"

"You must. I'm suffering. I'm hurting. I don't want to live like this anymore."

"I can't kill you, Mom." I was full-on crying now. I couldn't believe what she was asking of me.

"We're still snowed in and your father's missing," she whispered. "I'm not going to last until the storm breaks, you know this. Each day, each breath, hurts more than the last. Please."

She cried as she whispered 'please, please, please' repeatedly, until I finally nodded in reluctant agreement.

She suggested that I use the longest and sharpest knife we had. A quick stab into her brain and she would be at peace. I brought the knife in from the kitchen, shocked that I was actually going to do this.

"You know how much I love you, Zach, but I still have to say it again. I love you so much, son. You've been my pride and joy since the day you were born."

"I love you too, Mom," I managed to get out between the sobs.

"The storm hit so quickly that I didn't get all your presents in time to wrap them," she said,

"There are a few that were coming in the mail, but no mail was running once the storm got bad. I got you that video game you wanted so badly. The Mario Cart. It'll show up when the snow clears. There's also some shirts and something for your dad. I ... can't remember what else I got him. Tell him not to open it until Christmas morning."

She was becoming incoherent and I didn't know what to say. I let her babble, watching her wince in pain with every movement. I think she'd forgotten what she'd asked me to do and I wasn't going to bring it up. Relieved, I knew I wasn't going to kill her. I couldn't. She's my mother. She stared off and whispered more nonsense, so I took that moment to replace the knife in the block in the kitchen. When I came back, the heavy silence coated the room. The only sound I heard was the wind blowing through the hole in the attic above.

"Mom?" I ran to her.

She was still, her eyes open, finally relaxed and without pain. "Mom? Please don't die. Please."

I shook the mattress lightly, but it had no effect on her. She was gone.

I howled like an animal! My sorrow enveloped me and I thought I might explode from it. I was angry, scared, and sad.

I was alone.

When I came to, I was face down on the carpet. My head hurt horribly... from the hangover, or from something else? I felt around my head, looking for lumps or cuts. *Seemed to be intact.* I pushed up to a sitting position and noticed my wrist encased in the hospital ID band. My mouth opened and closed like a fish, not a sound coming from my throat. I didn't know how much more I could take.

I ran into the kitchen and picked up a knife to cut it off. The blade was between it and my wrist when I realized how much worse it could get if I removed it. I stared at my skin, lightly rubbing the flat of the knife back and forth.

Could I? Should I?

Since that day, I'd never had any suicidal thoughts. Even while I was in the... hospital?

I dropped the knife, barely missing my big toe.

I *was* in a hospital! How could I forget that? I looked closer at the wristband.

MIDHAVEN PSYCHIATRIC HOSPTIAL

Now it all came flooding back to me. I was in *that* hospital. After the storm ended, when the rescuers found me, they took me away to Midhaven. I was there for what— three, five years? I couldn't remember. How could I forget something like that so completely? I remembered everything that happened to my Mom and Dad, even if I did push the memories to the back of my mind. I did have those memories. Why did I block the memories of the hospital?

I sat back down on the sofa, noticing, of course, the other presents sitting on the table as if they belonged there. In a daze I turned on the TV and saw little Ralphie shooting a BB gun.

That's right! They played this movie repeatedly for twenty-four hours before Christmas. Even as I watched, his glasses flew off his face. The movie was almost over and I looked at the clock, stunned to see it was almost midnight, almost Christmas.

Had I been lying on the floor the entire day?

The camera zoomed out and the credits began rolling down the screen. Out of the corner of my eye, I saw the clock hit midnight.

December 25th – Christmas Day

With a low little *pop,* the power went out. Everything was dark and silent. I couldn't even hear traffic outside. I groped for my cell phone on the table to get some light, but I couldn't find it. Actually, I couldn't even find the coffee table. I started to panic as I dropped to the carpet, which didn't feel like carpet anymore, holding to the sofa I just left. On my knees, I reached out with one arm, waving frantically, trying to feel something.

Nothing.

I fell forward and used my other arm to help balance myself. When I reached back for the sofa, it was gone too. I patted the ground with both hands; it felt warm and rough, like a parking lot after a hot day. I couldn't see my fingers in front of my face, and I wiggled them close enough to flick my eyelashes. The darkness was thick and dense. Instinctively, I sucked in deep, thinking the air was gone, too. A light began coming towards me and enlarged as it got closer. I realized it wasn't just a light; there was a scene unfolding before me. I choked back a sob at the sight of my fifteen-year old self.

I was sitting on the floor in front of a dead fireplace. I ignored the loud knocking at the door in this cold and freezing house. Finally, the door was broken in, but my younger self didn't even flinch. Two firefighters and a police officer walked into the room. The officer turned back to the open doorway and waved in someone else. A clattering, metallic sound went unheard by me as a gurney was wheeled in, a paramedic at each end.

"Son, are you all right?" the officer asked, coming closer and putting his hand on my forehead.

He was shocked how cold it was and yet I wasn't frozen or dead. The only movement I made was to blink, involuntarily, not even shivering in the coldness.

"This boy is nearly frozen," the police officer said. "Let's get him to the hospital, fast."

The paramedics picked me up and strapped me in. One moved his finger back and forth in front of my empty eyes. "I think he's catatonic."

He nodded to the other and they hurried me into the ambulance. The snow was only a couple of feet deep now. At some point, the storm had abated and it had warmed up enough to melt down the high drifts. I didn't know when that was, as I wasn't sure of the day. I didn't know how long I sat there after my mother died and the fire went out. I didn't know anything.

I didn't care.

The paramedics had checked my mother's vital signs while the officer had been talking to me, so they knew she was dead already. The firefighters and police officer took in the scene. The horribly burned, dead woman. The blackened fireplace opening and charred carpet; the broken and partially burned furniture.

"They tried to hold out," one fireman said. "She just didn't have that much time."

"How sad," the other firefighter commented, then added, "and the man we found outside was obviously the boy's father. It's a shame he got buried in the snow and had a heart attack. He might have made it out. He died trying to save his family."

The police officer sighed, "As long and as bad as that storm was, I'm afraid they won't be the only casualties we find."

That scene faded and the white light turned to grey.

"Ho Ho Ho!"

A cackling, booming laugh brought my apartment back into view. I looked around and saw the evilest Santa I'd ever seen. Instead of red, his suit was black with red trim—like the bows, like my mother's face. His skin was dark, but appeared to shift and blur; I couldn't get a good look at his face.

At this point, nothing shocked me. I mean really nothing, anymore.

"Why are you doing this to me?" I asked, beginning to anger.

"Ha ha ha!" he laughed back at me in the same tone. "Why not? It's Christmas. I thought I'd dress in a familiar outfit. Of course, I don't buy off the rack, so it's been altered to fit my unique personality."

I just sat there dumbly. I didn't have a clue who he was or what to say to that.

"Come on, Zach!" he barked out, lightly smacking my shoulder with his palm. "You and I are old friends who just missed our connection. You were suppose to come with me back then."

He waved his hands around and a movie seemed to play, floating in the air in front of me. It was fifteen-year old me again, sitting, unmoving in front of the dead fire. To my left was a black, hooded figure, his skeletal hands just reaching for me when the knocking came at the door. This time I could hear him cursing as he missed his chance. At the time, I had no idea he was even there.

"I'm done with the games and charades," I said as I stood up. *Now I'm pissed.*

"Good," he replied with a wink. "I hate all this holiday shit, too."

He threw off the Santa costume and it disintegrated in the air with a red poof. He was there in his true self.

Death.

The Grim Reaper.

"You've been playing with me and I'm sick of it," I yelled. "Why now? Why did you wait twenty-five years?"

"Yes, I have," he laughed. "Why do humans get to have all the fun? Especially at Christmas. You had completely blocked the memory of the hospital, I had to make you remember that. It's made you whole again. I don't take anything unless it's full value. It's way beneath me."

Smugly, I turned my back on him. "You've lost your power over me, now. I'm not afraid of you anymore."

"Hmm. You're right about one thing," he said, tapping his bony fingertips on his chin, making little clicking sounds. "I can tell you're no longer afraid. However, about the other thing. Your belief in me makes no difference when I come for you. It's inevitable."

I turned around in time to feel his hot and bony palm placed on my forehead.

The End

The Joys of Christmas
By
Lisa Morton

I know it's hard to believe now, as you look at my Swarovski crystal snowflake brooch and my sweater patterned with reindeer and sleighs, but I didn't always love Christmas.

Once upon a time, I was a twenty-year-old college student majoring in Privilege. Well, technically my major was Political Science (after I got my Bachelor's, I wanted to get my Master's in Constitutional Law), and yes, at the time I was passionate about it, but I was still attending college on my parents' money and not much worried about my future. Like probably most twenty-somethings, my parents baffled me. Dad worked for a big health insurance company, Mom was a teacher, and they were both obsessed with being perceived as younger than they were. They had friends over to the house once a month for barbecues (with only free-range and non-GMO foods), and after dinner they sat in the living room smoking grass and talking about diversity and intersectionality.

Sometimes I'd listen in for a few minutes only to leave the room wincing.

And they were both obsessed with Christmas. Every November, the day after Thanksgiving was devoted to decking the halls. Dad and my brother, Josh, would work outside, stringing up enough lights to quintuple the power bill, while Mom and I set up the tree and decorated the house. Mom was really proud of that stupid tree – it was tall, reasonably realistic, and pre-strung with lights that could be programmed to change color or flash in a particular sequence. "Be careful with that," Mom would caution as I'd struggle with screwing the effing thing together, "we paid a lot of money for that tree!" December would thus be spent living in a twinkling wonderland of green, red, gold, and white. World War III could've started and they wouldn't have noticed.

And Titan was there through it all.

Titan, the world's biggest company. Titan, who would have anything you wanted to your front door in thirty minutes. Titan, whose reach was so ubiquitous that they claimed a nomad on the steppes of Mongolia could call out something he wanted, and they'd have it to him before he reached the next watering hole.

Josh and I didn't especially share either our parents' Christmas mania or their Titan shopping compulsion, at least not then. Sure, as kids we'd rampaged through our gifts on Christmas morning with the same fervor that other upper-middle-class American children had, but when we reached our teens Christmas started to seem less interesting somehow. Since I'd been at college, my parents had sent me a prepaid Titan card every year with the idea that I'd use it to buy Christmas presents, but I'd opted instead for small, handmade items (a calendar of pics of Josh and I as tots, a thumb drive of Christmas electronica) and used the money for a blow-out holiday party in the apartment I shared with three roomies.

So it was when I came home for Christmas in my third year of college, more focused on catching up on reading and paper-writing than Christmas. "Kathryn," my mother said (she'd never called me "Katie" or "Kate" or anything less Elizabethan), "would you like to help me with some wrapping?"

"Sorry, Mom, can't right now." The truth, of course, was that I *could*; I just didn't want to.

Mom's BFF was a first-grade teacher named Hannah. I'd always liked Hannah; she got sarcastic when grumpy and took some of Mom's political correctness with a grain of salt. It was genuinely nice to see Hannah when she dropped by on Christmas Eve, by herself – her husband of seventeen years had just divorced her to run off with a woman only two years older than me.

"How's Christmas treating you this year, Hannah?" I asked, as we exchanged hugs.

"Everything's better with Christmas!"

I laughed, thinking it was Hannah's good old wit, but when I looked at her, her eyes held not a twinkle of irony, no sense whatsoever that this was a jest. I was still staring at her, waiting for the wink or lip-curl, when she turned away to wrap my brother in a bear-hug, which was also not her style.

I tried to join in the conversation with Hannah and Mom and Dad over the next hour, but something was *off*. Hannah just wasn't her old self. She *bubbled*. She blathered about junk she'd bought from Titan as if her first grandchild had just arrived...although she probably could have bought one of those from Titan, too.

I think even Mom was taken aback by her friend's behavior, because at some point she leaned forward over their glasses of rum-spiked eggnog and asked, "How are you holding up on your first Christmas without...you know who?"

"Well," Hannah answered, without skipping an effervescent beat, "at first I thought it would be rough, but it's actually been great! I went to an amazing movie today – oh, you *have* to see it – called *The Joys of Christmas.*"

Mom perked up. "Oh, I saw the commercials for that. So it's good?"

"It's better than good," Hannah answered, without explanation.

After Hannah left, I asked Mom if she thought her friend was okay.

"I think she might be having a breakdown," Mom replied, making me feel better.

Christmas morning arrived, and we dutifully exchanged gifts (in Titan boxes) while those same tired old songs played in the background. Josh barely looked up from his phone the whole time, apparently mesmerized by the news feed. I tried to seem enthusiastic when gifted with a completely ludicrous Rudolph hat, but I'm sure they could tell it was forced.

"Say," Dad said, as we were in the post-unwrapping/post-orgiastic phase, relaxing with coffee and cookies, "your mom and I thought we'd do something special as a family today."

Josh grunted without looking up. I tried to fill the void. "Sure. What'd you have in mind?"

Mom said, "Remember that movie that Hannah mentioned – *The Joys of Christmas*? We thought maybe we could all go see it."

Josh muttered, "You're kidding, right?"

I recognized Mom's defensive tone when she was quick to answer, "Did you see the commercials? It's supposed to be a wonderful celebration of Christmas all over the world."

"I don't watch television," Josh said. I didn't, either. For some reason, my parents still did.

"Come on," Dad said, just a hint of don't-talk-back-to-your-father in his tone, "how bad would it be to put your phone down for two hours?"

Josh set his phone aside and finally raised his head. "Look – I can set my phone aside here without having to go to a theater."

In a desperate effort to keep this from escalating, I threw in, "Besides, won't the theaters be jammed?"

"I bought tickets already," Mom confessed.

That made it a done deal. Even Josh had to sigh in defeat. "What time?"

"A two p.m. matinee. We don't have to rush to get ready, in other words."

I rose, walked to Mom, and gave her a little kiss. "Sounds nice, Mom."

The truth, of course, was that it sounded like utter and total *shit*. It was the first movie under a new arm of Titan Productions, so I was guessing it was one big commercial. One night my friend Kendra had brought the trailer for it up on her phone, and we'd laughed even while my stomach turned at one shot after another of frolicking children and half-licked candy canes and old men dressed in faux red fur carrying stacks of Titan boxes. What would Kendra say if she found out I'd seen this thing? I seriously considered suddenly acquiring a winter cold, or remembering the overdue midterm paper that had a deadline of tomorrow, but as much as I hated the notion of enduring *The Joys of Christmas*, I hated disappointing Mom more.

So we got dressed, packed into Dad's car (Josh more sullen than usual), and headed to the local multiplex. It was crammed with patrons dressed in silly hats (like mine, which I'd worn to please Mom); a lot of them had the same do-we-have-to-do-this attitude that Josh and I did. But we kept quiet as we took our places in line. At least it hadn't snowed for Christmas, so we didn't have to freeze our asses off on top of enduring this sugary tripe.

The previous show must have ended, because a horde of people abruptly exited the theater, moving past us on the way to the parking lot.

And they were happy. I mean, really, *really* happy. Laughing and grinning. One family of four were singing "Frosty the Snowman" out loud. Even Josh looked up from his phone.

"What the fuck is *that*?" he whispered to me.

I whispered back, "Shoot me now."

"I heard that," Mom said.

One of the last groups out of the theater, however, didn't seem quite so happy. It was a group of four young women, all about my age. Three of them were like the rest of the crowd – animated, laughing, bright-eyed.

But something was wrong with the fourth one.

She tagged along with her friends as if pulled by their gravity. Her expression was dazed, her eyes vacant. Her mouth hung open slightly in a kind of half-smile, and her footsteps seemed mechanical and wooden. The other three didn't seem to notice her.

As the four passed right by us, for just a second I locked gazes with the stunned-looking woman, and in that instant her eyes came alive – but not with joy. With utter, all-encompassing *terror*. I caught my breath, but then something flickered across her face, and her eyes took on that 'nobody's home' look again. They passed by us, leaving my stomach clenched in dread.

"They were kinda hot," Josh half-whispered.

"Did you see the expression on the one, though? She looked... I don't know, really freaked out or something. Just for a second, then..."
"I didn't notice."

Mom looked at us, one eyebrow cocked. "What are you two talking about?"

"Nothing," I said.

Our line began to move. As we entered the theater, we were confronted by a huge display for *The Joys of Christmas*: big brightly colored Titan cardboard boxes stacked up fifteen feet high, with an elf in the front grinning and waving. A blurb at the top read, "You won't just love this movie while you're watching it – you'll bring home the spirit of

Christmas!" The blurb was attributed to "Santa Claus, CEO of Titan."

"Cute," I muttered.

As we approached the ticket-takers — two poor kids forced to dress like the elf in the display — we saw huge red velvet bags next to them. When they took a ticket, they reached into the bag and produced a small wrapped package, which they handed to the customer.

"Oh, look," Mom exclaimed, sounding like an excited five-year-old, "we each get a *present!*"

When the pimply kid in the elf costume handed me the box, I stared at it curiously. It was just a few square inches, so it couldn't hold much, but it rattled when I shook it. It was secured with a twinkly ribbon, and a tag on the top read, *"Open in the theater! Merry Christmas!"*

"Huh," Dad remarked, as we shuffled toward the theater doors.

Josh leaned over to me and said softly, "It's probably too much to hope it's ear plugs."

I snickered, but cut it off when Mom glanced at us.

We filed into the theater, took our seats, and joined the rest of the crowd opening our little boxes. Inside was a gaily-decorated, cellophane-wrapped cookie. Each one was different: I got a poinsettia, Josh got a star, Dad got a Santa face, and Mom got a reindeer. They all had little "EAT ME!" stickers on the cellophane, right next to the Titan logo.

"Oh, that's almost too pretty to eat!" Mom said. I had to agree with her; the quality of the decoration was impressive, almost like a fine painting.

Just then, we heard a cheerful commotion behind us. We craned our necks around to see that ushers had entered the theater with more of the big red bags, but this time they pulled out mini cartons of milk, like the ones they pass out to little kids in elementary schools. "Free milk for your cookies," the ushers called out.

Even Dad smiled at that. "Boy, they thought of everything."

"Screw the milk," Josh said, as he tore the cellophane off his star and crammed it into his mouth.

"How is it?" I asked.

"Pretty good."

Mom, Dad and I each took a carton of milk, unwrapped our cookies, and chowed down.

It was better than pretty good; it tasted as incredible as it looked. The sweetness coursed into me like a drug, like something I could feel in every cell. I was enveloped in a state of bliss, where nothing negative could enter.

"Wow," I heard Dad mutter around a mouthful of dough and icing.

"I'd love to get *this* recipe," Mom said.

The lights went down, and the movie started. There were no trailers, not even the usual "Turn off your phones" reminder. The instant it was dark, the screen lit up with *The Joys of Christmas*.

I should have hated it, because it was a celebration of everything I disliked about Christmas:

crowds of shoppers streaming out of a Titan store, juggling their purchases as they smiled along to seasonal music. Tiny tots in Rudolph-patterned pajamas maniacally ripping open presents and then squealing with joy when they pulled out the doll or game. People my age riding in sleighs, the boy shyly producing a tiny wrapped Titan box and the girl crying when she saw the ring. Middle-aged moms at home merrily pulling delicious-looking roasts out of an oven as a huge, gleaming Christmas tree could be seen in the background.

It was, in other words, a propaganda film for the world's greatest consumer holiday, produced by the world's greatest consumer supplier.

And yet I joined the rest of those in the theater laughing and aww-ing at the right moments. Some small part of me – a part that had somehow avoided the cookie's saccharine influence – knew I shouldn't be enjoying this. That part remembered the woman who had passed us as we were filing into the theater—the one who looked like some brain circuitry had been fried. But that memory seemed to grow tinier with each passing second, just like the inner voice that tried to scream that there was more to this movie than just clever filmmaking. There were instances when it almost felt as if my consciousness had just had a direct injection of the movie, a supercharged shot right to the id.

The phrase *subliminal advertising* popped into my thoughts. I remembered hearing something about how it had been tried in the '60s – how a single frame featuring a suggestive product image would be inserted into a movie – but hadn't achieved much.

But if this was subliminal advertising, it had come a long way, because it was working on *me*. I wanted to find the nearest department store Santa and hug him. I wanted to kiss somebody under artificial mistletoe. I wanted to log onto Titan's website and buy *everything*. I wanted another cookie.

The cookie...

There'd been something in the cookie. Just like there was something in the movie.

Something Titan.

But it didn't matter what, because by then I knew everybody else in the theater felt the way I did. A kid next to me whose piercings looked older than he did openly sobbed at the sight of a little girl cradling a teddy bear on Christmas morning. The kid's father, with tattoo sleeves going up both arms (and dressed in an inappropriate tank top for December weather) grinned like a fucking carnival clown at the sight of a tyke teetering on a new bike.

And I loved them for it.

I don't even remember the rest of the movie. All I know is that it ended, and the audience got up to file out before the next showing, and I couldn't wait to hit Titan's after-Christmas sales and stock up on decorations and gear for next year.

When I left that theater, I fucking *loved* Christmas.

***

That was a while back.

I'm older now, but I've never gotten over that love of Christmas. Dad died last year, but Mom and I are still hanging his stocking and filling it with his favorite candies. Mom's friend Hannah lost her house and wound up on skid row, but at least she had some really sturdy Titan appliance boxes to live out of. My brother Josh is married and already has two kids; he'll be bringing them by on Christmas morning so we can shower them with gifts. I haven't found my perfect partner yet, but I have a good job as a legal clerk for a medium-sized firm. Oh, I never quite graduated with my own law degree; somehow my passion for it just ran out. That, and I racked up huge credit card debts every December that made it impossible to keep up with college tuition.

But every Christmas, Mom and I go to the Titan store, wade through the cheery crowds, and add more onto those credit card bills. We don't mind; when we see ourselves in our new red-and-green dresses with the Santa-patterned trim on the hem, or set out the limited edition ceramic set of eight tiny reindeer, we realize that cost doesn't matter.

The only bad part about Christmas is the nightmares. They come every year now. I'm not sure what the bad dreams are about – the only thing I remember is the terrible feeling of being locked away in someplace that's dark and airless. But once I get up in the morning, the dreams fade, pushed out by the season's good cheer.

And every year we watch *The Joys of Christmas* on Titan's streaming service. Sure, we've heard the rumors, about how it was actually Titan's experiment in mind control, that it was so successful it resulted in a twenty-five percent boost to Titan's revenues, but I don't believe that silliness. What I believe in is what I can buy at Titan. What I believe is that I was once a stupid college girl who thought she was going to save the world. Well, I learned that you can't save the world, but maybe you can make it a little bit happier every December by buying gifts. You can even order cookies to be delivered on December 24th. Josh's kids have never seen *The Joys of Christmas*, so we ordered two extra cookies this year to go with our living-room screening. Josh says the kids are already breaking his bank accounts, but I'm sure he won't mind when they join us for the traditional post-Christmas shopping spree.

It's one of the joys of Christmas, after all.

The End

Afterword

When I put the first 'Collected Christmas Horror Shorts' together, I had no idea it would do so well. I had never put an anthology together before and had no idea what the outcome would be.

I managed to get a lot of great authors involved and I picked my favourite stories to go in the book. Lisa Vasquez created a lovely cover for it and it went on Amazon. It managed to go to number 1 in the horror anthology charts in the US and UK and it stayed there for quite some time. What I didn't expect was for it to hit the number one spots a second year running.

I get asked a lot when I am going to do follow ups to several of the books I've released but the Christmas one was the one that I always knew I would revisit. Christmas is such a special time of year and it's just fun to play with and set horror stories in. I think all of the authors in the book have outdone themselves. What you hold in your hands is my favourite of the stories I was sent. As always, everyone has different tastes but I hope that you enjoyed our collection and I hope we have convinced you to pick up other books by the authors.

From everyone involved, we wish you a very Merry Christmas!

Made in the USA
Middletown, DE
26 November 2018